THE CONSTRUCTION OF CHEER

Shiloh Ridge Ranch in Three Rivers, Book 3

LIZ ISAACSON

AEJ
CREATIVE WORKS

The Glover Family

❧❀❧

Welcome to Shiloh Ridge Ranch! The Glover family is BIG, and sometimes it can be hard to keep track of everyone.

Here's how things are right now:

Lois & Stone (deceased) Glover, 7 children, in age-order:

1. Bear (Sammy, wife / Lincoln, step-son)
2. Cactus (Allison, ex-wife / Bryce, son (deceased))
3. Judge
4. Preacher
5. Arizona
6. Mister
7. Bishop

DAWNA & BULL (DECEASED) GLOVER, 5 CHILDREN, in age-order:
1. Ranger (Oakley, wife)
2. Ward
3. Ace
4. Etta
5. Ida

BULL AND STONE GLOVER WERE BROTHERS, SO THEIR children are cousins. Ranger and Bear, for example, are cousins, and each the oldest sibling in their families.

THE GLOVERS KNOW AND INTERACT WITH THE WALKERS of Seven Sons Ranch. There's a lot of them too! Here's a little cheat sheet for you for the Walkers.

MOMMA & DADDY: PENNY AND GIDEON WALKER

    1. RHETT & EVELYN WALKER

    Son: Conrad

    Triplets: Austin, Elaine, and Easton

    2. JEREMIAH & WHITNEY WALKER

    Son: Jonah Jeremiah (JJ)

    Daughter: Clara Jean

    Son: Jason

    3. LIAM & CALLIE WALKER

    Daughter: Denise

    Daughter: Ginger

    4. TRIPP & IVORY WALKER

    Son: Oliver

    Son: Isaac

    5. WYATT & MARCY WALKER

    Son: Warren

    Son: Cole

Son: Harrison

6. SKYLER & MALLERY WALKER
Daughter: Camila

7. MICAH & SIMONE WALKER
Son: Travis (Trap)

Chapter One

Bishop Glover looked in the mirror and adjusted his bow tie. He'd been praying for a solid month for two things: that the barn would be finished in time for today's weddings, and that the weather would be perfect.

The barn had literally been finished last night when Bishop himself had hung the mirror in the bride's room. As the project had commenced, he'd realized they'd need more than just a huge open space for dancing or eating and a kitchen.

They needed bathrooms. They needed a furnace room. They needed dressing rooms, especially if the barn was going to be used for weddings, which it obviously was.

His cousin had spilled the beans to his brother about the barn project, and Bishop had been annoyed in the beginning. As the construction got started and it outgrew his own vision for it, Bishop had been grateful Bear knew about the barn renovation.

He'd suggested Bishop contact Micah Walker, who'd designed and built the new mansion-like homestead for the family.

Bishop had, and Micah could see way beyond what he could.

So the barn now had bathrooms, dressing rooms, a kitchen, a mudroom, and a control room, where the music and lighting could be programmed or changed with a few taps and presses of a button.

There were two hot water heaters in the barn, an industrial kitchen they'd probably use several times a year, beautiful barn doors that sectioned off the back of the barn for the dressing rooms and bathrooms, and a hardwood floor throughout.

Bishop loved the barn with his whole soul. If he could put a bedroom in the loft, he'd live there.

As it was, the loft was just for show. There was no ladder to get up to it, and it sat above the kitchen and looked pretty with the new posts and pillars Bishop had carved by hand.

In the end, almost everyone—except the two groomsmen for today—who worked on the ranch had put in some labor on the blue barn, which Bishop had affectionately named True Blue.

He'd gone to his mother's and looked through the old photo albums she had, and together, they'd found several picture of his father and his uncle working on the barn. They'd built it with their daddy and a few cowboys who'd worked Shiloh Ridge Ranch at the time.

Bishop had taken the photos and gone to the

genealogical society in Three Rivers. He'd asked for the best way to enlarge them and frame them so the memories wouldn't be lost. A very nice woman there had helped him, and Bishop had hung those pictures last night too.

"Come on," someone said, pounding on his door. "We're going to be late."

"Coming," he yelled as he left the bathroom. He exited his suite to noise coming down the hallway from the living room. Until last week, he'd lived in the west wing of the mansion-slash-homestead, but he and his oldest brother, Bear, had switched places.

Bear was going to be married today, and his wife and step-son were coming to live on the ranch.

Bishop's suite had a large bedroom, a full bath, and a private living area. It was enough for him right now.

His cousin, Ranger, who was also getting married today, already lived in the east wing, and once he and his wife returned from their honeymoon, they'd live upstairs together too.

Bishop looked around at the chaos in the house and thought forward about twelve hours. All of this would be done. The brothers and sisters and cousins and aunts and uncles would all go home. The weddings would be over.

Bishop could order dinner, drive down to Three Rivers to get it, and come sit in a quiet house by himself.

Sort of.

His eyes caught on his only sister as she turned toward someone entering the kitchen. Arizona was coming to stay in the house with Bishop while the two newlywed couples were on their honeymoons, because her house needed to be sprayed for termites.

Mother was going to go stay with her sister-in-law in town, and she had plenty of sons to help get her there and back any time she wanted to come to the ranch.

"It's time to go," Cactus yelled, and he could have a loud voice when he wanted to. He'd really come out of his prickly shell in the past four or five months, though he still hadn't found a woman he wanted to go out with more than twice.

The men and women in the house started to move out, and Bishop joined the flow. They could get almost all the way to True Blue on a road, so most people loaded into vehicles and started rumbling down the gravel lane.

Some people walked.

Bishop caught up to Zona and asked, "Want a ride?"

"I'm going with Duke," she said, looking up at Bishop. "Do you want to ride with us?"

"Sure," Bishop said. He liked Duke Rhinehart just fine, though he knew there was something that had happened with him in the past. Bear didn't seem to mind him, and Bishop tried very hard to only make judgments based on his own personal experiences with someone.

He climbed in the back of Duke's extended cab truck, finding his younger brothers there too. "Howdy, fellas," he said. "You guys lookin' for more work?"

"No, sir," one of them drawled. "Our place keeps us plenty busy."

The other one nodded, his eyes round like Bishop

would force him to come work at Shiloh Ridge after they finished their chores on their own ranch.

"Maybe in the summer," Bishop said, pinning his grin in place. "If y'all have friends who need a job, send 'em up here. We always have more work than we can do ourselves."

"That so?" Duke asked, looking in the rear-view mirror. He'd been waiting for his turn, and he finally eased out onto the road.

"Yes," Bishop said, already tired and summer was still a month or two off.

"I might know some guys."

"We've got seven empty cowboy cabins," Bishop said. "I'm trying to get Bear and Ranger to fill them this year. They'll be busy with their new families, and I'm tired of working fifteen hours a day."

He loved Shiloh Ridge, and he didn't want to be anywhere else. He never had. He'd always seen himself working this generational land that his ancestors had cultivated and loved. He just wanted time to sleep too. Time to date. Time to watch TV. Was that so wrong?

A frown filled his face, and he looked out the window.

In a truck, getting to True Blue only took about five minutes, and Bishop got out with everyone else when they arrived. He noticed Duke coming around to Zona's side and helping her down as she was in a pretty dress the color of evening clouds. Sort of pink, but also sort of peachy, and maybe a little gold. The dress shimmered, and Bishop watched as Zona smiled up at Duke and laced her arm through his.

They made a cute couple, and they'd been dating since just before Christmas.

Bishop himself had been on many dates since Christmas, but nothing seemed to stick. Even with the women he really liked, he couldn't seem to make a relationship launch. Familiar frustration built within him, and he strode inside as a bit of a breeze picked up.

The Lord had heard his prayers about the weather, though he knew he wasn't the only one who'd been praying for such a blessing. The whole Glover family had been, and it certainly seemed like the rain would hold off for a few more hours.

Bishop slowed as he neared the barn. She'd gotten a fresh coat of blue paint, and she gleamed in the sunlight. The doors had been widened, and new ones fashioned and fitted on the tracks. They could lock, but right now, they'd been thrown wide open.

A tall vase of flowers and greenery stood sentinel on either side of the open doors, with a small podium next to one. People paused there to write their names in the two guest books, but Bishop didn't.

The scent of roses blew toward him from inside the barn, and he stepped from dirt to a wide rug that would help clean people's boots and shoes as they transitioned from outdoor to indoor space.

The hardwood stretched beyond that, and the huge serving window Micah had suggested in the kitchen had been rolled up. Trays and plates sat there, and people moved in and out as they got appetizers and snacks before the wedding began.

The altar was immediately to his left, with the rows of chairs filling what could also be a dance floor. The middle aisle ran straight back to another set of hand-planed and hand-stained barn doors. Through those sat the dressing rooms and bathrooms, and the brides and grooms would exit back there, walk down the aisle, get married at the front, and be able to walk out the doorway where he stood easily.

It was a genius layout, really. Bishop had gotten them eighty percent of the way there.

"This place is incredible," Ace said, coming to a stop beside Bishop. The two cousins looked at one another and smiled. "I can't wait to get married here."

"Yeah? Are you gonna ask Bea?"

Ace's smile turned a bit mischievous. "You never know." He entered the barn, making a beeline for the kitchen window in the back corner, and Bishop shook his head. He knew what *you never know* meant.

It meant no.

Ace was currently dating Beatrice Gates, but he was really smitten with another woman.

Soft music played from the speakers high above the floor, and Bishop had installed those himself too. He could lean his head back and find them easily, though neither Ranger nor Bear had been able to spot more than one or two.

"Afternoon, Bishop."

He turned toward the male voice and found Pastor Summers. "Heya," he said, smiling and extending his hand to shake the pastor's. "Mrs. Summers. Good to see you." He shook her hand too.

"This is beautiful," she said, gazing around. She had blonde hair that had started to lose its color, and eyes the same as all the Glovers: blue. She had a kind soul, and Bishop had literally never seen the woman upset. "Are y'all renting it out?"

"I don't think so," Bishop said.

Her eyes came to his. "Our daughter would *love* to get married here. Don't you think, Curtis?"

"Hmm, probably," Pastor Summers said.

Mrs. Summers looked at Bishop again. "We need to talk some more."

"Okay," Bishop said, but he wasn't sure why she was talking to him. He was the youngest male in the family, and he literally had no say about how things were run on the ranch. Sure, sometimes Ranger and Bear sent emails or texts about big purchases or major projects, just to get feedback from everyone. In the end, though, they got to decide what happened at Shiloh Ridge.

"Excuse me," a woman said into the microphone. "It's time to take your seats, if you would, please. Our first bride will be coming down the aisle in only ten short minutes."

Bishop did what his cousin said to do, his seat decided up front. Both Bear and Ranger had opted for a wedding party in pictures only. Only the brides would be escorted down the aisle to meet their waiting groom. The wedding party would stand at the front for a moment, and then sit in the first couple of rows.

He got a fancy flower for his lapel too. He supposed that counted for something.

Bishop took his spot at the end of the row for his family, his four older brothers and Zona already there. The only one missing was Bear.

And Daddy, Bishop thought, a momentary pang of sadness gonging against his heart. He'd only been eighteen years old when his father had died, and Bishop sometimes felt like he had no idea how to be a man because his daddy hadn't been there when he'd become one.

He swallowed against the emotions and looked to the other side of the aisle. Samantha Benton's family sat over there, but it was just her mother and a few friends. Her father and her son would be walking her down the aisle to Bear.

Sammy owned the mechanic shop in town, and all of her mechanics and their families had come. Bishop liked seeing them there, as they sure did feel like family for Sammy.

The music paused, and the very air itself seemed to pause. Then, a new song started, and the crowd got to its feet as Bear pushed open the barn doors at the back of the hall. He beamed out at the crowd, his face softening even more as he cocked his elbow for Mother to put her hand on.

They walked down the aisle together, and Bishop could not stop grinning. Once they'd reached the altar, Mother straightened Bear's tie and hugged him tight. His siblings surged forward, all of them seeming to step at the same time.

Bear chuckled as they did a group hug for him, and then they stepped back to their places, Cactus holding onto Mother now.

The music paused again, and Bishop spun toward the open doors. Sammy appeared, her dress simple and elegant. It hugged her close to the hip, and then flared into a traditional wedding dress shape. Her train was long, and her son helped her fan it out behind her.

Then Lincoln disappeared again, and when he returned, he held onto his grandfather, who limped and wobbled on his feet. He managed to get to Sammy, who secured her hand in his, a wide smile on her face.

Lincoln moved to her other side, and then the three of them marched down the aisle. Bishop reveled in the reverence and spirit in the barn, a sense of family and love so permeating he felt himself start to choke up a little.

Pastor Summers could really get going during some of his sermons, but today, he kept the ceremony simple and to the point. He spoke of love and forgiveness, and, "Most of all," he said. "Be willing to talk to one another. Don't be afraid to tell your partner how you feel. Most issues can be resolved through proper communication."

Bishop thought about his failed relationships. Maybe that was what he'd been doing wrong. Not saying what he should say.

"Bartholomew Stone Glover, do you take Samantha Eden Benton to be your lawfully wedded wife, to love, to cherish, and to weather life's storms with?"

"Yes, sir," Bear said, causing a few twitters among the crowd.

Pastor Summers smiled at him and switched his gaze to Sammy. "Samantha Eden Benton, do you give yourself to Bear, and taken him unto yourself, to be your lawfully wedded husband, to love, to cherish, and to weather life's storms with?"

"Yes," Sammy said.

"I now pronounce you man and wife," the pastor said, and Bear turned toward Sammy. He dipped her down as cheers erupted, and they kissed. Bear lifted her up, and they faced the crowd.

Bear stepped over to Mother and hugged her while Sammy separated from him and went to her mom. Once another round of congratulations had finished, Bear and Sammy took their places in the audience.

The music paused. Ranger appeared in the doorway, and he wore a darker suit, a darker cowboy hat, and plenty of joy on his face. Bishop loved his cousin almost as much as his brother, and he let himself get lost in the happiness pouring from him.

Ranger walked down the aisle himself, kissed his mother on the cheek, and took his spot at the altar.

His bride, Oakley Hatch, appeared in the doorway too, and she also did not have an escort. Bishop glanced at Ace, who frowned. "I thought her father was coming," Bishop whispered.

"Me too," Ace said, looking at Ward. He too wore a concerned look, and they all turned to look at Ranger.

Bishop wanted to race to the back of the barn and offer his arm to Oakley. *Should I?* he wondered.

He didn't feel like he shouldn't, so he nudged Ace.

"Let's go. Get Ward." With that, he turned and went down the aisle on the outside of the chairs. He didn't care who saw him or what they thought. He was not letting Oakley walk down that aisle by herself.

She took the first step, and Bishop raised his hand. She caught sight of him coming toward her, and her eyes widened. Bishop arrived a moment later and offered his arm to her.

"Bishop," she said, her voice breaking.

"If you hate me for doing this, I'll go back to my seat," he whispered.

She shook her head, and then Ace crossed in front of them and took Oakley's other arm. Ward joined them, stepping behind Oakley and putting his hand on her shoulder.

Bishop looked up to the altar, where Ranger stood. He'd come forward a few steps and waited beside the first row of chairs.

All of the chairs were empty, because every Glover had followed Bishop. They formed a halo around Oakley now, who let out one sob and turned around.

Bishop looked at Ace, and they quickly stepped into the aisle to shield her from all the guests. Ward leaned down and said something to Oakley, and she nodded. He smiled at her, and Oakley handed her flowers to Zona and took a moment to wipe her eyes. Ida and Etta fretted over her for another few seconds, and then they nodded their approval.

Oakley took her flowers, took a giant breath that seemed to fill her whole body, and turned around.

Guilt tripped through Bishop. He should've stayed at his seat. He'd made her cry. "I'm sorry," he whispered.

"Don't be." She reached for him, and he and Ace took their positions on either side of her. The entire family walked down the aisle with Oakley, and they all gave her to Ranger. Really, they were giving Ranger to her, and Bishop actually thought it was a beautiful moment.

Another simple speech, and with less theatrics, Ranger kissed his new wife amidst the same loud cheering that Bear and Sammy had received.

Bishop drew in a deep breath and admired the men in his life he'd always looked up to. He sure did hope he could find someone as amazing as Sammy or Oakley, and he took a moment to close his eyes and offer up a simple prayer.

Thank you for showing me what true love is.

BISHOP GOT HIS QUIET SOLITUDE THAT EVENING. THE next day too, as it was the Sabbath, and everyone seemed exhausted from the previous day's events.

On Monday morning, Bishop had just set the coffee to brew when the doorbell rang. He whipped his attention that way, wondering who in the world would be out this way this early. Arizona hadn't gotten up yet, and if it was anyone else, they'd have just come in the house.

Bishop wasn't worried as he padded through the enormous kitchen, under the wide, arched doorway, and into the foyer. He pulled open the door to find a beautiful blonde woman standing there.

His mind said hello, but his voice stayed mute. He could only stare at her, taking her in piece by piece.

Pretty face, with plenty of personality in those vibrant blue eyes. She wore a black jacket over her shirt, which looked to be pink, red, and white plaid. She wore jeans and work boots, but the thing that caught Bishop's attention the most was the tool belt strapped around her waist.

His mouth turned dry.

She was an angel straight from heaven, crafted just for Bishop Glover.

"Good mornin'," she drawled, but he could tell instantly she wasn't from Texas. *Doesn't matter*, he thought. *It's a minor negative. Very minor.*

He still couldn't get his voice to work, and the woman slid her eyes down his chest, immediately bringing her gaze back to his. "Uh…I'm Montana Martin, and I'm wondering if you have any need for an extra hand with any construction projects. I have a certification in cabinetry, as well as a decade of experience with one of the biggest builders in San Antonio."

Bishop nodded, his vocal cords unknotting. Finally. "I could've used you three months ago," he said.

"Oh." Montana's face fell. "You're all caught up now?"

With the cabin remodels, the whole barn renovation, and the Ranch House set to get work done too, Bishop had hired multiple temporary workers to get the jobs done.

"We're never caught up," he said, curling his fingers over the top of the door and leaning into the frame. "I'm sure I can find something for you to do."

And if he couldn't, he'd invent something. Maybe a new

chicken coop needed to be built. No matter what, he needed to keep Montana nearby so he could get to know her better.

Montana's face burst into a smile, and it dang near made Bishop groan. She was stunning, the morning light streaking toward her across the front porch. When it touched her, she'd light up like a flame, and Bishop really wanted to see that.

"Do you have a minute to talk?" he asked. "I don't have to be out on the ranch for a bit."

Montana swallowed and nodded, her fingers tightening around that sexy tool belt. "Do you live alone?"

"No, ma'am," he said. "My sister's here with me. I'll get her to come down." He was a proper gentleman, after all.

Montana relaxed, her hand releasing the tool belt, and she nodded. "Okay. I can stay for a few minutes. Could you, uh, maybe put on a shirt?"

Bishop's eyes widened. Horrified, he looked down at himself. Sure enough, his torso was bare, and a bomb of heat exploded through his body. Still, he thought he sounded pretty cool when he said, "Sure. C'mon in and help yourself to a cup of coffee while I get dressed."

Chapter Two

Montana Martin entered the house after the tall, muscled man, realizing she hadn't gotten his name. She knew where she'd come though, and she knew the Glover family owned Shiloh Ridge. She didn't know all of their names, or even if they all lived here. She'd come to the first and biggest house on the ranch, assuming she'd get the owner.

She couldn't believe she'd made it through the front door. None of her other solicitations at other ranches had earned her more than a, "Sorry, we've got all the help we need," and a sympathetic smile.

Everyone in Texas sure was polite, she'd give them that.

She looked around the house, taking in the enormity of it. The ceiling here in the foyer stretched for two stories. The work on the banister leading up the double-wide stairs was custom and hand-made. Montana frowned at it, because she recognized the superior craftsmanship.

"Micah Walker," she muttered under her breath. The man had opened his custom home construction business at literally the same time Montana had. He had more money and more charisma, and his business had taken off while hers had whimpered in the darkness.

The only reason she'd survived for the past couple of years was because of her aunt and uncle's generosity and kindness. She'd had a job with a construction firm that had finished their subdivision three months ago, and Montana still hadn't found consistent full-time work.

The building boom in Three Rivers seemed to be slowing down a little, but she didn't want to leave town. She liked the stability she'd earned here, and she wanted to maintain some level of that for herself and her daughter.

Things had started to pick up in the past couple of months since she'd landed on a list in the Two Cents app, and Montana had been using that during some of her pitches.

What are you doing here? she wondered as she looked at the carved name above the doorway that led deeper into the house. Everything about this place screamed wealth, that was what she was doing there.

She needed a job, plain and simple.

It had taken her thirty-five minutes to get here from her aunt's house on the east side of town, and that was way too far to drive every day. Aurora was still in school, but Montana liked to be home when her daughter got off the bus.

She'd basically be able to work half-days with a commute as far as this one.

He's the first person who's let you in, she thought, quickly changing her internal dialog into a prayer. *Please, Lord, help this to work out. I need this job.*

"I said you could come in."

She turned toward the man, who now wore jeans instead of gym shorts, a black and white shirt with plenty of checkers on it, and a deliciously black cowboy hat. "I was just taking in the beauty of this place," she said. "It can't be very old."

"A little over a year," he said, looking up at the ceiling and walls too.

"Micah Walker did it, didn't he?" Montana watched the man.

He smiled, which only made her want to roll her eyes. "He sure did." He met her gaze again. "Do you know Micah?"

"Doesn't everyone?" she asked, realizing too late how bitter she sounded.

He didn't seem to notice though. His smile stayed hitched in place, and he stared at her in a way that almost had her walking right back out the front door, job or not. He blinked, and Montana saw a hint of redness creep up his neck.

"Sorry," he said with a low chuckle. "I'm not properly caffeinated. Come in, come in." He turned and went into the kitchen, and Montana decided to follow him.

"I'm Bishop, by the way," he said. "I realize I never even told you that." He stood in the biggest kitchen Montana had ever seen. The house seemed to go on and on, and the massive dining table against the far wall intrigued her.

The living room held four couches and three more loveseats, a huge flatscreen TV, and even a couple of beanbags. She half-expected a little black dog to come trotting up to greet her, because she'd entered a fairytale where all dreams came true.

Her daughter really wanted a little black dog, and that would've been heaven for Aurora.

"Coffee?" Bishop appeared in front of her, a mug extended toward her. "I'll get the cream out. Sugar is on the counter there."

"Thanks," she said, taking the mug. She didn't know where to look next, and she took a sip of the coffee. It was mighty good too, even without sugar. She still stepped over to the counter and spooned in the good stuff. She sighed as she sat at the bar and watched Bishop doctor up a cup of coffee for himself.

He turned, his face already beaming, and walked over to her. "What's your schedule like?" he asked.

"I'm pretty open," she said, glancing at him. "I have a small job at the college to finish up, and then I'm all yours." She realized what she'd said and pressed her eyes closed.

"Hmm, I like the sound of that," Bishop said.

Montana's eyes flew open, and she faced him. "What?"

"Nothing," he said, lifting his cup to his mouth. He sipped and asked, "Where else have you worked? Do you have a general contractor's license? Business insurance? That kind of stuff?"

"Yes," Montana said. She went on to detail her latest job with Liberty Homes. "I do have a general contractor's license, and I'm a master carpenter." She watched his eyebrows go up. "I can do anything you need me to on your ranch, Bishop. Sir."

He burst out laughing. "You do not need to call me sir," he said. "And I'm—"

"Bishop," a woman called, and a moment later, she came running into the kitchen. "Have you seen that blasted lizard? Link says it's not in his room, and he swears it was last night when he went to bed."

"Haven't seen 'im," Bishop said, clearly unconcerned about the lizard. "Are you taking Link to school today?"

"Yes," the woman said, and Montana ducked her head as she realized she'd met this woman before—and not under good circumstances.

"My sister," Bishop said. "Arizona." His face lit up, and he got to his feet. "Hey, you guys both have state names." He looked from his sister to Montana and back.

Arizona finally noticed her, and Montana decided to simply stare back. If she was going to work here— and she hoped and prayed she was—she'd have to deal with the woman. If only she'd known she was a Glover.

"This is Montana," Bishop said, indicating her. "She's gonna work around the ranch for us."

"Us?" Montana asked at the same time Arizona scoffed and then started laughing.

"Right," she said as she moved into the kitchen and started pouring herself a cup of coffee. "I don't think so."

"No?" Bishop asked, clearly confused.

Arizona turned around and took a long drink of her black coffee, her eyes never leaving Montana. She finally ducked her head, because she couldn't withstand the loathing coming from Arizona.

"No," Arizona said. "She's not."

"Why not?" Bishop asked.

"I wasn't hitting on him," Montana said at the same time Arizona took a breath in.

"She hit on Duke right in front of me."

"No," Montana said again. "You just blew it all out of proportion."

"I did not," Arizona said. "You came right over to our table and asked him to dance as if I wasn't even there."

"I just wanted to ask him about a job." Montana flicked her eyes in Bishop's direction. She didn't need to be right here. She could let this go. "*He* asked me to dance. I said yes."

"Why would he do that?" Arizona asked, throwing her hands into the air. "It makes no sense."

Montana could see the situation from her point of view, and Arizona was right. Duke Rhinehart's behavior last week made no sense. "I don't know." She glanced at Bishop, who now wore confusion in the slant of his eyebrows. He seemed to be made of light on dark, and Montana sure did like the golden color of his skin, the way his hair was brown, yet also highlighted with blonde. He had light blue eyes the color of the flowers she'd had in her first wedding bouquet, and as she'd already seen him with his shirt off, she knew the man had muscles in all the right places.

His strong jaw reminded her of her brother's, though her feelings for Bishop weren't anything brotherly at all.

She looked away from him when she realized she even had feelings for him.

She didn't know if she should sit back down or leave. They hadn't agreed on a wage, nor had Bishop invited her back to his ranch so she could look at the projects they were doing. Montana clenched her jaw and held her ground.

"I apprenticed for Marion Thurgate," she said. "I don't know if you know him, but he's—"

"Only the best woodworker in the state," Bishop said, his charm and charisma returning in a single heartbeat.

Montana couldn't help the beam of sunshine that shone through her body too. She smiled at him. "I think so too. I worked with him for four years."

"Where are you from?" he asked.

"Alabama originally," she said. "But I've been in Texas for a while now. Fifteen or sixteen years."

"Alabama," Arizona said. "Fifteen. Sixteen. It doesn't matter." She glared at Montana and then Bishop. "You're not hiring her. What is she going to do anyway?"

"We've got cabins and the Ranch House," Bishop said easily. He barely looked at Arizona and her animosity toward Montana only seemed to bother the two of them.

"Bear will never approve another full-time carpenter," Arizona said.

"Bear's on his honeymoon," Bishop said coolly. He looked at Montana again. "What's your rate?"

"I—"

"You can't just hire her," Arizona said, a hint of desperation in her voice now.

Montana kept her head down, a healthy dose of embarrassment making her feel too hot. The barstool was way too hard. She should leave.

"I can," Bishop said.

"You don't own the ranch."

Montana looked up then. "You don't own the ranch?"

Arizona burst out laughing, and Bishop blinked a couple of times. "No," he said. "I never said I owned the ranch."

"Yeah, but you made me think you did." Montana got up, tired of these games already. She'd never survive out here. "Sorry to waste your time." She started for the foyer, saying, "I'm sorry, Arizona. I was not hitting on your boyfriend, and I apologize that you thought I was."

Her momma had taught her that it wasn't always easy to apologize, but always worth it. Not only that, but she could do so even if she didn't think she'd done anything wrong.

"Wait," Bishop said, jumping to his feet too. He followed her into the foyer, saying, "I have full authority to hire for my construction teams. I don't need to own the ranch to give you a job."

Montana took a deep breath and faced him. "What do you pay?"

"Tell me what you charge."

She folded her arms. "Depending on the project, of course, but I typically earn one-fifty per day if I'm working on a project you have going. If I'm designing and building custom pieces, it doubles."

"I can do that," he said without breathing or blinking.

Montana's eyebrows went up, but she didn't challenge him. No sense in that, when the man had agreed to her fees so readily. "My schedule is pretty crazy," she said.

"You just said it was wide open after this small job at the college."

"Yeah." Montana shifted her feet. "I may need to go back and forth a little. Don't worry, Mister Glover. I can get whatever needs to be done, done. It just might not be during conventional work hours."

He cocked his head and studied her, and wow, Montana had the sudden urge to flirt with him.

"Explain that," he said.

She'd really rather not. She'd rather have her name signed in ink on a contract before she told him about Aurora. But he wasn't going to budge an inch, and the scent of Arizona's dislike of her hung heavy in the air too.

Before she could speak, Arizona called from the kitchen. "Stop flirting with her and come talk to me about this note Sammy left for Lincoln."

"I'm not flirting," Bishop called without removing his eyes from Montana's.

"We need to find that lizard too," Arizona said. "I'm not sleeping in this house with that thing on the loose."

"I'm hiring a construction team member," Bishop said, as if having two different conversations with his sister was normal.

Montana could not *believe* Arizona was his sister. What rotten luck.

"I am gonna need your number," Bishop said, a smile

gliding across his face. "I'll call you, and we'll work out the details of the contract. Okay?"

Montana nodded, reached into one of the pockets on her tool belt, and pulled out a business card. "That's my cell and my business number."

He took the card but didn't look at it. "You're going to have to tell me about your unconventional hours."

"All right."

"Maybe over dinner tonight?" He grinned at her and leaned closer. "Maybe I am flirting a little now."

Montana's eyes opened wider in surprise. It had been a while since a man had flirted with her, but she was glad she still recognized it. Of course, he'd come right out and *said* it, and Bishop Glover was unlike any man she'd ever met before.

"I have to ask my—" Thankfully, she managed to mute her voice before she could say "aunt." She wasn't twelve years old. She didn't need permission to go to dinner with a handsome cowboy.

"Assistant," she said, filling in the blank. "See what my schedule is."

"Oh, I see," he said, taking a step closer. "You'll have your people call my people, is that it?"

Montana had no idea how to respond. She looked at him, and he finally chuckled and shook his head. "You're a tough nut to crack, Montana. I like that."

He did? What exactly did he like?

"I'll call you later, okay? Check with your assistant so we can set something up."

"I knew you were asking her out," Arizona said,

appearing at his side. "Can you stop it already? I need help with that note. None of it makes sense." She gave a final glare to Montana and went back into the kitchen.

Montana turned and reached for the door, but Bishop jumped between her and it. He opened the door for her, and Montana's pulse spun cartwheels through her chest. "Okay, thanks," she said, finally getting her voice to work.

"See you soon," he said, and Montana walked away from the huge homestead, her blood running a little warmer in her veins and her head spinning a little bit.

As she drove away from Shiloh Ridge Ranch, she wasn't sure if she'd gotten a job or a date.

"Or both," she said to herself, seizing onto the idea of that and liking it very, very much.

Now she just had to wait for Bishop to call.

Chapter Three

Bishop ignored his sister's tirade as she started in on him and how he couldn't just go around town getting every blonde's number.

"This says he has soccer practice at four today," Bishop said. "What's so hard about that?" He looked at Arizona, who quickly turned toward the kitchen sink with her coffee mug. "Oh, I see. You just wanted to be annoying because I was talking to Montana."

"Montana," she said, most of the word a scoff. "What a dumb name."

"About like Arizona," he said, as he could hold his own with his sister. With any of the Glovers, really.

"Hey, I didn't name myself."

He took another sip of his coffee and waited until she turned to face him. "I don't imagine she did either." He lifted his eyebrows and grinned when Zona rolled her eyes. "Why don't you just ask Duke why he asked her to dance?"

"Because, Bishop, then I look and sound jealous."

"You are jealous."

"I am not." Zona glared at him. "Come help me find the lizard."

"Where's Link? Is he looking for it already?" Her and that lizard. She lived in the wilds of Texas, on a ranch with lots of bugs and critters. She should be able to handle a lizard.

"He said he was, but ten bucks says he's drawing in that sketch pad Mother gave him." She sounded cross about it, but Bishop knew she wasn't. Everyone loved Lincoln, himself included. He was a sweet boy, with a lot of talent with a pencil and a piece of paper. Mother had seen it and done something to cultivate it, just like she did with everyone.

Bishop went upstairs with his sister and into Bear's suite. He'd only been living there for a week or so, and Zona was staying in the third bedroom with Link while Bear and Sammy were on their honeymoon.

"Bishop, I can't find my other shoe," Link said when Bishop entered the boy's bedroom. It looked like a box of clothes had exploded, and he paused, taking in the scene.

"No wonder," he said, his skin starting to crawl already. Bishop liked a tidy room, that was for sure. He never left dirty dishes out, and he sprayed more air freshener than anyone ever should. He couldn't stand smells, and his nose wrinkled as he definitely caught a whiff of something decaying in the Lincoln's room.

"It's black," he said. "We have to leave soon."

"You look for the lizard," Bishop said. "I'll find the

shoe." He started picking up clothes, and he couldn't help folding them and laying them on the bed. Only three shirts in, he found the black hightop.

"Here you go, bud. Put it on." He turned to find Link stuffing his folders in his backpack. He seemed stressed, and Bishop stepped over to him. "Hey," he said. "What's going on?" He put his hand on Lincoln's shoulder, and the child finally stopped moving.

He sighed and sank into the chair in front of his desk. "I don't have anyone to come to Career Day this week."

Bishop's eyebrows went up. "That's not on the list your mom left."

"I didn't tell her about it."

"Lincoln." Bishop didn't mean to sound condescending or frustrated, but he was afraid he'd come off as both. "Why not?"

"Because then she wouldn't have married Bear, and I wouldn't be able to live here, and they wouldn't be on the beach right now." He looked up at Bishop with plenty of misery in his expression.

In that moment, Bishop realized how very smart Lincoln was. "Okay," he said. "I can come to Career Day. Or what about your grandpa or grandma? They could come."

Lincoln shook his head. "I don't want to ask them."

A dog barked from somewhere down the hall, and Zona shrieked. Bishop flew toward the bedroom door and caught the black and white spotted dog Link had gotten Sammy for her birthday racing right toward him.

He barked again, and Bishop saw the lizard as it went

streaking by him. "Grab it," he called to Link. "Benny found your lizard." He spun and closed the door, the lizard gone. Benny started rooting through the clothes, the puppy barking every other second.

"Too loud," Bishop said over him. "Leave it. Leave it alone." He tried to pull the dog away from the laundry, wondering if it was clean or dirty.

"Got him!" Lincoln yelled, and Benny lifted his head. He seemed to know what that meant—he couldn't chase the lizard anymore. He trotted over to the aquarium with the red heat lamp and sniffed at it.

Bishop needed to get out of this room before he had a mental breakdown over the cleanliness of it. He said, "Good job, Link. Get your shoe on and come downstairs. We can't have you bein' late on your first day your momma is gone." He stepped back into the hall, yelled to Zona that they'd caught the lizard, and went downstairs.

He made a sandwich for Link and had just tossed it into a paper bag when he and Zona appeared. "Applesauce or pudding?" he asked Link.

"Both," Link said, and Bishop put them both in his bag. He stooped to get a snack-size bag of cookies out of the cupboard and added those to the bag before rolling down the top and handing it to Link.

Lincoln grabbed onto him and hugged him, and Bishop's heart melted. He loved this boy, and he hugged Link back. "Be a good boy today, Link," he said. "And get me the information about Career Day."

"Yes, sir," Link said, and he and Zona left the house.

Bishop breathed in the silence and picked up his phone

to check what he needed to work on that day. Maybe he could call Montana right now and find out if she'd spoken to her assistant. "Too desperate?" he wondered under his breath as he put her number from the business card into his phone.

He tapped on his calendar to see where he'd be for most of the day. Sometimes he worked clear into the evening, especially as summer drew nearer. No sense in calling the woman if he wouldn't even be able to see her.

"Oh, buckets and barrels," he said when he saw the calendar.

He shoved his phone in his back pocket, swiped the keys to his truck from the drawer, and ran out of the house. Ten minutes later, he screeched to a halt at the Ranch house, where three of his brothers lived.

Judge stood on the roof with a couple of other guys, and Bishop whistled up to them. They all looked down at him. "Sorry," he called. "I lost track of time this morning. We had a lizard on the loose."

An internal sigh moved through him when he realized he'd left Benny at the homestead in his haste to get to the Ranch House for the roofers. The pup would need to go out soon, and Bishop liked having him around as he worked on the ranch.

"It's fine," Judge said. "C'mon up so you can see what's going on."

Bishop didn't see a way around it. He'd have to make another excuse after he saw whatever was on the roof, and head back to get Benny.

He climbed the ladder and joined them, immediately

seeing the problem. Hollow wood, and what looked like wood shavings, right there in the roof.

"Termites," he said, his heart sinking all the way to his toes. He might have authority to hire whoever he wanted for his construction crew, but he didn't own the ranch the way Bear and Ranger did, and only they could decide if this house should be sprayed and salvaged, or if the termite infestation was bad enough to have it razed and rebuilt.

"This isn't good," he said.

"Nope." Judge looked at him. "What are we going to do?"

"We can't just re-shingle," one of the men said. "The whole roof needs to be repaired or replaced. Then we can talk about shingles."

"Do you guys do that?" Bishop asked.

"Replace the entire roof on a home?" The man shook his head before he even finished speaking. "No, sir. We pull off old shingles, do minor fixes to the underlying sub-roof, and put on new shingles."

"So you're saying this isn't a minor fix." Bishop was kidding, of course. Anyone with two eyes—heck, probably only one—could see that the damage from the termites was major.

The man smiled, and Bishop did too. "I guess we don't need you today."

"We can pull the shingles off, at least," he said. "Demo it up so you can see what you're dealing with."

"Might as well," Judge said, his voice quiet and low. "They're already here, and we need to know what we're dealing with. Bear will insist on pictures."

Bishop nodded, because Judge was one-hundred percent right. Bear would want to see it all.

"Let's demo at least," he said to the roofers. "How long will that take?"

The man surveyed the roof. "A house this size? Three of us? We'll have it done before lunch."

"Great," Bishop said, already heading for the ladder. "Thanks so much." He thought about what replacing the roof would do to his schedule. They were only supposed to re-shingle today and tomorrow. Then everyone who worked on the ranch would come help move things out of the house. He'd scheduled painters to come. He was laying a whole new hardwood floor himself.

New textiles were arriving in three weeks. The entire kitchen was getting gutted and rebuilt, with a new configuration that made sense and made the kitchen more useable.

Delays were the name of the game in construction, but Bishop didn't have to like it. He frowned the whole way back to the homestead to get Benny too, because he suspected he wouldn't be able to get away from the ranch anytime that week to meet with Montana.

Take Montana to dinner?

He'd definitely flirted with her there at the end, and his tactics usually worked. Women ducked their heads and giggled, and Bishop knew he had their interest. Montana had just looked at him like he'd suddenly grown a second head.

She intrigued him, and Bishop thought that maybe he didn't want a giggly blonde. Perhaps that was why every single relationship he'd tried in the past few years had ended after only a few months.

"A few months at the most," he muttered to himself. He pulled up to the house and ran toward the front door. Inside, he called, "Come on, Benny. Let's get to work," still wondering how he could see Montana that week.

If they had to rebuild the whole Ranch House, he needed her. Badly.

The dog came hopping down the steps, and Bishop scooped him into his arms. "Can't lie around all day, you lazy dog," he said, smiling at the canine. "We work on this ranch, dogs and all."

Hard work had been instilled in him by his mother and father, and Bishop thrived on a full day's work. As he put Benny in the back of the truck and headed toward the cowboy cabins in the south sector, an idea popped into his head.

If he couldn't leave the ranch to see Montana this week, perhaps she'd come to him. A smile curved his lips, and he could barely wait until he got to the trio of cabins near Zona's and Mother's house to call her.

"Montana Home Designs," she said, and Bishop's grin grew.

"Hey there," he said. "It's Bishop Glover."

"Oh," she said.

He chuckled, mostly to get his nerves to settle. "Bet you didn't think I'd be calling so soon."

"Well, no," she said. "It's been what? Thirty minutes?"

"No idea," Bishop said. He didn't care about time. When the sun came up, he got up. When his stomach grumbled, he ate. When the sun went down, he went home. "I'm wondering how terribly busy you are. I've got a lot going on up here, and I'm afraid I won't be able to get down to town this week."

"Oh, well, we can meet next week," she said.

"No," he said. "I might need to build an entirely new house. We just found termites in the roof where my brothers live."

She whistled in a way that said, *Oh, boy, you're in trouble.*

They were; or rather, that house was. Bishop wouldn't call Bear or Ranger until he had all the facts and all the pictures. They deserved some time away from the ranch. He might not even call them at all.

Preacher, Mister, and Judge could find somewhere else to stay if they needed to. He could get a pest control company out to the ranch by tomorrow, and Bishop could handle this without bothering his brother and his new wife.

"Have you had a chance to talk to your assistant yet?" he asked.

"In the last thirty minutes?" she asked, her voice like a magical melody in Bishop's ears. "I'm surprised your call went through, honestly. The service out there is terrible."

"After thirty minutes, you should be back to town," he said, his curiosity piqued. "Where are you?"

"Almost back to town," she said. "I'm just saying, it's dead out there."

"And yet, I'm calling you." He grinned when she laughed lightly.

"Touché," she said.

"Well, we could have dinner up here and talk about your contract. Or you know, your schedule. Or your pretty eyes." He grinned, thinking himself so clever. "Whatever."

"Dinner?" she asked. "Will Arizona be there?"

"Nah," Bishop said, thinking of True Blue and the kitchen he'd built there. "I know a place we can go for privacy."

"You know, you're just digging yourself deeper and deeper with everything you say," she said.

Bishop watched a deer walk in front of his truck. "I am?"

"First, your pick-up line about my eyes? Pathetic," she said, though she distinctly had a teasing quality in her voice. "Second, you know a place we can go for privacy? That sounds like you're a total creeper."

"I just meant, I know somewhere we can get away from Zona."

"That's the only good thing you said."

"She really is nice once you get to know her."

"I'll take your word for it." Montana sighed, and Bishop could hear the frustration inside her. "Am I bringing this dinner up to you?"

"No," he said. "I'll cook."

"You cook?" she asked. "Of course he does. *Of course* he cooks."

Bishop grinned, wondering if she knew she was talking out loud. "Just tell me any allergies and what time you can come. I know it's a bit of a drive, but I really am swamped —and I really do need you."

"No allergies," she said. "Can I text you for the time? I haven't even gotten back to my office yet."

"Oh, all right," he said, laughing lightly afterward. "Text me when you know."

She said she would, and the call ended. Bishop got out of the truck, still whistling, and went to make his final assessment on these cabins. Their men had stayed here during the main cabin remodel, and they'd turned in quite a long list of items that needed to be fixed.

Bishop took a ton of pictures and notes, prepping for the family ranch meetings he sometimes attended with Ranger and Bear. Sometimes Ward and Cactus were there too. No matter what, Bishop would have to have details about the damage and repairs needed for these cabins if he wanted the projects approved.

They usually put their construction projects on a rotation. That way, all the cabins and houses on the ranch got updated periodically. The load across his shoulders and the rest of the Glovers was minimal, and he didn't find himself with more construction than he could handle. The past few months had just been insane because of the barn project, and he'd voluntarily agreed to that.

He opened the back door to the first cabin, the scent of mold nearly knocking him down the short flight of steps he'd taken. "Dear Lord," he whispered. "Is everything going to go wrong this week?"

Putting on his brave face, he entered the cabin. He wasn't sure they could repair this place. It might need to be replaced, which went against their core family motto. Heck, the Ranch House might need to be rebuilt from the foundation up, and there wasn't any recycling, reusing, or repairing that could save a house from a massive termite infestation.

He'd do the work here, snapping pictures and taking notes. Then he'd return to the Ranch House to do the same for the roof. Then he'd know what he was dealing with. Plain and simple. Easy as pie.

As he worked, all he could do was keep a prayer in his heart that he'd hear from Montana about dinner before too much of the day slipped away from him.

Maybe his line about her eyes was a little pathetic. Maybe he did get every blonde's number he could. Maybe he'd have to do something different with this woman if he wanted a different result.

But what? he asked himself. After all, Bishop was just Bishop, and he didn't know how to be anyone else.

As he left the first, moldy cabin, his phone chimed, and Montana's name sat there. A smile filled his chest and radiated from his face, especially when he saw her text.

Dinner at seven okay?

Dinner at seven is perfect, he typed and sent, his smile almost clownish. *See you then.*

/ # Chapter Four

Montana pulled up to her aunt's house just as her daughter started up the front steps. She scrambled to get out of a truck that had seen better days. It had been the vehicle she could afford, and it had served her well here in Three Rivers.

"Aurora," she called just as her daughter started to dig in the pocket of her backpack for her key. Montana hated that with every fiber of her being, and if she hadn't pulled over to check her schedule and then text Bishop Glover, she'd have beaten Aurora back to the house.

"Hey, Mom," she said, and Montana smiled at her before turning back to get her backpack.

"How was school?" Montana walked toward the front porch, her keys still out. Aurora didn't seem to notice or care that she sometimes had to unlock the door and go into a house that wasn't her own. Alone.

Montana knew it. She felt it keenly every afternoon,

and she worked to push away the bitter feelings that crept through her from time to time. She climbed the steps, clearing her head with each breath. "Hello?" she asked as she glanced to where her daughter stood.

Aurora didn't even look up, and she had her back to Montana, as she'd walked away from the door and toward the railing to say hello.

Irritation fired through Montana, but she fitted her key into the lock and twisted to get the door open. "Who are you texting?" Montana noticed how her daughter's head came up lightning-fast, and she turned back to her.

"No one."

"Yeah," Montana said dryly. She held out her hand. "Let me see."

"Mom," Aurora said with plenty of attitude.

"If you're not going to tell me, I get to see," she said, still waiting for her daughter to put the phone in her palm. "And none of these silly names like chicken nugget or luke-warm water." Montana cocked her head and smiled at her daughter.

Aurora smiled back, and she giggled in the next moment. "I really liked Sam," she said. "He stopped texting." She sighed as she put her phone in Montana's hand, and Montana started flipping it over in her fingers.

"I know, baby," Montana said. "But you've got your back-up boys, right? What about that boy in your drama class? Daniel? Dexter?"

"David," Aurora said, grinning. "I still like him. He's *so cute*, Mom." She pretended to swoon and go weak in the knees, and she bumped into Montana.

Montana grinned at her daughter, though her patience had already started to wear thin. She had no idea how to parent a fourteen-year-old, boy-crazy girl. She'd liked boys as a teenager, sure. But she'd never had a serious boyfriend. She went out with a lot of different boys, and she had a friend group of boys and girls that didn't date each other.

Aurora was forever telling Montana about how so-and-so liked this one boy, and they were holding hands at lunch. Then one of them would friend-zone the other, and before she knew it, the boy was texting Aurora or someone else in the group. Not only that, but once they "broke up," they kept hanging out.

Montana didn't understand any of it. She looked at Aurora's phone while her daughter started telling a story about how she saw David in the hall, and she'd been brave enough to say hi.

"Wow," Montana said. "Look at you being brave." She glanced up from the boy her daughter had been texting. She held up one hand so Aurora could give her a high-five. "Who's Ollie?" She looked at the texts again, but she didn't understand this kind of flirting. "He's invited you to his house in the afternoons."

Aurora reached for and took her phone from Montana. "He's a boy in my French class," she said. "He's really good at pretty much everything, and I...maybe...sort of...got a D on my last French test."

Montana gave her daughter a glare. "What? We went over the vocabulary. You knew it." She put her backpack on the kitchen table. "Those flashcards were for French, right?"

"Yes," Aurora said. "She did something weird on the test, and I didn't understand any of it." She sighed. "Don't worry, Mom. I can go in one day before lunch and retake it, but...." She looked away from Montana and opened the fridge.

"You want to go study at Ollie's." Montana had seen several of the texts.

"His dad picks him up every afternoon, and they live out on this lane off the south highway. He said he'd ask his parents if I could come tomorrow, and you can just come get me after you get done at the college. It's on that side of town."

"You have it all worked out, don't you?" Montana asked, plucking an apple from the bowl in the middle of the counter.

Aurora turned around with a can of soda in her hand. "Yes," she said. "It's close to the college, Ollie said."

"What's Ollie's last name?"

"Osburn," Aurora said. "Please, Mom? You can stay as long as you want, and you won't have to rush home at three o'clock to meet me here, and I'll get to study."

"Mm hm," Montana said, trying to decide how to phrase the question she wanted to ask. She took a few more bites of her apple while she popped the top on her soda and took a drink.

"And Ollie's just a...friend? Or we think he's super cute too?"

"Oh, he's super cute," Aurora said, squealing a little bit. "And, Mom, he's tall. And dark, and you're always telling me I need some height and some color so my kids aren't pale dwarves."

Montana laughed with her daughter, finished her apple, and drew her into a hug. "I love you, bug."

"I love you too, Mom."

"I'm...." Montana didn't know how to tell Aurora about Bishop. "I have a business meeting tonight," she said, the words only a little false. "I might have found another job that could help us get a place of our own."

"I like living with Aunt Jackie and Uncle Bob," Aurora said. "I have my own room, and the yard is big enough for a dog...." She lifted her eyebrows, such hope in her eyes.

Montana shook her head, but she kept a smile on her face. "We're not around enough for a dog, sissy."

"I know." Aurora left her can of soda on the counter, where Montana would likely pick it up, dump whatever she hadn't drunk down the drain, and put the can in the recycle bin. "So, what's the new job?"

"Oh, it's this ranch south of town," she said. "They need a full-time carpenter for a while." She hoped. She should probably pray, but she didn't want to hitch everything to hope and prayer.

"South of town is perfect for me to go to Ollie's after school...." Aurora said.

Montana shook her head. "You can go tomorrow," she said. "But you're not going every day."

"Maybe I could, though."

"Aurora." Montana shook her head again, stronger this time. "His parents are going to be home tomorrow afternoon?"

"Yes," she said.

"And you know we don't go in a boy's bedroom."

"I know."

"If he sends you pictures of himself, you…."

"Mom, I know."

"Tell me as if I don't know." Montana sometimes felt uncomfortable talking to her teenager about boys and hormones and sex, but it had to be done.

"I show you the picture, and then I tell him not to send me things like that, and then I block him."

"Good," Montana said. "But before that, you tell him your mother is coming over with an assortment of hammers."

"Mom." Aurora laughed and rolled her eyes. "Okay, I'm going to go do that English essay that's due tomorrow."

"Okay," Montana said, not really registering what her daughter had said until she was halfway down the hall. "Wait," she called. "I thought you finished that."

"Almost done," Aurora said, and the next thing Montana knew, her bedroom door clicked closed.

"That girl is going to be the death of me," Montana muttered. She looked up to the ceiling. "It would be nice if I could get some help with her."

Montana had prayed for help in every stage of Aurora's life. When she'd come home from her apprenticeship one day and found her husband had brought someone else home, Aurora had been four years old.

She'd finally packed their bags, and it had just been the two of them for the past decade. Most of the time, Montana was just fumbling her way through the darkness.

She turned to the fridge too, because as part of her rent, she made dinner every night. She'd gotten a package of chicken breasts out of the freezer that morning, and she set them on the counter so she could put a stock pot on the stove with plenty of salted water.

Once she had the pasta boiling, she got to work butterflying the chicken breasts and dredging them in flour and then panko breadcrumbs. They sizzled in the hot butter and oil, and once they were crispy and brown, she put them on a plate and added flour to the fat in the pan.

She'd just whisked in cream, cream cheese, and parmesan cheese when her phone rang.

Aunt Jackie's name sat on the screen, and Montana tapped with a clean knuckle to connect the call. "Hello," she said. "Dinner's almost done."

"I'm getting the bread," Aunt Jackie said. "And you're fine to go to your meeting tonight."

"Okay," Montana said. "Thanks."

"Bob should be there any minute. Remember he's got that boy with him."

Montana's mind blanked for a moment, and then she remembered that Uncle Bob was looking to hire someone to do the yard work this year. "I told him we could do it," Montana said. Cooking and yard work were how she could sleep at night, knowing she couldn't pay her aunt and uncle much in rent.

"Apparently, this boy has some magic system Bob wants to try." Aunt Jackie sounded like she'd believe it when she saw it.

"Okay," Montana said. "But I feel bad."

"You can still feed the chickens and milk the goats," Aunt Jackie said. "Don't worry, Ana. There's plenty to do." Something scratched on her end of the line, and she said, "Oops, I have to go. See you in a few minutes."

"Yeah," Montana said, letting her aunt's nickname for her flow through her. She hadn't been called Ana in a long time, and the name took her back to sweltering Texas days like the ones she'd experienced last summer.

Aunt Jackie and Uncle Bob had lived in Three Rivers for a very long time. Montana used to come visit her in the summer when her mother would take all the children for an extended vacation.

Later, Montana had realized that her mother got the kids out of the house for as much of the summer as possible so Daddy didn't kill one of them.

She had three siblings, and they'd all somehow landed in Texas.

None as far north as her, though, and they didn't live with long-lost relatives while trying to raise a teenager by themselves.

Montana loved her siblings. What they'd done carried enough blame to keep her from texting them very often, and she didn't like dwelling on the cracks in her family relationships.

She finished putting together dinner just as Uncle Bob walked in the back door. "Somethin' smells amazing," he said, his Texas drawl as thick as honey. He grinned at her, and she hugged him.

He was a big, tall, wide wall of a man, and he ran an outdoor outfitters store in town. Aunt Jackie did some work with him on the weekends, but otherwise, she worked as a nurse at the hospital in town.

"It's all ready," she said. "Aunt Jackie said she'll be here any minute with the bread." She started for the hallway, where a narrow doorway led to a set of even narrower steps. Her room sat at the top of those, and Montana could admit she didn't hate it. Only two bedrooms and a single bathroom existed on the second level of the farmhouse, the rest of it a sprawling one-story rambler.

Her bedroom had a slanted ceiling on one side, and Aurora's had a mirrored slant on the other side of her bedroom. The bathroom sat between them, and Montana felt like she and Aurora could get out of her aunt and uncle's hair with their second-floor bedrooms. She'd loved the slanted ceiling as a child, and she did now as an adult too.

"Don't wait for me," she said. "I'm eating at a business meeting tonight."

"Okay," Uncle Bob called after her. "I'll be outside with Steven for a bit."

"All right." Montana went upstairs and started searching through her closet for something to wear that said professional business meeting and that wasn't made of denim.

MONTANA PULLED UP TO THE MASSIVE MANSION-LIKE homestead at Shiloh Ridge and found Bishop sitting on the top step as if men like him did such things. "Play it cool," she told herself.

She hadn't been able to go downstairs wearing a denim skirt like she'd planned. She'd be peppered with questions from everyone in the house, including the lawn man Uncle Bob had hired and then invited to stay for dinner. Didn't they all understand that she'd rather not admit that this business meeting was really dinner with a good-looking cowboy?

That good-looking cowboy rose to his feet and came down the steps, making Montana's breath lodge somewhere behind her tongue. He'd said some pretty cheesy lines that day, but Montana hadn't been flirted with in a while, and she hadn't minded them so much.

She finally opened her door when she realized she was still sitting in her truck.

"You look nice," Bishop said as he approached.

Montana looked down at her clothes. They were clean, at least, but she'd ended up wearing a practically white-washed pair of jeans with a blouse as green as an emerald. It had pure white stitching on the sleeves, collar, and hem, and Montana wore it when she wanted to draw out the color in her eyes and provide strong contrast for her sometimes embarrassingly blonde hair.

"That's hardly a compliment," she said. "But thank you."

"It's not?" He seemed genuinely confused.

"Nice?" she repeated. She looked from the sexy black cowboy hat on his head down to his boots. They were dark brown and tucked up under a clean pair of dark wash jeans.

He wore a belt buckle that glinted in the evening sunlight, and a pale green dress shirt, open at the throat.

He was perfection, and Montana started having thoughts about him she hadn't had about a man in a long, long time.

"Amazing then," Bishop said. "You look amazing." He grinned at her, and it was clear the man went out with a lot of women. Did she really want to be another one?

"That's better," she said, teasing him. *Teasing* him. She didn't even know who she was anymore. "Are we staying here? Or...?" She left the sentence there, because she didn't want to eat under the same roof as his sister.

"Nope," he said. "It's about a ten-minute walk. We can drive in five." He looked at her truck, no judgment on his face. "So walk or drive?"

"We can walk," she said.

He nodded and gestured for her to turn and go in front of him. She did, and when they reached the wider lane beyond the truck, he came to her side easily with those long legs.

"It's a nice night," he said.

"Yes," she said. "And that, cowboy, is the proper usage of the adjective nice."

He looked at her, those light blue eyes dancing and lighting up with stars. In the next moment, he burst out laughing, and Montana felt like she'd conquered the world.

"I think we're gonna get along just fine, Montana," he said, grinning at her. "Let's go over the most pressing jobs I've got here."

He started to detail a termite infestation at what he

called the Ranch House. "Three of my brothers live there, but we're going to relocate them during the construction. My eldest brother is on his honeymoon, and the co-owner, my cousin, is as well."

"Did they marry each other?" Montana asked, smiling at him.

He didn't laugh this time, and foolishness spread through Montana. Maybe he was just a happy-go-lucky guy. Maybe he hadn't been flirting with her at all.

Bishop hadn't tried to touch her or hold her hand, and Montana turned serious. She couldn't blow this job because he was tall and dreamy in a cowboy hat and a belt buckle.

But oh, the belt buckle....

Montana steadfastly refused to look at it as he stepped in front of her and turned around to walk backward. "There's a barn up here," he said. "I did a lot of the work on it, and that's where we're eating dinner."

"And signing contracts," she said.

He nodded and reached up to press his hat further onto his head. "Yeah, I imagine if you want to clean up a nest of termites, I'm not gonna object." He fell into step beside her again, leaving her view wide open as a blue barn peeked its way around the corner of another building.

"My goodness," she said, her steps slowing. Everything about the scene in front of her should be on the front cover of a magazine. Perhaps one about old barns or country living or the perfect cowboy wedding.

"You did this?"

"Not all of it," he admitted. "I worked with some family members on it."

Montana cut a look at him, and he was almost as stunning as the old grain silo that had rust stains in the aged cracks. She adored old things, and especially old farm things. "How many family members do you have?"

"Six siblings," he said. "Me and five other boys, and then Arizona."

No wonder she was just *so pleasant* to be around. Montana kept her sarcastic and biting words beneath her tongue. It wouldn't do well to badmouth the man's sister.

"And my cousins. Three men, two women. My mother lives here on the ranch too. With Arizona."

"Oh, so she doesn't normally live in that mansion?"

Bishop chuckled and shook his head no. "What about you? You said you were from Alabama. Do you have family there still?"

"Believe it or not, we all live in the Lone Star State now."

"Well, Texas *is* the best," Bishop said without missing a beat. "Who's we?"

Montana swallowed, finding her throat sticky. "I have two sisters and a brother." *And a fourteen-year-old daughter.*

She took in Bishop's rugged jaw and deeply tanned skin. He wasn't a boy, but he couldn't be much older than thirty either. Aurora was almost half that.

"Parents?" he asked.

"Divorced," she said. *Just like me*, she added silently. "You said your mother lives here. Is your father...?"

"He died when I was only eighteen," Bishop said, looking toward the blue barn now. They approached the doors, and he slid the extravagant, carved piece of art to the side to reveal a spacious hall inside.

This was no barn, that was for sure.

"This is incredible." Montana wanted to walk around and simply touch everything. Feel the energy of it and smile when her heart got full. "I mean, just stunning." She couldn't look everywhere at once, and she hated that she might miss something.

"I can give you a tour later. Dinner is hot right now." He led her across the space to a single table that had been set up with two chairs. A flurry of bluebonnets peeked out from inside a stone vase, and Montana wasn't sure she was fit to sit on furniture this nice, inside a barn that was easily four times as big as the house she'd left behind in Austin.

"Sit, sit," Bishop said, and she realized he'd left and gone somewhere to get the two plates of food he now carried. He put one down in front of her chair and rounded the table to his. He'd just sat down when his phone rang. He glanced at it and swiped the call to voicemail.

"Sorry," he said. "I'm kind of on-call right now. My brother might call and want to know about the house. And well, our cabins have mold in them. I recommended we raze them and start over, and well, Bear doesn't like that. Goes against the family motto." He said the last two words in almost a cartoon voice, his head definitely bobbling in a way that wasn't entirely human.

"What's the family motto?" she asked, picking up her fork.

"Recycle, reuse, repair," he said. "We don't just replace. We work something to death, finally admit defeat, and *then* we replace." He grinned as he lifted a speared green bean to his mouth. After he'd eaten it, he said, "We don't use ATVs or anything besides trucks and tractors out here. When it's time to round up the herd, we do it all from horseback."

"Wow," she said. "How traditional."

For some reason, there was something very untraditional about Bishop she wanted to unwrap layer by layer.

His phone rang again, and Montana put a slice of steak in her mouth. A moan came out automatically, because this piece of meat had been properly seasoned and cooked to a perfect medium temperature.

"Where'd you get this food?" she asked as he once again swiped the call to voicemail.

"I made it," he said, looking up at her. His expression was so perfect—open and vulnerable.

"Oh, that's right. You cook," she said, no question in sight.

"Yes," he said. "You?"

"Yes," she said. "But I don't particularly enjoy it."

"I do," he said. "It's a nice release from the other stuff I do."

For some reason, she could see him relieving his stress by pounding out some bread dough, and it was a good picture in her mind.

His phone rang again, and Bishop snatched it from the table. "I'm going to kill him." He stood up. "Excuse me for two seconds." He turned his back on her and lifted the phone to his ear. "What, Ward?"

He stilled, and Montana lowered her fork.

Something had happened.

Something bad.

Sure enough, Bishop spun back to her, all the razzle dazzle gone from his expression. He looked straight ahead as he hurried forward. He gestured for her to get up and come with him, which she did.

"What is it?" she asked.

"Yes," Bishop said. "I've got the retardant. I'll call Wade." He lowered his phone as they spilled back into the evening air. He took a big breath, and Montana suddenly felt like she should too.

"Fire," he said. "There's a fire raging on Seven Sons Ranch."

Montana's first reaction was horror. Everyone knew fire in the Texas Panhandle spelled disaster. They were coming out of winter though, and perhaps a few things would still be wet.

Her second thought she would take to the grave with her. Everyone in Three Rivers and all neighboring counties, states, and countries loved the Walkers.

They owned Seven Sons Ranch, and even Montana could admit they were all drop-dead gorgeous. How a family got blessed with that many good-looking men, Montana didn't know.

Some dark seed in her heart hoped the fire would burn down Micah Walker's office. The one where he ran his custom home builds and kitchen remodeling business.

Jealousy and bitterness swirled within her, and she prayed the dangerous and malicious feelings would leave.

God granted her a miracle, because she suddenly no

longer felt envious of Micah and his business success she'd spent many hours wishing was hers.

"We have to go help them," she said.

"I'm getting the retardant we have," he said. "Wade Rhinehart next door has a drone. We can drop it from above." Bishop flew into action then, and it was all Montana could do to keep up with him.

She could pray while she lugged a bag of fire deterrent, so she did that, hoping the Walkers wouldn't suffer too much damage to their ranch, their animals, or their homes.

Chapter Five

Bishop pulled up to the pile of trucks parked right in the middle of the highway leading into Three Rivers, his heartbeat bouncing through his veins. "They closed the road," he said, stating the obvious.

"That's because that fire is gonna jump any second," Montana said. She didn't unbuckle her seatbelt the way Bishop did.

About a hundred yards down the road, all three of Three Rivers's fire engines had been parked there, lights flashing and hoses out.

"They're not getting that out in the next few minutes," Montana said.

"It's grown," Bishop said.

"Things shouldn't be terribly dry," Montana said as Bishop opened his door. "I don't get it."

"Probably tons of dead grass underneath the new growth," he said, heat licking his face from the fire despite his distance from it. The scent of ash and smoke filled his nose, and he choked and coughed. "You should stay in here."

"I will, unless you need help," Montana said.

This was not the way he'd imagined their evening would go, but he couldn't turn his back on friends—good friends—because he'd been hoping to ask a pretty blonde on a real dinner date. Tonight, they'd barely sat down to eat before Ward had called. His stomach was unhappy with only green beans for dinner, that was for sure.

He hadn't even gotten out the contract he needed to go over with her, but he supposed that made tonight less professional, and he wondered if maybe he had been on a date for twenty minutes before Ward's phone call.

He lowered the tailgate as Wade Rhinehart pulled up in his truck. His sons spilled out of the truck without much delay, including Zona's boyfriend, Duke. They all moved to the back of the truck too, and Bishop hefted a bag of fire retardant onto his shoulder and took it over to them.

Wade poured it into the drone's bucket, and he used a giant remote control to get the drone off the ground. "What do you think? The road?"

"If it jumps the road, it can come up the hill," Bishop said. Shiloh Ridge and Hidden Hill—the Rhinehart's place —were up in those hills. A few minutes down the road, a couple of lanes of homes sat on that side of the road.

"We need to keep it on this side," Wade said. "I feel bad, because I'm sure the Walkers would like it to leave their land." He looked at Bishop, concern in his eyes.

Bishop wasn't going to consult the man. He was thirty

years his senior, and Wade could make his own decisions. Before he could get the drone dropping any retardant, shouts filled the air, and one of the fire engines honked its horn, the sound nearly deafening.

Bishop spun to see flames shooting into the air, ash raining from the sky.

"Holy cow," he said, his heart pounding now. He shouldn't be here at all. There was nothing he could do to stop this, or even to help the Walkers.

He looked east, hoping they hadn't lost homes or barns or animals. A man came over a fence, and Bishop started toward Jeremiah. The man looked utterly exhausted, and he had dirt and soot on his face and clothes.

More shouts filled the air, and Bishop heard, "It's on the other side!"

He couldn't help looking, but his attention turned back to Jeremiah quickly, especially when he stepped to his side. "What happened?" Bishop asked.

"It's our fault," Jeremiah said. "I wish I could say it was lightning or a truck with a dragging chain." He sighed and took off his cowboy hat. His hair was remarkably clean as he ran his hand through it. "But we were working on a tractor out in a field, and the welder sparked. That caught the grass on fire, and it grew like, well, like wildfire."

He hung his head, and Bishop wanted to tell him stuff like this happened all the time.

"Not near the houses and barns, I hope, if you were out in the fields."

"No," Jeremiah said. "Praise the Lord. That's where all of us are—forming a line between the fire and fields and the rest of the ranch. We haven't lost any animals or structures." He looked past Bishop. "If it gets to the houses over there...." He trailed off, but Bishop heard the regret and agony laced in his voice.

"They'll make sure it doesn't," he said to reassure Jeremiah. He turned back to Wade, who was just now lifting the drone into the air. "Maybe you should dump that on the other side of the road, other side of the fire. Keep it from burning down the road toward the houses there."

Wade nodded, and he raised the drone into the air. Bishop moved over to the truck and transferred the bags of retardant he'd brought to the Rhinehart's truck. He called Cactus and told him the fire had jumped the road, and they needed eyes on their northeast borders to make sure the fire didn't burn onto their land.

He finished a phone call with Ward, who'd been on his way down but turned back when Bishop said there wasn't much to do down here.

He'd just sighed when Montana came marching toward him. She wore a look of fury on her face, and Bishop paused. She was absolutely stunning with that fire blazing from her eyes. The red and orange flames had made the normally-blue hue in them seem navy and purple, and Bishop waited for her to come closer.

She had a storm preceding her, and he felt her energy ram into him and flow over and around him for a few steps until she arrived. "They're saying the road is going to be closed for hours now."

"I'll bet," he said.

"I can't stay on this side of the line," she said. "I have to

—I have—" She glanced at Jeremiah, her distaste growing. Bishop looked at him too, and if he felt the animosity Montana Martin had for him, he didn't show it. Perhaps he didn't care.

Bishop assumed he was simply overwhelmed with that evening's events, and he met Montana's eyes. "We have plenty of room at Shiloh Ridge. My cousin's suite is empty."

She shook her head. "No," she said firmly. "There has to be another way back to Three Rivers."

"If you go all the way down to Pampa, you can come back north on the fifty-seven," Jeremiah said. "A couple of turns, and you get to the forty-two, which comes in on the east side. It's probably over two hours."

"You can't drive for two hours tonight," Bishop said. "It's really fine. There are tons of bedrooms at Shiloh Ridge." He didn't understand the panic pouring from her. She was like a sieve, though; he could feel everything she did.

"I'm not worried about a bedroom," she said, her teeth clenched. She turned her back on Jeremiah and took a few steps away. Bishop went with her, his curiosity rising with every breath he took.

He put his hand on her lower back and pressed in close to her. He wished he was doing so only a moment before whispering something sweet and flirty in her ear, but he'd have to save that for another time.

"What's the matter?" he asked.

She shook her head, a long sigh coming out of her mouth. "You're going to find out anyway."

Bishop just waited, his mind whirring. Maybe the source of her anxiety was the same reason she'd have odd hours on the job.

Montana tilted her head and looked up at him. Oh, she was close, and she somehow smelled like something he wanted in his life, despite the ash and smoke and flames. The heat flowing through him wasn't all from the fire now burning on both sides of the highway.

"I have a daughter I need to get home to."

"Oh," Bishop said, surprised but not to the point where he needed to freak out. He'd dated single moms before. "You don't have a neighbor or someone you can call?"

"I don't need to," Montana said. "We live with my aunt and uncle." She dropped her chin toward her chest then, and Bishop slipped his hand along her waist and into hers.

He didn't know what to say, so he kept quiet. This was a new skill he'd started working on in the past couple of months. He'd lived most of his life trying to get his voice heard. As the youngest in a large, loud family, he'd had to fight for his opinion to matter.

As a teenager, his mouth had gotten him in trouble more times than he could count. As an adult, he'd learned to stand out by joking and calling attention to himself. But his loud mouth had ruined his last few relationships, and he was determined not to say everything that came into his mind, nor to insert himself into every conversation.

Sometimes, he just needed to listen and let someone else have the spotlight.

"How old is your daughter? Can you call her and let her know you're safe?"

"I've already spoken to her and my aunt," Montana said. "I just…I don't like being away from them."

"I understand." He noticed that she'd dodged the question of how old her daughter was. But she could obviously talk on the phone, so she had to be at least four or five. "What's her name?"

"Aurora," Montana said. "She's fourteen."

"Fourteen?" came out of Bishop's mouth before he could school the tone. His shock was loud and clear, and Montana nodded by the light of the fire. Darkness had settled over Texas, and Bishop just wanted to go back to the barn and pretend like they could have a normal dinner and sign the contracts.

In that moment, he realized he was still holding Montana's hand, and he slipped his fingers away.

"Yes," Montana said, shifting away from him. "Fourteen."

"I don't think you're old enough to have a fourteen-year-old daughter," he said.

"I am," she said, but she didn't volunteer her age.

"I'm thirty-three," he said. "Older or younger?"

"Older," she said.

"More than a decade or less?"

"Less."

Bishop nodded. "That's all I needed to know."

"Why do you need to know that?" she asked, and Bishop backed up a step. Had she not noticed the fire sparking between them? Was she not present when he'd held her hand and touched her back? He thought he'd been blatantly obvious, but maybe he hadn't. Maybe the electricity he felt zipping from her to him and back was only in his experience.

"No reason," he said, because he was done making a fool of himself in front of pretty women. "I don't think we need to stay down here. We're just in the way." He stepped toward the back corner of the truck. "Want to go back up to the ranch?"

Montana got in the truck, and Bishop did too. It smelled more like her already, and she'd ridden in it for twenty minutes.

Twenty more, and he reached the T-junction on the ranch. The land spread before him, their main barn directly in front of him. Right, he'd park at the homestead. Left, and he could get almost all the way to True Blue. "Do you want to go finish dinner? The contracts are out there too."

"We might as well do that," she said, and Bishop turned left. A few minutes later, he pulled up to the stables and got out of the truck. He made very sure not to get too close to her or to touch her as they made the quick walk to the barn.

Their dinners still sat on the table Bishop had set up. One look at it, and Bishop could see the romance hanging in the air. How did Montana not see it?

Idiot, he chastised himself as they continued toward the table. "I can heat it up," he said.

"I'm sure it's fine." Montana sat down and immediately took a bite of steak. "Still good." She smiled at him, and Bishop swore the gesture was flirty.

Her signals were all over the place, and Bishop made a

decision to keep things strictly professional tonight. Get the contract signed. He did need her help on the ranch.

He shoved some steak in his mouth and stood up as he chewed. He went into the kitchen and collected the folder with their standard independent contractor contract in it, swallowed, and returned to the table.

"This is pretty basic," he said. "But you can have a lawyer look at it before you sign."

"Do I need to have a lawyer look at it?" she asked.

"No," he said. He set the folder in front of her.

She opened the folder and took out the top sheet. She seemed to read every word, and then she asked, "Do you have a pen?"

"Sure thing." Bishop plucked it out of his jacket pocket and handed it to her.

She signed the contract and handed it and the folder back to him.

"Great," he said. "I'm still hiring people, but you can come up tomorrow if you'd like. I can put you to work in the south cabins for now."

She nodded, but she didn't pick up her fork again. He felt the weight of her gaze on his face, but he didn't look up.

"What changed?" she asked.

"What do you mean?" Bishop did raise his eyes then, wishing he could just say what came into his mind.

"I mean, you changed. You went all cold."

Bishop searched her face, finding genuine interest and confusion on her face. "When's the last time you've been on a date?" he asked.

Her eyebrows flew up, and she leaned back, folding her arms. "Excuse me?"

"I've been flirting with you since the moment you showed up on my porch. I held your hand down there. Tried to figure out if you were a lot older than me or a little, because I don't mind an age difference, but I didn't want it to be, you know, creepy."

His mouth was going to get him into so much trouble tonight, and yet, he couldn't stop it. "And you were all, 'why do you need to know that?' as if you have no idea when a man is flirting with you. So I thought, maybe she hasn't dated in a while. I don't know. Maybe the fourteen-year-old prevents that. Maybe you're not looking for a boyfriend or another—" He finally got his voice to stop.

Montana's eyes had been steadily widening, and she gaped at him, her mouth open slightly. In the next moment, she snapped it shut, her arms still tightly clenched across her chest. "It's been a while," she said. "Since I dated."

"You seriously didn't know I was flirting with you?"

"I'm rusty, not oblivious."

Bishop nodded, his face starting to heat now that he'd blurted out the entirety of his thoughts.

"I'm thirty-seven," Montana said. "Four years isn't very much."

Bishop ducked his head and looked at his food. It wasn't appetizing cold, and he'd definitely need to eat something more than he had. "No, ma'am, it is not."

She hadn't said she was looking for a boyfriend or another husband, and Bishop found himself needing to know. "If a flirty cowboy with a really big mouth asked you to dinner, would you check with your assistant so you could go?"

"I don't have an assistant."

Bishop's gaze flew back to hers. A smile spread across her face, and she started giggling. That grew into real laughter, and Bishop grinned too.

"Liar, liar," he teased, chuckling with her.

Montana pulled out her phone and looked at her calendar. "Depending on the evening, I think I could say yes to dinner with a flirty cowboy who has an *honest* mouth."

Bishop's chest finally expanded properly when he breathed, and he grinned at her. "Great," he said. "Let me know if one asks you out."

Chapter Six

Montana went down the immaculately carved steps, slowing as she neared the first floor. She wasn't so bitter that she couldn't appreciate Micah Walker's skill with wood, even if she silently vowed to never say so, to anyone, out loud.

The front of the house had a long, wide hallway, but the only way to go was into the kitchen, so Montana bypassed the extra-wide front door and the huge windows, and went under the arched walkway that led into the kitchen.

She expected to see Bishop there, whipping up a hot breakfast before a day of hard work on the ranch. Only the faint morning light greeted her. Well, and plenty of silence.

Montana stopped again and took in the vastness of the space here. She'd always wanted a fifteen-foot-long island, and this kitchen had that. There were cupboards every-where, and they weren't quite white, but more of a freshly-churned-butter-yellow. They made the whole room lighter, and someone had put cheery blue and gray curtains to dress up the windows.

If she kept going straight, she could exit the house through another door that led out onto a deck. To the right of that sat the long table she'd admired yesterday. She moved over to that, tracing her fingertips along the wood. It spoke to her soul in a way nothing else, save motherhood, ever had.

She wasn't sure if that made her strange or wonderful that she loved her daughter only slightly more than she enjoyed taking a rough piece of wood and turning it into something as functional and beautiful as a family table like this one.

In her mind's eye, she could see the joy this wood got to absorb as people sat down for holiday meals. She felt the bond brothers had with brothers, and mothers with sons, and daughters with mothers. The sibling energy flowed through her, and she realized she'd closed her eyes.

She quickly snapped them open, because they were not her personal feelings. She pulled her hand away from the wood, and her mind cleared. Turning away from what was surely a magnificent place to be for any meal, Montana drank in the family room. Bishop had said his family was big, and this room looked like it could house them all.

Beside the fireplace sat a closed door, and she assumed wherever it led filled the rest of the first floor. The wing where she'd slept last night was directly above her head, and when she looked out the windows at the back of the house, she saw the deck went all the way around.

"This is an incredible house," she said aloud. She wasn't

sure if she'd ever be able to design anything like this, and she once again could appreciate Micah's talent. "You just need to think bigger."

She went into the kitchen, that thought in her mind, and started making coffee. She could at least do that while she waited for Bishop to wake up. She'd signed his contract last night, and she couldn't wait to get started here at Shiloh Ridge. She'd texted her crew at the college and said she'd be late that day, due to the fire, and her boss had told her to get there when she could.

She let herself imagine the way her bank account would benefit from the work here. Soon, she and Aurora would be able to move into their own place, and finally, Montana would be able to start living her own life.

She'd felt in limbo for so long, and she'd been praying for something like this that would help her achieve her goals. "Thank you, Lord," she whispered as she measured grounds and poured water into the coffee maker.

"Bishop doesn't like it when other people cook in his kitchen."

Montana gave a startled cry and turned around. Arizona stood there, fully dressed and ready for the day. She wore jeans and a belt, just like most cowboys. Her shirt was pink and yellow flowers, though, and Montana had never seen a man wear a shirt like that.

It went all the way to her wrists, and Arizona had taken her hair and pulled it all up on top of her head. How she'd put a hat over that, Montana didn't know.

"Sorry, I was just making coffee." She tried on a smile and added, "Good morning."

Arizona folded her arms and cocked her hip. After several long seconds of appraisal, she said, "Good morning."

Montana didn't want awkwardness between them. Not today, and not tomorrow, and not in a month when she was still here working on the ranch. "I sincerely apologize about Duke," Montana said. "I realize I shouldn't have approached you at dinner, but...." She paused for a moment, because she wasn't sure how to admit this. She just had to say it. She'd marched up to the door and knocked on it. She'd looked into a gorgeous man's face, and asked him if he needed help on his ranch.

She could tell Arizona anything.

"I needed a job," she said. "Desperately. The Rhinehart's had put a listing on the Three Rivers Classifieds, and Duke did text me to say he'd be in town that night at Double Spurs. I thought...." She sighed. "I honestly don't know what I thought. I thought maybe he'd take a minute with me, and that he'd told you, and I'm sorry. I didn't mean—"

"I know," Arizona said, finally holding up one palm toward Montana. "I called him last night. He said all the same things you just said." She rolled her eyes. "Men can be so dense sometimes." She walked over to the nearest barstool and sat on it, the inkling of a smile forming on her face. "I literally had to tell him that a heads-up about a job interview during our dinner date was warranted."

Montana giggled with Arizona as the first drips of coffee started to scent the air.

"There are eggs and bacon in the fridge," she said, nodding toward the huge, industrial-sized fridge.

"Yeah?" Montana's eyebrows went up. "You're going to get me in trouble."

"Bishop needs to know he's not the only one who knows how to fry an egg." Arizona grinned again and shrugged one shoulder. "Plus, I'm hungry."

"Mm hm." Montana retrieved the eggs and bacon from the fridge and took a pan from the rack hanging over the built-in stovetop in the middle of the island. She set it over the flame and turned it on. "Kitchen shears?"

"Probably in one of the drawers," Arizona said, her attention switched to her phone.

Montana opened all the drawers in the island before she found the kitchen shears, and they looked expensive and like no one ever used them. *Lonely things*, she thought, and she used them to open the package of bacon while Arizona giggled at something on her phone.

She started looking through cupboards, finding bread and peanut butter. Montana could fry an egg, but she'd rather have peanut butter bacon toast.

"Are you married to having an egg for breakfast?" she asked Arizona.

She looked up from her phone. "No. What are you thinking?" She took in the new ingredients on the counter-top. "I'm intrigued."

"Great." Montana picked up the shears again and started snipping the strip into smaller bits. She'd made toast with strips of bacon in the past, but it was hard to bite through, and she'd developed a new way of piling on all the bacon she liked and not having to bite so hard to get the saltiness in every bite.

The fat sizzled as it hit the hot pan, and she barely had enough time to get a couple of pieces snipped before she needed to find a pair of tongs and stir things before they burned. She did that, turned down the flame, and got back to snipping.

"What is happening here?"

She looked up to find Bishop pulling a shirt over his head as he walked through the living room. He rounded the couch and came toward her, and he seriously looked like he'd just rolled out of bed.

"I thought all cowboys rose with the sun," she said, realizing how flirty she sounded. She tossed a look at Arizona, whose fingers flew across her screen.

"I normally do." Bishop came into the kitchen and started to pour himself a cup of coffee. "But I'm sort of in a stand-still for today." He stepped next to her, and it wasn't fair that he had access to all his toiletries and clothing, and she still only had yesterday's deodorant and jeans. At least she'd dressed nicely for their "meeting," though she normally wouldn't wear a blouse to work the ranch.

"Stand-still?" she asked, glancing up at him briefly as she reached for another chunk of bacon. Snip, snip, snip.

"I've never seen someone use scissors to cut bacon," he said, his voice full of curiosity.

"You've obviously never had to use a knife so dull it can't even cut paper." She finished with the bacon and looked at him fully. Big mistake, as time froze. Even the scent of bacon and coffee—the two best smells in the whole wide world—disappeared.

There was only Bishop and his gorgeous smile. His light eyes that shone like a spring sky with bright sunlight. His laughter filled her ears, and when he put his hand on her waist, everything in the world rushed forward again.

"You're right," he said, still chuckling. "I probably haven't."

Montana pulled in a breath at his familiar and yet oh-so-new touch. His hand fell away, and he put a more appropriate distance between them. "What are you making?"

She picked up the tongs and stirred the bacon around the pan, some of it already starting to crisp. This stove was astronomically better than any she'd used before too. "Peanut butter bacon toast."

He picked up the jar of peanut butter. "You've got to be kidding."

"I am not," she said. "I never joke about bacon."

"Oh yeah? Is that your favorite food?"

"That's right." Montana couldn't allow herself to look directly at him again, so she kept busy by putting four slices of bread into the toaster, just so it would be ready. "You're not going out on the ranch today?"

"I need to go do an interview in town," he said. "Then I was going to meet my mother for lunch. Be back here in the afternoon to do a little bit of demo on one cabin that isn't full of mold. I'm meeting the exterminators at the Ranch House at four."

"So you don't need me up here today." She did look at him then, and he wore a slightly alarmed expression.

"You could come back in the afternoon, after you shower and everything." He looked down to her bare feet, quickly pulling his eyes back to hers. "If you wanted. But no, your contract starts Monday."

"Okay," she said, ducking her head and letting her hair fall over her shoulder. "This only has a few more minutes." The last of her words got drowned out by Lincoln as he came skipping into the kitchen, singing at the top of his lungs.

"Zona," he said. "I have both of my shoes, and Benny's already been outside."

"Good boy," she said, smiling at him. "But you're goin' with Bishy today. He's taking you to school and then he's taking Benny to the garage. Remember?

"Bishy?" Montana asked before she could stop herself. She looked at Bishop, grinning like a fool. "Like Bishy Wishy Fishy?"

"Stop it," he said, though his own smile stretched across his whole face.

She laughed as she reached for the paper towels. He handed her a plate, and for a moment, Montana felt like this was normal. The two of them working together in the kitchen, moving around each other easily, as if they'd done it countless times in the past.

She laid the paper towels over the plate and started tonging the crisp bacon pieces onto it. She set the bread to toast and got out a knife.

A few minutes later, she said, "There's an art to the bacon piling." She picked up a healthy pinch of bacon and mounded it right in the center. "See? It falls all to the side, and then it's perfect." She lifted the piece. "Who wants the first piece?"

She watched Bishop look at Arizona, who looked back at him. They wore identical expression of doubt, and Montana shook her head. "Lincoln, then. Here you go, bud. Show them they won't die."

The boy took the toast and bit into it without hesitation. His eyes got big and round, and he tried smiling and chewing at the same time.

Montana laughed and mounded another handful of bacon onto the next piece of toast. Her mouth watered at the sight of the melty peanut butter and the scent of that salty bacon.

She passed out the toast, and raised hers to Bishop and Arizona, who hadn't taken a bite yet. Montana did, the crunchy toast slightly softened on the top because of the peanut butter. It was creamy and rich, and the bacon cut through it with grease and salt.

A groan started in the back of her throat, and she closed her eyes in bliss. She chewed and swallowed and said, "I love this stuff."

Bishop nodded, licked his lips, and said, "It's delicious." He took another bite that was practically half of the piece of toast, and Montana looked at his sister.

"Best thing I've ever eaten."

"Please," Bishop said with a scoff. "Better than that chocolate pie I made for Christmas?"

"Yes," Arizona said. "Better than that." She took another enormous bite too.

Montana was pretty sure she'd only said that to antagonize Bishop, and it had worked. She grinned at Bishop, who shook his head as he finished his toast. "Is there more?"

"Sure," she said just as her phone rang. "Oh, it's my daughter." She pushed down the bread. "You just slather on peanut butter and do that mounding technique."

"I can handle it," he said dryly, and Montana grinned as she turned away from him.

"Hey, sweetie," she said to Aurora. "You're up and getting ready for school?"

"Yep," Aurora said, her voice already pitched up.

Montana braced herself for whatever came next. Her daughter probably needed something from her, and she quickly ran through what she was supposed to do last night that she hadn't been able to do because she hadn't been able to get back to town.

She couldn't think of anything.

"Listen, I don't know if you'll be back this afternoon or not, and Ollie said I could come over for sure after school, and you never said if I could go or not...."

Montana frowned, but she honestly wasn't sure what her afternoon looked like, as she still had a job at the college to finish, and it would be nice to not have to worry about Aurora. "His parents will be there?"

"Yes, Mom."

"I get to ask questions," Montana said, pacing further from Bishop and Arizona and Lincoln, though Arizona and Lincoln seemed engaged in teasing Bishop about his bacon mounding technique.

"I know."

"Are you going to brush up on your French?"

"Yes," Aurora said. "And we have chemistry together too. I'm sure we'll just do homework and watch TV. Just like I do here."

"His parents said it's okay?"

"Yes." Aurora's impatience came through the line, and Montana knew she should stop. The problem was, once she gave her permission, the call would end.

"Okay," Montana said. "I'll keep in touch, so I can get his address and let you know when I'll be picking you up."

"Thanks, Mom." Aurora squealed, and Montana pressed her eyes closed for an entirely different reason now.

She prayed for patience quickly, adding a quick note about being strong. "Aurora," she said. "When you're studying French, that does not involve kissing."

"Mom, come on."

"No, you come on," she said. "You know boys want to kiss."

"What if I want to kiss him too?"

"Aurora, don't make me say you can't go over there."

Her daughter sighed like Montana was requiring her to rip off her own arm before she went to school. "Fine, Mom. We'll just study French vocabulary. Not French kissing."

"*No* kissing," Montana said. "Of any kind."

"Mom, fourteen-year-olds kiss."

"Have you been to his house before?"

"No."

"Has he been at any of the houses where you've been hanging out this year?"

"No," Aurora said, her voice slipping into resignation.

"Then you need more time to get to know this boy before you start kissing him."

Aurora didn't answer, which meant she knew Montana was right.

"I'll keep in touch so I can get his address and let you know what time I'll be there." She turned around and found Bishop watching her, his second piece of toast almost gone. "Tell me the safe word."

"Spaghetti," Aurora dutifully recited, and Montana nodded.

"Good girl. Have a good day at school. I love you."

"Love you too, Mom."

Montana ended the call and slipped the phone into her pocket. She stepped back over to Bishop, who was alone in the kitchen.

"No French kissing?" he asked, those eyes aglow.

His spirit lit something inside her that she'd thought long dead. "Oh, my daughter likes this boy, and she's going to his house this afternoon for the first time."

"Sounds scandalous."

"Be honest," Montana said, settling at the bar and looking at him across the wide island. "When you were fourteen, and you liked a girl enough to invite her over to your house to do *French* homework, you were thinking about kissing her."

Bishop didn't even blink. "Absolutely," he said, grinning.

Montana shook her head, even as a decent amount of worry snaked through her. She reminded herself that

Aurora had a good head on her shoulders. "I don't think much has changed with you, Mister Glover."

He leaned his palms into the counter, his smile the most glorious thing Montana had ever seen. "I'd love for you to come up here in the afternoon, since you don't have to be in town with your daughter." He raised his eyebrows, his invitation clear. "I'll pay you for the day. And maybe...." He dropped his gaze to the counter in front of him, and he was the most adorable man Montana had ever met. She tried to press on the brakes of her feelings, because she'd felt this way before. In fact, new relationships always tingled and sparked. This one was nothing new or different.

"Maybe you and I could go to dinner together tomorrow night."

Before Montana could answer, more male voices filled the silence. At least three, maybe four. She turned and watched as two men came through the arch, both of them talking at the same time.

"That's all I'm saying," one said, and he clearly belonged to Bishop somehow.

The other did too. "I know what you're sayin'," the second man said, wiping his hand down his face. "I just don't think it's going to work."

They looked at Montana and Bishop at the same time. "There's bacon?" one said, and he made a beeline for the counter.

"There *was* bacon," Bishop said, grinning. "How's the fire?"

"Contained, finally," the first man said. "Can you make

us some eggs or something? Ward and I have been out there all night."

"Preacher and Judge are out there now," Ward said, sitting down at the end of the counter. He glanced at Montana, and she opened her mouth to introduce herself.

"This is Montana Martin," Bishop said, practically leaping over the countertop as he threw up his arm so she wouldn't speak. "She's my new crew for the construction around here." He smiled at her. "My cousin, Ward. My brother, Cactus."

"Nice to meet you," Montana said, feeling like a speck of dust among all these tall, dark cowboys.

"What is this?" Cactus asked, picking up a half-eaten piece of peanut butter bacon toast.

"It's the food of the gods," Montana said at the same time Bishop said, "It's your funeral."

Chapter Seven

Bishop couldn't help grinning like a fool at Montana as she made an indignant sound. Ward and Cactus would be able to see that this pretty blonde woman had already smitten him, but he couldn't get himself to stop.

Finally, the spell broke when Link came bounding into the kitchen, and Ward grinned as he scooped him into his arms.

"You smell like smoke, Uncle Ward."

"That's because I've been out watching the fire all night." He set Link back on his feet. "Can I take Benny today?"

"Bishy was gonna take him to the garage, because he's not…something."

"I'm not here most of the day," Bishop said, glancing at Montana. "The guys at the garage like him, and I figured he'd be out of the way there."

"I'll take him," Ward said. "I'm going to shower and

sleep as much as I want." He gave Bishop a weary smile and started for the steps. "Ace and I are okay in Ranger's rooms until he gets back?"

"Yeah," Bishop said. "Montana was in there last night, but—"

"I cleaned everything up," she said quickly, rising. "You won't even know which bed I slept in."

Ward nodded at her and then Bishop and left the kitchen. Bishop looked at Cactus, who was just polishing off the last bit of Lincoln's toast. He looked like he wanted to talk to Bishop, but thankfully, he needed to get Lincoln to school.

"Come on, bud," he said. "Get your backpack and let's go. I refuse to let you be late on my watch."

"Career Day is tomorrow, Uncle Bishop. You can still come, right?"

Bishop put his arm around the boy and looked at Montana, who was scurrying to his side and away from Cactus. "Yes," he said, though he had no idea what tomorrow would bring. "I can still come. What time?"

"It's after lunch," Lincoln said as he stooped to get his backpack from just outside the kitchen. "I got you that paper."

"Right, the paper," Bishop said, but he couldn't recall where he'd put it at the moment. All he could focus on was the blonde at his side. He'd asked her to dinner, but she still hadn't said yes. Not that she'd had the opportunity to do so.

Don't ask again, he told himself. *She already knows you're interested. It's fine.*

He went outside with the two of them, Lincoln skipping ahead to go down the steps. "You really could come out this afternoon," he said. "In fact, it might be good for you to be there when I meet with the exterminator. Then you'll know what we're dealing with at the Ranch House too."

"Four o'clock?"

"I should be back here about two," he said, pausing at the bottom of the steps. "Get in a couple of good hours of demo."

"Nothing better than demo," Montana said, her smile lighting his pulse on fire. "Thanks for letting me stay up here, Bishop."

"Of course."

She ducked her head and started toward her truck. Bishop wanted to say something witty and fun, but he held back. He didn't need to make a fool of himself by asking again.

She'd been flirting with him right in front of Zona, as his sister had so not-casually pointed out while Montana had been on the phone. Bishop had told her if she really cared about him, she'd take Link upstairs for five minutes so Bishop could ask Montana to dinner.

Turned out, Zona did care about him, and she'd done as he'd asked. If only Bishop had known he needed to text the whole blasted family that he needed two minutes alone with a woman.

He wrenched his eyes away from Montana and got in his own truck, settling and buckling his seatbelt. "Ready, bud?"

"Yep," Lincoln said. "Bishy, could you bring your big hammer tomorrow?"

"Only if you stop calling me Bishy," he said, cutting the nine-year-old a look out of the corner of his eye.

BISHOP HAD BARELY PULLED UP TO THE ASSISTED LIVING facility where his aunt lived when his mother came out the front door. He grinned, laughed, and swung out of the truck to go hug her.

"Momma," he said, the only son to call her that. He picked her right up off her feet as she laughed.

"Bense," she said, reverting to his real childhood nickname. "Put me down, child. I'm far too old for such things."

He did as she said, grinning at her. "Sorry, Mother."

She swatted at his bicep, still smiling. "You're taking me to that place with the good salads, right?"

"Yes, Mother," he said. "Same as always." He didn't particularly enjoy Bella Vita, but his mother loved the garden crunch salad, and he'd do anything to make his mother happy. Anything.

"Maybe they'll have that brisket again. You liked that."

"I did like that." He opened her door and helped her get up. She wasn't as old at Aunt Dawna, and she had quite a bit of her normal mobility. She lived in a cottage with Zona on the ranch, and Bishop usually brought her the salad and they ate at her house.

He wasn't sure if the other brothers knew he had one-on-one lunches with Mother, and he didn't care if they did. He needed them, and he wouldn't apologize for centering his soul and aligning his thoughts when they got crooked and out of place.

"I heard about the fire," she said, and Bishop glanced at her before he looked over his shoulder to pull out.

"Yeah," he said. "It's still burning, but it's contained. There aren't any more houses in danger, and we've got men watching our borders to make sure it doesn't come onto Shiloh Ridge."

"Donald said they'd have it out by tonight," she said.

"Oh, have you been callin' in your favors with the fire chief?" Bishop asked, teasing her.

Mother reached up and patted her perfectly set hair. "Perhaps."

"Momma," Bishop said. He'd expected her to admit it, but he hadn't expected her to be so proper about it. He stared openly as a hint of a flush worked its way up her neck and into her face.

"Momma," he said again, his heartbeat crashing against his ribs. "Are you sweet on Donald Parker?"

"Pish posh," Momma said, scoffing as she turned away from him. She curled the fingers of one hand around the back of her neck. "I just don't want the fire to reach Shiloh Ridge."

Bishop started to chuckle, though he honestly wasn't sure how he felt about his mother having a crush. She was seventy-eight-years-old, and Daddy had been gone for fifteen years.

As far as Bishop knew, none of her children had ever

asked her if she wanted to date again. She'd never brought it up. He'd been so young, and he hadn't even started his year of living like a cowboy on the ranch, earning the same rate they paid their men, and living in the same cabins.

After he'd done that, he'd moved back into the homestead with Mother, Arizona, and Bear. That had only sufficed for a couple of years, and then Bishop had finished his carpentry training and finished the cottage where Zona and Mother lived now.

"I think you just lied to me, Mother," he said. His chest squeezed tightly though. He cleared his throat. "If you marry him, can I still go to lunch with you?"

"I'm not going to marry him," Mother said with so much force that Bishop believed her. "Even if I did, you would always be able to come have lunch with me." She reached over and put her hand on his forearm. "I know how much you need them."

He nodded, because he couldn't argue with her.

"So tell your mother what's eating at you this time."

"It's nothing, Mother," he said, though it was something.

"I don't judge, Bishop," she said. "You best take your cares to John if you want someone to make a judgment."

"He doesn't judge either, Mother." It was why John went by Judge. He was like the apostle—any judgments he did make were righteous, and always spot-on. Bishop had never gone wrong when he'd gone to Judge for help.

"I know," she said. "None of you do, which is why it's troubling to me that you feel like you don't fit."

"It's just that everyone has a person," Bishop said,

trying to find the right way to explain it this month. It wasn't like this was the first time he and his mother had spoken of this.

"Ward and Ace. Judge and Mister. Bear and Ranger. Cactus and Bear. Heck, Ward and Bear. Ace and Bear." He turned away from his mother. "Everyone loves Bear."

"Of course everyone loves Bear," Mother said. "He messes up all the time, son. And he's real, and he's apologetic, and he works hard to do better. That endears him to them."

"So you're saying I have to be meaner? And then apologize?"

"No," she said. "I'm saying you have to be Bishop, not Bear."

"That makes no sense, Mother."

"You have a person too," she said. "Ace."

Bishop nodded, because he and Ace did get along really well.

"And Cactus. That man would be lost without you, and don't you forget it," Mother said, her voice turning dark. "I don't think it's any coincidence that he lets exactly two people come to his cabin—you and Bear. You're more like your eldest brother than you think you are."

Bishop didn't respond, because he didn't know what that meant either. He and Bear were nothing alike. In fact, Bishop had done as much as he could to stand apart from Bear. He loved his brother; he did work hard around the ranch to make Bear proud.

After Daddy died, it was Bear he needed to impress. Bear who checked off his work. Bear who'd taken him in and loved him like an equal even though he'd been a teenager trying to be a man.

"Bishop."

"I'm done talking about it, Mother," he said, glancing at her. "Okay?" He smiled. "Thank you, but I don't need anything else."

She wore worry plainly in her bright blue eyes, the source of where all of her children had gotten their lighter features. Of them all, Bishop was the most like her coloring, and she often told him he was her favorite son.

"You're my favorite son, remember?" she asked, smiling.

He smiled too and turned into the parking lot for her favorite restaurant. "Yes, Mother," he said. "But I'm pretty sure you say that to all the sons."

"I do not," she said huffily, her hand going right back to pat her curls. "Now come help me out of this truck like a proper gentleman. I see our new pastor coming out, and you'll want to make a good impression."

Bishop laughed as he got out of the truck and went to help his mother. He let her clutch his arm and act utterly delighted to meet the new pastor who'd come to their church to help his brother, who's suffered a fall a month or so ago.

He smiled and he made small talk, playing the perfect Texan cowboy gentleman, but inside, a storm swirled, and Bishop needed a way to release it before it consumed him whole.

As Mother sat down and got situated, he sent a quick text to Cactus. *I asked Montana to dinner right before you guys came in, and she didn't answer. Do I ask again?*

Cactus's response came instantly. *You're asking me? How would I know?*

Come on, Bishop said. *You know.*

You like her?

That's a hard yes. In fact, Bishop had done the interview with the other cowboy this morning, but he wouldn't be able to hire him for more than day work, which only paid fifty bucks a day, because he'd blown his whole budget on Montana's contract.

When Bear found out....

She knows you like her?

Yes. If she didn't, Bishop didn't know how to make it more obvious.

And you met her when?

Yesterday morning.

Then give her a minute, Cactus said. *We're a lot to handle—you're a lot to handle, Bishop. Handsome, tall, strong, good with your hands. Maybe you intimidate her. Maybe she needs a minute to breathe after getting a job at our ranch and meeting you literally less than twenty-four hours ago.*

A minute to breathe, yes. Maybe Cactus was his person, despite their age differences, and Bishop smiled as he read the text again. He looked up from his phone to find Mother's eyebrow cocked at him, asking, *Are you going to be on that thing the whole time?*

"Sorry, Mother," he said, setting the phone face-down. "Now, tell me more about Donald, because I *know* you like him."

Chapter Eight

Cactus Glover couldn't help feeling like he was doing something wrong. He'd put his extra-wide-brimmed cowboy hat on for this trip to town, and he wasn't even sure why. Who was he hiding from?

Himself, that was who, and he frowned at the faint reflection of himself in the passenger window as Ace pulled into the tack and feed store.

Cactus had mentioned that he needed to go on the family text, and the next thing he knew, Ace had set it up, claiming he needed to get down there too.

As if driving thirty minutes to the town of Three Rivers was so dang hard for any of them to do.

Cactus yawned, his all-nighter from a couple of days ago still dragging him down. He didn't recover from anything as easily or as quickly as he once had. When he'd smashed his thumb while working on a cabin in January, it had taken a month for it to start to feel better.

He glanced at the appendage now, where the nail was just barely starting to grow back in. The moment he'd turned forty, his eyesight had started to dwindle, and now that he'd be forty-four this year, he couldn't do anything without lights bright enough to see from space.

"Let's go," Ace said, getting out and slamming his door before Cactus had even registered that he'd parked. He strode away from the truck without waiting for Cactus, who narrowed his eyes at his cousin.

"What is goin' on with him?" he asked himself. He too got out of the truck and followed Ace, not really trying to keep up with him. He glanced left and right like he might try to rob the place and he wanted to make sure there weren't any cops nearby.

He wasn't sure why this energy needled below his skin, only that it was there, and it was making him jumpy.

Inside the tack and feed, he got his own cart, because Ace had conveniently disappeared. It was just as well, because Cactus needed new leather to make reins, and Ace needed chicken feed and goat pellets. The two items were on opposite sides of the store.

Cactus started to relax as he went down the first aisle. He didn't use shopping as therapy, but he did like looking at everything in the tack and feed. He liked to get raw leather and braid his own reins, though he could just buy a pair of ready-made leads.

He needed something to keep his hands busy at night, which was why he'd learned to crochet, knit, and whittle over the years. He'd been braiding reins since the age of seven, when he'd sit beside his father and listen to him talk to Mother about the ranch, about their children, and about his dreams. Sometimes Uncle Bull would take Mother's spot in the living room, the fireplace flickering onto their faces as Cactus kept his mouth closed and his hands busy.

He was extraordinarily good at keeping quiet. He'd learned early on in his life that he didn't have to talk all the time. Even if he disagreed, he could keep his thoughts to himself. He didn't have to voice his opinion. He didn't have to be heard.

He thought of Bishop as he turned down the aisle filled with outdoor cooking equipment. The man's birthday was coming up, and while Cactus wasn't going to get him a heavy-duty Dutch oven, Bishop would probably like something new to make the family meals he, Etta, and Ida put together week after week a little easier.

Cactus pulled out his phone and set himself a calendar reminder for the following day. *Get Bishop something for his birthday.* He looked up when he heard familiar laughter. His heartbeat bumped over itself while he first thought it was one of the women he'd chatted with over the past few months.

"Don't be stupid," he muttered. He'd never spoken to them on the phone or in person. There was no way it could be one of them. There were only three, and Cactus wasn't sure what he'd done wrong with each one to make them all eventually go silent.

He'd concluded that he just wasn't that interesting. Bishop had looked at one of his conversations, and he'd had nothing to say. No suggestions for what Cactus could've done differently.

It had taken all of Cactus's courage to show Bishop just one conversation, and he wasn't putting himself through that again.

He'd deleted his profile on the dating app, and since no one asked him what his plan was to meet a woman, he didn't have to have one.

The woman laughed again, and Cactus definitely knew her. He inched around the corner and looked down the aisle to find none other than Ace wearing a smile the size of Texas itself as he flirted with a pretty brunette.

Of course, Cactus thought. Holly Ann Broadbent stood with one hand on Ace's cart, clearly holding him in place. Cactus wasn't sure why Ace and Holly Ann hadn't worked out a few months ago. He was clearly smitten with her, and as she pealed out another round of laughter, it was obvious she was thrilled to be talking to Ace.

He'd gotten her number at the Christmas movie three months ago. Cactus hadn't followed up with him, so he wasn't entirely sure what had happened. He relied on Bear and Bishop for the ranch gossip, and Bear was a poor choice as he hated drama and gossip as much as Cactus hated that he'd lost his infant son and then his wife.

He pulled in a breath while he waited for the anger and humiliation to grip his heart. Today, though, it only blipped through him. The humiliation especially dried up quickly, and the anger felt more like a slow burn than the instant fury he'd experienced in the past.

He pushed his cart past Ace and Holly Ann, whisper-ing, "Bless him with whatever it takes to be happy."

That was all Cactus really wanted. For himself, for all of

his family members, for everyone. Didn't everyone deserve to have some measure of happiness?

He couldn't help thinking that perhaps he'd used up all the measure God was willing to give him. He'd had it all once. The wife. The child on the way. The ranch life he loved.

It had been so long since any of that, Cactus wasn't even sure what happiness felt like anymore.

He made it to the leather section and picked out the strips he wanted. At the end of the aisle, several bridles had fallen to the floor, and Cactus bent down to pick them up.

"Watch out!" someone called, and he looked up just in time to see a pig bearing down on him. "Grab him!"

Cactus dropped the bridles and braced himself to get hit by the oinker. He thought for sure it would turn left—the only direction to go—before it would just ram into him.

He thought wrong, and it just kept coming.

He widened his stance a moment before the pig seemed to finally realize he was a person and not an escape route, and it tried to turn.

His hooves slipped and slid, and Cactus grunted as he wrapped both arms around the ungulate and lifted the pink pig right up off its feet.

Everything happened so quickly after that. "Thanks, Mister," the man who'd called the warning said. He clipped a lead around the pig's neck and added, "Clarence, you can't run off in the store."

A worker arrived a few moments after the man, out of breath and wearing a hat very much like Cactus's. He was an older gentleman, and he too scolded the pig. Cactus had no idea what had just happened, or how a pig called Clarence had come to be so clean—and on a leash.

The man and the worker walked away as quickly as they'd come, both of them talking over the other, and Clarence trotted along beside them. He wasn't a full-grown pig, but as Cactus turned back to the dropped bridles, his back estimated he'd lifted about a hundred pounds of pork.

A groan came out of his mouth as he straightened, and he still had his hand on the bridles when a woman said, "Excuse me? Can you help me find the rabbit feed?"

Cactus turned toward the angelic voice, his throat narrowing as he tried to pull in a breath. It was like trying to scuba dive with only a straw to breathe through, and he thought he might have wheezed.

The most beautiful woman he'd ever seen stood in front of him, her red hair mixed with plenty of light brown. It fell to her shoulders, and framed her face perfectly. She looked at him with perfect hope in her blue-green eyes, and once Cactus looked there, he couldn't look away.

She carried a basket—as if that was all she needed to get rabbit feed—and wore a pair of jeans with a bright green sweater. A piece of vanilla cake sat across her chest, with a halo over the wide end with plenty of frosting.

"Sure," he said, completely abandoning his cart of leather straps. "The feed is over here."

A smile lit her face, and Cactus immediately started thinking of a way to find out who she was. Could he ask her name? Would she give him her number?

All of the lessons Ace and Bishop had given him

melded together, and Cactus looked over his shoulder as he walked. "How many rabbits do you have?"

"Just two," she said. She smelled like lemons and cupcakes, and Cactus absolutely had to have more of both in his life.

"For now," he said. "They tend to have a lot of babies."

"That they do," she agreed, her voice like cool water on a hot day.

"Have you owned rabbits before?"

"No, sir," she said. "And I guess they're not really *my* rabbits."

He turned down the feed aisle, trying to look at her again. If he kept that up, he was going to fall down in front of her, and that would be more embarrassing than smelling like the pig he'd just wrestled.

"They're not?" He arrived in front of the rabbit feed and started scanning for the brand he'd use.

"They're my niece's," she said. "I told their father I'd help with them, and it was the only way he'd let them get the bunnies." She smiled at Cactus, who forgot what he was doing for a moment.

When he realized he'd posed as a tack and feed employee, he panicked. He had to get away from her before she realized he didn't wear a name tag.

"How old are they?" he asked, his throat so dry.

"The rabbits or the nieces?" She grinned at him again, and Cactus almost wished she wouldn't.

He wasn't going to blurt out anything embarrassing. He tucked all of that away, under his tongue, and looked at the feed again. "Both," he said.

"The rabbits are little," she said. "Maybe a couple of months old? The nieces are six and seven."

If Cactus knew anyone in town, that might help him figure out who she was without having to come out and ask. "Baby rabbits," he said. "You'll want these smaller alfalfa pellets, I think." He plucked a bag from the shelf and looked at her basket. It might fit in there, but it might not.

"I probably needed a cart." She put the basket down and took the bag from him. "How long does this last?"

"Depends on what else you feed them," he said. "They can eat all kinds of fruits and veggies."

"Mariah actually told me that." She shifted the bag to rest on her hip, which curved in the most delicious way. Cactus yanked his eyes back to hers. "She's one of the nieces."

He smiled and nodded. "Do you live with them?"

"Down the street," she said. "Don't ask me where." She trilled out a pretty little laugh. "We just moved here, and I have no idea which way to go when I leave here."

"Oh, so you're new." He kept his smile in place. "Well, welcome to Three Rivers, ma'am." He reached up and tipped his hat at her. "That should last you a few weeks, at least. I'd give them kale and apples, some carrots, tops and all. They love blueberries too."

"These rabbits are going to eat better than I do." The woman rolled her eyes, and Cactus sure did like her sense of humor. He liked her easy-going spirit. He had the distinct impression he should ask her if she was at least in her thirties, but he bit down on the question.

"Anything else I can help you find?" he asked, and he wanted to stuff his boot in his mouth. He couldn't be leading her all over the store, showing her their various products. Someone would catch him, and his ruse would be up.

"No, this is all," she said, stooping to pick up her basket, where she had a water bottle for a rabbit cage he hadn't even seen before. "Thank you...." She looked at his shirt for that blasted name tag, and heat shot into Cactus's face.

"I'm Cactus Glover," he said, extending his hand toward her to shake.

Her hands were full, and she became flustered as she looked at his hand and tried to shift things around so she could shake it. In the end, she laughed as she simply dropped everything.

"Willa Knowlton," she said, finally shaking his hand. "My brother is the new pastor, and I'm here to do some stand-in preaching for him and to help take care of Pastor Summers."

"Oh, right," Cactus said. He'd heard that Pastor Summers had fallen and been injured. He hadn't been to church in a while, but as he gazed at Willa, he suddenly had a very good reason to go back.

Stop staring.

He wasn't sure where the voice had come from, but he dropped his head and cleared his throat. "Let me take this up front for you."

"Oh, you don't have to do that." But she let him pick up the bag of feed. Then she bent to get the basket, she tucked her hair, and when their eyes met again, Cactus swore they had even more twinkle than before.

Was she flirting with him? How could he possibly know?

He walked her up front and set the rabbit pellets on the counter. "There you go, ma'am."

"Thank you," she said, and he tipped his hat and walked away. He hadn't gone far when she said, "You have very helpful employees here."

He increased his pace to get around the corner, and he'd just made it when the clerk said, "He doesn't work for us."

"Don't stop," he muttered. "Don't go back. Don't stop. Don't stop. Do *not* stop." He made it back to the leather section of the store, and by some miracle his cart was still there. He couldn't just go back up front and check out, in case Willa was still there. So he turned his back on the rest of the store and huddled over his phone as if he had anyone to text.

Instead, he opened his notes app and typed in *Willa Knowlton*. His pulse pounced against his ribcage just looking at the letters in her name.

Now, he just had to figure out why he'd need to talk to her again, and how he'd get her number to do that.

"There you are," Ace said, and Cactus turned around. "I've been looking everywhere for you." He glanced down at the phone in Cactus's hand. "Why didn't you answer when I called?"

"I didn't get a call," Cactus said. "There's no service in this corner."

Ace looked in Cactus's cart. "Did you get what you needed?"

"Yes," he said. "Are they really busy up front?"

"No one," Ace said. "I almost had them page you."

Cactus stared at him, horror moving through him.

Ace laughed and shook his head. "Relax. I didn't. But I'm ready to go."

"Yeah?" Cactus asked. "Did you get back in Holly Ann's good graces?"

"I—you—she just happened to be here."

Cactus grinned at him and grabbed onto his cart. "Right. You're a really bad liar." He led the way toward the front of the store to check out. "How did you know she'd be here?"

"She works here," Ace said. "So keep your voice down. I'll tell you once we're in the truck."

"Great," Cactus said. "I have something to tell you too. We'll get Bishop on speaker, because I'm going to need all the help I can get."

Chapter Nine

Montana scrubbed the smoke and the last couple of days out of her hair and off her skin. Once she finished showering and had gotten dressed, she went into the kitchen to get another cup of coffee.

"Morning, Aunt Jackie," she said to her aunt, working over a journal at the kitchen table.

She glanced up, her perpetual happiness radiating from her bright, dark brown eyes. "Morning, darling." She got up and hugged Montana, who smiled and laughed as she put her arm around her aunt's waist. "I'm glad you made it home okay."

"Me too," Montana said, reaching for a mug as her aunt went back to the table. "Thanks for taking care of Aurora."

"Oh, we love having her here," Aunt Jackie said. "Both of you." She picked up her pencil again and got back to work.

"Doing the scheduling?"

"Yes," she said with a sigh. "No matter what I do, someone will be upset." She scratched in a couple more names. She struggled with the scheduling every month, but she was the one who'd taught Montana that everything worked out in the end.

So when Montana said it this time, Aunt Jackie laughed with her. She put sugar and cream in her coffee and sat down across from her aunt and stirred her spoon through the dark light brown liquid.

"I signed a contract at Shiloh Ridge Ranch," she said. "Doing remodeling and rebuilds."

Aunt Jackie looked up, her eyes wide and sparkling. Joy filled them as she said, "Montana, dear, that's wonderful."

"It's a long commute."

"We'll get Aurora off to school," she said. "As I'm sure you'll get up there early, especially as the summer months approach."

"I'm sure that's true." Montana started worrying about summer already, and not only because of the heat. Aurora would be fifteen by then, and there was nothing more dangerous than a teenager without something to keep her busy. Very, very busy.

At the current moment, Montana didn't have anything to keep Aurora busy in the summer. She also might not have a job then, either. She had no idea how long it would take to get the remodeling and rebuilding done at Shiloh Ridge, and a second pit opened in her stomach.

She took a sip of her coffee, unsurprised when Aunt Jackie said, "It'll do you no good to worry about it now."

Montana opened her mouth to deny she was worried about anything, but she'd protested in the past, and Aunt Jackie hadn't believed her. She had a gift for knowing how someone felt; it was one of the reasons she was such a good nurse.

"I can't help it," Montana finally said. "Aurora is a good girl, but she needs a lot of attention or she'll veer down the wrong path."

"Oh, she has a heart of gold." Aunt Jackie smiled and looked down at her journal again. "I don't worry about her at all."

"Who do you worry about?" Montana asked.

"Tracey," Aunt Jackie said instantly. "She never sleeps, and I worry about that. Uncle Bob, because his blood pressure is too high, and he works too much at that store. You." She gave Montana a faint smile.

"Why me?" Montana said.

Aunt Jackie kept her pencil moving as she said, "You're a wonderful person, Montana, and you don't even know it."

"I...." She didn't know how to finish, because she'd never thought she'd thought of herself all that negatively.

"I worry that you'll work yourself to the bone only to prove a point, but really, no one is waiting for you to do anything but what you're already doing."

Montana focused on her coffee, a pinch starting in her chest. "Is it wrong to want a place of my own? For me and Aurora?"

"Of course not," Aunt Jackie said. "But who are you going to call when you move in?" She looked up then, her eyes much sharper now. "Your mother? Georgia? Paris?"

"Okay," Montana said.

"Johnny?"

"Okay," Montana barked, her mood dark as night now.

Aunt Jackie didn't back down, though. She held Montana's glare for several long moments before she sighed. "I just want you to be happy. Bob and I love having you here. You are not a burden. We love it."

"I know." Montana dropped her gaze too, not wanting to argue with her aunt. No, she would not call either of her sisters to tell them about her new house or apartment. And she hadn't spoken to her ex-husband in a decade; he wouldn't care about her getting into her own place other than how much it cost. If he determined he could get anything from Montana—even a simple ten-dollar bill, he'd do it.

"Aunt Jackie?" she asked.

"Mm?"

"If I...I mean, do you...do you ever talk to your sister?"

Aunt Jackie brought her head up again. "Yes," she said. "Your mother and I speak often enough."

Montana nodded, nothing else to ask, because she hadn't intended to ask about her mother, but Bishop Glover. She bit back the question as if Aunt Jackie would mind if she started dating for a reason she could not name. She and her aunt had never spoken of men, and Montana figured she probably put off some vibe that said she wasn't interested in meeting someone new and trying to fall in love again.

She could admit she'd been beyond sour on men when

she'd come to Three Rivers. Not only had her husband broken her heart and her trust, but after Montana had finally gotten back into the game of dating, her own sister had played a cruel, cruel card.

"What are you thinking, my darling?" Aunt Jackie asked, and Montana looked up from her coffee.

"Nothing," she said, putting on the brightest, biggest smile she could. "I have to go up to the ranch this afternoon and meet with the exterminator. Aurora is going to a friend's house. I don't know if we'll be home for dinner."

"I'm on the swing tonight," Aunt Jackie said. "I'll text Bob and let him know to pick up a burger on his way home."

Montana nodded and got up, a groan pulling through her throat as a pain shot up her back. "I'm okay," she said before Aunt Jackie could ask. "I think that bed up at that ranch was actually *too* nice for me." She took a couple of hobbling steps before her gait evened, and she thought everything about Shiloh Ridge Ranch was too nice for her —including Bishop Glover.

Maybe she should just maintain a professional, working relationship with him and nothing more.

Nothing more, echoed through her head as she lay in her own inferior bed and prepared to get the sleep she'd missed last night.

MONTANA PULLED UP TO THE RANCH HOUSE, AS BISHOP called it, complete with capital letters. It looked like a normal house, only bigger, and it overlooked the entirety of Three Rivers. When she got out of her truck, she turned and looked out over the side of the hill, the town below and to the north.

"This is incredible," she said. If she lived somewhere like this, she'd sit on the front porch and sip coffee every morning, imagining what the people in town were doing. Who was late for work, and who was impatient to get their coffee so they wouldn't be late for work.

Who'd just made it through the green light, and whose car wouldn't start. She smiled to herself, stories flowing through her mind. The rumble of another truck interrupted her, and she turned her gaze to the road she'd come up to find two more vehicles coming.

The first was Bishop, in that big, black, sexy truck she'd ridden in last night. Right behind him came the exterminator, with a truck so wide, she felt sure it wouldn't fit in the driveway.

She got out of the way so Bishop could park next to her, realizing this place had plenty of space, just like the homestead. If she thought Bishop was handsome and adorable and sexy without his truck, all of those were amplified with him behind the wheel.

He grinned at her as he pulled in, and she smiled right on back. The man had asked her out to dinner for tomorrow night, and she hadn't answered him yet. Could she bring it up this afternoon? She wasn't particularly skilled when it came to men, that was for sure.

She knew she possessed a look a lot of men liked—the blonde haired, blue-eyed look. Most didn't mind her muscles or the extra twenty pounds she carried because of that look. In the end, though, there was always something about her that drove the men away.

Or rather, there was something more alluring about someone else.

"Hey," Bishop said. "You found it."

"I sure did," she said. "It's a whole house on the side of a hill. Wasn't hard to find." She grinned at him, glad when he chuckled. He stepped to her side as she turned to look at the house. Three-car garage. Wide front porch that touched the garage and wrapped around the front corner of the house.

"How many bedrooms?" she asked.

"Six," he said.

"Who lives here?"

"Three of my brothers," he said. "Mister, Judge, and Preacher."

"Y'all have interesting names," she said.

"That we do," he said. "None of them are real." He reached up and pushed his hat further down. "I'll have to tell you about mine sometime." With that, he turned toward the two guys who'd gotten out of the extermination truck.

None of them are real? Montana wanted him to turn back around and tell her about his right now. If Bishop wasn't his real name, what was it? And why did he go by Bishop?

Intrigued, she followed him and shook hands with Ralph—clearly the one in charge—and Peyton, who looked to be no older than Aurora.

"Let's see what you've got," Ralph said.

"It's on the roof," Bishop said. "Or you might be able to see things from inside. I don't know what you're looking for."

"You sounded sure it was termites," Ralph said.

"Well, there's significant damage to the roof," Bishop said, leading the way along the side of the garage toward the back of the house. "I'm not sure what else it would be."

"Peyton," Ralph said, and Montana turned back to the pair of them. Ralph was looking at the ground, and Peyton bent down to examine something almost against the cement foundation of the house.

"Mud tubes," he said, looking up at the older gentleman. Peyton straightened, his eyes serious and his mouth straight. He turned toward Bishop. "Sir, you have termites."

"On the ground?" Bishop crouched down to look at the mud tubes.

"It's a sign," Ralph said. "That's how they get from their nest to your house. They're subterranean termites." He looked out toward the stand of trees several feet away. "Their nest'll be out here somewhere. Beneath the earth. They travel back and forth."

"And they've eaten all the way to the roof?" The level of horror in Bishop's voice wasn't lost on Montana. She wished she could step to his side and take his hand in hers. Perhaps a little bit of comfort would go a long way.

"Let's go see," Ralph said.

Bishop squared his shoulders and his jaw, nodded, and continued to the ladder on the back deck. He went up first, and Montana gestured for Ralph and Peyton to go in front of her. She arrived last to find the roof had been stripped of its shingles. A lot of the wood looked fine to her, but there were some definite patches that needed to be repaired.

Bishop and the others stood around a particularly bad wound in the roof, and Ralph crouched down and ran his fingers along one of the beams. Montana could see all the way into the attic, and it sure did seem full of dust and sawdust, all of it covering the insulation there.

"You have drywood termites too," he said, looking up at Bishop.

"You have got to be kidding me," Bishop said.

Ralph stood and showed him the sandy stuff on his fingers. "This is called frass. It's their excrement."

"It looks like sawdust," Peyton said. "This type of termite lives in a nest inside your house."

Bishop took a deep breath, and Montana's heart pinched at the unrest pouring off of him. "So you're saying we have subterranean termites that live in nest beneath the ground and travel into the house. And we have drywood termites that nest inside the house. And they all eat wood."

"Yes, sir," Peyton said, glancing at Montana.

Bishop blew out his breath and looked at her too. "So what next? You guys get rid of them, and we start repairing? Do you think this house is so far gone we should strip it and start over?"

Montana couldn't hope for the worst for him, even though it would allow her to work at the ranch longer. She tried to smile, and she simply let herself do what was natural. Her hand slipped into his, which caused a blip of surprise to cross his face. He didn't let go of her fingers though.

"We'll do a full assessment," Ralph said, nodding to Peyton. "It could take a while. This place is big, and it's got a basement."

Bishop nodded and said, "Let's get 'er done. Then we'll know what we're dealing with."

Once they were all down on the deck again, he asked, "Do we need to be here?"

"No, sir," Peyton said. "We'll call you when we're done to make sure we have your email. We'll send our treatment plan there, and you can take some time to look over it."

"It's not going to be cheap, Bishop." Ralph looked concerned, but Bishop just nodded. "Okay, Pey. Let's call Momma first and let her know we'll be a couple of hours up here. Then I want you on inspection, okay?"

"Yes, sir," Peyton said, and Montana's heart warmed at the father-son team. Her blood lit on fire when Bishop took her hand again and leaned closer to her.

"Want to go look at the cabins for a minute? I can catch you up on that project too, if you have a minute."

Montana cleared her throat, praying her voice would work while she held hands with this gorgeous cowboy. "I have a minute," she said, her faith that God answered prayers absolutely whole as her voice came out full and normal.

"Great," Bishop said. "You drive."

A WEEK LATER, MONTANA WOKE BEFORE THE SUN. THAT was a little unusual, as Bishop had said he didn't want to leave the homestead until seven-thirty in the morning. The sun was well-up by then, and she'd wondered if they'd move their schedule to earlier as summer arrived.

As it was, they still had a week left in March, and the weather in April was usually the best of the year in Three Rivers.

Today, though, Montana needed to finish the bid she'd been working on for two straight weeks and get it submitted. The deadline wasn't until next Wednesday, but she didn't want to leave it until the last minute.

Three Rivers was in desperate need of a new library. The town had grown and expanded the last several years to the point where some of the local services needed to be updated as well. The building had slowed, though Montana had enjoyed a couple of years of steady employment in Three Rivers.

The new library would need a designer and a builder, and Montana wanted to be both. Her horizons had been broadened by being at Shiloh Ridge this week. The ranch up in the hills was enormous, with every structure and every fencepost exactly where it was supposed to be. The men and women there took care of their land and buildings, and the pride Montana felt emanating from them and the very ranch itself had renewed her soul.

She and Bishop had eaten lunch in the barn where he'd

first taken her for dinner. He called it True Blue, she'd learned, and he'd designed it himself. Montana had been embarrassed when he'd finally given her that tour and then fed her a quick lunch of black bean quesadillas and spiced crema.

Watching him cook was even better than watching him work, and Montana's crush on the man had multiplied and intensified in the few days she'd been working with him.

She'd redrawn most of her plans in the evenings this week, after tasting and seeing what truly expensive and expansive spaces could look like. That was a gift Shiloh Ridge had given her already, and gratitude filled her as she read through her bid one final time.

"Anything else?" she asked, looking up at the ceiling the only room in the house where she could have any privacy. Aurora slept next door, and Montana was glad they each had a place they belonged.

The Lord didn't sway her to add anything else, nor take something out of the bid, so Montana saved it and started uploading each piece to the website accepting proposals from contractors and construction crews.

Twenty minutes later, she'd done it. A strange sense of accomplishment came over her, though she'd not really done anything all that special. Still, putting together a bid with sample schematics to show vision was hard work. Most companies that would take on something like this had dozens of employees, and a whole department that dreamed up concepts, spacious libraries with tons of sunlight pouring in, and luxury spaces for meetings, book nooks, and teen activities.

Montana had done it all herself. She didn't like discussing her plans and drawings with anyone, and she hadn't told anyone that she was even planning to put in a bid on the new library build.

She sat back from the computer and thought about Bishop. If there was someone she wanted to know about what she'd done, it was him.

A smile formed on her face, and she reached for her phone. *I just submitted a complete concept and build bid for the new library in town.*

She wasn't sure what time he got up, but a message came in while she mulled over what else to send him. They hadn't gone to dinner last Friday. He hadn't asked about it again, and she hadn't known how to bring it up.

With his brother and cousin gone, Bishop was running a lot of things on the ranch, taking care of Lincoln, and dealing with two nests of termites from two different species and colonies at the Ranch House.

A decision regarding that house had not yet been made, and he and Montana had been working on gutting the cabins for the past four days since her contract had started.

They're not going to steal you from me, are they?

Montana grinned at the phone. *It takes months for a bid to be accepted*, she tapped out. *I think we're good.*

She looked up from her phone. Were they good? She'd reasoned that he was busy, and she was still trying to work out the commute up to Shiloh Ridge with Aurora. There really wasn't more time to be spent showering, putting on lipstick, and going to dinner with the man she saw all day long.

They had not held hands again, and in fact, Montana realized as she sat in her bedroom, he hadn't flirted with her much that week, nor had he asked her to dinner again.

"Maybe you blew it already," she grumbled to herself, especially when Bishop didn't respond again.

Chapter Ten

❧

"All right," Ranger drawled. "That just leaves Bishop and his, uh, *personal item*."

Bishop felt that uh way down deep in his soul. He shouldn't have put that on the Friday morning meeting agenda, but at the same time, when he'd been praying to know what to do, that had been the thought inside his head.

He looked across the table to Bear, who gazed steadily back. Ranger leaned out from behind his computer, his gaze flitting from the monitor there to Bishop and back every few seconds. Cactus sat on Bear's right, as did Ward.

He loved watching the four of them converse and come to an agreement about projects on the ranch. Bishop had been specifically invited to this meeting to present on the southern sector cabins, as well as the Ranch House.

He couldn't wait to tell Montana how it had gone, despite the fact that she hadn't asked him to update her after the meeting that morning. He'd told her about it at least a half a dozen times, and—

"Are you going to say anything?" Bear asked. "We have work to do."

Bishop shifted in his seat and looked at Cactus, who nodded. "I met a woman," he said.

"Another one?" Ward teased.

Bishop smiled along with the rest of them. "She's different," he said. "She makes me nervous, and while I've already asked her out—maybe two or three times—she's never really said yes."

Bear folded his arms but otherwise said nothing. Ranger closed his laptop and gave Bishop his full attention.

His nerves settled further. This was exactly why he'd put this item on the agenda for this meeting. They weren't making fun of him. This was important to him, and therefore important to them.

In moments like these, he didn't need to go to lunch with his mother ever again. Ranger was his person, and so was Bear, and so was Ward, and so was Cactus.

"We always get interrupted, or you know, I've made a joke of it."

"I can't imagine either of those," Cactus said dryly. "Do we interrupt each other around here?"

Bishop shot him a look and kept going. "I'm frustrated, because I usually know if a woman likes me, and with her, I don't know."

"Who is it?" Ranger asked. "You've been working a lot. Perhaps the timing just isn't right to get off the ranch and go to dinner with her." He raised his eyebrows as if asking if that could be the issue.

Bishop drew his shoulders back, ready to spill the secret. "It's Montana."

"Montana?" Bear asked, leaning forward now. "The woman you hired at *three times* our daily rate to work construction with you?"

"Yes." Bishop dropped his chin toward his chest.

"The woman he hired," Bear said. "*The woman he hired* who made it impossible for him to hire anyone else."

"I have plenty of people to hire," Bishop said, the fire inside him licking its way up his throat. He raised his head and glared at Bear. "If you'd just release more of the budget."

"We gave you an appropriate budget."

"The Ranch House is *infested* with *two* colonies of *two* different types of termites," Bishop shot back. "You did *not* give me an adequate budget for construction personnel for that." He'd had to reschedule everything from the painters to the furniture delivery. That had taken days to accomplish, and Bear just assumed Bishop snapped his fingers and magic happened.

"He needs more budget," Ranger said, causing Bishop to whip his attention to his soft-spoken yet fierce cousin.

"I agree," Ward said.

"Thank you," Bishop said. "Despite my...rash hiring of Montana—which I'm not wrong about, by the way. She's amazing with a hammer and a power drill." In fact, he had to stop speaking so how amazing he thought she was while working with power tools wouldn't show in his voice.

"I'll bet you think so," Bear said, smiling.

Bishop wished he had his bagel back so he could throw it at his smug brother. It had taken him months to ask Sammy to dinner, and their first date had been so horrid, neither of them had called for another.

He would never actually rub that in Bear's face, because Bishop knew what it was like to want to call a woman and feel like he couldn't. He also knew what it felt like to wish a woman would call him, and she didn't.

Bear started to chuckle, and Bishop wasn't sure what the joke was. Probably him. He'd felt like a loser for a solid week, after attending Career Day at Lincoln's school and learning what amazing lives and jobs all the other moms and dads had.

He'd been late getting back to the ranch, and that had prompted him to stay silent about the dinner he'd asked Montana to have with him that night. She never had confirmed, and he'd simply let it slide into the past.

Before he knew it, everyone at the table was laughing except for him, and Bishop looked around at all of them.

Benny jumped up and put his paws on the table, and Bear growled at him and pushed him down. "No," he said, and the puppy came to Bishop's side. He curled onto his feet while the laughter subsided, and Bishop looked around at his brothers and cousins.

"So how do I do it?" he asked. "Text her? Call her? Maybe then there wouldn't be any distractions. Maybe we'd have time for the part where she says yes or no."

"And what if she says no?" Ranger asked. "You're going to keep working with her?"

"And paying her triple the rate," Bear added.

"Yes," Bishop said. "I can be a professional." He nodded at Ranger, then turned his attention to Bear. "If the salary bothers you so much, I'll pay her from my personal account. She's worth it, Bear. She apprenticed with the best woodworker in the state. She does beautiful work, and it's not even hard for her." He leveled his gaze at his oldest brother. "If I'd have quoted her fifty bucks a day, she'd have laughed and walked right out the door."

"I have an idea," Cactus said, and everyone turned their attention to him. He didn't speak up as much as others, especially in meetings like this one. When he did, everyone listened, especially Bishop.

He trusted Cactus with his whole might, mind, and strength, and he'd seriously consider his idea.

"He asks her out again." He glanced at Bishop. "Just call her, Bish. Call her as soon as we're done here and don't get off the phone until you guys have something set or she definitively says no. It's obviously eating at you, and you'll feel like a new man if you know one way or the other."

Bishop nodded, his chest suddenly so tight.

"If she says yes," Cactus continued. "He gets to work with her on the construction projects around the ranch and offer her a raise."

"What?" Bear asked, his voice on the border of a bellow.

"If she says no," Cactus said as if Bear hadn't spoken at all. "He gets the extra budget that three of us agree he needs, and he can hire the extra people so he won't have to see her as much."

Bishop immediately knew where Cactus was driving. "So you're going to give me an increased budget no matter what."

"I think we should," Cactus said. "Ranger and Ward already agreed." He looked across the table to Ranger, who nodded. "If Montana says yes, she can have the extra budget for her salary, and you two get to work exclusively together. The projects will take longer...." He let the sentence hang there, and Bishop got lost in a fantasy for a few moments.

Him and Montana, working on all the construction around the ranch. Together. No one else. It was always sunny but never too hot. She held his hand on rooftops and beneath trees, and he kissed her with a summer breeze blowing across his shoulders, his cowboy hat pressed against her back as she cradled his face in her hands.

"He's gone," Bear said, and Bishop blinked his way back to the meeting.

"Sorry, what?"

"I hope it was a good vision," Bear said. "Because I just agreed to this crazy plan of Cactus's, and you didn't even hear me."

Bishop's eyes widened, and he looked at the other men at the table, all of them either nodding or chuckling too. He swallowed and said, "It *was* a good vision, thanks."

The five of them laughed together then, and Bishop stood up to leave the conference room with everyone else. "Thanks, Bear," he said, stepping to his brother's side.

"Of course," Bear said. "Bishop, if you need more

budget, just say so. You never even said." He paused to let the others exit first.

"I was embarrassed," Bishop admitted in a near-whisper. "I know how important it is to you to maintain the integrity of our daddy's procedures."

"Daddy never had to deal with two termite infestations in one house." Bear clapped his hand on Bishop's shoulder. "Or a beautiful blonde with impressive carpentry skills."

"Yeah," Bishop said, needing this moment to be lighter. "He had to deal with Mother."

Bear burst out laughing, though they both loved their mother very much. "And six unruly boys, and Arizona."

"No wonder he went to an early grave," Bishop said, though that wasn't funny at all.

He and Bear sobered, and Bear looked him right in the eye. "Let's go out to the cemetery on Sunday morning before church. Just you and me."

The lump in Bishop's throat choked him, so all he did was nod. How did Bear know that Bishop needed exactly what he'd just suggested? That he needed to feel connected to Bear *and* his father, and he couldn't if they weren't all together?

"All right," Bear said, his voice gruff. "Now go call that woman and see what she says." He grinned at Bishop, who suddenly had more confidence than he needed to make the call.

Outside, in his truck, he looked at his phone. He didn't want to call, though he could. He knew right were Montana was, and that she was expecting him in the cabin they'd started yesterday in only ten minutes.

He should at least call and let her know he was running a little late. He backed out first, then tapped to get the phone ringing.

"Hey," she said after only one ring. "Let me guess. You're running late."

"Only ten minutes or so," he said, wondering if he was really always running late.

"Did you happen to get any of that candy you mentioned?"

He looked at the bag of chocolate-covered mint patties he'd taken from the conference room. "Yes, ma'am. A whole bag."

"Thank the Lord above," she said with a sigh. "Because I pulled out the stove, and Bishop, you're not going to like what I found."

His heart started to pound, and he started up the lane toward Mother's too fast. "What is it?"

"There's a huge hole in the wall here," she said, her voice moving further from the speaker and pitching it down. "I'm surprised you can't see it from outside."

"Great," he said, his mood suddenly foul again. "Listen, can we forget about the hole for a second? I want to ask you something."

"Okay." Her voice centered again. "What is it?"

"It's about us going to dinner," he said. "Is that ever going to happen? I know we've both been busy. The ranch is sort of a mess right now, and we work hard all day. You go home to Aurora in the afternoons, which you totally should. I'm not saying you shouldn't. Then, when you come back, I'm gone."

He exhaled, not quite sure why he'd given such a long soliloquy. He should've just stopped after *Is that ever going to happen?*

"But I'm frustrated," he admitted. "I think you're incredible, and beautiful, and I want to get to know you while I'm not wearing a mask to protect myself from mold, and literally the ugliest pair of kneepads ever created."

There. He'd said it all. Now, if she'd just say yes, Bishop could get back to living a normal life. Well, as normal of a life as he'd ever had while dating a pretty blonde woman.

"How about when you get here," she said slowly. "We get my assistant on the phone and make a plan?"

A smile burst onto Bishop's face. "I'll be there in ten."

The call ended, and Bishop couldn't stop smiling, despite the news of a hole in the wall creeping back into his mind. It didn't matter. He and Montana were tearing these cabins all the way back to their studs and floorboards. If they had to put in a new one, so be it.

The rest of the drive seemed to take forever, but he finally pulled in next to Montana's gray pickup. He'd barely gotten out of the truck when she came rushing out onto the porch. "Come see this, Bishop."

He just wanted to see her, but her wide-eyed excitement had his heart pounding triple time. The sight of her made his pulse double every single time, and he drank in her tank top of choice today.

This one was purple, which played nicely with her hair and eyes, and had a very grumpy cat on the front of it. She wore the funkiest shirts he'd ever seen, and that was one of the things he'd really like to ask her about while they sat across from one another at a nice restaurant, all thoughts of Shiloh Ridge somewhere else.

He took the steps two at a time and followed her into the cabin. They'd started in the kitchen, so he didn't have to step from floor stud to floor stud to get to her. She turned just as he arrived at the bank of cabinets they'd pried off the floor yesterday but hadn't removed from the cabin yet.

A small, black safe sat there. "This was in that hole," Montana said, her voice animated in a way he'd never heard before. He simply stared at the safe, which was probably two feet wide and two feet tall. She pointed to the top of it. "There was this piece of tape here, and it had these numbers on it. Looked like a combination, so I figured, why not? I put them in, and it opened."

He met her eye, and she carried pure joy and wonder in her expression. He found her made of light and beauty, and he wanted to see what she'd found inside that safe more than almost anything.

Almost.

This is another distraction, a voice in his head said.

He put his palm against the door of the safe and turned his hip into it. "I want to see what's in this. I do." He met her eyes again and swallowed. "But I really want to go out with you, and I'm not going to let another distraction prevent that from happening."

Surprise entered her eyes, quickly followed by a bit of shyness.

"Just tell me I'm not the only one whose heartbeat goes crazy when I see you."

She dropped her gaze to her hands, and Bishop wanted to make her look at him. He reached out and took both of her hands in his. "That came out wrong. Of course your own pulse doesn't go crazy when you see yourself. But me. When you see me, do you react at all? I mean, I don't need a huge compliment or anything, but I just...." He sighed. "I'm making a big mess of things."

He so wasn't the calm, cool, flirty cowboy he usually was with women. Ace would be downright horrified by everything he'd just admitted to, and Cactus would wish he'd gotten it all on video.

She looked up at him then, her eyes the crystal clear blue of a pure lake of fresh water. "I think you wanted to know when a sweet, charming, handsome cowboy asked me to dinner."

Bishop could only search her face, his hope skyrocketing with every moment that passed. He'd used the word flirty to describe himself. Not sweet, or charming, or handsome.

"One did," she said. "I'm going to say yes."

"Is that right?" he asked, his voice scratchy and rusted.

She nodded and gently pulled her hands away from his. "Let's see what my assistant says we should do this weekend." She took out her phone and tapped on something. She stepped closer to him, bringing the scent of green apples, sweat, and wood with her. He breathed it in, his blood turning to liquid lava in his veins.

She held her phone out so they could both see it. "Have you used this app? Two Cents?" She looked up at him, her face so close now that all Bishop would have to do was dip his four inches and he could kiss her.

Don't, he thought, and he just looked back at the app.

"I think your cousin owns it," she said. "He sent a really sweet message to his girlfriend a few months ago."

"That he did," Bishop said. "I've used it a few times."

She tapped once and then paused. "Most romantic first date spots."

"Let's look at that," he said, his voice as quiet as hers had been.

She dropped her thumb onto it, and Bishop tensed in the half-second it took to load the list.

"Couples massage," they read aloud.

Bishop looked at Montana, and she turned her head to look at him too. They burst out laughing together, and she said, "Okay, so maybe number two."

He kept chuckling as she read, "Hike to Apple Falls and eat dinner as the sun goes down." She looked up at him again, and he again thought of kissing her. "I'd do that. It sounds fun."

"Tonight?" he asked, dropping his head six inches instead of four and skating his lips along her jawline.

She drew in a stuttering breath and said, "I need to talk to my aunt first."

"So you *do* have an assistant," he murmured, straightening so he wouldn't make his heart explode for how fast it was currently beating.

"Give me five minutes." She stepped away from him. "Look inside that while I'm gone." With that, she walked away from him. Bishop watched her go, enjoying every moment.

He felt like whooping, like ripping his cowboy hat from his head and tossing it in the air for joy. Instead, he opened the safe, not sure what he'd find.

A wooden box sat on the left side, and it was completely crusted in grime and dust, along with broken cobwebs. Montana must have pulled it out already, because it came easily and left behind a clean portion of the bottom of the safe.

The lid opened fairly easily, with only a slight squeak of protest from one of the hinges. Letters sat inside. Old letters, with curling, strong cursive writing on the envelopes.

He sucked in a breath, his pulse spinning as wildly as his thoughts. He knew what these were, but he still reached delicately inside to take out the top envelope.

The letter was addressed to Lois Mather, and Bishop closed his eyes as he pressed the old paper with his father's beautiful handwriting on it to his chest.

"Thank you, Lord," he whispered. Mother had been looking for her love letters from Daddy for years. Over a decade. Since Daddy had died, actually.

He'd taken them from her to be preserved in a book, but he'd passed away before he'd ever presented her with the gift.

She'd cried for days after his death, and most of that was because of these letters that she'd lost.

Bishop opened his eyes, the love between his mother and father a palpable being in the room with him. In fact,

Bishop looked up as if Daddy himself would be standing on the other side of the countertop. "I feel you, Daddy," he whispered. "Mother is going to be so happy."

Take care of your mother, son.

Bishop nodded now, the same way he had the last time he'd spoken to his father. His dad had taught him to love and respect his mother, claiming that she'd gone to the edge of death to bring him into the world, and she'd done it because she loved him ages before she even knew him.

Daddy had loved her so much too.

He reached into the box and took out all of the letters. There had to be at least fifty, and he wanted to read every one of them. They needed to be cleaned and salvaged, and Bishop immediately thought he and his siblings should do it for their mother's birthday, which was only about six weeks away now.

He tucked the letters back into the box, intending to get them into something cleaner as soon as possible, and returned his attention to the safe.

A legal-sized envelope sat on the other half of the safe, and Bishop's fingers trembled as he reached for it. He knew what it contained before he'd opened it. After Daddy's death, he and the other children had found envelopes with money in them all over the house.

This one held money too—a lot of money. More money than Bishop could count with a glance or even a few minutes.

Several sheets of paper accompanied the money, and Bishop pulled them out to look at them.

"To my son Bartholomew," he read aloud, realizing this

was a letter for Bear. Cactus had one. Judge, Preacher, Arizona, Mister, and Bishop. His sat on the bottom, the last child, but not the least.

"I'm good for tonight," Montana said, and Bishop looked up from his letter, having only read the first line.

He felt heaven shining through him as Montana came toward him. "This is incredible."

"They're love letters," she said, her countenance beaming too.

"My mother's been looking for them for years and years." He slid the letters back inside the envelope to keep them somewhat clean. "Thank you." He drew Montana into a tight hug. "This is like striking gold. Thank you."

"I didn't do anything," she said, though she did wrap her arms around him too. "I just moved a stove and found a hole."

He didn't care. To him, she'd done something, and he was grateful.

"Did you hear me say I was good to go tonight?"

Bishop pulled away and looked at her. So many things were said between them, though neither one of them said a word. "Yes," he said, his voice slightly cracked. "Should we say six? That should give us enough time to hike to the falls and get set up."

"Six is great."

Bishop couldn't believe how much difference a half an hour and a phone call could make. His life felt like someone had turned it inside out since the meeting ended, and he couldn't wait to get back to the homestead and show his siblings what he had.

"Let's see if we can get everyone to come to the homestead to see what you found," he said.

"Really?" she asked, glancing around at the cabin. He knew what she was thinking, because they did have a lot of work to do.

"Yeah," he said. "This is more important." He pulled out his phone and dialed Bear.

"Yep," Bear said.

"First off," Bishop said. "She said yes, and we're going out tonight." He grinned at Montana as her eyebrows went up and Bear cheered for him. "Second, I found Mother's love letters, and I think we need an emergency sibling meeting at the homestead. I'll head back now and make the chicken and gnocchi soup, if you can get everyone there for lunch."

Silence poured through the line, and Bishop couldn't help laughing.

"You really found the letters?" Bear asked quietly.

"Montana did," Bishop said. "She'll be at lunch too." He reached for her hand, letting her close the distance to slip her fingers between his.

He lifted her hand to his lips as Bear said, "I'll get everyone there." And when Bear spoke like that, Bishop didn't doubt him for a second.

Chapter Eleven

Bear Glover leaned against the column at the top of the steps on the front porch, anxious for Bishop to arrive. His nerves had been singing since his brother had called a half an hour ago, and he sincerely hoped he wasn't waiting while Bishop kissed Montana.

He told himself even Bishop wouldn't do that before even going out with a woman, but Bear knew hormones and blondes did strange things to his youngest brother.

He'd sent a text to the family string the moment he'd hung up with Bishop, and he'd called Sammy only a few seconds after that.

She'd been elbow-deep in someone's engine, but Logan had promised he'd tell her about the love letters and the lunch at the homestead, and Bear was still waiting for her confirmation that she'd be there.

She was a Glover now, and Bear wanted her here more than anything.

Bishop had texted during the phone call that he had an idea for how they could clean up the letters and present them to Mother for her birthday, and Bear had scratched that phone call off his list.

With her house freshly fumigated and inspected for termites, Mother had been back in the cottage for a couple of days now, and she had no reason to come down to the homestead. She rarely drove anywhere by herself anymore anyway, and Zona had confirmed that she was out in the bullpens and wouldn't go home to get Mother for the luncheon.

Bear's heartbeat skipped, and he wasn't even sure why. Something huge felt just out of his reach, and he wanted it so badly. He supposed that could be the reason why.

Finally, Bishop's big black truck came rumbling down the dirt lane that led up to the southern sector, where the cabins and Mother's cottage were located, and Bear's muscles spasmed as his need to get down the steps to the truck kicked into gear, but he told himself not to move a split-second later.

Bishop pulled into his normal spot in front of the homestead, and he looked at Montana, who rode in the passenger seat.

Bear hadn't even met her yet; he'd only heard of the woman Bishop had hired and who'd been working on the cabins with him every day this week. He watched as Bishop got out of the truck and waved to him. "You want to come see?" He gestured to the back of the truck, and Bear allowed himself to go down the steps now.

Montana got out of the passenger side, and Bear met the two of them at the tailgate.

"First off," Bishop said. "Montana, this is my oldest brother, Bear. Bear, this is your new construction manager, Montana Martin."

"Manager?" Montana asked at the same time Bear extended his hand toward her to shake.

"Oh, you're the manager," Bear said. "From what Bishop tells me, your talent exceeds most we've had out here."

She put her hand in his and shook firmly. Bear sure did like that, and he could see exactly why Bishop liked this woman. Not only did she have the blonde and blue-eyed features he loved so much, but she was strong, with personality and drive. She wasn't one of the simpering women he'd brought home in the past, and Bear had the very distinct feeling she'd teach Bishop exactly how she wanted him to treat her.

Not that Bishop wasn't a perfect gentleman with the women he went out with. He was—that was the problem. They wanted someone with more alpha-male qualities, and they broke up with Bishop and then expected him to chase them. To show up with flowers and dinners and beg them to have him, that there was no one for him but them.

The problem was, Bishop didn't do that. And when he didn't, those other women found him weak, or took his ability to give them space as him saying he wasn't interested in them.

Bear had never told Bishop that, and he never would. But this Montana...she'd already ignited something inside

Bishop that made him fight for what he wanted. Just his glaring and words at the meeting had told Bear that.

"I thought this was a temporary job," Montana said, looking at Bishop. "The cabins and the Ranch Home."

"Well, those two things could take a while," Bear said, looking away from her as a clank sounded. Bishop had opened the safe, and Bear's mouth was suddenly full of cotton.

"Here they are." Bishop took a box out of the safe that Bear recognized instantly. He got thrown back in time thirty years, and he could remember distinctly when his father had made this box.

"Oh, wow," he said reverently, taking the box from Bishop. He looked at his brother and found his eyes shining the same way Bear imagined his were. "Daddy built this box the day he showed me how to use the table saw," he said. "I was fifteen years old, and we spent the afternoon in the wood shop together."

Bishop's throat worked, and Bear knew Bishop had had plenty of afternoons like that with Daddy. He'd taught all of his boys to work with wood, but none loved it more than Bishop. None had more talent than Bishop. None had bonded to their father over shavings and carvings the way Bishop had.

"He made it for Mother's birthday," Bear said. "He said she was going to love it, because she loved to keep and store little trinkets." He lifted the lid and looked at the stack of letters inside. He sucked in a breath, because he honestly hadn't believed they'd be there, despite what

Bishop had said. "Dear Lord," he whispered, letting his eyes fall closed as they burned. "Thank you."

"Have you read the letters?" Bishop asked.

Bear shook his head. "She'd never let us as kids. She didn't want them to get ripped." He opened his eyes and looked at Bishop and then Montana, who watched them with a supporting smile on her face. "After that, I guess I just...forgot about them."

"I was only eighteen when he died," Bishop said, and Montana stepped around Bear to his side. She linked her arm through his, and Bishop ducked his head to look at her, creating a safe space for the two of them behind the brim of his cowboy hat.

Oh, yeah, she already had sharp teeth in his heart, and Bear let the happiness he felt flow through him. He wanted everyone in his family to find a forever love the way he had, and no one more than Bishop.

"That's not all," Bishop said. "Should we go in?" He glanced toward the house and took out a large, orange envelope. "Is anyone else here?"

"No," Bear said. "I came straight back after you called. I texted, and everyone in our family confirmed. Ranger and Ward are coming too. Haven't heard from the twins or Ace."

"Well, it's not their mother."

"They'll still want to see them," Bear said, closing the lid on the box. "If they can. I called Sammy. I hope she can come."

"Me too," Bishop held up the envelope. "There's money in here."

"Big surprise," Bear said with a smile. "I'll stick it in a closet for y'all to find after I die."

He grinned at Montana. "My grandmother did that, and we found money in the strangest places after she passed. Daddy picked it up from her."

"That's sweet," Montana said. "You guys clearly love your father. And your mother."

"Yes," Bear said, because what else could he say? He had loved his father with all he had, and he still did. Mother had a special piece of his heart as well, and Bear wasn't going to apologize for it.

"I go to lunch with Mother at least once a month," Bishop said. "Just me and her. It's...." He looked at Bear, a measure of fear in his eyes.

"I didn't know that," Bear said. He started for the homestead, hoping Bishop would say more but suspecting he wouldn't.

Sure enough, Bishop fell silent, and together, along with Benny, they went inside the homestead. Bear's phone chimed, and Sammy had texted with, *I'll be there, Bear.*

His love for her multiplied, and Bear didn't think that was possible. He'd enjoyed their engagement immensely, and the wedding had been all of Sammy's dreams. His too, if he'd ever had any fantasies about his wedding.

The honeymoon had been warm and wonderful, and Bear missed the bright blue ocean and the big ship they'd ridden on to get to it. He missed the golden sand and lying next to Sammy under the sun without a care in the world.

He still got to kiss her goodnight and wake up with her

curled into his side, and he could be anywhere with her and be happy.

He'd been screened for colon cancer the day after they'd returned from the Caribbean, and his test had come back clean. Once Sammy had learned that disease had taken Daddy from the ranch and the family at such a young age, she'd insisted he get scanned every year, starting now.

"People die from that, Bear," she said. "Obviously. And they die young. Your daddy got sixty years, but I know people who've died at forty-three."

He'd do anything to make her happy, and if that meant going to the hospital for an uncomfortable test, he'd do it. He should've been doing it anyway, and he needed to tell all the men in his family to do the same.

"Okay," Bishop said, and Bear lifted his head from looking at the box. "There are letters for each of us in here." He opened the envelope. "I don't want anyone to read mine. I think we should each get to read them privately first, and then we can choose to share or not."

"Of course," Bear said. "Were there instructions for them?"

"No." Bishop dumped the money on the counter, and Montana ogled it. Bear didn't care about money, but he knew her reaction was more normal.

"Looks like Daddy was thinkin' of starting a savings account for something." Bear picked up one of the stacks of cash, the band around it saying there was five thousand dollars of fifties there. "There's nothing that says anything?"

"Not in here," Bishop said. "Was there anything in the

will?"

"Not that I recall," Bear said. "But it's been a while since we read it." He had not gone back to it since the day they'd hosted the lawyers at the homestead. Daddy had a pour over will, which meant everything went to Mother, except for certain things that had already been transferred.

Bear had already taken over the ranch on paper by then. After Daddy's death, he'd taken over in every aspect. A few years later, Ranger had joined him at the helm, and after Uncle Stone's death a handful of years ago, they'd been running Shiloh Ridge together.

Uncle Stone also died from colon cancer, he thought, and he couldn't believe he'd missed it before. Did he really think himself immune from the troubles and trials of the world? Of course he wasn't.

"Here's yours," Bishop said, handing him a single sheet of paper. "They're all just one page, surprisingly."

"Well, Daddy never did mince words," Bear said. "Did you read yours?"

Bishop shook his head, and Montana said, "Come on, Benny. You come outside with me, and I'll throw you a ball." She'd said the magic word, and Benny perked right up as Montana picked up his toy and headed for the front door.

"She's great," Bear said once she'd left. "I see why you like her so much."

"Do you?" Bishop looked so hopeful, and Bear smiled at him to get him to settle down.

"Absolutely." He looked at his letter. *To my son Bartholomew.*

His chest hitched, and he said, "I'm going to go read this upstairs."

Bishop didn't answer, but he had a single sheet of paper in his hand too, and he moved toward the living room and through it to the door that led into the main level suite.

Bear did go upstairs and all the way into the bedroom he now shared with Sammy. He sat in the recliner she'd brought from her place and took a long, deep breath.

To my son Bartholomew,

Your mother and I started calling you Bear after my momma told me you had a heart of a champion. I'm not sure she ever told you that story, so I'll tell you.

You were probably four or five years old, and we'd just brought home Judge from the hospital. Mother was drowning with more children than adults, and I was working an incredibly difficult birthing season that year. Gone all the time, and your mother met me at the door one night, long past dark.

She told me she couldn't keep doing what we were doing. She was upset with me, and looking back, she had every right to be. You were a rambunctious child who wasn't in school yet, and Cactus has always been a bit spiny. Judge cried all the time, and Mother gave me the baby and said, "I get to go work the ranch tomorrow. You'll be the one at home."

I didn't believe her. But when I got up in the morning, she was dressed already in her pants and shirt and winter coat. She looked at me and said, "Good luck," before she left.

I marvel at her strength and faith. I could've literally killed you three boys that day, because I had no idea what I was doing. Mother hadn't left me a list of when you ate, your activities, or even what to feed you.

I had nothing but myself and you three boys, two of whom couldn't even talk.

You could, though, Bear, and you got up first and found me in the kitchen. You asked me what was for breakfast, and I asked you what Mother usually made.

Pancakes. I managed to make some of those, but no one would eat them. I gave you all juice and turned on the TV. You lasted about five minutes. Then you asked if you could go fishing. I said no.

On and on this went. You'd ask to do something; I'd say no. I didn't dare leave the house. I didn't even know where your shoes were, and none of you were dressed in anything but what Mother had put you in for bed the night before.

Finally, you climbed onto my lap, despite the fact that I had Cactus in one arm and Judge in the other, both of them fussing over something I didn't understand.

You took my face in both of your little boy hands, and you said, "Daddy, they need to eat and go outside. Let's go play."

I don't remember what I said, but I remember what you did. You said, "I'll help you, Daddy."

And my dear Bear, you helped me the rest of the day, and every day since. By the time Mother came home, long after dark, I'd fed you boys two meals and managed to give you baths too. I wept and begged her to never leave me alone with the children again, and she told me of course she would.

They were my children, and if I'd love them half as much as I loved Shiloh Ridge, I'd be a better man. She expected me to be that better man.

I didn't know how to do that, but I wanted to. For her. For all you kids, but mostly for you, Bear. I can still see those bright blue eyes only inches from mine. I can hear your tinny, childlike voice saying, "I'll help you, Daddy."

Every day, you taught me something new, all the way to today when I watched you gather all the children together outside in the hallway. I watched them look to you the way I have so many times, and I watched you lead them in prayer before you came in.

You have a powerful, powerful personality. Grandmother saw it instantly, and when I told her what Mother had done, she said, "Good for her. You better learn to treat her right, Stone. Your children are watching you. God sent you a bear of a man inside that little boy. He's a champion. Do not stifle him."

I've tried not to stifle you, Bear. Lord knows I've tried.

I am not going to be here much longer. I can feel it in my bones and in my very soul. I want you to know I love you with all the energy the Good Lord will let me have. I trust you beyond measure to take Shiloh Ridge into the future and pass it along to your son or daughter. I believe you will know how to treat the woman you find to love much better than I treated Mother in those early years.

I am grateful for the gift of forgiveness. I am grateful for my family and the time God has given me with them. Oh, how I wish I could have more, but I cannot.

Please, watch out for Bishop. I fear for him the most, because we are so very important to one another, and he will need your champion heart in the days and years after I am gone.

I leave you with the words of Grandmother, whom I know you loved.

Do not stifle him. Do not stifle yourself, Bear. Do not stifle Bishop. Do not stifle that championship spirit you were named for.

Embrace it, and you will never be led astray.

I love you, and I pray that anything I have done that you resent or are bitter about will be forgiven in the future.

Daddy

BEAR SOBBED AS HE FINISHED READING THE LETTER, letting go of it with one hand as he released all the tension and nervousness from his body.

He rarely cried, but the powerful emotions washing over him and through him could not be released any other way.

Great sobs wracked his chest, and he thought he'd never get another proper breath. He missed his father so much that anger descended upon him that God had taken him so soon.

Just as quickly as that had come, it all faded.

Bear quieted, and he wiped his face clean and dry.

"A champion heart," he whispered. "Thank you, Grandmother." He'd loved her too, and he loved this story he'd never heard before. He didn't remember being home with his father that day, and Mother had never said a word about such things.

"Bear?"

He looked up as Sammy pushed the door in one inch at a time. "Can I come in?"

Bear's tears started anew at the beautiful, calming sight of her. "Yes," he said, gesturing her forward. "Come and read this letter."

She hurried toward him, pure alarm on her face. "You're crying, Bear."

He took her right onto his lap and buried his face in her chest. "I love you," he said. "I love you beyond anything else."

"You're scaring me," she whispered.

"It's good," he said, trying to get his eyes to stop watering. He handed her the letter. "Read it. It's good. Nothing to be scared of."

She took the paper but didn't start reading. "This is one of those times when the grief sneaks up on you, isn't it?" She wasn't really asking, and Bear didn't really need to answer.

He just closed his eyes and said, "Read it, my love. Tell me if you think he's right."

A COUPLE OF HOURS LATER, SAMMY SMOOTHED THE HAIR from Bear's forehead. "We should go down, Teddy. I'm sure everyone's here by now."

Bear opened his eyes and looked into his wife's. She was so good and so kind, and Bear did love her with his whole champion heart. "Okay," he said. After she'd read the letter and told him that yes, he had a heart made of gold, she'd tucked him into bed and said, *Rest for a while, baby. You don't rest enough.*

She'd tucked herself into his arms, and Bear had thanked the Lord for his multitude of blessings and dozed. At some point, he'd smelled the beginnings of lunch, which meant Bishop had come out of his room.

Bear groaned as he sat up and he took a moment as the

room spun to give it time to settle. "I just need a minute to wash my face." He went into the bathroom and drenched a washrag with cold water. After wiping it down his face to clear away the evidence of tears, he looked into his eyes. "I don't want to cry in front of everyone."

Bear couldn't even remember the last time he'd cried. Probably the day they'd buried Daddy, over fifteen years ago.

Sammy appeared in the doorway, and she was soft and strong at the same time. Their eyes met in the mirror, and she held up her phone. "I screened this. You have a ton of messages, but none of them are essential for you to read right now. The only one I'd respond to is the one from your mother."

Bear turned toward her and took the device. "Thank you." For some reason, he was having a hard time maintaining eye contact with her.

"You don't have to be embarrassed with me," she said. "I know it makes no sense to you what happened this morning, but I understand it. I understand it, because I've lived it."

He wrapped her in a hug and stroked her hair, his words stuck somewhere in his chest.

"Come on," she said. "Bishop's started texting me now."

When Bear arrived in the kitchen, every eye swung his way, and most of them carried plenty of anxiety. Bishop wore a navy blue apron and looked up from the casserole dish. "Finally," he said, taking off the oven mitts and tossing them on the counter. "Okay, everyone. Quiet down."

No one was talking, and Bear thought of the day they'd all gathered to this spot of land. The house was different, but this was the same place where Daddy had once lived and died. He had kept them in the hall and said he'd like to say a prayer before they went in to visit him.

It wasn't the last time Bear had visited his father, but he'd known his dad wouldn't survive the moment he'd opened his mouth to say that prayer. He hadn't known what he was going to say then, just as he didn't now.

Last time, he'd just opened his mouth.

Maybe this time, that was all he had to do again.

"Thanks for coming," he said. "Bishop and Montana have been working on the cabins in the southern sector, and they've made a very exciting discovery."

Bishop moved over to stand next to Bear, and everyone tracked him. Montana sat at the large kitchen table, smartly out of the way.

"Well?" Cactus growled. "What is it?"

"Just spit it out," Ward said.

"Okay," Bishop said, his grin giddy. "Now, it's a bit of a mess, but I'm going to clean it all up. The box and the letters and everything."

Zona sucked in a breath and covered her mouth.

"Montana found a safe hidden in the wall that has the box full of Mother's love letters from Daddy." Bishop smiled around at everyone. "There was an envelope with money and—"

"*The* letters?" Preacher asked, cutting him off.

"Are you sure?" Judge took a step closer, his eyes firing with hope.

"I'm quite sure," Bishop said, and he reached up to the cupboard above the fridge. "They're right here." He pulled out the box, and everyone crowded around, even Ranger and his brothers. Etta and Ida must not have been able to make it.

"But you guys," Bishop said as everyone started talking again.

"Bish," Bear said. "Give them a minute."

Bishop nodded and glanced over to Montana.

"She's probably overwhelmed," Bear said.

"Yeah," Sammy said. "Or she doesn't have a family that's like this."

"Go make sure she's okay," Bear urged.

Bishop moved that way, and Bear spoke to the others as they said things to him. At one point, Cactus left the group surrounding the letters and stepped over to Montana and Bishop. He handed an envelope to Bishop, who looked at it and then up at Cactus.

He said something and stood up, embracing Cactus. Bear wanted to know what that was about, and he wanted to show Bishop his letter so he'd know he'd loved Bishop and taken him as his long before Daddy had asked him to.

Later, he told himself. They had a date at the cemetery, and Bear would bring his letter with him then.

"All right," he said. "There's more. Bishop?"

Bishop turned away from Cactus and surveyed the group. "I'm going to clean up the box and letters and give them to Mother for her birthday. So it's a secret for now, okay? Not a word to her." He sought out Arizona and cocked his eyebrow. "Zona?"

"Fine," she whispered, her tears obvious in her eyes and voice. "Not a word."

"Daddy had a bunch of money in the envelope," Bishop said, looking at Bear. "We're not sure what it's for, but I think I'll use it for the restoration of the letters, and maybe to bind them in a book."

"Good idea," Bear said.

"And Daddy wrote us each a letter," Bishop said, picking up the envelope. "Bear and I have ours, and we've agreed that everyone should get to read their letter in private and only share what you want with who you want." He pressed the envelope to his chest. "So we can eat first or you can take your letters now."

Mister took a step toward Bishop, his choice obvious. "I love your food, Bishop, but I want my letter."

Everyone did, and Bishop handed them all out, and in only a matter of seconds, Bear and Bishop stood with Ranger, Ward, and Ace. Sammy had wandered over to Montana, and Bear felt a new kind of peaceful spirit enter the homestead that he hadn't felt before.

"I wonder if my father wrote us letters," Ranger said, his eyes bright.

"I'm sorry, Ranger," Bear said, grabbing onto his cousin and one of his best friends. "This can't make things easier for you. I shouldn't have invited you."

"I'm glad you did," Ranger said. "Sometimes I just miss him, you know?"

Boy, did Bear know. "Yeah," he said, his voice thick. "I know."

Chapter Twelve

Montana cocked her head to the left to put in her earring. Her heart beat unnaturally, because it was ten minutes until six, and then Bishop would be standing at the door. She'd given him the address to her aunt and uncle's house against her better judgment. She'd let Uncle Bob take Aurora to get ice cream for a party she was going to that night.

"Ollie Osburn," she muttered. She'd told Aurora she needed to meet the boy soon, and Aurora had asked why. Actually asked *why* Montana needed to meet the boy she was crushing on and spending so much time with.

She'd been over to his house just the one afternoon, but they spent a lot of time texting, and this was the second party at the boy's house. It was just as well, because Montana was not ready to introduce Bishop to her daughter, or her daughter to Bishop.

She was mildly horrified to have to introduce her aunt.

If she lived alone, there would be no introductions. Just a handsome cowboy on her doorstep, with a picnic basket in his big truck.

Right on time, the doorbell rang, and Aunt Jackie must've leapt from her chair in the kitchen, because it banged into the wall behind it. "I'll get it!" she yelled as she came jogging into the living room.

Montana stared at her, her stomach suddenly cramping. "This is a bad idea."

"Oh, you look beautiful." Aunt Jackie's hand fluttered near her mouth.

Montana had chosen to wear jeans, as they were hiking. They were form-fitting jeggings actually, and she'd tucked them into a pair of black boots with great traction that went all the way to her knee.

She wore a short-sleeved shirt in dark blue, because that color made her eyes brighter and her hair stand out. A simple silver necklace lay against her collarbone, and large hoops dangled from her ears.

She wasn't sure if this was what one wore on a hiking date, but she wanted to be able to move if she needed to.

Aunt Jackie's voice sounded, and Montana realized she'd moved to the door. "Come in, come in."

Bishop appeared, and he too wore jeans and a short-sleeved, button-up shirt in light blue and white. He looked around, and when his eyes met hers, he lit up like a Christmas tree. "Hey, there," he said.

"Hey yourself," Montana said. "You look nice."

Bishop came toward her, his energy and charisma infectious. "You look absolutely stunning." He touched her shirt first, right on the cuff of the sleeve. "You should always wear this color. It's amazing on you."

"Thank you."

He leaned down and swept his lips along her cheek. "I have everything in the truck. Are you ready?"

"Yes, sir."

"Oh, come on." He laughed. "What did I say about the sir business?"

Montana grinned up at him. "You said not to call you that at work. We're not at work."

"No, we are not," he murmured, turning toward Aunt Jackie. He tipped his hat as they passed. "Nice to meet you, ma'am."

"Likewise," she said, her excitement palpable too.

Montana managed not to giggle on her way out the door, and once she sat in Bishop's truck, everything felt more normal. She breathed in while he rounded the truck and out as he got behind the wheel.

"Ready?"

"Yes." She glanced at him. "You promised me the story behind the names."

"I haven't even left your driveway." He looked at her with some shock in his expression.

"I'm anxious," she said. "After seeing everything earlier today." Montana shook her head and swallowed. "Your family is absolutely amazing, Bishop. I can't even fathom having the kind of relationships you have with them. The names are very clearly part of that, and I want to know what."

"You seem to have a good relationship with your aunt," he said as he backed out of the driveway.

"Yes," Montana admitted. "She and Uncle Bob are, in fact, the only family members I'm currently speaking with. At least for longer than it takes to update them that I'm still alive."

Bishop looked at her fully then, despite driving down the sleepy streets of Three Rivers. "I want to hear all about that."

Montana knew he would, because Bishop wanted to know everything about her. He'd come right out and said as much, and Montana had remembered keenly why she hadn't been overly anxious to begin dating again.

"Maybe," she said.

"Maybe?"

"It's date number one," she said, folding her hands in her lap. "I want it to be fun, and light-hearted and memorable. If you decide you still want to know more, we can try a second date."

"I already know I want to know more."

"What if I don't want to know more?"

Bishop just blinked at her, as if such a notion was preposterous.

Montana laughed, because the man really was something else. "You're so confident," she said.

He looked away from her. "I'm actually the opposite," he said. A brief smile touched his lips. "I put on a good front at least."

Montana wanted to know more about that, but she

wanted the story on the names first. She waited, because she'd already asked once.

"My real name is Benson," he said. "After my great-grandmother. It was her maiden name." He glanced at her. "Mother says I carry some of her can-do spirit in my soul, and I can't say she's wrong." He shifted in his seat, clearly trying to gauge how Montana would take his story.

"Benson," she said. "It's an unusual first name, but I like it."

"That's why I go by Bishop," he said. "Daddy wanted to honor his great-grandmother, but he didn't want a son with two last names."

"He knows Bishop can be a last name too, right?"

Bishop chuckled and shook his head. "You know, I'm not sure he knew that. Daddy really didn't get off the ranch much."

"Come on," Montana said. "Surely he knew Bishop was a last name."

"All right, he did." Bishop made a turn and accelerated as they went down the highway west of town.

"So how did you come to have it?"

"All the names in the family mean something," he said. "For example, Judge's name is John. Mother believed in traditional names, and we've got John, Michael, Paul, Charles. You get the idea."

Montana tried to match up the traditional names with the men she'd seen in the homestead at lunchtime. She'd met several of them previously, but she'd had a devil of a time keeping them all straight. Not only did Bishop have five brothers, but he had three male cousins.

She knew Bear, as he'd been kind and impossible to forget. She remembered Cactus too, because he scared her slightly. She'd seen softness in his eyes for a moment after Bishop had hugged him, but his shutters had flown right back into place, and when he'd looked at her, Cactus's eyes had gone back to the hard, nearly navy marbles they'd been before.

"I get the idea," she said, because Bishop had stopped talking.

"Right." He cleared his throat. "Each child got a different name, based on certain qualities or traits our grandmother saw in us." He looked out his window, and Montana found his vulnerability more attractive than his confidence.

Too bad she didn't have the confidence to tell him that.

"I got Bishop, because Grandmother said I needed something to live up to. A bishop is an overseer, I suppose, and she said by giving me the name, I'd rise to my birthright and become a great leader."

"Wow," Montana said.

Bishop scoffed. "I'm not sure my grandmother was all there when she said all of that, to be honest."

"Overseer," Montana said. "I think it fits, Bishop."

"You do?" He turned to look at her. "I spent a lot of years wondering what she meant by giving me that name. I'm the youngest. I'm quite literally overlooked most of the time."

"Not today," she said. "I saw all of them looking at you. They asked you where Bear was. They looked to you for answers."

"Only because I'd found the letters," he said. "The cooking doesn't hurt."

"Cactus likes you."

"Cactus and I have a unique friendship," Bishop admitted. "Even when—" He shook his head. "Cactus is part of my soul." He flashed her a smile. "Bear too, if you must know."

A deep, yawning sadness pulled through Montana, and she found herself looking out her window now.

"I've made you upset," Bishop said quietly. "I apologize. I didn't mean to."

"It's not your fault," Montana said, but she couldn't face him. "I do not...my family is the polar opposite of yours." She wasn't sure how she could say more. She didn't wish to speak unkindly about her sisters, so she simply said nothing at all. It was a good rule she'd abided by for a while now.

"Why don't you speak to them?"

Montana drew in a deep breath and found her well of confidence. "I have two sisters. We're all named after places—Georgia and Paris. I'm the oldest girl. I have an older brother named Dakota."

"Interesting," Bishop said.

"I think it's weird," Montana said. "But interesting is probably a nice way to say that, and you're kind, so."

He chuckled and made another turn, this one that would lead them to the trailhead. "Go on."

Montana cleared her throat. "I dated a man in Dallas, where I used to live with my two sisters. We were getting serious, at least in my head, and the next thing I knew,

Mason broke up with me. Literally, four days later, he and Paris started dating."

"You're joking."

"I wish." Montana crossed her arms, hoping to hold in the bitterness she didn't like to let out. "They dated for a while, and Paris honestly couldn't see the problem with what had happened. Then, when the exact same thing happened to her, she understood."

"Georgia went out with him?" The level of incredulity in his voice mirrored the way Montana had felt. She could admit she'd felt fairly vindicated too, but she didn't like to say so out loud.

"I tried to be sympathetic, but I'm not very nice. I decided I couldn't stay in Dallas, and that's when Aurora and I moved here."

"You should *not* have to be sympathetic to that," he said, and she appreciated his indignation.

"My mother has had her problems over the years," Montana said, not wanting to get into the whole nine yards there. "Let's just say I text her from time to time. She's my aunt's sister, and they talk regularly. I call my father on his birthday and on Father's Day. Aurora sends him cards and letters. He's still in Alabama."

She looked at Bishop. "It's just been me and Aurora for a while now. Ten years. We've been with Aunt Jackie and Uncle Bob for almost three years. I love it here, and I'm trying to save up enough to get my own place." The familiar bubble of excitement buzzed through her. "But Aunt Jackie doesn't want us to move out. She actually likes the teen drama and having someone to fuss over." She grinned then, because she did love her aunt.

"Does she have children?" Bishop asked.

"No, sir. She and Uncle Bob were never able to have any."

"Do you want more children?"

Montana's voice dried up, and even when she tried to speak, she couldn't.

"Cactus is going to love this," Bishop said, saving her.

"What do you mean?'

"I mean, he's trying to get back into the dating pool too, and he loves it when I make mistakes."

"Was that a mistake?"

"You literally couldn't answer." He turned into a dirt parking lot where only two other cars sat. "It's fine. It's a question I shouldn't have asked on the first date." He parked and smiled at her. "That's why Cactus will love it when I tell him I stuck my cowboy boot so far down my throat before we even made it to the trailhead."

He grinned, still so confident. So handsome. So charming and likable.

Montana focused on unbuckling her seatbelt as if such a task required extra attention. "Maybe you asked it because it's important to you to know the answer."

Bishop pulled in a breath. "Maybe I did." He opened his door. "Let me come around and help you."

Montana didn't need his help getting out of the truck, but she let him jog around the hood and open her door. Bishop definitely possessed an energy she craved, and she smiled down at him. He took her hand, and she slipped to the ground, keeping her fingers laced through his after she'd found her balance.

"Thanks," she said. He stayed right where he was, and she added, "Can I have a little more time to give you an answer to that particular question?"

"Sure," he said, his voice too casual to actually be casual.

"I suspect you want children," she said. "Just from being around your family. I have Aurora and she'll be fifteen in a few months. It's hard for me to think I'm going to go back to diapers and getting up in the middle of the night and first steps and all of that."

"I understand," he said, but Montana didn't believe him. There was no way he could possibly understand. Not only did he not have children of his own, but he was the youngest. He'd never had to care for a baby in any capacity.

"Let me get dinner," he said, practically jumping away from her and toward the tailgate. He collected a classic picnic basket, complete with the red-and-white checkered cloth peeking out the sides. "I hope you like slightly warm pizza." He grinned at her, and Montana had a feeling she'd eat cardboard just to spend a little bit of time with him.

"There's pizza in there? You didn't cook?"

"It's been a draining day," he admitted, and she saw his exhaustion for the briefest of moments. "So I ordered and picked up only a few minutes before I stopped by your aunt's."

"Oh, so even you have off days," she teased.

"So many," Bishop said.

"We don't have to hike to the falls," she said. "I don't even know how far it is."

Bishop paused and turned back to her. "What? We just drive here and eat?"

"Sure," she said. "You have a tailgate, right? Drop that thing, and we sit in the back of your truck. Legs dangling. The sun's gonna go down here just like it will up there." The more Montana spoke, the more she wanted to do what she said. "In fact, I'm kinda tired too."

"Yeah? I didn't think you got tired."

She looked at him, surprised. "What? Of course I get tired."

"You just seem to go and go," he said. "It's one of the reasons I really like you. It's just that...it makes you more human."

Montana had no idea what to say. "I'm one-hundred percent human," she said, and that summed up everything. "But let's stay here. It's a great view already."

"Deal," he said, and Bishop led her back to his truck, where Montana ate room-temperature pizza and delicious cinnamon twists, laughed with Bishop, and leaned into his side while the sun said goodbye to Texas for another day.

"THAT'S THE LAST OF IT," MONTANA SAID, HEFTING another armful of debris into the Dumpster she and Bishop had filled several times over in the past couple of weeks. He currently looked at his phone, a frown between his eyes.

"Thanks," he said, definitely distracted.

Montana needed a drink like she needed oxygen, and she made one last trek inside the cabin and retrieved her water bottle from the windowsill. She sucked at the cold liquid inside, her throat thanking her instantly.

She grabbed Bishop's bottle too and glanced around this last cabin. The stripping had taken so long, because they had to deal with mold the whole time, and that required constant checks and paperwork with the health department.

A restoration company was scheduled to come tomorrow to treat whatever remained in the three cabins they'd been working on. A foundation for a fourth had been poured, and she and Bishop had spent days framing and getting it to the stage the others were at.

That way, as they ordered supplies, they could do it in bulk.

"You okay?" she asked as she approached Bishop again. She was very comfortable with him, because they spent hours together every day. He took her back to the homestead at lunchtime, where they'd only eaten alone once or twice. Bear was almost always there, usually with Ranger and Ace, and Montana had seen the way the four of them interacted.

She'd felt like an outsider, though literally no one treated her that way. Quite the opposite, in fact. She hardly saw Arizona at all, and while Sammy had spoken to her at the luncheon after they'd found the love letters, Montana hadn't seen her again.

Out of everyone, she saw Ranger and his wife, Oakley,

the most. She owned and worked at Mack's Motor Sports, and she worked a lot of afternoons and evenings. Since she lived in the homestead, she was often there when Bishop and Montana showed up for lunch.

"Bishop?"

"Yeah," Bishop said, looking up and tucking his phone in his back pocket. "Things are okay." He took his water bottle from her. "Thanks. It's just Agatha. The foal isn't dropping, and the vet thinks he might have to do a C-section on her."

"That's not good."

"He's trying to get it to turn." Bishop reached for her hand. "I'm distracted today. Can we just go to the stable?"

"We're done here anyway," she said. "You left me to haul out all the trash while you texted about your horse." She smiled up at him, her eyes focusing on his mouth. She'd thought about kissing him, which did surprise her slightly.

"Sorry," he said, his voice quiet and his eyes on her mouth too.

They'd been out a couple more times, and Montana needed to have a conversation with her daughter about Bishop. She couldn't get herself to think of him as her boyfriend, though she probably should.

"We can go to the stable," Montana said, but neither of them moved.

"There's something I want to do first." Bishop took her easily into his arms, and she put her hands flat against his chest. "Do you know what it is?"

"I think I have an idea," she said, one hand moving up

to his collar. She stalled there, her eyes drifting closed as she breathed in the scent of him. Cotton, and dryer sheets, and cologne. Wood, and work, and wonder.

She curled her fingers around the back of his neck and put pressure there so he'd lower his head. She kept her head tilted back, and as the moment lengthened and Bishop still did not kiss her, Montana's need for him to do so rose exponentially.

Finally, his lips touched hers, and Montana felt like lightning crackled through her veins. His kiss lasted only a second, and then his touch was gone.

"That was terrible," she whispered, opening her eyes to look at Bishop. He gazed down at her, so much adoration in those golden brown eyes. He ran his fingers up the side of her face and tucked her hair behind her ear.

"I've never been told I'm a terrible kisser."

"That wasn't a kiss, Bishop."

"No?"

She shook her head, almost laughing. If her heart wasn't sprinting so fast, she might be able to do more than breathe in and out.

"No." She tipped up and pressed her mouth to his. His hands tightened along her waist, and Montana and Bishop breathed in together, the kiss growing more passionate as it continued.

Now that's a kiss, she thought, hoping it would last a lot longer.

Chapter Thirteen

❧

Bishop had been dreaming of kissing Montana since almost the day he'd met her. He'd not waited this long to kiss a woman he liked before, but there was something different about Montana Martin.

Something very different in a very good way.

They'd been out three or four times, and they worked together every day, of course. They'd had great conversations, and times when she'd say, "I don't want to talk about this right now."

He wouldn't push her, and he got to say the same thing if she asked him something he didn't want to talk about. The only topic he'd passed on was his father. She'd told him little about her first marriage, her daughter, and he still didn't know if she wanted more children or not.

He suspected she didn't, and that was something Bishop was going to have to face sooner or later.

Right now, he didn't care, because right now, he was

kissing Montana.

Kissing Montana erased all his nerves and worries, and everything in the world felt absolutely right.

She finally pulled away, and Bishop opened his eyes, the sunlight suddenly too bright. He looked at her, and she met his eye for only a half-moment before she ducked her head, a giggle coming from her head.

Bishop let the smile coursing through him manifest itself on his face as he held her. "I guess you're right," he said. "That was a better kiss than the first one."

"Yeah, what was that?" she asked.

"An experiment," he said.

She stepped away from him and searched his face. "What?"

"I wanted to see if you'd make my blood sizzle."

She opened her mouth, but words didn't come out. Only a scoff.

"Don't be all like that," he said, grinning at her. "You do, by the way. Everything about you makes me come alive in a way I don't understand."

Bishop wanted to shove a boot down his throat. He'd told Cactus about the children question when he and Montana had gone to hike to the falls, and Cactus had simply looked at him.

He'd given Bishop a gift certificate to The Baker's Dozen in town, where Bishop could buy any item for the kitchen he wanted. He'd appreciated the gesture, because come Sunday in a week or two, the whole family would gather to the homestead and celebrate his birthday, but no one would bring a gift.

They simply didn't do a lot of gifts in the Glover family. A name-draw exchange at Christmas, and that was it.

But since then, Cactus had been closed off, more like the man he'd been before Thanksgiving last year. He glared more. He spoke less. Bishop hadn't been able to get anything out of him regarding the change, and even Ace couldn't get Cactus to leave the ranch anymore.

"Let's go to the stables," he said, turning away from Montana, who hadn't said anything after his confession. They got in his truck, and Bishop realized he had one more thing he needed to say to her.

"Listen," he said, wondering if a person could survive without their vocal cords. "I understand that you're protective of Aurora. I do." He cut a glance in her direction, not truly looking at her. "But I'm ready. I'm ready to meet her. Whenever you're ready to share her with me."

He cleared his throat while he waited for Montana to say something. "And it's my birthday in a couple of weeks, and I'd love for the two of you—and your aunt and uncle if they want to come—to come eat with us at the homestead."

"What day?" she asked, her voice raw and hardly her own.

"Sunday," he said. "First Sunday in May."

She nodded, her lips pressed together. Bishop had said something to upset her. He knew; he'd seen her shut down like this before. This time, though, he didn't press her. He'd learned over the past few weeks of working with her that sometimes Montana just needed a few minutes to think before she continued the conversation.

This time, though, they rode to the stables in silence, and Bishop let his worry over Agatha's delivery take over his nerves that he'd said too much and revealed too much to Montana.

"TALK TO ME, BABY," HE SAID A WEEK OR SO LATER. HE and Montana had been texting for a solid fifteen minutes, and Bishop needed to get out to the equipment shed where Bear and Ace were waiting for him.

Montana sighed, and Bishop simply waited for her. "I just don't know what to do with her," she finally said.

"So you got home," Bishop said. "And you were a little late, because—" He cut off and cleared his throat. He may have kept her a little longer than he normally did, because he couldn't stop kissing her. She seemed to enjoy kissing him too, and Bishop grinned as he walked down the path.

The sun was bright and hot today, and Bishop only had a week until he turned thirty-four. Montana had not confirmed if she would be there. Alone, with her daughter, or with her aunt and uncle. Nothing. Bishop didn't want to press her again.

After their kiss last week, when he'd told her he was ready to meet her daughter, she'd gone quiet for a little while. Later, she'd told him she needed to talk to Aurora first, and she was still trying to figure out how to do that.

Bishop knew she'd dated since her divorce, but he had no idea how to have a conversation with a teenager about dating, so he hadn't asked again.

"I was late, cowboy, because you wouldn't stop kissing me." her voice dropped to a whisper, and she giggled quietly.

"You liked it," Bishop said, laughing with her.

"I did like it," she said. The moment sobered, and Bishop slowed his step. "I really like you, Bishop."

"I like you too, Montana." And he did. Oh, he did.

"Anyway, I got home, and I knew she was here, because her backpack was right inside the door. Her shoes. Everything. You never have to guess where she's been. She leaves a trail of stuff." Montana's frustration coated every syllable. "Anyway, in the kitchen, I saw an extra can of soda on the counter, and I was like, who else is here?"

"Mm hm." Bishop got going again. She'd said all of this in the text. "You went and checked by the front door, and there was another backpack."

"Yes," Montana said. "So I called for her, and she didn't answer. I called her phone, and she didn't answer. I was going upstairs to her room, seriously praying out loud."

"She's smart," Bishop said. "She wouldn't take a boy up to her room."

"Think of yourself at fourteen," she said. "Girls are just as hormonal as boys."

"Okay," Bishop said. "I'm just repeating what you've told me. You said she's smart."

"She is."

"Okay, then. Where were they?"

"Thankfully, they weren't in her bedroom, but I looked out the window and saw her and Oliver in the hammock together."

"Oh, the hammock," Bishop said. "That's not bad."

"Have you ever laid in a hammock with another person?" Montana demanded. "She was practically on top of him. I swear my heartbeat flew up my throat."

"What were they doing?"

"Reading."

"Reading?" Bishop burst out laughing.

"Bishop, this is serious."

"I know," he said through his chuckles. "I know it is. So you went down there, hopping mad, and...."

"She—I don't want to say now."

"Come on," he said. "I didn't mean to laugh. I was just expecting you to say they were making out. Reading felt so...tame." He remembered what he and Montana were doing right before she left, and reading a book was nowhere near Bishop's mind.

"She reacted the same way you did," Montana said miserably. "She said they weren't doing anything wrong. He was reading the book they have to do an analysis on for English, and she was taking notes so they could get the assignment done."

"You were just surprised."

"I forgot he was coming home with her," Montana admitted. "You distract me, Bishop Glover."

He started to laugh again but cut it off quickly. "In a good way, right?"

"Depends on what I need to remember and how late I am."

"I won't do it again," he teased.

"Mm hm," she said dryly. "That girl needs a job." She sighed. "I just don't know what to do for her. She'll be fifteen in a few weeks, and who's going to hire a fifteen-year-old?"

"Lots of people," Bishop said.

"Really?'

"If she's willing to work," Bishop said. "There are tons of farms and ranches who are always looking for hands." He entered the equipment shed, and Bear turned toward him with a growl on his face. He needed to wrap up this conversation quickly. "I'll ask Bear and Ranger, okay? They always know stuff like that."

"Would you?"

"Of course," he said. "And you don't need to come back up tonight. There's nothing to do at the Ranch House, and the floors are done at the cabins."

"You sure? I can just work on the cabinets."

"It's up to you," Bishop said. "I'm good either way."

Montana fell silent for a few moments, and Bishop opened his mouth to say he had to run when she said, "Would you come to a family dinner party for Aurora's birthday?"

A strange, strangled noise came out of Bishop's mouth. He quickly coughed and turned his back on Grizzly Bear. "Of course," he said. "Absolutely. One hundred percent yes."

Montana laughed and said, "Okay, Bishop. I got it."

He pressed his eyes closed and begged the Lord to know what to say. He opened his mouth, still hoping God would just put the right words there. "Does this mean you'll come to my family dinner birthday party thing next week?"

"Yes," Montana said. "We're all going to be there…just as soon as I figure out how to tell my daughter—who I just told she needed to be smart with boys and not be alone with them—that I've been kissing you."

"She knows we've been out, right?"

"Sort of?" Montana hedged, and Bishop didn't like that.

Behind him, Bear called his name. "I have to go," he said. "I'm sorry, but Bear's in a mood about the tractor, and apparently, I'm the only one who can fit underneath it."

"No problem," she said. "I'll call you later."

"Okay." He hung up and turned toward Bear. He gave him a glare that said, *I know what's going on. I needed five minutes.*

Bear held up one hand as an apology, and Bishop once again found himself with a burning curiosity about his brother's letter. His letter from his father had left Bishop feeling like he'd been loved and appreciated, and that he still had a lot to live up to. He'd wanted to share his letter with Bear, as he was in it, but Bear said he wasn't ready yet.

Ace grunted from underneath the tractor, and Bishop bent down. "Status."

"I can't reach the blasted thing." Ace slid out, his face filled with irritation. "I can't get underneath far enough, and I can't extend my arm far enough." He took Bishop's hand and let him pull him to his feet. He handed the wrench to Bishop. "Good luck. That thing is impossible."

"I don't know why they make these things so hard to work on," Bear said.

"You don't have to watch," Ace said, glaring at him. "Don't you have something else to do?" He and Bear entered a battle of wills, and Bishop stepped between them.

"You two need to go to your separate corners." He looked from Bear to Ace. "What's going on?"

"He yelled at me about the catering for Aunt Lois's party."

Bishop looked at Bear. "You did? Why? You put Ace in charge of the food."

"He hired his girlfriend, and she has the lowest reviews in town."

"She's brand-new," Ace shot back. "There's one review, and it's from her next-door neighbor who ordered the lemon bars when he thought he'd ordered the lemon chiffon cake. She showed me the order form and everything." Ace's chest heaved, and Bishop actually put out one hand as if Ace would fly at Bear and start swinging. "And she's not my girlfriend."

"Ace," Bishop said. "Is it Holly Ann?"

Ace finally tore his gaze from Bear. "Yeah."

Bishop leaned closer. "She's not your girlfriend? I thought you guys have been out a few times now."

"Yeah, well, so did I," Ace mumbled. He pushed his cowboy hat forward and fell back a couple of steps. "The food is going to be great," he said louder.

"I'm sure it will," Bishop said, looking at Bear. He lifted his eyebrows, and Bear dropped his glare.

"I'm sorry, Ace. I'm stressed about a lot of things." He held up his hand as Bishop opened his mouth. "I know that doesn't give me the right to say mean stuff. I just want everything to be perfect for Mother's party."

"It will be," Bishop said. "The barn is beautiful, and I talked to Ari at the restoration shop, and she said the letters cleaned up great, and they're already onto preservation. It's going to be ready on time."

Bear nodded, and Bishop understood the slightly different nod where he looked toward the door. Bishop lowered the hand he still held toward Ace and he took several steps away, Bear going with him. "What's going on?" he asked. "I know most of the stuff around the ranch, and we're not that stressed right now."

"Besides this tractor."

"We always have maintenance in the spring," Bishop said.

"And the Ranch House."

"Which you don't live in." Bishop could do this all day. Perhaps Bear did carry a heavier load than some of the others, but Bishop still didn't know of anything so crazy-stressful that would drive Bear back to being a grizzly.

Bear rolled his neck. "I haven't been sleeping well."

"I'm sorry," Bishop said.

"Let's go to the cemetery tonight," Bear said, and Bishop immediately nodded. "Bring your letter if you want to share it with me," his brother added. "I'll bring mine."

"Okay."

Bear nodded and called, "I'm sorry, Ace," before turning to leave the equipment shed.

"Yeah," Ace called, and Bishop watched Bear leave before he returned to Ace.

"Holly Ann?"

"Her neighbor is eighty-nine years old and in the early stages of dementia," Ace said, a dark look still in his eyes.

Bishop blinked and burst out laughing. "I don't care about the review," Bishop said. "I—she doesn't think you're dating?"

"She said she needed to focus on her catering business," Ace said, staring over Bishop's shoulder. "I suggested lots of different options before you start doing that too. In the end, she flat-out said she liked me, but she needed to focus on her business."

"Ouch," Bishop said. "I'm sorry, Ace."

"Yeah, well, me too," he said, softening. "Now, can you please fix this so Bear will calm down?"

"I'll try." Bishop gripped the wrench and slid under the tractor. He was able to get further underneath it than Ace had been, and he searched for the bolt that would open the compartment where the filter went.

"Have you noticed Cactus going to church?" Ace asked.

"Yes," Bishop called out to him. He fitted the wrench around the bolt and strained against it. "What's with that?"

"I have a theory."

"Let's hear it."

"He only goes when the new pastor preaches. He's always late, and he always leaves early."

"Wow, you've really been watching him." The bolt suddenly moved, and Bishop grunted. "Got it."

"Of course you did," Ace said, and while he didn't sound happy about it, he really was.

The panel came with the bolt, and the next thing

Bishop knew, it fell toward his face. He yelped and tried to put his hand between his nose and the panel, but he couldn't.

Pain exploded through his face, and he immediately started pulling himself out from underneath the tractor. Ace's voice crowded in his ears, but Bishop couldn't distinguish the words through the screaming nerves of his nose.

Ace shoved something into his hands, and Bishop held the rag to his face. Moment by moment, the pain lessened, and he realized his nose was gushing blood. He groaned, and Ace said, "I'll finish it. Go wash up."

Bishop got to his feet and tipped his head back to get the blood to stop. When it finally did, he went over to the sink against the wall and washed up. By the time he was done, Ace had the tractor running.

Bishop returned to the machine, smiling. "Good job."

"I just need you to get the panel back on."

"Okay," Bishop said.

Ace stared at him. "You're going to have a black eye."

Bishop reached up and touched his face. "It's not broken at least."

Ace grinned at him. "You're going to have a shiner for your birthday."

Horror filled Bishop. "No," he said, his voice made mostly of air. "Montana is bringing her daughter and aunt and uncle to my birthday dinner."

Ace sobered and shook his head. "Bad luck, Bish."

Bishop took the wrench from him. "Let's just get this done so I can go ask my mother how to make this go away fast."

Chapter Fourteen

Montana took the last tray of cookies out of the oven and pressed the cancel button to turn everything off. She couldn't help noticing the time, and that Aurora would be home any minute.

With Oliver Osburn.

After Montana had found them reading in the hammock a few days ago, she'd been talking to Aurora every evening about boys and boyfriends and hormones and kissing. She'd spoken to Ollie for a few minutes before he'd had to leave, and Aurora had spent the next thirty minutes arguing with Montana about what they'd been doing in the hammock and how it was fine.

Montana had finally sat her down and told her that boys did not think the same way as girls. Period. The end.

Aurora still liked the boy, and honestly, Montana could see why. He was tall, and he wore a black cowboy hat like a pro. He looked at Aurora with stars in his eyes, and he'd been able to have a real, mature conversation with Montana before his mother had come to get him.

Montana stiffened as voices filled the air and then the front door closed. She untied the strings on her apron and pulled it over her head just as Aurora came into the kitchen. She looked like Montana had just thrown a bucket of ice water in her face, and Montana couldn't blame her.

"I was able to leave the ranch at lunchtime," she said, smiling as Ollie crowded in behind Aurora. He put his hand on her waist, and Montana saw it. Aurora knew she saw it, and she edged away from Ollie.

Another boy appeared, and surprise moved through Montana. She looked at Aurora, her eyebrows high.

"Mom, you remember Ollie," Aurora said. "This is Charlie. He has Jensen for English too, and he lives out by Oliver."

"Nice to meet you," Montana said, nodding to the other boy. He didn't wear a cowboy hat, but he smiled at her.

"Nice to meet you, ma'am. Thanks for lettin' us come to your house. My mama just had twins, and it's kind of a circus at my house."

"Of course," Montana said, deciding not to correct him on the house thing.

"Ma'am," Oliver said, stepping forward. "My uncle was at my house the other day, and—"

"Ollie," Aurora said, jumping in front of him. She said something else, but Montana couldn't hear what it was. Oliver wore surprise in his eyes, but he ducked his head, and his cowboy hat hid his face at that point.

"She's gonna find out," Ollie said, looking past Aurora to Montana.

Montana's heart started flopping around, because her daughter was keeping secrets from her. They'd talked a lot about that too, and Montana had said they couldn't have secrets.

Too bad she hadn't told Aurora about Bishop yet. She was running out of time, too, because his birthday party was in four days.

"You guys go out back," Aurora said loudly. "I'll bring out the cookies."

Charlie grinned at Montana and nudged an unhappy Oliver. They did what Aurora wanted, and Montana waited until the back door clicked closed before she looked at her daughter.

"Chocolate chip cookies, Mom?" Aurora turned and got a plate out of the cupboard. "You're making it seem like—" She cut off, but Montana heard the rest of the sentence.

"Like I'm a good mom?"

"No," Aurora said, keeping her eyes down. "That's not what I was going to say."

Montana knew it was, but she didn't want to argue. She sighed. "We really did get done early at the ranch today. The painters are behind schedule, and there's nothing else to do until we get the new lumber for the Ranch House."

"Great," Aurora said. "We have that English report to finish."

"What was Oliver going to tell me?" she asked.

Aurora stilled, but she raised her blue-gray eyes to look at Montana. "I don't want to tell you."

"I have something to tell you too." Montana swallowed. "You go first."

"I have two things." Aurora looked like she might throw up. She was always a little pale, because she had Montana's nearly white-blonde hair. Her eyes were darker than Montana's, and she had a better ability to tan due to her father. She got dozens of freckles when she spent too much time outside, and she had Johnny's long, straight nose.

"Start with the easiest one," Montana said.

"I know I said—" Aurora swallowed and looked toward the back door. "I have kissed Oliver."

Montana pulled in a breath, but she refused to fly off the handle again. If she wanted her daughter to tell her things like this—and she did—she had to be approachable. Montana had never been particularly approachable, but she was willing to work on this.

"Okay," she said. "When?"

"I don't know. After a party a while ago."

"So you were alone with him."

"For a few minutes," she said. "It wasn't a big deal, Mom."

"Sweetheart." Montana stepped around the counter to Aurora and drew her into a hug. "It is a big deal." She stroked her daughter's hair. "Did you like it?"

"Yes," Aurora whispered. They both burst into giggles, and Montana's pulse kept sprinting while she tried to figure out what to say.

"Have you kissed him again?"

"Yeah," she said. "It's not gross, Mom. We're not making out or anything."

Montana thought about the last kiss she'd shared with Bishop, mere hours ago. He'd pressed her into the strong, beautiful barn door in True Blue and kissed her until she couldn't breathe. She'd had no idea how much time had passed, and she'd been riding a buzz all the way to the town's border before she'd been able to focus.

"But you have to be alone to kiss him, right? You're not kissing in front of other people?"

"Yeah, but it's like when you come get me, he walks me to the door and kisses me real quick."

"He's a very cute kid," Montana said, taking a deep breath. She thought of what Bishop had said when she'd called him to talk about her daughter. "You're smart, and I trust you." She stepped back and held Aurora by the shoulders. "I still want you to try to get a job this summer. I have to work, and I can't be worried about you all the time."

"I don't know how to do that."

"I do," Montana said. "I've asked my boss at the ranch if he knows of any other ranches that are hiring teens, and he said they're always looking for people to come help work with the horses at Bowman's Breeds."

Aurora looked doubtful, but she didn't immediately argue, so Montana was going to count that as a win.

"Okay, your turn," Aurora said.

Montana suddenly knew the desire to look anywhere but at her daughter. "Uh, okay." She raised her head. She wasn't embarrassed of her relationship with Bishop. "You—

I'm dating Bishop Glover. He's my boyfriend. I, uh, he, well, he walks me to my truck when I leave the ranch and kisses me good-bye, like how Ollie walks you to the door when you're leaving the party."

Aurora's eyes grew wider with each word Montana spoke, until she gaped at Montana. "Mom."

"What? I've dated before."

"Not here." Aurora shook her head, sending her long hair swinging. "Not for a while. Not while you're lecturing me about being alone with boys."

"Okay," Montana said, working hard not to roll her eyes. She took as much sarcasm out of her voice as she could as she added, "I'm not fourteen, with my first *very cute cowboy* boyfriend."

Aurora smiled, the gesture suddenly popping onto her face. A squeal followed, and she launched herself into Montana's arms. "That's so great, Mom."

"Really?"

"Yes, really." Aurora stepped back, her eyes glinting with happiness. "I've always said you should date."

Montana nodded, because Aurora had said that. "Nothing is going to change with us," she said. "Okay? He's not more important than you."

"I know that, Mom."

"He wants to meet you," Montana said. "I think I'm ready for him to meet you." She watched Aurora for her reaction, and she clapped her hands together. Good sign.

Then she gasped and covered her mouth with her hands.

"What?" Montana asked.

"If he wants to meet me, you must've been dating him for a while."

Montana shrugged, knowing she wouldn't get anything by Aurora. "I mean, sort of. A while now. Maybe a month or so. Five weeks."

"Mom, you've only been up at that ranch for six weeks."

"Yes, well, he's very handsome."

Aurora pealed out a string of laughter that made Montana's joy double and then triple. She let her carry on for a few seconds, and then she said, "I'm glad you're so happy about it. We're going up to the ranch for lunch on Sunday. It's his birthday tomorrow, and I'm going out with him. You'll meet him then."

Aurora quieted. "Not tomorrow, Mom. I'm going to the roller rink, remember?"

"Right," she said. "I meant Sunday."

"Oh, Sunday, okay," she said. "I'm excited. Do you have any pictures of him?"

"Uh, maybe." Neither Montana nor Bishop took many pictures, of one another or themselves. She swiped on her phone, her memory firing. "He did send me one of him while he was picking out curtains to see what I thought." She navigated to the photo, a smile taking over her soul as she looked at him.

He had the curtain draped around his shoulders like a fancy fur stole, and he wore a look of playful worry on his face. She turned the phone toward Aurora, who took it and studied the picture of Bishop with sparkling eyes.

"Mom," she said, gasping. "He's gorgeous." She handed the phone back to Montana. "Okay, I have to get out there. Those two barely know how to read." She grinned and picked up the plate of cookies. Before Montana knew what was going on, Aurora had gone out the back door while Montana was still looking at the picture of Bishop.

"Wait," she said, but her daughter was gone. "What was the other thing?" she asked anyway, having the very real feeling that her daughter had just tricked her by getting her talking about Bishop.

"Clever girl," she muttered, turning back to the sink. It was full of dishes and utensils she'd used to make the cookies. No wonder she hated baking, and she braced herself against the counter.

"Dear Lord," she prayed. "Help me to navigate things with Aurora. Please, please help her to be safe. Help her to be smart." Montana paused, because she didn't know what else to say. Her desperation tasted bitter in the back of her throat, and surely the Lord could feel that and know what Montana needed for her daughter.

Because Oliver Osburn was very cute, and she didn't believe for a moment that he couldn't read. He was smart too. Otherwise, Aurora wouldn't be attracted to him.

Montana made a deal with herself—she had to do the dishes before she could migrate over to the window and spy on her daughter with the two teenage boys in the back yard.

"Okay," Montana said, pulling up to the homestead. At least half a dozen extra trucks sat in the parking area out front, and her nerves started to sizzle.

"Wow, Montana," Aunt Jackie said. "Look at this house."

"It's a mansion," Uncle Bob said. "I'd heard the Glovers had rebuilt their homestead. I just didn't realize how big it was."

"Three of them live here," Montana said, feeling the need to defend them all. She wasn't even sure why. Aunt Jackie and Uncle Bob weren't judgmental people, and neither of them really had to deal with the Glovers all that much.

If Montana were being honest with herself, she'd started thinking about living out here at this ranch too. Then her aunt and uncle would have more of a reason to see the Glovers more often.

She pushed those thoughts away. It was barely May, and Aurora had been right when she'd said Montana and Bishop had started dating almost the moment she'd been hired here, and not very much time had passed since then.

Not even two months yet.

"Mom," Aurora said from the back seat. "You didn't say he was rich."

"Well, they are," Montana said. "They're all rich, okay?" She turned and glared at her aunt, and then Uncle Bob and Aurora in the back seat. "Does it really matter?"

"Not at all," Uncle Bob said easily. "The Glovers are good people."

"Bear bought all that food for everyone last year," Aunt

Jackie said. "And Stone Glover used to sponsor the entire Shop for Santa event every year."

"That's Bishop's father," Montana said. "Can we all agree just one more time that we're going to be on our best behavior?"

"Yes," all three of them chorused together, and Montana couldn't tell if Aurora was being snarky or not.

"There will be a lot of people here," Montana said, still looking at the house. "We're nice people too. It will be fine." Properly pumped up, she unbuckled her seatbelt and got out of the truck. The rest of her family joined her, and she took the card and small gift she'd gotten for Bishop from Aunt Jackie.

"Don't worry, darling," her aunt said, smiling kindly at Montana. "I've taken Uncle Bob to parties before, and he's very charming."

Montana laughed and that got her nerves to settle down. She climbed the steps and found a note on the door that said *just come in. We might not hear the door.*

So she turned the knob and stepped into the house. "Kitchen this way," she said unnecessarily. The noise coming from the kitchen would've told a deaf person where the party was. By the round of laughter filling the rafters, Montana estimated them to be the last to arrive, but when she led the way into the kitchen, she found only a few people.

Bishop stood in the kitchen, a knife in his hand as he laughed. He was gorgeous and glorious, that was for sure. Montana smiled just looking at him, her people pressing in behind her.

"Bish," Ranger said, smiling at Montana. He stepped away from his brothers and came toward her. "Hey, Montana. I'm so glad you could make it." He gave her a quick hug, which sent surprise through her, and looked at her family. She stepped next to him, turning her back on the party.

"This is my aunt and uncle, Jackie and Bob Kent."

"I know Ranger," Uncle Bob said, adding a hearty laugh and a handshake. Montana relaxed, because Uncle Bob did know a lot of people. Her aunt and uncle had lived in Three Rivers for a long time, and so had the Glovers.

A hand slid along her back, and Montana tipped her head back to look at her boyfriend. "Hey," she said, smiling.

He looked down at her, anxiety in those delightful eyes. "Hey."

She turned back to her family. "Everyone, this is Bishop Glover, my boyfriend. Bishop." She took a breath, glad her voice had remained steady and strong. "My aunt and uncle, Jackie and Bob Kent." She hadn't even been able to introduce her daughter to Ranger, and she stalled as she looked at her beautiful girl.

"And my daughter, Aurora." She extended her hand toward Aurora, who wore a little mascara and lip gloss today and practically glowed as she stepped over to Montana.

"Aurora," Bishop said, the name perfect rolling off his tongue. "So nice to meet you."

"You too," she said, shaking his hand. "You really are as gorgeous as my mom said you would be."

"Aurora," Montana said. She glanced at Bishop, "I didn't say that. She did."

"Hey, I'll take it," Bishop said with a laugh. "Now, don't try to remember all the names." He gestured everyone further into the kitchen, solidly securing his hand in Montana's. She liked how he claimed her in front of everyone, and she was doubly grateful her family was there to see it.

"There are a lot of us, and my father and my uncle had a lot of the same characteristics. You met Ranger, my oldest cousin. This here is the youngest male cousin, Ace."

"She's got a gift for you, Bish," Ace said, nodding to Montana's hand.

"Oh, right," she said, thrusting the gift toward Bishop. "Don't be impressed. It's nothing special."

He took the gift, a sense of wonder entering his eyes. "I should've told you," he said. "We don't really do gifts."

"Oh." Montana's face heated, as if this kitchen wasn't already hot enough with all these bodies in it and something bubbling away on the stove. "I'm sorry. I didn't know."

"It's fine." He smiled down at her. "Can I open it later, though? Away from all of...this?"

"Bishop," a woman called from the kitchen. "Your timer is going off."

"Duty calls," he said with a smile. He bent down and kissed her quickly before bustling off to take care of the timer.

Aunt Jackie and Uncle Bob had joined Ranger, Oakley,

and Ace in conversation, and while Montana knew almost everyone here, she didn't know where to go.

"Montana," someone said, and she turned toward Sammy.

She smiled and said, "Come let me see your pretty daughter."

Relief rushed through Montana, and she joined Sammy and her son, Lincoln, on one of the couches, Aurora right at her side. As she chatted with Sammy, then surprisingly, Arizona, Montana had a glimpse of what her future could look like.

Bishop in the kitchen while she tried to find a place for her and her daughter to belong.

At Aunt Jackie's, they already belonged, and Montana worked to keep her smile hitched in place.

Chapter Fifteen

Bishop kept one eye on Montana as he finished up with the hot chicken dip. He'd tried to get out of cooking for his own blasted birthday luncheon, but Etta wouldn't have it.

He'd been thinking about who he could set her up with for days, as Ida had bowed out of cooking because she'd rather spend time with Brady. She'd cooked for Christmas while he was there, and she hadn't liked it.

Bishop knew exactly how she felt, and he quickly got out three bags of chips and took off his apron. "I'm done," he said. "You're leading the show."

"Bishop," Etta said, clearly frustrated.

"I'm not announcing my own birthday, Etta," he growled. "Okay?"

She frowned, but she nodded. "Okay. Go on. I know this is about Montana and not lunch."

"This is the first time I've met her daughter," Bishop

said. "I said two words to her, with twenty other people yelling nearby." He watched them laugh with Sammy and when Arizona sat beside Aurora, Bishop sucked in a breath.

"Go," Etta said. "I have a bad feeling about that."

"Yep." Bishop strode through the kitchen, dodging cousins and brothers, a dog, and Oakley's yowling cat before he reached Aurora and Montana. "Hey." He sat beside her and took her hand, then looked at Aurora. "Your mother says you're interested in writing."

"Yes." Aurora smiled at him, and it was no wonder she had boys interested in her. She was a beautiful girl, with plenty of that same blonde hair her mother had. "I've been working on a book for a couple of years." She reached up and tucked her hair. "Do you write?"

"Heavens, no," Bishop said. "But my father did. He was always scrawling something in some notebook." He grinned at her. "I picked up woodworking from my dad. If you want to talk to someone with the writing gene, you want Mister there." He nodded to his brother on the end of the other couch, who was currently talking to Preacher.

Aurora followed his gaze. "Which one? The one in the brown hat or the slightly browner hat?" She looked at Bishop and then her mother, giggling all the while.

"Oh, boy," Bishop said. "I see what we've got here."

"What?" Montana asked, and her hand tightened in his.

"A real smarty pants," he said, grinning at both of them. "The one in the brown*er* hat." Before he could call to Mister, Etta whistled, which only set people off more. The complaining about the piercing, shrill sound rose like a tidal wave, and Bishop's heartbeat skipped a couple of beats.

"Well, settle down, you lot," Etta said. "Then I wouldn't have to do that."

Bishop was glad he wasn't standing in the kitchen, because there were a lot of sharp looks going in that direction.

"Happy birthday to Bishop," Etta said with a smile. "Stand up now, Bish."

"I'm fine," he said, though he did stand up. "I didn't make it around to everyone, though. Uh, most of you know Montana Martin. She works with me on all the construction around the ranch." He'd released her hand, and she hadn't stood up with him.

His throat felt as if he'd glued sand to it. "We're dating, and she's brought her daughter, Aurora and her aunt and uncle, Jackie and Bob Kent, to celebrate with us." He smiled at her aunt and uncle across the room. "So be nice to them, okay? I'm trying to make a good impression."

"Shouldn't have invited them to a full family party, then," someone said, almost like they were trying not to be heard, but definitely loud enough to be heard.

"Oh, stop it, Cactus," Etta said as Bishop sat down. He wasn't sure where Cactus was standing as he couldn't see him right now. Part of him worried that he'd done something to upset his brother, and a strong prompting told him to get out to Cactus's that day.

"Welcome, everyone," Etta said brightly. "Since it's Bishop's birthday—or it was on Friday—and he loves potatoes and good meat, we smoked brisket and made mashed potatoes and gravy, scalloped potatoes with extra cream, and fried potatoes with a bit of spice. There's potato salad and potato chips, and Ida even brought potato rolls from Heidi's." She beamed at the spread of food on the counter.

Bishop couldn't help grinning, and he retook Montana's hand in his. He did love potatoes, and there was no reason not to eat them for every meal, though he did like that bacon peanut butter toast Montana had made for him once.

She'd told him once that she loved toast, and she dressed it up in different ways as often as she could. Something had happened at the cabin where they'd been working, and the conversation had been interrupted.

"I didn't know you were such a potato freak," Montana whispered, and Bishop shrugged as cowboy hats got removed, and Bear asked Judge to say the prayer.

He pressed his hat to his chest, his hand still secured in Montana's, and looked at her until she bowed her head. Her silky hair fell between them, and all Bishop could think about was opening that tiny box she'd brought him and kissing her until she whispered that she better go find her daughter and get on home.

Then he'd kiss her again, just so she'd know that he didn't like it when she left him here at Shiloh Ranch by himself.

He wasn't sure where his feelings had come from, or how they'd gotten so strong so fast. He knew Montana was strong and sexy, kind and hardworking. She loved her daughter, and she loved wood, and she wanted to make her aunt and uncle happy.

"Amen," everyone chorused, and Bishop tacked his on at the end, because he hadn't been listening at all.

"Do we swarm or wait?" Montana asked.

"I'm going to swarm," Aurora said, jumping to her feet. She went off on her own, and Montana looked after her.

"She's great," Bishop said. "She talks to people like she's an adult."

"She's quite mature, yes," Montana said, standing. Bishop went with her, and right behind the couch, he came face-to-face with Cactus. He knew the look, and he shook his head.

"I have to," Cactus said.

"I'm coming by later then," Bishop said.

Cactus reached up and pushed his hat forward and down. "You do what you have to do."

"Will you let me in?" Bishop hadn't had to ask to enter Cactus's house for months now, and he felt like the whole world was spinning the wrong direction.

Pain radiated from Cactus, and Bishop leaned toward Montana. "I need five minutes. You go on ahead and just save me a spot, okay?"

She looked from Cactus to him, nodded, and followed her daughter, though Aurora had already been surrounded by Glovers.

Cactus stepped out the nearest door, and Bishop followed him. He didn't know what to say, and sometimes letting Cactus start the conversation was better.

But Cactus said nothing. They went away from the table under the shade and around the front of the house.

"You'll bring me some cake later?" Cactus finally asked.

"Two pieces." Bishop leaned against the railing. He let out a long sigh. "I'm worried I did something to upset you."

"It's not you," Cactus said.

"Is it me dating Montana?"

"No, she's great."

"You just don't want to be around it, because it makes you sad?"

"No." Cactus bit the word out and then exhaled heavily. "It's none of that. It's just...I met a woman, and I really liked her."

"Cactus, that's great," Bishop said.

"No, it's not great," he said. "I managed to get her number, though she didn't give it to me. She said she's not ready to start dating. Wants to get settled in first."

Bishop thought of Ace, who was experiencing something similar. "Is this why you won't go to town anymore?"

"No," Cactus said. "I won't go to town with specifically Ace, because he keeps throwing himself at that Holly Ann, and I think it's pathetic."

"Ouch, Cactus. Tell me how you really feel." Bishop grinned at him, and Cactus softened slightly. Enough to come stand at the railing and lean against it too.

"I don't want to do that," he said softly. "I see how he acts around her, and what he does, and I don't want to do that."

"You can come to town with me."

"You never go to town."

"No, what I think you mean is I don't track who the pastor is each week, and I go to church even if it isn't Willa

Knowlton." He tensed, waiting for Cactus to whip him with his tongue, stomp off, and yell back to him not to come out to his cabin later.

It was a great testament to Cactus that he didn't do any of the above. He did turn to stare at Bishop. "Dear Lord, is it that obvious?"

"It is to those of us watching you," he said. "Ace actually told me. He's worried about you too."

"I texted him an apology after I sort of snapped at him last time he wanted me to go to town with him."

"Mm." Bishop became keenly aware of how long he'd been gone from his own luncheon. "I'll bring you a whole plate of food later, if you want."

"Thanks," Cactus said. "I don't know why I can't today, only that my skin was crawling in there."

"Think about that," Bishop said. "Because I thought that was getting better too."

"I'm going to talk to Judge," Cactus said.

"Good idea," Bishop said, though he thought Cactus should go to a licensed therapist once a week, not his brother who'd started his psychology degree and never finished. "Love you, brother. Take care of yourself, okay? I'll bring cake to make up the rest."

He started to turn away from Cactus, but his brother grabbed him and held him in a tight hug. "You're a good man, Bishop. Happy birthday." He stepped back as quickly as he'd grabbed him, and Bishop could only stare at his brother's back as he strode away.

"Please help him iron everything flat," he begged the

Lord. "Please. He's suffered enough. Can't you let Willa Knowlton know that? She could help him so much."

"ARE YOU SURE WE CAN JUST LEAVE?" MONTANA whispered, looking around at everyone still hanging around the homestead.

"Yeah," Bishop said in an equally low voice. "Aurora's got five grown men hanging on her every word. Your aunt and uncle are here. Come on." He stood and nodded at Jackie, retrieved the small box and card from the top of the fridge, and led Montana outside.

He couldn't even breathe it was so hot. "Okay, so this is a bad idea," he said. "Let's go to the barn. It's air conditioned."

"Okay." Montana followed him to his truck, because he wasn't about to walk in this heat and humidity, even if it would only take ten minutes. He'd be soaking wet by the time he got there, and he already had plenty of days like that to look forward to.

The barn wasn't locked, and he slid the door open easily. He and Montana had snuck several kisses right here in this barn, but today, Bishop slid the door closed and stepped over to the thermostat. He turned it down and faced her. "Thanks for a gift," he said.

"I didn't realize you guys didn't do gifts."

"Mother brought me one on Friday," he said, smiling. "And Cactus actually gave me something a couple of weeks ago."

Montana looked at the box. "Aurora wrapped it. We did the best we could."

"I'm already in love with it," he said, gazing at the blue and white striped paper. He lifted his eyes to hers. "Surely you know by now how smitten I am with you."

She smiled and reached up to cradle his face. "I have a little bit of an idea." She nodded to the box. "Open it. Then you'll know I'm a little bit smitten by you too."

"Will I?" Bishop's anxiety and excitement doubled. "All right. Here I go." He tore off the paper and stalled. "Wait. Should I open the card first?"

"You're really bad at opening gifts," Montana teased. "You just open it."

He met her eye. "A terrible kisser and bad at opening gifts. Why are you still with me?" He grinned and chuckled, especially when she shook her head.

"That wasn't a real kiss," she said, which was what she said every time he teased her that she'd called him a terrible kisser.

He finished taking the paper off the box to find a box without any markings on it. "Intriguing," he said.

"Aurora said you get boys what they like," Montana said.

"Are you seriously trying to justify your gift?" he asked. "And did you just call me a boy?"

"Stop it," she said, laughing. "I'm nervous about this."

"Why?" He opened the box before she could answer, and after peering inside, he pulled in a breath. "Montana Louise Martin." He looked up, his eyes wide. "Did you get me the new smartMeasure?"

"Yes, sir." She looked at him with apprehension in every particle of her being.

"You're going to get me in trouble with Bear," he murmured, taking her into his arms. "Thank you so much. I love this." He wanted to say he loved her, but he didn't. It was far too soon for that, and he wasn't in love with her anyway.

He liked her very, very much, though, and in soft, wonderful, private moments like this one, that could feel a lot like love.

"Remind me to tell you about Bowman's Breeds," he said, and she pulled back to look at him again.

"Tell me now."

"No," he said with a grin. "Now, I'm going to kiss you." He did just that, and the way Montana melted into his arms meant a great deal to him.

She only kissed him for a few seconds before she pulled away and said, "Oh, and my middle name isn't Louise."

He laughed lightly. "I know. I just made that up. What is it?" He traced the tip of his nose down the side of her face and placed a kiss below her ear.

"Jewel," she said.

"Mm." He kissed her again, thinking she was exactly the jewel his life had needed, and his gratitude that a loving Lord knew exactly what he needed, and when, grew.

Bishop found Bear sitting at the bottom of the stairs, his eyes closed as he leaned against the bannister. "You ready?" he asked.

Bear's eyes opened, and he looked tired. "Yeah," he said.

"Are you okay?" Bishop asked. "I'm worried about you."

"I'm okay," he said, standing. "I'm going to take tomorrow off, though. Ranger has everything I need to do."

Bishop knew then that Bear wasn't okay. "What aren't you telling me?" He paused with his hand on the doorknob so he didn't miss a moment of Bear's reaction.

"Being married is full of challenges," Bear said with a smile. "How's that for a start?"

Bishop wasn't sure if he was kidding or not, though he suspected not. Bishop had never been married, but he'd seen his parents go through hard times.

"Come on," Bear said. "If we don't do this today, it'll just get put off again."

Bishop opened the door and Bear walked outside. Bishop's letter suddenly felt so heavy in his pocket, and he wasn't sure he wanted to show it to Bear. They walked in silence down the steps and sidewalk to the graveled area where everyone parked. From there, it was a straight shot across the street to the family cemetery, and once they'd stepped onto the grass there, Bear sighed.

"What did Cactus have to say this afternoon?"

"He's havin' a hard time," Bishop said. That was all of a report Bear ever got. Bishop didn't want to betray Cactus's confidence, so he delivered everything in terms of how he was doing. "I'm taking some cake out there after this."

"Good idea," Bear said. "He hasn't been staying for much at the homestead."

"He doesn't go to town anymore either."

"I wish there was something I could do to help him."

"I used to feel like that too," Bishop said. "But after a while, I learned that Cactus is the only one who can help Cactus."

Bear looked at him. "You sounded just like Daddy right there."

"Great," Bishop said. "Barely thirty-four, and already sounding like an old man." He tried to laugh, but Bear didn't even crack a smile.

He took out his letter and held it toward Bishop. "I don't want you to read the whole thing. I just want you to read the last little bit."

Bishop's heart started to pound. "Okay." He reached for the paper and Bear let him take it.

"It's the last five paragraphs. Starts with the word 'please'." Bear walked all the way to the fence and put his foot on the bottom rung. Bishop hung back and unfolded the letter.

The urge to read the whole thing as quickly as he could surged through him, but he forced his eyes to the bottom of the page.

Bear's letter was longer than Bishop's, and he tried not to let the envy steal through him.

Please, watch out for Bishop. I fear for him the most, because we are so very important to one another, and he will need your champion heart in the days and years after I am gone.

Bishop looked up at the strong back of his brother. There was no way Bear had seen this letter before, and he had watched out for Bishop from the very day Daddy had died.

He took a deep breath. He and Daddy *had* been so very important to each other, and Bishop re-read that line and closed his eyes. "I miss you," he whispered.

There was so much his father hadn't been able to witness. He hadn't seen Bishop prove his worth as a cowboy. He hadn't seen him take over the construction. He hadn't seen him design and build the barn, or any of the other dozens of projects Bishop had completed over the years.

He hadn't met Montana, and he hadn't been here for Cactus's wedding, or Bear's, or Ranger's.

He wouldn't be here for Bishop's, if he could manage to get down the aisle.

Bishop took a steadying breath and kept reading.

I leave you with the words of Grandmother, whom I know you loved.

Do not stifle him. Do not stifle yourself, Bear. Do not stifle Bishop. Do not stifle that championship spirit you were named for.

Embrace it, and you will never be led astray.

I love you, and I pray that anything I have done that you resent or are bitter about will be forgiven in the future.

Daddy

. . .

DADDY HAD ASKED BISHOP TO FORGIVE HIM TOO, AND Bishop hadn't found one thing he needed to forgive his father for—except dying so early.

He supposed that resentment belonged to the Lord though, and Bishop had never allowed it to sink too deeply into his heart.

He refolded Bear's letter and took out his own. He joined Bear at the fence, though they could wander among the headstones if they wanted.

"Thank you," he said, giving the letter back. "For letting me see it, and for doing exactly what it said to do before you even got it."

Bear nodded and tucked the letter back into his pocket.

"You're mentioned in mine," Bishop said. "You can read the whole thing if you want."

Bear glanced at the letter, obvious interest in his eyes. "Maybe another time. I'm still recovering from my own letter."

It had been a few weeks since Bishop and Montana had shown up at the homestead with the love letters, and as Bishop stood there with Bear, he realized that Bear's mood and demeanor had flipped a switch about the time the love letters had made a reappearance.

But it wasn't the love letters troubling Bear. It was Daddy's letter to him. It sure seemed like a good one to Bishop, but he hadn't read the whole thing.

"Bear, you've done right by all of us," Bishop said. "So if that's what—"

"It's not that," he said.

"Then what is it?"

"I can't explain it," Bear said. "I honestly feel like I'm grieving his death all over again." He went over the fence. "I just need some time to grieve him again."

"Okay," Bishop said, and he followed Bear over the fence and into the cemetery. Together, they cleaned up Daddy's grave, and then Uncle Bull's. The two brothers were buried right next to one another, with space on the outer sides for Mother and Aunt Dawna.

Once Bear was satisfied with the cleanliness of the headstones, he straightened. "You and Montana make a real nice couple."

"Thank you," Bishop said. "I sure do like her, and that Aurora is quite the character."

Bear chuckled, and when he looked at Bishop this time, he had some of the sparkle and happiness he'd had for much of the past year back in his eyes. "She sure is. Mister said something about how he wished she was older so he could ask her out. You should've *heard* Judge rip into him."

Bear shook his head.

"What are we going to do about those two? They can't move back into the Ranch House together. Things have been better since Mister's been livin' up in that cabin."

"I know," Bear said. "I think Mister will take one of the cabins in the southern sector for a permanent residence. That's probably what I'll suggest to him."

"Smart," Bishop said. He bent down and brushed a tad more dirt from the S on Daddy's name. Daddy had counseled Bishop to look to those around him and to emulate their best qualities.

He'd always tried to do that, starting with his father.

"Love you, Daddy," he said, stepping back to Bear's side. "Thanks, Bear."

"I haven't stifled you, have I, Bishop?"

"Not even a little bit."

Bear nodded, lost somewhere inside his own head. Bishop let his thoughts wander too, most of them lighting on Montana, Ace, and Cactus. He had a lot left to do today, and he finally stepped away from Bear, saying, "I best get out to Cactus's before it gets too late."

"Yep." Bear stayed in the cemetery, and as Bishop went back over the fence, he said a prayer for Bear too. It was a good reminder for Bishop that even the mighty Bear, who seemingly had everything on the outside, struggled with things too.

Chapter Sixteen

Montana bent to do her side of the table while Bishop pulled out the legs on his. "Bishop, Bowman's Breeds is at Three Rivers Ranch. It's a forty-five-minute drive from the edge of town, and it takes ten just to get there from my aunt's house."

They righted the circular table, and their eyes met across it.

"I know," Bishop said, turning to grab another table-cloth. The whole family would gather in True Blue for Lois Glover's birthday party. Why they were using the barn this time when they'd used the homestead for Bishop's birthday, Montana didn't know. She hadn't asked.

Bishop had said they needed to get the barn set up for the party, and then he was going to spend the afternoon at home, relaxing and resting while Holly Ann, the woman Ace had hired to do the food for the party, set up in the barn. Montana would go back to town like she always did, to be there for Aurora in the afternoon, and then she and her family were coming back to the party that evening.

"I can't drive her to Three Rivers and then drive back here," Montana said. "It would take me over two hours."

Bishop tossed the cream-colored cloth across the table and Montana grabbed it to straighten it out. "I know that."

"Can you say anything besides 'I know'?" Montana glared at him. She'd been so excited about the prospect of Aurora getting a job at Bowman's Breeds. Even Aurora was excited about it, and Montana did not want to have to tell her that it wasn't going to work out. Montana already felt like a failure in so many ways when it came to parenting Aurora. She did, and always had, wanted the best for her daughter.

The truth was, as a single mom with limited resources, there were spaces she simply couldn't fill. As Aurora got older, Montana told her appropriate things to help her daughter understand that Montana tried to fill those spaces as best she could.

But many remained, and Montana felt the weight of them every single day.

Bishop smiled, and that only aggravated her further. He didn't understand those gaps, and he'd likely never experienced them.

Not fair, she told herself even as they went to work on another table. His father had died when he was eighteen years old. There had been gaps in his life; they were simply different than the ones in Montana's or Aurora's.

"I've arranged a ride for her," Bishop said, his gaze

steady on the underside of the table, as if he'd never seen anything like it before.

"What does that mean?" Montana pulled out the legs on her side and gripped the edges of the table. They set that one up, and Bishop retrieved another tablecloth.

He sighed as he spread it across the table and Montana pulled it flat on her side. They stayed there for a few seconds, looking at each other.

"You won't like it."

"Then why did you do it?"

"Because it's a perfect solution, and it allows your daughter to work at the training facility and you to keep working here." He smiled, and it wasn't his cocky *I-know-I'm-gorgeous* smile. It wasn't his playful smile. It wasn't his joyful smile. And it wasn't his flirty, coy smile.

Montana had seen all of those, and they were all wonderful. But this one was twice as amazing, because it spoke of his sensitive side. The side that cared about people and wanted them to be happy.

He cared about *her* and wanted *her* to be happy.

"What is it?" she asked softly.

"Wyatt Walker works at Three Rivers a few times a week," Bishop said, and Montana stiffened, her back moving to be perfectly straight. "See?" He shook his head. "I knew you wouldn't like it, but Montana, it works."

He came around the table and cradled her face in one hand. "I know you don't like Micah Walker all that much, but what could you possibly have against Wyatt?"

Montana clung to the bitterness she held for all Walkers, though she knew she needed to let it go. She simply didn't know how.

She hadn't known how to keep living with her sisters as they each dated her ex-boyfriend. She hadn't known how to forgive her ex-husband for cheating on her and bringing home both men *and* women while their daughter slept in the room next door.

She hadn't known how to keep talking to her mother when she'd sided first with Johnny and then with Paris and Georgia.

If she couldn't figure out how to let go of all of that, she certainly couldn't figure out how to release Micah and his whole family from the cage of her resentment. She wished she'd never said anything about him to Bishop, but the man was pretty perceptive, and she'd wanted to share with him.

"Anyway," Bishop said, leaning down and touching his lips to her cheek. So he wasn't going to play fair. Montana remained completely still. "He lives way up in the east hills, close to you, actually. He said he drives right past your place to get to Three Rivers, and he'll pick up Aurora on his way."

"She can't ride with him alone," Montana said. "I don't even know him."

"She won't be alone," Bishop said, whispering right in her ear now. "Tripp said Ollie's got a job up there too, and he'll bring him to your place too. Wyatt will take them both."

Montana shivered with the nearness of Bishop, the

tantalizing scent of his cologne and the sweet minty scent of his breath.

She could kiss him in a minute, because there were still plenty of questions to be answered.

"Tripp?" she asked. "Why would Tripp bring Ollie to my place?"

Bishop pulled back and looked at her, clear confusion in his eyes. "Why wouldn't he? Ollie's his son."

Ollie's his son.

Those three words filled Montana's bloodstream with ice. Her eyes widened as her mouth dropped open. Horror and betrayal and disbelief snaked through her, filling the spaces the ice left behind with darkness and fear.

"No," she said. "Ollie's last name is not Walker." Unless Aurora had lied about that too. She shook her head, because she couldn't stand the thought of Aurora lying to her at all. "It's not. Aurora introduced him as Oliver Osburn."

"Yeah," Bishop said. "But his mom remarried after her divorce. She married Tripp Walker. They live out on Quail Creek, down the road from Rhett and his family, and like ten minutes from Seven Sons." He searched her face, and Montana wondered what he saw there. "You've never gone to pick her up there?"

"I have," Montana said. "I've never seen Tripp Walker." Her emotions had morphed to anger now, and she turned around, surveying how much work they had left to do. She wanted to leave now and get to Aurora. Grab her by the shoulders and demand she tell her the truth.

You already know the truth.

She pressed one hand to her chest, trying to calm her heartbeat, and the other to her mouth, trying to contain the moan. Her eyes drifted closed too, as she suddenly felt sweaty and like she might faint.

She swayed on her feet, and Bishop said, "Okay, I've got you." He took her into his arms, his chest pressing into her back and keeping her on her feet. "Montana, love, I'm sorry. I thought you knew."

She shook her head, but with her eyes closed and her heart still racing, the motion only disoriented her further. Tears pressed behind her eyes, and she hated that stupid Tripp Walker had caused them.

Turning, she pressed her face to Bishop's chest as her eyelids couldn't hold back her tears any longer. "I'm sorry," she said, her voice high-pitched and her next breath wheezing into her lungs. "I'm sorry. I don't know why this has upset me so much."

"It's fine," Bishop murmured, his hands firm and steady against her back. He rubbed in large circles, his heartbeat clear and strong in her ears.

Montana focused on his touch and looked up at him. "How do I carry this burden? I can't do it anymore. How do you let go of it all?" Tears streamed down her face, and Bishop smiled at her with pain in his eyes. He wiped her face with his tender yet tough hands and shook his head.

"I would take it for you if I could, sweetheart." His smile wobbled on his face. "The only thing that's worked for me is to give it to the Lord. He takes it, and He shoulders it somehow—at least for a little while." He swallowed, his vulnerability matching hers in that moment.

Montana took a deep breath, trying to find her faith. She nodded and rubbed the tears from her eyes, making white sparks shoot through her vision she pressed so hard. "Yes, like Pastor Knowlton said on Sunday. We just have to come unto the Lord, and He will make our burdens light."

Bishop nodded too, his jaw so, so tight.

"I've got to figure out how to do that," Montana said. "I go to church. I read the Bible. I pray. I try to live a good, Christian life. Why don't I know how to do this?"

Bishop drew her into his chest again, and Montana gripped him tightly. The storm inside her threatened to rip her apart, the winds so strong she felt sure she'd be swept out onto the prairie and never heard from again.

"I go somewhere quiet," Bishop said, his voice low and husky. "Usually my dad's grave. I talk to him for a while, and then I talk to the Lord. I beg Him—literally *beg* Him—to take the burden from me. He always does. Like the pastor said, it's His nature to do so. He can't *not* care for us. He can't *not* take it."

Montana needed to go right now. She stepped away from Bishop and looked around the barn, her anxiety and need to beg the Lord to take her burdens almost making her frantic.

"I'll go with you," he said. "If you want. The cemetery is a peaceful place. It could be your place too."

Montana drew in a deep breath, her thoughts finally quieting. "Let's finish here first. I know you wanted to rest this afternoon, but maybe you could at least walk me there?" Her insides shook again. "I'm not sure I'm brave enough to go by myself."

"Baby," Bishop said, his voice strong and with all the confidence he usually possessed. "You're the strongest woman I know."

She shook her head, those stupid tears gathering again. "I'm really not."

"Physically, you are." He ran his hands down her shoulders and arms to her hands, where he laced his fingers. "Have you seen your muscles?"

"Men don't like my muscles," she whispered.

"I love them," Bishop said, smiling that flirty, coy smile at her. "I think they're sexy and beautiful."

"Stop it," she said, her tears spilling over again. No one had ever told her all the muscles in her arms and back were sexy. They made her thick and manly and she knew it.

"I won't," he said, though his smile dropped. "You've been raising Aurora alone for a decade. That takes emotional and mental and spiritual strength I don't understand. But I can feel it."

Montana shook her head. "I don't even have my own house."

"So what?" he asked. "You have done exactly what you needed to do for her and for you. You shouldn't be embarrassed of that."

Montana wasn't embarrassed of that, but she still wanted her own place. "I have so much I carry about my family," she said. "I need to release all of that. I need to find a way to forgive them all." She kept crying, but she didn't care. There was so much to tell Bishop; so much he didn't know about her.

"My mother took my ex-husband's side in the divorce. I

haven't spoken to her in a while. She sided with Paris and Georgia when they started dating my ex-boyfriend. She's told Jackie she shouldn't support me so much."

She shook her head. "I'm not sure what I did to make her dislike me so much, but I stopped caring a while ago. I just haven't been able to forgive her."

"You can," Bishop said. "I know you can. The Lord can carry all of that for you."

Montana nodded, the air conditioning in the barn suddenly too cold. She shivered, and Bishop gathered her back into his arms.

"My ex-husband started seeing other people when Aurora was only three years old," she said. "And not just women. I finally got enough courage to leave and file for divorce when he brought his boyfriend into our house."

Bishop gasped, his whole body tightening and tensing next to hers. A moment later, he released it all. "I'm so sorry, Montana."

"He didn't fight me on full custody. He doesn't talk to either me or Aurora. I know it hurts her, and I don't know how to heal it."

"You don't have to heal it."

"I think I might hate him," Montana said. "I'm not supposed to hate people, right?"

Bishop didn't answer, and Montana regretted telling him that she might hate Johnny. But she did. So many times, when she really thought about how she felt about what her ex-husband had done, it came down to hatred.

"I can't answer that, sweetheart. People inflict wounds on us that take a long time to heal."

"It feels like it will never go away," Montana said, everything open now and about to gush out. "I don't like my sisters. I don't ever want to see them again. I came here, and I fit here with my aunt and uncle, and it's always been enough. Then all this stuff happened with Micah, and I just feel like I'm not meant to ever have more than what I do now. It doesn't feel fair. I work hard—I have worked *so hard*. I have more training than Micah Stupid Walker. I should be the one designing and building million-dollar houses in Three Rivers. Not him."

"I know." Bishop rubbed those circles on her back, but they didn't comfort her the way they had a few minutes ago.

"And now my daughter's dating a Walker? And I was doing so good with you, and I like you so much, and now you know all these horrible things about me, and—" She cut herself off and shook her head.

She had to leave. Now.

She stepped out of his arms. "I'm sorry, Bishop." She wiped her face and pressed her palms against her eyes. Horror filled her at all she'd said. "I have to go." She strode away from him, her breaths coming in great gasps now.

"Montana, you don't have to go."

But she did. She ran the last few steps to the barn door and slid it open easily, using those muscles she had. She didn't bother closing it, which only allowed Bishop to catch up to her faster.

"Please don't go," he said, latching onto her arm as she reached his truck. "I'll drive you to the cemetery right now."

She couldn't look at him. She couldn't speak. The strength of his fingers around her arm meant she couldn't leave either.

"Montana," he said.

"I can't," she said.

"You can." He gently put his hand on the side of her face and guided her attention to him. "I do not think badly of you for how you feel. Not even a little bit."

"I don't believe you," she said since she'd said everything else she'd been hiding.

Bishop blinked, as if no one had ever spoken to him like that before. "You'll have to work on that too, then. It's not your fault the things that have happened to you." He wore a fierce look in his eyes. "Come on. Let's go to the cemetery."

Montana wanted to tell him no, but she didn't have the energy. She let him lead her around to the passenger side of the truck and help her up. He got behind the wheel and drove to the cemetery. She let him lead her to where his father and his uncle lay side-by-side, with several other graves in the small family cemetery.

He held her hand in his and told a story about his father and how he'd once ran his hand through the table saw.

"I was only fourteen," Bishop said. "I had no idea what to do. There was blood everywhere, and just me and him in the shop. I panicked, like *panicked*, and all I remember was rushing over to my dad with the only towel I could find, praying out loud the whole time."

Montana just listened, her emotions almost numb

again. She preferred the numbness, actually, though she knew that was why she hadn't been able to let go of any of the negative things she'd been carrying for so long.

"My dad looked me in the eye, and said, 'Son, keep prayin', but get my fingers, and go get Mother.'" Bishop gave an unhappy chuckle. "He said, 'You're going to have to run as fast as you can. Get them on ice, and come get me. Have someone call the hospital. You can do this.'"

He paused in the story then, and Montana just traced the letters of his father's name on the headstone. Stone. His brother's name was Bull.

"Are those their real names?" she asked.

"They are," he said. "My father was like a stone. A big, heavy stone that could not be moved. He was strong in his convictions and his faith. The strongest."

"Did you save his fingers?"

"I did," Bishop said. "Both of them. I ran as fast as I could while praying. I got the fingers on ice while Mother radioed out to Bear and everyone else on the emergency channel. Uncle Bull was close to the wood shop, and he got Daddy. Mother and I drove the fingers to the hospital and met them there." He stared straight down at the stones, and Montana wondered what he was really thinking. His voice was so...dark.

"We saved the fingers, and my dad was back to a limited work schedule within a week. Mother was not happy." A smile touched his face then. "Bear and Ranger cleaned up the wood shop while we were at the hospital. I have a very, very good family."

"Yes, you do," Montana said. It was all Aurora and Aunt

Jackie had talked about since Bishop's birthday party, and they were thrilled to be coming back to Shiloh Ridge tonight.

"At that age, I did not think so," Bishop said. "I wanted to wrestle. I wanted to play football. I was a fast runner, and I resented that I had to use it to run from the wood shop to the homestead instead of running to score touchdowns." He finally looked away from the graves and out over the horizon. "I fought with my dad about it several times, until he finally exploded and told me to do whatever I wanted. If I was so smart, I could do whatever I wanted."

Montana looked at Bishop, because she'd never heard him say anything bad about his father. Ever. He'd never said he didn't get along with his family. Everything about him was plated in gold, and Montana should've known there was something more real underneath.

Everyone had a past, and everyone had things that hadn't worked out for them. Even Bishop, she was now realizing.

Her perfect Bishop, who she'd started falling in love with.

"What did you do?"

"I wrestled, and I played football," Bishop said, his voice haunted now. "I missed the time I usually spent with Daddy, and I missed the first signs of his cancer. If I hadn't...." He left the sentence there.

"There was no way you could've known," Montana said.

"I could've if I'd been around," Bishop said. "Instead, it was Mister who was with Daddy when he doubled-over with abdominal pain and told Mother. It wasn't the first time. Daddy had been experiencing pain like that for several months, and if I'd been around instead of at practice, we would've caught it sooner."

"Bishop."

"I quit my senior year and spent it with Daddy as he fought as hard as he could. But even a stone cannot overcome cancer when it's as advanced and as wide-spread as Daddy's was." He hung his head, his regret filling the sky around them. "I didn't mean to turn this onto me," he whispered. "I just want you to know, my sweetheart, that things happen sometimes that we cannot control. It took me a decade to come to terms with my behavior and that what you said a few minutes ago is right. There was no way for me to really know. My father's death is not my fault."

He looked at her. "Just like your husband's cheating is not yours. And your mother's decisions are not your fault. They're not your burden to carry."

Montana nodded and released his hand so she could put her arm around his waist. She wanted to be as close to him physically as she was emotionally, and she relished the feeling of his arm around her shoulders, tucking him against her side.

"I've never told anyone about Johnny or my mother," she said. "I would appreciate it if you kept it to yourself."

"Who am I going to tell?" he asked, his chuckle back to light and airy. "I've never told anyone what I just told you, either. Not even Bear, though he probably suspected I blamed myself for Daddy's death for a while."

Montana bent down and traced *Stone Nelson Glover* with her fingers. "I can feel his spirit," she said. "He is strong."

She straightened and faced Bishop this time. "I just have to tell you one more thing."

"Anything, love." He gazed at her with such an expression of love too, that Montana knew he was falling for her too.

"I am very cautious with my heart," she said. "I know better than most that sometimes a person can think they're in love when they're just in pain."

Bishop nodded. "I suppose you do."

"Even when you're engaged, that doesn't mean you're in love. You can even be married and not be in love." Montana looked at him, hoping he understood. She should just spell it out. "So I'm falling in love with you, Bishop Benson Daniel Glover, but I'm going to need time to make sure I'm really in love with you and not just feeling so great because our relationship is so much better than my real life."

Bishop's eyes couldn't get any wider, and then he burst out laughing. He took her into his arms and crushed her to him. "I'm falling for you too, Montana," he said sobering. "And my middle name isn't Daniel."

"What is it, then?"

"Flint," he said, and then he kissed her. Montana matched him stroke for stroke, the intensity in the kiss slowing the longer it lasted. This was a whole new kind of kiss that spoke of their passion for one another, as well as their mutual respect, and all the emotion they'd just shared.

Montana was definitely falling in love with him, but she clung to the edge of the cliff, because she'd spoken true earlier. She knew what it was like to think she was in love when she wasn't, and she wasn't going to do that again. She was not. She was going to make sure she was one-hundred percent healed and in love with Bishop before they talked about diamond rings or weddings.

Chapter Seventeen

Ace approached the barn, frowning when he saw the door was wide open. "Bishop?" he called, because his cousin was crazy about making sure the barn was kept closed. They weren't paying to air condition the state of Texas in June, after all.

Bishop didn't appear, and his truck wasn't outside the barn either. Inside, only a few tables had been set up, and Ace paused, searching for some evidence of an injury. Something to indicate why Bishop had obviously been here but wasn't now.

Ace turned and looked back outside. Something had definitely happened, because the plan was that he and Montana would get the barn set up that morning, and Ace would meet Holly Ann to make sure she could get into the kitchen and prepare the food for that evening's party.

Ace pulled out his phone and called his cousin, hoping he wasn't interrupting something, good or bad.

Bishop didn't answer, and Ace pocketed his phone. Something niggled in his mind that Bishop wouldn't run off and leave the barn unfinished if it wasn't important. Ace could set up tables and chairs, and he'd arrived early, hoping to catch Bishop and talk to him about Holly Ann for a couple of minutes.

"Might as well work off the anxiety," Ace muttered to himself. He'd been getting up at four a.m. to run off the nerves, but they came back by lunchtime. He'd been avoiding the homestead for meals, though he usually ate lunch there. Instead, he'd been returning to the house he and Ward shared and eating alone while he contemplated his options.

Keep waiting for Holly Ann. Or get back on the dating app and find someone new. Keep going to town parties, dances, and festivals, and meet someone else. Ace also considered simply doing nothing.

He didn't have to wait for Holly Ann. He didn't need to update his profile and change his status back to single. He didn't have to go to town. He could just keep being himself, and working Shiloh Ridge Ranch, and enjoying his family.

He'd had plenty of girlfriends over the years, and he'd never doubted that he'd find The One and have what his father had had. A wife, a family, a life he loved on the ranch. He'd come close once, but his proposal to Jeanie had been met with a no.

Ace hadn't even waited a month before he'd asked someone else out. Maybe he just needed to slow down.

Footsteps sounded behind him as he set another table on its feet. He turned to find Royce and Max coming into the barn. "Hey," he said. "Sorry, I meant to come back to the field. I just wanted to check on the barn, and Bishop isn't here." He looked around at the half-finished space.

"He called me," Royce drawled. "Sent us to help." He smiled, and he and Max moved over to the supply closet. "How many tables are we puttin' up?"

Bishop likely had a map for tonight's party, and Ace actually looked around for it. He wondered why his cousin hadn't called or texted him back. *He probably doesn't want to talk right now*, Ace thought. It was easier to send help than to get into a conversation about why he wasn't there. Royce and Max didn't need an explanation; Ace would.

Ace did some quick calculations. "Probably six," he said. "They hold six chairs each, too. Tablecloths are right here."

"All right," Max said, and with the three of them, they got the tables and chairs set up quickly.

"Thanks," Ace said. "Holly Ann should be here soon with the food. I'm gonna check on the kitchen."

"I'm still okay to take off at four, right?" Max asked, his eyes bright with hope. "I'm almost done with this class, but it's got a couple more weeks."

"Sure," Ace said. "You won't be at the party?"

"I'm gonna have to miss it," he said, his face falling. "I'll have to stop by Miss Lois's another time."

Everyone on the ranch loved Bear's mother. She mothered all of them, even Ace, and he loved that about her. She was good to the cowboys that lived on the ranch, Ace knew that. He'd caught her leaving one of the cabins a few nights ago, a couple of empty dishes in her hands. He suspected she'd dropped off new meals, and those were just the pans and casserole dishes from the last time she'd brought food to the cowboys.

"How's your mother?" Royce asked, glancing at Max.

"She's doin' okay," Ace said with a quick smile. "Etta and Ida will bring her up tonight."

"I'll stop by when I get back," Max said. "Maybe she'll still be here."

"Anything is possible," Ace said. "You know how the family is." He smiled at the two cowboys, and they smiled back.

"We sure do." Royce tipped his hat. "We'll get the field tested and leave the results for you, okay?"

"Okay," Ace said. "Thanks, guys."

They left, and Ace walked over to the kitchen door. It opened without a key, and Ace faced the huge space with all this equipment he didn't really understand. He could put things in the fridge, and he could make coffee. He could usually make toast that wasn't too burnt and he could heat cans of soup or chili in the microwave.

Other than that, he was pretty helpless. Luckily, Ward could cook decently, and they only lived a few hundred yards from the homestead, where there was always something to eat and something happening.

Ace loved the homestead, especially now that it was redone. But he sure did like having a quiet place he could retreat to, and he could relate to Cactus on that front.

"Ah, Cactus," he said with a sigh. Bishop had been able to get out to the cabin on the edge of the ranch to visit him a couple of times since his birthday party, and he'd reported that Cactus just needed some time. Again.

Ace actually missed him, and he pulled out his phone to text his cousin. *You're coming tonight for your mother's party, right?*

Yes, Cactus sent back almost instantly.

Ace's fingers hovered above the screen as he tried to figure out what else to say. Cactus didn't like long conversations, and he rarely gave more than one-word answers. He didn't like to be pressed on things, and because Ace respected him immensely, he didn't normally do anything Cactus wouldn't like.

He'd been deep inside his head for the past couple of months, though, and he couldn't get out without saying something.

If I did something to upset you, I apologize, he typed out. *Really, Cactus. Just tell me what it was, and I won't do it again.*

He read over the text and decided to delete the last couple of sentences. He didn't have to know what it was, though it would be nice so he wouldn't repeat whatever it had been to drive Cactus back to his cabin and back into his silence.

So he typed the sentences again and sent them without triple-guessing himself. Quickly too, he added, *I miss driving to town with you. Please let me know when you're ready to go again so we can go together, if you want.*

He read it, deleted *if you want*, and sent that message too.

To his surprise, Cactus called, and Ace turned away from the pristine kitchen to answer the phone. "Hey," he said. He held back from immediately launching into another sentence. He'd said everything he wanted to say in the texts. Cactus was the one who'd called.

He sighed and said, "You have nothing to apologize for, Ace."

Ace nodded, his throat tight. He didn't want to blame Cactus for anything, so he said nothing.

"I'm...a mess, frankly," Cactus said. "I've talked to Judge, but he's not a real therapist."

"No, he's not."

"Would you—could you help me with something?"

"Of course."

"I can't seem to make myself call a real counselor, and I know I need to. I'll even let you drive me to the appointments."

Ace smiled as a ray of light filled his soul. "You'll *let* me drive you?" He scoffed and gave a light laugh that only lasted a moment. "I'll drive you, otherwise you won't go."

"That too," Cactus whispered.

Ace's heart tore and bled for his cousin. "We'll get it done tomorrow, okay, Cactus?"

Cactus didn't answer, probably because his own throat was too dang tight.

"Okay," Ace said, hearing a car pull up to the barn. "I think someone just got here, and it might be Holly Ann."

"Good luck with her," Cactus said, every ounce of sincerity he owned in the words.

"Thank you, Cactus," Ace said, meaning it too. "I'm trying not to be too pathetic with her."

"Just be yourself," he said. "I think you and Bishop told me that once."

"Yeah, and you got a date," Ace said, though he knew he wouldn't get a date with Holly Ann unless he hired her again. Which wasn't a bad idea.... They were forever having parties up here, and Ace could simply say he'd take care of the food.

"I did not get a date," Cactus said. "I got a phone number for a twenty-three-year-old."

Ace chuckled, glad when Cactus did too. "We're going to find the right woman for you," he said as Holly Ann entered the barn. His heartbeat rioted, and with the sunlight shining into the barn behind her, haloing her in light, she was an angel straight from heaven.

Ace thought she was his One, and he felt it way down deep in his soul. If he had to wait for her to realize that he was her One, he could do it. He absolutely could do it.

"You've gone silent. Go talk to your girl," Cactus said, and the call ended.

Ace shoved his phone in his back pocket and smiled at Holly Ann. "Hey," he said, wishing he could add *baby* or *sweetheart* to that sentence. Instead, he added, "Do you need help bringing things in?"

"Yes, please," she said, returning his smile. She'd pulled her dark hair into a ponytail that sat on top of her head, and she wore a pair of shorts that were barely long enough to cover the pockets and a black sleeveless shirt with a floral print.

Ace followed her back to her van, where she started directing him which bins to take. She worked with him, and he asked her how the business was going, how her father and sister were, and what her next job was.

They'd never had a problem keeping the conversation going, and Ace did love talking to her. He loved the sound of her lower voice and rolled Texan accent. He loved learning about her and feeding off her excitement for things like ham and cheese sandwiches and brown sugar squares.

Once she had everything she needed in the kitchen, she sighed and faced it all. "Thanks, Ace." Her eyes met his, and Ace's throat turned dry.

They had gone out a few times over the winter, but not for a while now. She knew he liked her though, and when she looked at him with that glinting sparkle in her dark eyes, he suspected she liked him too.

"Sure," he said. "Bishop put the best of everything in this kitchen, so you should have everything you need."

"It's seriously the nicest kitchen I've ever seen." She gazed around at all the stainless steel and sturdy oak cabinets. "Your brother is somethin' else."

"He's my cousin," Ace said. "Just the two brothers, remember?"

Holly Ann's face flushed, and that only made her more attractive to Ace. "Oh, right," she said. "Sorry. I just think of you guys up here like one big, happy family."

He smiled at her, so she'd know he understood. "Well, that kind of fits too." He tucked his hands in his pockets and told himself to leave. She had what she needed, and he didn't need to hang around. He'd only be in her way, and she'd made her feelings for him clear.

"Listen," she said, dropping her eyes to where her hand pressed into the steel tabletop. "I meant thank you for the job too."

"Sure thing," he said, his voice pitching up on the last word.

"Because you booked me, I've had several other jobs come my way, all of them because of you."

"Oh, you don't know that," he said.

She looked up and right into his eyes. Hers were wide and earnest and filled with an emotion he couldn't quite grasp. Did she...? Maybe he could ask her out again and she'd say yes.

"I do know that," she said. "Every one of them said you referred me."

"Oh." Him and his stupid mouth. Why couldn't he keep quiet? Even posts on forums and comments on Two Cents were "talking."

"Ace, I—" She shook her head. "I know you like me."

"Mm hm." He wasn't going to deny it, but he didn't need to open the door to his heart and invite her inside to carve it out with one of her fancy knives either.

Holly Ann took a step toward him, and he couldn't help letting his gaze slide down the height of her body. She was curvy and delicious and everything Ace wanted physically in a woman. He licked his lips as he returned his gaze to hers.

"Would you be willing to take me to dinner sometime?" she asked.

Surprise shot through Ace at the speed of light.

"What?" came out of his mouth instead of, *Yes, of course. Let's go right now.*

Holly Ann ducked her head and smiled, which so wasn't fair to Ace's pulse. "Did I speak too fast, cowboy?" She stopped right in front of him and raised her hand to fiddle with the collar on his shirt.

He held very still, though he knew this particular female tactic very well. She was touching him—a very good sign. She was in his personal space—another good sign. A very loud sign. All he had to do was take her in his arms, say yes, and kiss her—and she'd probably let him.

All the signs said so.

"You've asked me to dinner before," she said slowly, her eyes trained on that blasted collar, though it was nothing special. In fact, there was very little special about Ace, and he knew it. He blended in amongst all the other Glovers, many of them with bigger, brighter personalities. He'd tried competing with Bishop and Bear and Ward for a while, but he'd given it up in recent years. He'd still gotten dates, though the women he typically attracted were fairly average themselves.

Not Holly Ann. Everything about her was above average, and she was way out of his league.

She looked up at him, her eyes boring into his while she said, "I'd like to go to dinner with you. Would you be willing to take me on a dinner date?" Once she finished, her eyes dropped to his mouth, and Ace quickly read all the signs one more time.

She was still touching him.

She was leaning into him now.

She'd just asked him to take her on a date.

And she was staring at his mouth.

Can't get any clearer than that, he thought.

"Absolutely," he said. He wanted to ask what had changed. Find out if her business really was as stable as she'd made it sound while they'd brought in her ingredients and equipment.

Instead of asking her any of that, he simply did what she wanted him to—he took her into his arms, leaned down, and kissed her.

They both pulled in a breath through their noses, and then Holly Ann kissed him right on back.

Chapter Eighteen

Holly Ann couldn't believe what she'd just done, though she'd been rehearsing her speech for three solid days. She hadn't believed she'd actually go through with it. Faced with Ace Glover, she almost hadn't.

But he was so charming, and so good-looking, and just plain good. She could really only say no to him when he wasn't live and in-person. It was much easier to deflect his invitation to dinner while they texted. Even over the phone had been easier, though not as easy as texting, to tell him she needed to focus on her business.

He'd stopped asking after that, and weeks had gone by. With every new client she got because of him, he buried himself a little deeper into her heart.

She'd known she was in trouble with the tall, dark-haired cowboy the moment he'd sat down in front of her at church, months ago now. As if he'd been drawn by her, he'd turned around and looked at her, a small smile accompanying the hat-tip she'd gotten.

He'd stuck around after the sermon to chat for a minute. He hadn't asked for her number, and Holly Ann hadn't seen him the next week. It wasn't hard for her to figure out who he was. He sat with all the Glovers, and everyone in Three Rivers knew the Glovers. She knew they lived and worked at Shiloh Ridge Ranch, and that it was one of the most successful cattle ranches in the Texas Panhandle.

It had won Ranch of the Year three times in a row before Seven Sons had taken the honor. This year, Wade Rhinehart had won the coveted award, but his sons were far too young for Holly Ann.

As she kissed Ace, she tried to pour the same care and feeling into her touch that he possessed in his. Bethany Rose had told her exactly what to say, where to stand, how to flirt with a cowboy like Ace.

And Bethany Rose knew, because she'd roped her own cowboy only a couple of years ago, and they were living happily-ever-after on his small farm just north of town.

Holly Ann had always wanted a cowboy for a husband. Always, always.

Don't go too fast, she told herself, and that was good advice for this kiss and for this relationship with Ace. She slowed the movement, finally breaking it, and both she and Ace drew in another simultaneous breath.

She giggled hers out while Ace just kept her contained within the circle of his arms.

"Sorry," he murmured. "I think that was a huge distraction from why you came up here." He stepped away and bent to retrieve his cowboy hat. He dusted it against his jean-clad leg and settled it on his head, the brim low so she couldn't see his eyes.

Her blood burned through her whole body. He'd apologized? He'd obviously read all the signals Bethany Rose had taught her, so why was he apologizing?

"You don't distract me, Ace," she said.

He looked up then, and Holly Ann's stomach flipped. "Those were the exact words you used."

"In April," she said. "It's June now, and things have settled down." Had she blown things with him already? She'd tried to tell him she wanted to see him, but right when she was starting up a brand-new catering business wasn't the best timing. She still worked at the tack and feed store, and she had to juggle her schedule on a daily basis.

Kissing him was probably a bad idea. She'd just wanted to so badly—and she had for a long time.

Ace just looked at her, and he was so different than the fun, flirty cowboy who'd sat right next to her at the Christmas movie and finally asked her for her phone number. She'd given it to him without hesitation, and he hadn't wasted any time using it.

"Look," she said. "I'm going to say something that's going to embarrass me. It might freak you out. I don't know." She wiped her hand across her forehead, because it was so dang hot in here. He'd promised air conditioning, and she knew she wouldn't be boiling if she hadn't just experienced the single best cowboy kiss ever.

"Go on, then," he said. "I'll do my best not to freak out." He actually took another step backward, though, and folded his arms. Body language—completely closed off. Bethany Rose would tell her not to tell him, but she'd already committed.

Holly Ann opened her mouth when she should close it. She knew that, but she couldn't stop herself from doing it. With clients, she could. With Ace, she babbled about *everything*.

"I like you a whole lot," she said. "I knew the minute you sat yourself on down on my blanket at that movie that we'd be great together." She gestured to him and back to herself. "This is me saying I'm ready to be together."

The tightness in her chest released, and she drew in another breath. "That's it. That's all I'm going to say." She turned away from him and took off the lid on the nearest bin. Her brain spun, and it took her twice as long to catalog what she was looking at. Buns. That was right. She was making hot meatball sandwiches tonight, from scratch. She needed to get those in the oven so they had time to slow-cook to perfection.

She started taking everything out of the bins, and Ace stepped over to help her.

"Would you please say something?" The words just burst out of her mouth, and they sounded so loud in this echoy kitchen.

"What do you want me to say?" he asked, his voice the complete opposite of hers—calm, quiet, in control. He was her complete opposite in a lot of ways, actually. She could barely lift a gallon of milk, and he could probably lift her right up over his head. She talked too much; he never said more than needed to be said. She always wanted to be outside, and he said he'd rather spend evenings indoors, as he worked outside all day long. She'd told him about her pillow obsession, and he'd said he used one pillow on his bed. One.

Holly Ann had pillows on the back seat of her sedan, for crying out loud.

"I want you to say you like me too, and that you want to be together with me too," she said, throwing him a darted look. "Or I want you to say you don't like me a whole lot, and that you'd rather I just made this meal and we can just say the kiss was a mistake of the heat."

She swallowed, because if he said the second thing, she wasn't even sure she could stay to make the meal.

"Holly Ann," he said, really hanging onto the vowels in her name in a sexiest way possible. Had he practiced that? Had he called Bethany Rose and asked her how to say Holly Ann's name so she'd swoon? Bethany Rose would've told him, Holly Ann knew that. She'd dated Ward Glover once, and she'd been infatuated with all the Glover men since.

When she'd found out it was Ace who'd sat down on the blanket during the Christmas movie, Bethany Rose seemed more excited than Holly Ann.

"I thought it was pretty dang obvious that I liked you a whole lot," he said. "Was that part not clear with all the texting, and calling, and me hiring you to cater this party just so I could see you?"

She looked at him, and he did look a little perplexed. "A

girl likes to hear it too," she said, foolishness racing through her. "Especially after she says it right out loud to a frowning cowboy with his arms all folded."

Ace laughed, and Holly Ann basked in the wonderful sound of it. He stopped taking breadcrumbs out of the bin and swept her back into his embrace. "Holly Ann," he whispered, his breath trailing down her neck and making her shiver. "I sure do like you. A whole lot, like you said. I've thought we'd be great together since the day I missed my ride back to the ranch just so I could stay and talk to you after church."

With that, he dipped his head and kissed her again. Holly Ann let his touch sweep her away, because he really was the very best kisser in the whole wide world.

He stopped much sooner this time than last time, and he said, "I'm ready to be together, sweetheart. You tell me when you can go to dinner, and I'll be there to take you."

"Okay," she said, giggling. She playfully pushed him away. "Now get. I'm makin' dinner for your aunt, and it has to be perfect. I don't need you hangin' around makin' me nervous."

He chuckled, straightened his hat, and said, "Yes, ma'am," before leaving her alone in the kitchen. Holly Ann took a deep breath, giggled again, and got to work. Ace would give her a five-star review no matter what. But she wanted to earn it.

HOURS LATER, HOLLY ANN TOOK THE LAST TRAY OF coconut brownies out to the serving buffet. Ace and Ward had set them up for her, and she admired them in this gorgeous barn. This space was simply stunning, with a dark, rich floor, and pure white wood on the walls.

The exposed beams in the ceiling reminded everyone where they really stood, as did the scent of hay and dust. But the fixtures were high-quality, and all of the amenities top-notch. Even the bathroom she'd used a couple of times throughout the afternoon was nicer than anything she'd ever seen.

It helped that everything was brand-new and hardly used, but she loved every detail, down to the old barrels that had been restored and sealed and stood at the entrance to this big room where they had tables set up now.

She'd heard there'd been dancing here after the double-wedding in March. She hadn't come to the wedding, despite being Ace's semi-girlfriend. He'd asked her to come, but that was when she'd said she needed to focus on her catering.

Idiot, she told herself now. This place would steal her breath if it were decorated for a wedding. As it was, someone had put potted plants on the barrels, and they brought life into the barn where none had been before.

At some point, someone had hung a banner at the front of the barn that said HAPPY BIRTHDAY MOTHER in huge letters. A wreath of horseshoes hung there, and someone had tucked a few greeting cards through the loops created by the shoes.

She turned in a full circle, the cleanliness of this place speaking to how much someone cared about it. She took a couple of pictures of her fully filled buffets and wiped away a drop of sauce. Everything was covered so it would stay hot and ready for eating, and she wondered where everyone was.

The party was supposed to start in only five minutes.

Through the wide entrance to this room, someone opened the sliding door that had first captured Holly Ann's love. She wanted a barn door like that in her house, though it wasn't even big enough for such a thing. A small foyer sat beyond that door, so it didn't take long for Ace to appear. "Ready?" he asked. "They just did the surprise at the homestead, and they're literally seconds behind me."

"I'm ready," she said, sweeping her hand toward the buffet. "Look."

"Were you taking a picture?" he asked, noticing her phone. "Do you want me to take one with you in it?"

"Yes," she said. "By the desserts, okay?" She quickly swept the wispy hair off her face and debated removing her apron. In the end, she left it on. It showed the wear and tear of her work in the kitchen, and a chef should display their apron in any picture they took.

She pressed one hip into the buffet and away from the camera, as per Bethany Rose's posing instructions. She knew she carried more weight than other women with hot cowboy boyfriends, but she didn't mind that much. She thought her curves were beautiful, and she didn't want a man who didn't feel the same way she did about her body.

Besides, she didn't trust a skinny chef.

She did want to look good in pictures, though, and Bethany Rose had taught her how to put her weight away from the camera to hide their thick Broadbent behinds and accentuate their better features.

"Gorgeous," Ace said, stepping over to her and turning the phone so she could see it. "If I didn't hear my brother's voice right now, I'd kiss you again."

Holly Ann took her phone, her smile in the picture just as happy as the one still on her face. "Later, cowboy," she promised, and then she headed for the kitchen. "I'll be in here if you need anything. I'll keep an eye on the food from a distance."

That was the mark of a great caterer, and Holly Ann wasn't under any delusion that she was at this party as anything other than the woman who'd done the food.

She'd barely made it through the door when the noise level increased. Men and women talked and laughed, and she heard the moment when they entered the hall and found everything set and ready.

A rousing round of *Happy Birthday* filled the air, and Holly Ann dared to move back to the doorway to watch the Glover clan celebrate one of their revered members. She caught sight of Ace standing next to his mother, one arm linked through hers as he sang his heart out. He grinned and laughed when the song ended, and nearly everyone else clapped.

Ward stood on their mother's other side, and it was him who took her carefully to her seat. She sat right next to Lois Glover, and the two of them clasped hands. They clearly shared a special bond, and Holly Ann knew exactly what that looked like and felt like.

She had that with her sister and father. In fact, she couldn't wait to get back in her car and head down to town. She'd call Bethany Rose first, because that would be the longest conversation and she could end it when she pulled into her garage. Then she'd call Daddy and tell him she did the brave thing and told Ace how she felt.

He'd congratulate her and warn her not to go too fast with the man. He'd suggest she have him come pick her up at her childhood home, where he still lived, so he could meet Ace. She'd laugh and say no.

He'd make her promise that when Ace fell in love with her and wanted to marry her, that she'd make him come ask him for permission. Holly Ann would promise him and then she'd go inside, sigh, and flop down on the couch to relive the afternoon, starting with that very first kiss she'd shared with Ace....

"Amen," chorused through the barn, and Holly Ann hadn't even realized they'd welcomed everyone and said grace already. She sometimes lost a lot of time to her fantasies, another thing she was trying to tame. She failed at that too, but so far, it hadn't caused her anything too damaging.

"Maybe we can get her to come tell us what it all is," Etta said. "That's all I'm saying. That's what we do."

"No," Ace argued. "That's what *you* do. I was in charge of the food, and it's here. You can't look at it and see what it is?"

"Just ask her," Bishop said, and Holly Ann peeked out

of the doorway. "It looks amazing, and maybe Mother would like to know if any of it is spicy."

"Fine," Ace grumbled, and he turned toward the kitchen door. Holly Ann caught his eye and he gestured for her to come join him. "They want a quick run-down of the food."

Holly Ann looked out at the sea of men and women. Definitely way more men here than women, though a few dotted the crowd. She swallowed, because women tended to like her food more than men.

Customer service, she recited to herself while she hitched her smile in place. "Sure thing," she said, trying to tame her accent into something softer. "Ace said his aunt used to make an amazing hot meatball sandwich. So, because it's her birthday—" She paused and smiled at Lois Glover, who beamed back at her with the brightest pair of blue eyes Holly Ann had ever seen on a person. "I made a menu surrounding hot meatball sandwiches. So you've got the buns for those here. They're not terribly spicy, but they are made with pork, beef, and veal. They're slow-roasted and then slathered with homemade marinara sauce with a secret ingredient."

She continued to perform as she went through the rest of the menu, which was fairly basic fare for a meatball sandwich. "For a hot item, we have butter-lemon asparagus. There are three cold items, as it's summertime. This is a creamy cucumber salad. Very cool with mint and sour cream. It's perfect to put right on top of the meatballs, if you dare." She grinned out at everyone, noticing several other smiles.

"This is a classic green salad with plenty of veggies, and an Italian balsamic vinaigrette. Ace said Aunt Lois loves balsamic, so I made a reduction of it and that's over vine-ripened tomatoes and fresh mozzarella cheese chunks in a family-style Caprese salad. And lastly, there's a kale and broccoli salad with a creamy dressing that has craisins and sunflower seeds in it."

She moved down the buffet to her personal favorite part—dessert. "Aunt Lois loves coconut, I heard, so your choices for dessert are coconut cream pie. I understand Uncle Stone used to make this for your birthday every year, Lois, and I figured it would be okay if I tried my hand at it." She smiled at the older woman, the gesture wobbling when Lois Glover wiped her face as if she were crying. Her sons rallied behind her, and Holly Ann took her enthusiasm down a notch as she read the crowd.

She met Arizona's eyes, and while they didn't know each other well, Arizona nodded and smiled at Holly Ann, so she continued.

"There's a traditional chocolate birthday cake. It has five layers and is infused with a bit of coconut cream. And there are coconut Rocky Road brownies, which have marshmallows, plenty of chocolate—Ace said y'all are addicted to chocolate—and the addition of toasted coconut."

She surveyed her buffet again, her pride surging one more time. This was an amazing menu, and she needed to make notes of the prep it had taken, as well as the timing of the items to get them all out on time, hot things hot and cold things cold.

"I'd get one of these first," she said. "They're that delicious. In fact." She used a pair of tongs to pick up a brownie and place it on the delicate dessert plates she'd brought. She walked over to Lois and handed it to her. "Happy birthday, Lois. May it be filled with the love I can feel at this party for the whole year."

She hugged the older woman and stepped back. "Okay, eat. Enjoy. I have more in the kitchen, so I'll keep my eye on everything." With that, she walked into the kitchen and ducked around the corner.

She pressed her back into the wall and wiped the sweat from her forehead. She loved performing like that, but hated it at the same time. It drained her every time, and she needed to remember to pack a hygiene kit from now on. Something with a stick of deodorant, an extra blouse, and plenty of mint gum. Then she could freshen up before she had to present her food.

A presentation didn't happen at every event, but she had been doing them more and more, especially for the custom menus she put together, like this one.

"This is incredible," someone said. Holly Ann didn't know all of the men well enough to distinguish their voices.

"I apologize for thinking you shouldn't have hired her," another man said. "I want to eat all of this."

Holly Ann smiled as the chatter started to overlap and she couldn't hear more than snatches of it. She stepped over to the sink and washed her hands again, then got busy cleaning up the kitchen. She should be completely packed and ready to go by the time they finished eating. Then she could load up and get home. Most people didn't pay her to stay the whole time, and Ace had asked for an hour after the party started.

She looked up as someone entered the kitchen, and she found Lois Glover entering through the doorway. "Hello, ma'am," she said. "Everything okay?"

"No, it is not," she said, coming closer. "I don't have the recipe for these brownies, and I need it." She took the last bite, a smile filling her wrinkled and aged face. "I love them." She took Holly Ann into an embrace. "You are a Godsend, my dear."

"Oh." Holly Ann hugged her back. "Thank you. I can send you the recipe."

"I'd like that." Lois stepped back. "How's your father?"

"He's doing great," Holly Ann said, surprised Lois knew her dad. He wasn't quite as old as Lois, and he'd been single for the last twenty years despite Bethany Rose and Holly Ann telling him he was handsome and should date.

He claimed to have loved Mama too much to ever marry again, but he hadn't even tried. Holly Ann had given up talking to him about it, and they just talked about her sporadic love life now.

"Good." Lois patted her hand. "Now, there's a certain young man out there who would like you to come eat with him."

"Oh, no," Holly Ann said, holding up both hands. "I don't do that."

"I insist," Lois said, and she linked her arm through Holly Ann's. Since she could barely lift that gallon of milk, and with her surprise rendering her usually active vocal cords dormant, Holly Ann found herself getting towed back into the hall.

Ace had an empty spot next to him at the table with his brothers and sisters, and he gestured to her to come fill it.

You're doing all kinds of different things today, she told herself. *What's one more?*

So she filled a plate with her own food and sat down beside Ace. He introduced her to his brother Ward, then Ranger and his wife Oakley, then his twin sisters, Etta and Ida. Ida had her boyfriend with her, and Holly Ann nodded at all of them in turn, lastly Brady Burton, the cop that lived just across the street from her.

He gave her a look that wasn't hard to read, and Holly Ann dropped her eyes to her plate. He'd said she'd fit in soon enough, and that he knew how hard it was to show up with this family and not feel out of place.

That was exactly how Holly Ann felt, and she knew Brady had been dating Ida for a while now.

Then Ace put his hand on her knee under the table and squeezed, and Holly Ann suddenly fit right there at his side.

"All right," Bear Glover said. "Mother, we have a gift for you."

Holly Ann watched as he presented Lois with a carefully wrapped package. She fussed over the ribbon, finally untying it and peeling back the paper.

She looked up at the sight of the book, her eyes bright. "Children?"

"It's the love letters, Mother," Bishop blurted out,

hurrying forward. "We found them in that old cabin Daddy liked to hang out in."

Lois looked down at the book and opened it. She pulled in a sharp breath and traced one finger lovingly down the page. "Oh, my goodness. Stone."

The whole room held its breath, and Holly Ann enjoyed the presence of love and peace that came with this loud family.

"We think he was working on that cabin while he was gathering all of these for you," Cactus said. "That's why they were there. And then at some point, someone just shoved them in the wall, where Bishop and Montana found them."

Lois nodded as she turned the page, and Ace leaned toward Holly Ann. "They're letters from her husband." His soft, warm voice made her shiver, and Holly Ann nestled a little closer to Ace, where she'd like to stay for a good, long while.

Chapter Nineteen

Montana folded the top of the brown bag while Aurora sprayed herself with sunscreen on the back porch. She came inside and tucked the can inside her backpack.

"Here you go, sweetie." Montana handed her the lunch she'd packed, and Aurora put that in her backpack too. "What else do you need? Did you get your water bottle?"

"I got it," she said. "Sunscreen. I have my wallet. I have my phone and a battery. My lunch." She ticked things off on her fingers as she said them. "I think I'm ready."

She was starting at Bowman's Breeds that morning, and Montana's nerves had been buzzing for weeks.

After the emotional day in the barn and then the cemetery, she'd taken a few days to gather her emotions before she'd spoken to Aurora about the solution to getting up to Bowman's Breeds—and that Oliver was really a Walker.

Aurora had admitted that yes, he was. Not only that,

but she'd been to Seven Sons Ranch several times over the past few months as she spent time with Oliver. She liked Tripp and Liam, and they'd been teaching her how to ride a horse, which was one of Oliver's absolute favorite things to do.

Montana had cried after the conversation, not during it. Since then, though, Aurora told her a lot more about Oliver. She said when she kissed him, and she told Montana if she was at Seven Sons or Oliver's house. Oliver came to their house quite often, and in fact, Montana had invited him and his family for the Fourth of July barbecue that Uncle Bob did every year.

And they were coming.

She was hosting a Walker at the house where she lived.

When she looked at herself in the mirror now, she didn't even know the woman looking back at her. She wore happiness in her eyes in a way Montana had never done before—at least not for a long time.

She could smile with a simple text that had Bishop Glover's name on it.

She didn't hate anyone, even her ex-husband who had inflicted so much pain upon her. For some reason, the Lord had taken that burden the easiest, and Montana barely carried any thought of Johnny anymore.

She and Aurora had talked about him, and Aurora said the same thing. "I don't even think about him, Mom. I don't need him."

Montana feared she might need a father one day, and she didn't want it to be Johnny Martin. She'd started thinking that perhaps it could be Bishop Glover, but they were moving slow, just as she'd said she needed to.

She still saw him on a daily basis. They sat beside one another at church every week. He kissed her every chance he got. But they were not talking about marriage and diamonds and where they'd live once all of that happened. He was dealing with family issues himself, and Montana still had a long way to go to be the woman she wanted to be when she finally put on a white dress and walked down an aisle toward another man.

Someone knocked on the door, and Aurora spun toward it. "That's probably Ollie." She grabbed her backpack and hurried through the kitchen. Montana followed her, but she didn't try to go quickly.

It was Ollie, and Aurora let him into the house just as Aunt Jackie came into the hall. "Good morning," she said pleasantly to Oliver.

"Ma'am," he said, tipping his hat at Jackie. He met Montana's eye, and his lit up. "Morning to you too, Montana. Ma'am." He swallowed but kept his smile hitched in place.

"Good morning, Oliver." She smiled at him, because she genuinely liked the boy. He really was well-mannered and well-spoken.

"Uncle Wyatt said he's two minutes out," Oliver said. "Should we wait on the porch?"

"Sure," Aurora said, opening the door again.

Montana did hurry forward then. She gathered her daughter into a hug and slung one arm around Oliver too. "You guys be careful up there, okay?"

"We will, Mom," Aurora said.

"Work hard," she said next. "You're working with adults who expect you to listen and do what you're told. You're working with animals who deserve your respect." She stepped back and cocked her eyebrows at the pair of them. "This isn't summer camp or some sort of ranch date."

"Mom," Aurora said.

"No, ma'am," Oliver said. "You're right. We'll work hard."

"Be polite."

"Mom, stop it."

"I won't," Montana said, actually enjoying her daughter's embarrassment. "Remember who's name you carry. It's mine, Aurora. I might have a job at Three Rivers one day, and I don't want them whispering about how my daughter wasn't a hard-working, perfectly polite, absolute joy to work with."

"Mom."

"And your family surely expects something from you, Oliver," she said, looking at him.

"They sure do," he said. "We'll be polite."

"Perhaps you two could keep working there if you do a good job this summer," Montana said. "Never underestimate the value of connections."

"We won't, Mom," Aurora said, her eyes bright. She stepped into Montana and hugged her again. "I love you."

"Love you too, baby," Montana whispered. She nodded at Oliver, who smiled at her. "If you guys get a lunch, call me. I don't think I can stand to wait until tonight to hear how it's going."

"Okay." With that, Aurora stepped outside, with Oliver following her. He closed the door behind him, but it stuck, and it didn't latch all the way.

"She's so embarrassing," Montana heard Aurora say.

"Nah," Oliver said. "She's great, Rory. I like her a lot."

"I know," Aurora said while Montana thought *Rory? Who in the devil is Rory?*

"You're lucky you have her," Oliver said, and Montana pressed her face against the crack in the door, hoping to see them. She couldn't. "My step-dad gave me the same lecture on the way over. My mom did it over breakfast. They just care about us, and they want the best for us."

Oh, this Oliver was wise too. Good-looking. Charming. Hard-working. Smart. Well-spoken. And wise.

No wonder Aurora was head-over-heels for him, and Montana started to pray that he wouldn't break her daughter's heart. But they were fifteen. Broken hearts were inevitable at that age, weren't they?

"There's Uncle Wyatt."

Montana opened the door then and stepped out onto the porch as the teens went down the steps. Wyatt pulled parallel to the house and rolled down his window. "Morning, Montana."

"Thank you, Wyatt," she called to him, waving one hand above her head.

"I'll keep my eye on 'em," he said as they went around to get in on the passenger side. "I've got your number. You've got mine."

"Yep."

He waved then, and with everyone loaded, off they

went. Montana watched until the truck turned, and she couldn't see it anymore. "Dear Lord," she said aloud, but she couldn't continue the prayer. God knew what she wanted—protection, safety, help, blessings.

"Come on, darling," Aunt Jackie said. "You haven't even had your coffee yet, and you've got to get up to Shiloh Ridge. It's the last day of painting at the Ranch House, and then you'll get to install your cabinets."

Montana let her aunt guide her inside and serve her coffee and cinnamon-sugar toast. She hugged Uncle Bob as he rushed out to the store, and then she got in her truck and headed up to the ranch that had been a saving grace for her these past few months.

Not only was Bishop paying her a whole lot more than her daily rate, but she got to see her boyfriend every day. She got to feed off the energy of the land. She got to watch the cowboys work and realize how much she loved Texas, her country, and God, just like all of them.

She got to see Bear dote on Sammy, and she'd watched Ranger take soup up to Oakley when she wasn't feeling well. She'd watched him leave the ranch to check on his wife at the dealership she owned when she went back to work after her bout with the flu.

She loved the examples of good living and caring about others she saw at Shiloh Ridge.

And she got to do what she'd trained and loved to do more than anything—build. Design cabinets and pantries, then make them come to life out of flat planks of wood.

Bishop had given her free rein with the Ranch House, and she'd redone the entire bottom floor layout simply because she could. He'd said she could put it in her portfolio, and she was absolutely going to do that.

She hadn't tried to get another job yet, though she knew her time at Shiloh Ridge was going to end soon. Probably not for another month or two, but soon enough.

She'd need something else, despite the small nest-egg she had in her bank account now.

Her website for Montana Home Designs was functional, and she could add pictures from the Ranch House and really start to get her name out there. Perhaps she could pick up a job of her own, redesigning and then building that design for a family in Three Rivers. Perhaps she wouldn't have to go from ranch to ranch, knocking on doors and asking if they had any work for her.

She hadn't heard about the library bid either, and she needed to check the deadline on that. "Probably should've heard something by now," she told herself as she turned off the highway and onto the road she knew by heart at this point.

"Guide me," she prayed to the Lord. "I'll work anywhere, and if that's another ranch, help me get there. If it's a project for my own company, that's okay too." she took the road that led around a portion of the ranch to the house overlooking the town of Three Rivers. She loved the view up here, and she imagined God on His throne on high, looking down over the inhabitants of the world.

"Keep my daughter safe," she added to her prayer. "If possible and according to Thy will, Lord, keep Aurora safe in every sense of the word."

The road arced, and she couldn't see the town anymore.

"And bless Bishop, and Bear, and Ranger, and Ace. Ward, and Cactus, and Mister, Judge, and Preacher. Bless the cowboys who work up here. Bless Lois and Dawna Glover. Bless them all, please. I don't know what they need, but You do. They're good people, and I just want them to be happy. If You can, please."

Her mind churned, and Montana realized who she was thinking about now.

Tears filled her eyes. "And I know I haven't prayed for my mother in a while, but if You could watch over her too, that would be nice." Her heart pittered, sending a scattered beat through Montana's chest.

She literally felt the weight she'd carried on her spine for years release. "Thank you," she said, her tears spilling down her cheeks. "Thank you, Lord, for taking that burden."

She pulled up to the house, and while she was several minutes late, she took another one to send a quick text to her mother. *Love you, Mom. I hope you're okay. Let me know if you're not, and I'll see if I can help in some way.*

Looking up, she studied the outside of the house. From this view, no one would know the mess it was inside, or how long it had been under construction. She felt so much like it. On the outside, she looked put together and whole. On the inside, the Lord had been working on her constantly for a decade now. She looked back at the phone and sent the text, feeling a whole portion of her chest coming together just like that.

Fixed.

Done.

Relief filled her, and Montana got out of her truck and stuck her phone in her back pocket. She had the distinct realization that most people were exactly like her—no matter how perfect they seemed from the outside, on the inside, the Lord was working on them too. Everyone, everywhere, was in a constant state of construction. Some were a little closer to being restored, while others had just had everything knocked down so it could be rebuilt.

"That's right," a man yelled as he came out the front door. He nearly plowed into Montana, but she jumped out of the way just in time. She didn't even think Mister had seen her.

He pounded down the steps she'd just come up as someone else yelled, "You can't just move out."

"Yes, I can!" Mister yelled. "I'm not livin' with you anymore, Judge." He stormed over to his truck and stood on the rudder to climb in. He paused there as Judge came out of the house. He rose above the truck and wore a perfect mask of rage. "In fact, I hope I never have to talk to you again!"

With that, he got in his truck, slammed the door so hard Montana cringed, and started the vehicle. It roared as he stomped on the gas as he backed up. He laid on the horn as he drove away, and Judge said, "You're such an infant, Mister," in a cruel, cruel voice Montana didn't think he'd want anyone to hear.

Montana wished she could make herself very small so she could disappear into the windows behind her.

She couldn't, so when Judge turned around to return to the house, he looked right at her. "Hi," she said weakly.

"Bishop isn't here yet," Judge said, frowning as he strode back into the house. He slammed that door too, and Montana took that, along with his statement about Bishop not being there, as him saying, *don't come in until he is.*

Montana sighed and sat down on the top step of the porch. She could overlook the town from here, and she gazed down on it as her pulse calmed. Yep, everyone was just in some state of disrepair on the inside, no matter how put-together they were on the outside.

I'M HEADING IN NOW. I'LL CALL WITH AN UPDATE afterward. Montana sent the text to the group with Aunt Jackie, Uncle Bob, and Aurora in it and looked at Bishop. "I'm ready."

"You gonna text your mom?"

"Oh, right." Montana kept forgetting that things between her and her mother had improved over the past month, since she'd found a way to pray vocally for her and then text her. Her mother had texted back, and while they weren't sharing deep thoughts or feelings yet, they were speaking. That was something.

She sent a quick text to her mother about the meeting for the bid finalists for the library. With that done, she faced the current library, and it was a sad, little blue building in an older part of town. It looked like it had once been a house, and Montana wouldn't doubt that for a moment.

"It's going to be great," Bishop said. "You're one of the

top three. Even if you don't get it, that's a huge compliment."

"Yes," she said absently, trying to gather her strength and courage together. She'd debated dressing up for this meeting tonight, but in the end, she'd just put on a clean pair of jeans and a top with red, pink, and yellow flowers splashed across it.

"Go on, now," Bishop said, plenty of cowboy drawl in his voice. "I'll be right here when you're done."

She looked at him, an extreme sense of gratitude and adoration pouring through her. "Thank you, Bishop." She leaned toward him and found the last of her strength as he kissed her. "Go have fun with your mother."

"See you in an hour."

Montana got out of the truck and went inside the library. It wasn't hard to find the sign with a huge arrow and the words *conference room*. She went that way, pausing outside the only door in this short hallway.

"Whatever Thy will is, I will be okay," she whispered. "But I'd really like to get this design and build." It would catapult her to the top of the list of builders in Three Rivers. Everyone would know she'd designed and built the library, and thousands of people would use it. "I've worked my whole life for this."

So had a lot of other people, Montana knew. Just because she'd worked hard didn't mean everyone else hadn't. Her hard work didn't make her more deserving.

Bishop was right; even if she didn't get the bid, getting selected as one of the three finalists was a huge honor.

She opened the door and walked in, already scanning to

see who else was there. Her eyes landed on Micah Walker, and her heart plummeted to the ground.

Yes, Wyatt had been driving Aurora to Bowman's Breeds for about a month now. She liked Wyatt. He always had a smile and a laugh, and once he'd brought Montana a loaf of bread from his wife Marcy.

She'd hosted Oliver and his family at her aunt's house for the Fourth of July, and that had gone really well too. Tripp Walker was kind and actually somewhat soft-spoken. He wasn't Oliver's biological father, but he treated Ollie as his own. They acted the same. They spoke the same. They even wore the same hat—one of Wyatt's signature pieces, she'd learned.

Montana had been giving her burdens to the Lord for a couple of months now, and while she still wasn't quite to the place of forgiving her sisters, she'd been learning more and more about the Walkers, getting to know a couple of them, and she knew they weren't bad people.

Micah Walker didn't even know what he'd done to Montana's business. To her confidence. For him, he just wanted to start his own construction firm, same as her. The difference was, he had a lot more money and a lot more connections than Montana did.

He rose to his feet, his smile wide and instant. "Montana Martin," he said, his voice kind and deep and full of joy. "Micah Walker." He extended his hand toward her, and she found herself returning his grin as she shook his hand.

Her eyes went to the other man in the room. He wore a dark suit, and Montana did not recognize him, which meant he represented a big firm. He wouldn't get the job;

the library board and City Council would want it to go to a local.

She now had a fifty-fifty chance of getting it.

"Nice to meet you," she finally said to Micah. "I've heard a lot about you, as I'm sure you can imagine." She smiled again. "Wyatt drives my daughter to work with him, and my daughter is dating your nephew, Oliver."

"I've heard," Micah said, pulling out a chair for her. "In fact, I've met your daughter several times. She's real good with babies. Did you know that?" He smiled at her.

Montana's smile slipped. "I didn't know that. I know she's been to Seven Sons several times."

"We live right across the lane from the main ranch," he said. "My wife sometimes sits on the front porch with our fussy boy. Aurora took him once, and she had him laughing before she even left the driveway." He chuckled. "My wife said we should hire her to babysit, but we have so much family, we haven't needed to do that yet."

"Mm," Montana said, wondering if she'd let Aurora go babysit for the man she'd had ill feelings for over the course of at least a year. Maybe longer.

He's a nice guy, she thought. *How do I release these?*

"Hey, I wanted to talk to you," he said. "I gave Ollie my card to give to you ages ago, but he never did it." Micah cleared his throat, and Montana looked back at him. He wore nervousness in his expression, which completely took her by surprise.

"Your card?"

"I've heard nothing but good things about you," he said. "I thought maybe we could partner on some projects." He handed her a card then, and Montana switched her gaze to it, still too surprised to even read it.

Slowly, her wits returned, and she tucked the card away. It felt too heavy to hold as it was. "You have too much work, is that it?"

"I do okay," he said evasively. "But really, I'd rather design and then hire out as much of the work as possible. I'm good with cupboards and cabinets and things like that, but I have a family now, and I...." He cleared his throat again and this time, he leaned closer to her before he spoke. "I promised my wife I wouldn't work so much."

Montana had no idea what to say. "Your wife."

"Mm." Micah grinned and looked at the door as a woman walked in. "In fact, if I get this, I'm gonna have to turn it down or face a divorce." He stood up and grinned at the woman. "Howdy, Melissa."

He sure was working the library director for a job he wouldn't even take.

Montana did not want to get the job because Micah Walker refused it.

She shook Melissa Dailey's hand too and when she sat next to Micah again, he said, "I'd love to work with you. Again, I've heard nothing but good things, and your website shows real talent."

"Thank you," Montana said. "I'm most familiar with the homestead you did for the Glovers, and it's beautiful. The best work and design I've seen in a long time." She meant that compliment too, because Micah *had* done beautiful work at Shiloh Ridge.

His face lit up. "That was one of my first projects," he said. "I *love* that place. Love it."

"It shows in the work," she said. "That's what some people are missing. The love of the build."

"Not you," he said seriously.

"I do love the build," she said with a smile. "I'm seriously considering your offer, Mister Walker. I'm great with the build, but I'm still working on my designs."

"Yeah?" He possessed a boyish charm that Montana actually liked.

"Yeah," she said. "I'm working up at Shiloh Ridge these days, but we should go to lunch or I'll just stop by your place one day on my way home. We can talk more about this partnership you're thinking about."

Micah started to laugh, and she wasn't sure what she'd said that was so funny. "The Lord works in mysterious ways," he said, still chuckling.

"What do you mean?" Montana asked as another man walked through the door.

"I mean, I wasn't going to come tonight, but something kept telling me to be here." He gestured between the two of them. "Now I know why. I was meant to speak with you tonight."

"Thank you for coming," Melissa said. "Some of you probably know Councilman Scott. He's part of the library board this year, so I wanted him here."

Montana sat on the edge of her seat, every muscle tense. Would they announce who'd won the bid tonight? Need more information? The email she'd received had been quite vague on that point.

As Harold Scott started to drone, Montana's mind wandered back to Micah Walker. Not only was he a nice guy, he was an upstanding man. He'd done nothing wrong. The only person she was hurting with her bitterness and resentment was herself.

Please take this jealousy from me, she thought. *I have no need for it anymore. He doesn't deserve my resentment or bitterness or ill will either.*

The meeting continued, and when it ended, Montana shook hands all around, promised Micah she'd call and set something up, and hurried out to the parking lot. She had so much to tell everyone, and she couldn't wait to share her news with Bishop first.

Chapter Twenty

Bishop got out of the truck when he saw Montana burst through the library doors. She ran toward him, laughter trailing on the air behind her. "She got it," he whispered, his thoughts flying to the prayer he and Mother had given together.

"You got it," he said, jogging toward her too.

"I got it!" She squealed and launched herself at him. Bishop caught her in his arms and laughed as she did. "I got it, Bishop. Free and clear, I got it." He set her down and peered down at her.

"I knew you'd get it."

She wiped her hair out of her face, panting. "I can't believe it. Micah Walker was in there." She hooked her thumb over her shoulder just as the man walked out the doors.

"I see 'im," Bishop said.

"That's my second piece of news," she said, turning him away from Micah. "I got rid of my resentment for him. He's actually nice, and he would've never hurt me or my business on purpose."

Bishop smiled at Montana. She'd changed so much, and yet she was exactly the same woman he'd first met while she stood on his front porch and asked for a job.

"I'm not jealous anymore."

"Congratulations again, Montana," Micah called, and Bishop looked at him. "Oh, hey, Bishop." Micah detoured over to them, and Bishop slipped his hand into Montana's for Micah to see. "How's Bear?"

"He's great," Bishop said. "How's Jeremiah?"

"Oh, you know Jeremiah," Micah said with a smile. "Since the fire, he's gone all crazy about rules and frankly, I'm surprised Skyler hasn't killed him yet. There are count-less places to hide a body on that ranch." He laughed, and Bishop and Montana joined in.

"Hey, thanks for that number for the counselor," Bishop said, glancing at Montana. "We've put it to good use."

Micah looked between Bishop and Montana. "Yeah? You two? Doing marriage counseling before you get married?"

"What?" Bishop asked. "No."

"Not that," Montana said, looking up at Bishop with questions in her eyes.

"Yeah, well, it's not a bad idea," Micah said. "I wish Simone and I would've done it." He chuckled. "Then again, we got married during an audition and didn't even know it for three weeks. So. Probably wouldn't have worked out anyway."

"You what?" Montana asked, plenty of incredulity in her voice.

"I have not heard this story," Bishop said, intrigued.

"I'll tell y'all about it when we meet." He checked his phone. "I'm late. Sorry, I have to go." He walked away, with Bishop and Montana staring after him.

"We're meeting with him?" Bishop asked.

"Another bit of news," Montana said. "He asked me to do some partner work with him, and we're going to meet to talk about it."

Bishop could only stare at her. "How long were you in there?"

She laughed, and Bishop did love the joy coming from her. She'd been happy before, but this was a new level of that happiness. He fell further in love with her, and Bishop was pretty sure he was well below the line to consider himself able to say *I love you*, but he hadn't said it.

She'd wanted to go slow, and he'd agreed. He wasn't going to bring up marriage until she did. In fact, Bishop had decided not to bring up any serious topics until she'd broached marriage. None of the others mattered if they weren't going to get married.

In his mind, he could already see them married, living on the ranch somewhere with Aurora, and blissfully happy. They'd design their house together, and build it together, and live in it until the day they died. They'd be buried in the Glover family cemetery, and Bishop could imagine it all.

"Let's go to dinner," she said, tugging on his hand.

"Yes," he said, trying to focus on reality. He took her to The Rooftop Garden, which was one huge buffet of gourmet foods. Just their wall of desserts was worth the high price tag, in Bishop's opinion.

She talked about her family first, and then the bid, and then how far she'd come on her spiritual journey toward relying more on the Lord and releasing the burdens she'd been carrying herself for so long.

"I'm real proud of you, sweetheart," he said as he pulled up to her house. "You're so inspiring."

"Not really," she said, sobering now and reverting to her more normal, quiet self. "Someone inspiring would've been able to just go, 'take it all, Lord,' and move on. I've been working for months now."

"You're working on it," he said. "That's what's amazing." He had a few things to work on himself, but his progress was a lot slower than hers.

"How's your self-care going?" she asked.

"Good," he said. "And the counselor was for Cactus, though if you ever tell him I told you that, I'll deny it." He meant it too, but he chuckled anyway.

"You love Cactus," she said simply.

"Very much," Bishop said, looking at the light coming from the windows. "You want to sit in the swing for a bit?"

"Sure," she said, and she got out of the truck and met him at the corner of the hood. She took his hand and led him up the steps and across the porch to the swing there.

He sighed as he sat down, letting the country stillness seep through him. "We need more swings at Shiloh Ridge," he said. "This is real nice." He toed them forward and back, happy to have her curled into his side, a full stomach, and a beautiful summer night in Texas.

"Bishop?" she asked.

"Yeah, baby?"

"Remember how you asked me once if I wanted more children?"

He tensed, his foot stuttering along the surface of the porch. "Yes."

"If the man I fell in love with wanted children of his own—my children, *our* children—I'd have them if I could."

Bishop smiled into the gathering darkness and tucked her tighter into his side. He was definitely in love with Montana Martin, and he definitely wanted his children to be her children. He kept all of that to himself for now, and when it was time for him to head back to the ranch, he stood on Montana's porch and kissed her like a man in love with her.

He wouldn't have to say *I love you* out loud, because surely, she could feel it in every stroke of his mouth against hers.

BISHOP PASSED LINCOLN ON THE STEPS AS THE BOY streaked down them, in hot pursuit of his dog. "Give that back!" he yelled after Benny, and Bishop laughed. That dog loved socks, and he would not give it back without a significantly tasty treat in return.

At the top of the steps, Sammy smiled at him. "Hello, Bishop."

"Hey, Sammy."

"He's all yours this afternoon." She patted his chest. "Good luck. He's not in a great mood."

"Great," Bishop said darkly. "Why didn't you sweeten him up for me?"

"I'm perfectly sweet," Bear said. "Have fun with your parents, love." He cocked his head as Lincoln continued to yell at his dog to drop the sock. "What's that about?"

"Nothing," Sammy said. "I'll take care of it. Have fun with Bishop."

"Thanks again, Sammy," Bishop said as she went down the steps, one hand lightly on the bannister. He faced his brother, who certainly didn't look sweet as he came out of the suite and looked over the railing. "Benny stole a sock."

"Of course he did," Bear said, and he didn't sound sweet either. Maybe Bishop should abort this mission. Just as quickly as he'd thought it, he dismissed the idea. He'd been putting this off long enough as it was.

"C'mon in," Bear said. "I have chocolate ice cream."

"Perfect." Bishop followed his brother into the suite where he'd once lived. The space was completely different now, as a family lived there now. All the bedrooms got used. The living room. Even the kitchenette, where Bear had two bowls and two spoons beside a thawing container of chocolate ice cream.

He started to scoop the treat, and Bishop almost lost his nerve for a second time. *Who are you kidding?* he asked himself. This would be about the fiftieth time he'd lost his nerve.

"Bear," he said. "I have to say some stuff, and I just want you to listen to the end, okay?"

Bear paused and looked at Bishop. "Okay," he said slowly.

Bishop ducked his head, though he should be brave enough to have a face-to-face conversation with his brother. "I did resent you for a long time after Daddy died."

Bear pulled in a breath, and Bishop looked up. "Sometimes, I still look at you, and I wonder why you get everything you want. Why your life seems so perfect when I can't get a woman to call me back, and when I can't seem to catch a break, and when I'm an emotional mess but you're just fine."

"Literally none of what you just said is true," Bear said.

"I know," Bishop said. "Montana has this whole speech about outward appearances. I know it's not true. I know you and Sammy didn't hit it off right away. I know Daddy's letter devastated you." Bishop shook his head. "I don't know what I'm saying. I think, for me sometimes, you're perfect, and I wish I could be you. That's hard on me."

"What do I need to do?"

"Nothing," Bishop said quickly. "This is nothing about you. This is about me, and me trying to clear the air between us. But it's air I've poisoned, not you."

"It has to have something to do with me," Bear said. "Or else why would you bring it up?" He pushed one of the bowls of ice cream toward Bishop, and he put a spoon in his bowl and joined Bishop at the tiny bar. The two of them took up all the available space, and Bishop reached into his pocket and withdrew his letter.

He smoothed it out and set it between him and Bear. "Read it."

"Oh, I don't know, Bish. I might not be able to handle it."

"I've read it so many times, I have it memorized," Bishop said. "The creases I put in it were starting to rip, so I typed it up again, so I'd always have it."

"Good idea," Bear said. "I really don't need to read it, Bishop. I'm sorry if I've—"

"It's not you," Bishop said, sighing. This wasn't going the way he'd hoped it would. "In my letter, Daddy says to always make sure I'm being honest with myself and honest with everyone else. He said that honesty and integrity would become attached to me, and people everywhere would know my name for those traits." Bishop's throat closed slightly, but he was going to see this through to the end.

He thought of Montana—his beautiful, kind, strong Montana—and all the hurdles she'd overcome already in her own spiritual and emotional healing.

"He said to pay special attention to my relationship with you, Bear, because I would need it. He's right. I need it. He said to always come to you and confess how I felt, to make sure the air between us is clear, even if it's through no fault of yours."

Bishop picked up his letter and refolded it. "So I don't need you to do anything. I guess you'll have to listen to me when I need to come to confess to you."

Bear took a bite of his ice cream, and said, "I suppose I can do that."

Bishop swirled his spoon through the melting mess in his bowl. "I've been afraid to come talk to you, because you have been having a hard time this summer."

"You can always come to me."

"I've been afraid, because sometimes it feels like you don't have room for me anymore. You have Sammy now, and Lincoln, and you *should* be focusing on them." Bishop looked at him. "But how many times did we plan to go to the cemetery before we did?"

"Several," Bear admitted.

"How many times did you cancel because of Lincoln or Sammy?"

"Several," Bear said again. "I'm sorry, Bishop. I didn't realize that upset you."

"I didn't either," he said. "Our family is changing." And Bishop wasn't entirely happy about it. "I just miss you, I think. Like I said, it's my problem. You should be devoted to your family. Of course they come before me."

"Change is always hard," Bear said. "I don't think you're the only one who feels this way."

"No?"

Bear shook his head. "Mother texted me the other day

that just because I was married now didn't mean I could ignore everyone."

"You don't ignore everyone," Bishop said.

"I didn't think so either, but it doesn't really matter what I think. If someone feels like that, it probably has some merit." Bear finished his ice cream and got up to get more. "Sammy and I do eat up here quite often. The kitchen is just so loud, and we're tired. I'm old, and she just carries a lot of stress."

"You're not that old."

"Yes, I am," Bear said. "Forty-six is almost fifty, Bishop. Things happen to a person at forty that you don't understand yet." He smiled like he couldn't wait until Bishop experienced these "things that happen at forty."

Bishop took a deep breath. "My letter says to be appreciative too," he said. "Out loud. That people need to hear how appreciated they are, and I wanted you to know that I appreciate you, Bear. You did take me in when Daddy died, and I was so lost...." He trailed off, because memories from the days and months following his father's death rushed through his mind.

"You were the anchor for me in a very dark time," Bishop said. "And I appreciate that. Even now, just when I need something, you're there."

Bear nodded and took his barstool again. "What do you need right now, Bish?"

He took a bite of mostly melted ice cream. "I need you to tell me where I can build a house of my own."

Bear's shock wasn't hard to find. "A house of your own?"

"Well, I can't live with Montana in that one-bedroom suite."

His eyebrows climbed higher. "You're going to marry Montana?"

"Eventually," Bishop said, tapping to wake his phone. "Now, I know there's a house down here, on that other ranch that Daddy bought years ago, but I checked it out already, and it's almost falling down. Plus, there are no trees."

He glanced at Bear, who looked at the map on Bishop's phone. "I was thinking about up here, on the main ranch, behind True Blue."

Bear smiled and shook his head. "Just because you love that barn."

"I do love the barn," Bishop said, not seeing a reason to deny it. "There's room there for a house, and we'd only lose half an acre of hay at the most. Those fields are dormant right now anyway."

"Right at the beginning of the cycle too."

That was as good as a yes, but Bishop wanted to hear his brother say it.

"I'll talk to Ranger about putting it on the agenda," Bear said. "With stuff like this, Bishop, we have to have Cactus and Ward there too. Sometimes it takes a couple of weeks for all four of us to get our schedules to align."

"Okay," Bishop said. "Thank you, Bear."

Bear put his arm around Bishop. "I love you, brother. I honestly am sorry if I have added any poison to the air between us."

"I love you too," Bishop said. "I'm going to try to do

what Daddy said in his letter. I hope it's not too annoying for you."

"I can handle annoying," Bear said. "Just don't expect me to be a teddy about it."

They looked at one another, both of them bursting into laughter in the next moment. Bishop let the healing happiness move through him, and he felt the cleansing touch of the spirit of the Lord too, as his burden of negative feelings for Bear was lifted and carried away.

Chapter Twenty-One

Bear woke to the sound of Sammy humming to herself in the shower. A few times a week, she showered before him so he could sleep later and she could have all the hot water. He loved the sound of the spray as it twined with his wife's voice, and he closed his eyes to listen to it.

The water turned off at some point, waking him again. In the following seconds, Sammy cried out. Bear sat straight up and got out of bed, seemingly in the space of a single breath.

"Sammy?" He started toward the bathroom just as she appeared in the doorway. She wore a towel around her body and one in her hair, and her whole face was filled with light.

"Come see this," she said.

Bear wasn't sure if he should be excited or scared, and his heartbeat kept sprinting nonetheless. He approached her, but she didn't turn to retrieve anything from the bathroom.

"I'm pregnant, Bear," she said, giggling immediately afterward. "I'm late for my period—really late, but I had a touch of that flu Oakley had, and I just thought that was why I was a little sick in the morning. I haven't been throwing up or anything."

She did pace into the bathroom then, but Bear was still trying to process her first few words. He couldn't move and think so hard at the same time.

"And then we had all those parties, and I thought my stomachaches were because of all that rich food or whatever." She appeared in the doorway again, and this time, she held something in her fingers.

"But when I realized I should've had another period by now, I stopped at the store last night and got a pregnancy test." She was talking so fast, and Bear was still back on those first few words.

"It says to take it in the morning, because you know, that's when the hormones are the highest—that's why you're sick. Did you know that? I didn't know that—anyway. I took it and got in the shower, and it says I'm pregnant." She looked down at the stick in her hand and then back to him, her eyes wide.

Bear swept her into his arms, wonder and joy filling him now. "My sweet Sammy," he said. "I'm so excited."

"Are you?"

"Of course I am," he said, pulling back to look at her. "I've always said I wanted kids. We've been trying since we got married."

"It's August," she said. "But like I said, I think I've missed two periods now. I'm probably at least two months along. Which means I'll be due in…March? Maybe end of February."

"We have to go to the doctor today. He'll tell us, right?"

"I can't go today," she said. "I have that meeting this morning, and two cars I said I'd deliver today."

"Sammy," he said. "You're *pregnant*. The cars can wait."

She looked up at him, several emotions flying through her expression. "I'm pregnant."

He whooped and lifted her off her feet. She squealed too, the towel twisted in her hair slipping. "Bear," she laughed.

"You're not even going to work today," he said. "I'm calling the doctor right now." Not that he knew who to call.

"You're crazy," she said. "It's six-fifteen in the morning."

"So I have time to figure out which doctor to call. I think there's a specific kind you see when you're pregnant."

She laughed again, but Bear simply gazed down at her. He loved going to bed with her at his side. He loved waking up to his alarm and looking over to see if he'd disturbed her. He loved everything about Sammy, and while everything wasn't perfect between them, they were both working. They both tried to forgive. They both had honest conversations.

"I love you," he murmured, leaning down to kiss her.

She kissed him back, and Bear found his hand sliding down to her stomach as if he could feel the life there through the towel and all of her skin and muscle. "I can't believe you're going to have my baby," he whispered. "I love you so much. So, so much."

"I love you, too, Bear." She kissed him again, and Bear let himself get lost in the touch and smell and love of this good woman.

***

"THERE HE IS," RANGER SAID WHEN BEAR WALKED INTO the conference room in his suite. "How's it looking out there?"

"Good," Bear said, brushing his hand up the back of his neck again. He needed to shower again already, as cutting hay seemed to get the stuff everywhere. "We've almost got the north and west sections done. Royce is mowing the last field now."

They'd been out working all night, as Bear liked to mow when it was dark, so the fields were ready to dry in the hot August sun the moment it came up. He was getting too old to pull the all-nighters, but he had good men who could do it when he had to stop. He paid double the daily rate for all-night work, and the sign-ups for it never ended.

"I have two, no, three, things to add to the agenda," he said, glancing at Cactus as he sat down. "Hey, Cactus. Haven't seen you for a while."

"Same," Cactus said, a smile actually touching his mouth. "I have something for the agenda too."

"And you guys forgot how to text?" Ranger asked, frowning.

"You know about one of mine," Bear said. "It's the personal item."

"So that's not a new item," Ranger said, his pen poised above the paper. "How many things do you have?"

"I have the personal thing," he said. "And two more things."

"So two things for Bear," he said, making a note. "One for Cactus." He looked across the table to his brother, Ward. "Anything, Ward?"

"No, sir," Ward said, looking up from his phone.

"Let's start with you then," Ranger said. "And we'll move into the things that require all of us. Then you and Cactus can go. I know your time is short this morning."

"I just have that call at ten," Ward said.

Bear glanced at his phone. It was eight-forty-five. He'd been fifteen minutes late, and he instantly regretted it. "Sorry, Ward," he said, but his cousin just waved his hand.

"My only piece of business is the Walker family party at True Blue next weekend. They're bringing all the food and stuff, but they're using our tables and chairs. They said they'd consolidate into as few vehicles as possible, as there's not a ton of parking back there. I'm not worried about it."

"They're great," Ranger agreed. "And we're all going to that?"

"It's right here on our property," Bear said. "I'm planning to take my family." He looked around at the others. "Are we saying it's mandatory attendance?"

"I don't think so," Cactus said. "We don't even have

mandatory attendance for our own family parties. It's not our mother who passed the bar exam."

"Let's send a text so everyone knows they're invited," Ranger said. "Cowboys too." He looked at Ward with his eyebrows raised.

"Sounds good," Ward said. "I know the family wants a count for food by Monday. They're doing their family pictures here on the ranch too. When I talked to Whitney, she said they'd stick to the blue barn and the stables right next to it. They won't go all over the ranch. I didn't see a problem with that, so I agreed."

"I see no problem with that either," Bear said.

"They do have a lot of kids," Ranger said.

"They watch their kids," Bear said, shifting in his seat.

"I'm fine with whatever," Cactus said, clearing his throat. "I'm, uh, bringing a date to the Walker's party."

"Okay, so—" Ranger cut off, his gaze flying to Cactus as his brain caught up with what he'd said. "What?"

"Her name is Violet Hamshire," Cactus said. "We, uh, met at the therapist's office."

Bear leaned forward, his interest in Cactus ultra-focused now. "Is this your thing?"

"Yes," Cactus said. "Ace has been taking me to see a counselor. We go every Friday, which is why this has been hard to set up." He shifted in his seat and looked away, something Cactus rarely did. He knew who he was, and he didn't care if someone disagreed with him. He didn't look away during difficult conversations, and Bear wondered who he was looking at.

"I just moved to every other week," he said. "It's been,

uh, real good for me." He nodded and looked around at the other three men watching him. "Real good."

"That's amazing, Cactus," Ranger said. "Good for you."

"Yeah," Ward said, smiling. "Have you been out with Violet before?"

"Once," Cactus said. "It was a fast lunch date after my appointment. We've been talking a lot through text and calls for a few weeks."

"And you think a giant family party is the best idea for your second date?" Bear asked.

"I figure it can't hurt to expose her to the crazy right up front," Cactus said, grinning at Bear. "Besides, she knows most of the Walker women. She's got, uh, a son the same age as Rhett's oldest boy."

Bear's eyebrows flew up. "She's got a son."

"Yes," Cactus said, looking down now. "No one needs to say anything else, okay? I know what it looks like, and it's not that. I'm *not* trying to replace Allison and Bryce. I'm not."

"Well, maybe Allison," Ranger said gently. "You do want another wife and best friend."

Cactus looked at Ranger, something powerful passing between them. "Yes, I can agree to that."

Ranger nodded and made a check-mark next to something on his agenda. "Ward is good. Cactus is good. Let's talk about Bishop." He looked at Bear. "And your personal item, as they both require us all to be here."

"All of my items require us all to be here," Bear said. "Let's start with the easy stuff. I want to sponsor a booth at the Harvest Festival this year." He looked at Ranger. "An informational booth about Three Rivers, where we'll feature your app."

Ranger's eyes widened. "What? What does that look like?"

"We get signage made," Bear said. "Advertising the app. We can partner with some of the top businesses in town, and they can have reps on-site to answer questions, hand out fliers, give out coupons, or whatever works for them." Bear opened the folder he'd given to Ranger earlier to bring to the meeting. "I've already asked Oakley about having someone from Mack's there." He barely glanced at Ranger, because he wasn't sure if Oakley had spoken to him about it.

"She said yes. Montana is meeting with Micah Walker this week, and they might have a partnership to promote. Either way, she'll be there. Sammy is going to be there for her shop, obviously. I've called Heidi Ackerman, but she said the bakery is going to have their own booth." Bear looked at his list and back up at the others.

"I just went through the app and took the number-one rated businesses. I've got calls out to several people. Tony from Down Under has agreed, and he's bringing samples. Roberto from Pizza Pipeline will be there. I wanted more than restaurants, and I've got a confirmation from Camila Cruz for her plumbing services, as well as Karl Madrid from that custom glass shop."

"Bishop is putting his custom windows in the Ranch House," Ward said. "I was there yesterday while they started the install."

"Exactly," Bear said. "Oh, and Ace's new girlfriend will

be there for her catering company. I'm focusing on locally owned and operated shops and businesses. Montana is asking her uncle to represent the outdoor outfitters, and Holly Ann is asking her boss at the tack and feed store."

"Don't most people know about all of these places?" Cactus asked. "Especially because of Two Cents?"

"It's for advertising," Ranger said quietly. He hadn't looked at Bear during his speech. "Right? You're doing this because Ward and I were talking about offering paid advertising on Two Cents, and it'll be the local businesses who want that space."

Bear grinned at him. "Yep. And I think we should invest in Two Cents for our yearly donation this year."

"That's a conflict of interest," Ranger said.

"Is it?" Bear asked. "Why? We want our money to make more money. Your app is ripe for that, Range. Why can't our money make more money through your app? You win. We win." He looked at Cactus and Ward. "Maybe this is a full-family decision."

"I would think so," Cactus said. "Otherwise, why aren't we investing in Mack's? Or Sammy's shop? Or Montana's home designs? Or Holly Ann's catering? You know? We could invest in Micah's construction firm. Just give money to all of our friends." He looked around at everyone and reached for his bottle of water. "The whole family needs to vote on this one."

"I agree," Ward said.

"Okay," Bear said, frowning. "Can we agree to sponsor the booth at the Harvest Festival?"

No one said anything, which meant none of them

wanted to be the first to say yes or no. Ward and Cactus both looked at Ranger, who stared at Bear with a hard edge in his eyes.

"Fine," Ranger said.

"Okay," Cactus and Ward said together. The tension broke in the room, and all four of them chuckled.

"I want to see everything," Ranger said, tapping Bear's folder. "You should've told me about this before now."

"Sorry," Bear said, but he wasn't really sorry. Ranger wouldn't take the next step for Two Cents if he wasn't prodded a little, and Bear knew how to prod his cousin better than anyone.

"Up next—Sammy is pregnant." He couldn't say those words—or even think them—without grinning from ear to ear. Everyone else grinned at him too, and Bear chuckled and shook his head as the congratulations came at him. "She's due at the end of February, and I want to take time off the ranch."

He swallowed, because he loved Shiloh Ridge with his whole heart and soul. "I'll still be here. I'll still work. But I don't want to mow all night, and I don't want to work from sunup to sundown. I want to enjoy my wife and family." He cleared his throat. "I want to show Lincoln how to ranch, and I want to teach him how to fix tractors and I want him to know how very much he belongs to me, and that this ranch is important to all of us."

He blinked and stopped talking. He nodded. "I want more time to do those things." He looked at Ranger. "I imagine as more and more changes around here, we'll all want to find a better balance between ranch and family."

"I'm sure you can take time off," Cactus said. "Bishop just finished all those cowboy cabins. We have money to hire people."

"Yes," Bear said. "That leads me to the next item. I want to increase the cowboy pay."

Ranger muttered something about having so many big discussions in one meeting, but he gestured for Bear to go on.

"Our men work hard for us. I think we need to include them more in our lives here, and we need to pay them more."

"What brought that on?" Ward asked.

"The overnight mowing," Bear said. "I sent the signup for it, because it's an optional thing, and we offer double the pay. Everyone signed up within ten minutes. They all want the work, because they want the money." He looked at Ranger. "I think we should think about hiring a foreman —maybe two—and providing bigger and better homes for them. That way, they can bring their whole families to live here and work here as *career* cowboys. Not day laborers."

Bear took a deep breath. "I know this is a lot for one meeting, so we can table it for now. But Bishop wants to build a house for himself out by True Blue, and he told me there's a house on that ranch my father bought before he died. There's no reason we can't fix that up—it used to be a homestead for that ranch—and add a couple bigger places down there. Then our foremen can live there. They'd be permanent men or women we hire and treat like family. They'd come to these meetings. They'd essentially do what Ranger and I do, so we can do less. He can work on his app. I can be the husband and father I want to be."

"I'm writing all of this down," Ranger said. "But I do think it too requires a whole family discussion and meeting. Perhaps there's someone in the family who'd be willing to take on more of a leadership role you want to vacate." He nodded at Ward. "Yes?"

"Yes," Ward said.

"You do?" Bear asked.

"I'm not saying I do," Ward said. "I'm saying you and Ranger own the ranch, and you've been running it for fifteen years. If either of you want to turn over some responsibilities, that's great. Fine. But they should be offered to family first."

"I agree," Cactus said quietly. "I do like the idea of having a foreman or two, with a separate place for him to live and raise his family. That's smart."

"I'm tabling this for now," Ranger said. "Let's come back to it next time we can get together." He sighed and flipped his paper over. "I'm going to send a text for a whole family meeting. We'll discuss our investments, as well as this foreman idea."

He consulted his paper again. "No one sees a problem with Bear stepping back once his baby comes. And we're sponsoring a booth at the Harvest Festival." He looked at Bear. "Bishop's house?"

"Right." Bear pulled the printout Bishop had given him from the folder. "Bishop needs a place of his own. He wouldn't come right out and say, but he's pretty serious with Montana. If they get married, they can't live in a one-bedroom suite here in the homestead. He wants to build a place out by True Blue."

He set the map showing the location of it, with the bulleted points Bishop had put together. "We have to sign off on this. We'll lose half an acre of farmland that just entered its first year of rest. He wants to improve the road leading out there, and he'll want to pave and all of that."

"It's fine with me," Cactus said. "All of us might find ourselves in Bishop's position eventually." He looked at Ward. "Right?"

Ward's jaw jumped, and Bear wondered what other conversations had happened that he'd missed. "Right," Ward said.

"I'm fine with it," Ranger said. "I trust Bishop to maintain the integrity of the ranch." He pinned Bear with a glare though. "I am going to add an item of my own real quick, while we're on this topic."

Bear looked steadily back at him. "Go for it."

"I want a shed for my four-wheelers," he said. "I've already spoken to Bishop about it, and he's made some preliminary sketches. There's room right here, between this homestead and Ward's place." He glanced at Ward. "We don't farm that land anyway. It would actually be an addition to the construction and remodeling that needs to be done on the Bull House."

Bear gritted his teeth, his jaw suddenly tight. "We're not using those things here."

"We can store them here without using them," Ranger said. "Oakley is going to sell her house, because it's ridiculous to keep a mansion in town when we live up here."

"Bishop has that measuring app," Cactus said. "I see why we don't want to transition from horses to ATVs, Bear. I do. But there's no reason not to use the advancements the Good Lord has provided for us."

"Bishop has a measuring app?" Bear asked.

"Oh, boy," Ward said. "And we have electricity in the houses too, Bear." He leaned forward, his frustration plain on his face. "I don't want to use ATVs here either. I voted against it, and I would again. But I agree with Ranger—he can store them here. He and Oakley enjoy taking them up on the trails. Heck, I think I would too. There's no reason we can't use them for recreation while still holding true to our roots of using dogs and horses for our herds."

Cactus was nodding, and Bear could see their reasoning.

"Ace and I would like to talk about using apps and programs for our agriculture," Ward said, clearing his throat. "Add that to the list, Ranger. Whole family discussion."

"What kind of apps?" Bear asked.

"They have things to help us rotate fields," Ward said. "To maintain soil pH. To harvest at the most optimal time."

"You have systems for that."

"Yes," Ward said. "But computers and apps think faster than a man can."

Bear couldn't argue with that, especially as Ranger had two computers sitting in front of him and developed apps in his spare time. "Okay," he said, the word grinding through his throat. Bishop had spoken more true than Bear had thought—things *were* changing around Shiloh Ridge.

I trust you beyond measure to take Shiloh Ridge into the future and pass it along to your son or daughter.

He couldn't take Shiloh Ridge into the future by stifling himself—or anyone else—in the past. "I just want the original culture at Shiloh Ridge—I want what Daddy and Uncle Bull built—to be maintained."

"We can do that," Ranger said. "With careful and thoughtful and progressive discussion, among all of us." He looked around at the others. "Maybe we should be scheduling a quarterly family meeting, with everyone."

"I can second that," Cactus said.

"Third," Ward said, and Ranger looked at Bear.

He nodded, and Ranger wrote it down. He looked up and smiled around at everyone. "That's it, men. Good talks today. Real good."

Bear stayed in his seat as the others left, and when it was just him and Ranger, they finally looked at one another. "Who are you thinking for foremen?"

"Ward," Ranger said. "He wants it; I can see it in his face. He'll keep Bull House, because it's our father's. Ace will need somewhere else to live. Cactus too. He can't raise a family in that Edge Cabin."

"He won't leave that cabin," Bear said. "His son is buried there."

"Then it'll need a complete remodel and reconstruction," Ranger said. "Enlargement, expansion."

"We'll all sign off on that." Bear placed his palms flat against the table and stood, his all-night mowing session catching up to him. "I'll consult with Bishop on places we have now that need work—Bull House, Edge Cabin, the house down on that adjacent piece we own. We'll go through everyone and start working now to make sure everyone has the accommodations they need for a family."

"It's time," Ranger said, and Bear could only agree. He hugged his cousin, which took Ranger by surprise.

"I didn't mean to take over with Two Cents," he said. "I just know sometimes you can overthink things and not actually take the first step forward."

"I can," Ranger conceded, stepping back. "It's okay. We'll talk later. You look about five seconds away from passing out." He smiled at Bear. "Go to bed. Oh, and congratulations on your baby."

Bear's grin once again exploded onto his face. "Thanks."

Ranger turned away, but not before Bear distinctly caught a river of pain moving through his eyes. He opened his mouth to ask Ranger what was wrong, but a voice inside his head said, *Give it time. Now's not the time to ask.*

He walked toward the door, his thoughts racing now. What did he need to give more time to? Asking Ranger... what, exactly?

Chapter Twenty-Two

❦

"Oh, no," Penny Walker said with a moan.

Gideon looked up from his oatmeal, his eyebrows up. "What is it?" he asked.

She loved her husband so very much, and he made a little more progress every single day. She smiled gently at him, her mother heart so full and yet so fragile. "Rhett just texted to say that Penny died this morning."

She looked back at her phone. "He said Conrad's been crying for an hour, and he hopes Bill can take out bloodshot eyes in photos."

She set her device down and got up from the table, her stomach clenching. She did not want her grandson to have to endure pain and disappointment. Losing a dog was hard on everyone, and Penny suspected Rhett himself had shed quite a few tears. "He's had that dog for thirteen years."

"I'll call 'im," Gideon said, already getting up from the table. He loved dogs as much as Rhett, and he'd been through several in his life. She could still remember the two big mutts that had bowled her over at the park in Sweet Creek.

Their handsome owner had come running around the trees, calling for Moose and Mack, and that had been the first time Penny had met Gideon Walker. Those two dogs had changed the course of her whole life.

Tears came to her eyes as she looked out the window above the kitchen sink. Gideon now had two dozen miniature horses in the pasture behind their farmhouse, and she took comfort in the low drone of his voice as he spoke to their first-born son about the loss of his dog.

Penny could clearly see Gideon in that park. Gideon coming to her apartment while they dated in college. Gideon bringing doughnuts to her study groups on campus.

She saw him dressed in a sharp, black tuxedo, that stunning and sexy cowboy hat on his head while he waited for her to carefully step down the aisle on her father's arm. She'd been the first Aarons child to marry, though she was the youngest.

Her mother had dealt with three weddings in a twelve-month period, and then she and Daddy had passed away in a terrible trucking accident that had left Penny reeling for years. Even now, she wished her mother was there to guide her. She'd lost her very best friend and greatest mentor the day her mother had died.

Her tears fell, though over four decades had passed since that terrible day Darren had called in pure agony to tell her the news.

"I finally did it, Mama," she whispered to the back yard. She'd told her mother she wanted to be a lawyer since the age of twelve, and her mother had always supported her, though she certainly had a different idea of what Penny should dedicate her life to.

Sadness always came to her when she thought about the fact that none of her sons had known the beauty of her mother's spirit, and that none of them had learned from her father the way she had.

She and Gideon had not stayed in Sweet Creek, and the egg farm Penny had loved as a youth had disappeared from her life as her husband pursued his dreams in the field of technology.

She'd dropped out of college when she'd had Jeremiah, as he was only fifteen months younger than Rhett. With two babies in less than a year and a half, and Gideon working crazy hours, Penny had put her dreams on hold.

They'd kept too. For forty long years, they'd kept.

When she'd first told Gideon she wanted to go back and finish her degree, he'd been nothing but supportive. He'd studied with her, and encouraged her, and before she knew it, she'd finished the coursework.

Then came the bar exam. More studying. More prayerful nights. More work. She wasn't as quick in body or mind as she'd once been, but her bravery was just as strong. She'd signed up for the spring exam, and she'd passed it.

Her sons and their wives wanted to throw her another party, and she'd finally agreed—with one condition: They all had to do family photos before the event.

She wanted seven big, beautiful family photos on her

walls, with all of her sons, all of their wives, and all of her grandchildren. She wanted one with just her and Gideon, just as they were, with their wrinkles and gray hair and years of wisdom behind their smiling eyes.

No one had put up much of a fuss—except Jeremiah—and their family photos were getting taken up at Shiloh Ridge Ranch later today.

Gideon's touch ran along her waist, and Penny leaned into him. "How is he?"

"Not great," he said. "But I talked to Tripp, who's there with them. Oliver brought his girlfriend, and the two of them are entertaining the kids. They're happy enough for now."

"Oliver has a girlfriend?"

"Apparently," Gideon said. "Now, Penny, don't you go all Grandmother Bear on him. He's fifteen years old, and he's allowed to have a girlfriend."

"I was not going to go Grandmother Bear on him," she said indignantly.

Gideon chuckled. "How old were you when boys started showing up at the egg farm again?" He kept her tucked right against his side, and Penny loved how he'd always claimed her. How he'd always wanted her. He'd barely been able to leave for college, and he'd repeatedly asked her in the three weeks it had taken her to follow him if she'd been asked out by anyone else.

He'd asked her to marry him after only a few months of dating, because he didn't want anyone else to have her.

"Younger than fifteen," she murmured, leaning her head against his strong, broad chest.

"Exactly." Gideon stepped away from her. "I see Yellow Ribbon is all tangled in that dang rope again." He bent to pull on his boots again, though he'd already been out to the pasture.

"Gideon, we have to leave soon."

"I know, dear." He smiled at her. "I won't be long." He stepped back over to her and kissed her. "Tripp and Ivory are good parents. They know Ollie's girlfriend. She's over to the house all the time. Ollie goes to her house. Her mother knows him. It's fine."

"Of course it is," she said. "I'm not even thinking about it anymore."

Gideon laughed and shook his head. "I know you, Mrs. Walker. You're thinking about it."

Maybe she was. Oliver dominated her thoughts for the next several minutes while she kept an eye on her husband as he worked to get his precious miniature horse out of the mess it had gotten itself into. Oliver was not hers by blood, but he still belonged to her completely.

She picked up her phone as Gideon headed back in, and she sent a quick text to Ollie. *I heard you have a girl-friend, Ollie. How exciting. I can't wait to meet her. Please remember who you are when you're with her.*

That wasn't too Grandmother Bear, was it?

She wasn't going to ask Gideon, that was for sure.

I will, Grandma, came back quickly. *You can meet her at the party. She'll be there with her family.*

A smile adorned Penny's face as Gideon came back inside, bringing a blast of heat with him. "Let's go. Jeremiah needs help with the food."

"Right," Penny said, reaching up to wipe her eyes one more time. She'd forgone the makeup today. She was almost seventy years old, and she was going to spend the day weeping. She'd accepted it, and makeup would only be in her way. "Let's go. Whitney could use a break, I'm sure, and you'll get to hold your new grandson while I help Jeremiah with the cookie monster salad."

Her tears started afresh, because Jeremiah and Whitney had brought home their third child only a few weeks ago. There had been no complications, and Penny wept because they'd named him Jason, after her father, and his special spirit reminded her so much of the man she'd lost far too soon.

Chapter Twenty-Three

Bishop stayed close to Montana as people started arriving at True Blue. His job was to hand out the menu so everyone would know what had nuts in it, and what was gluten-free, and what wasn't.

He'd wanted something where he got to see everyone's reaction to True Blue, and he could safely say that his pride in the remodeled barn had swelled and grown with every man, woman, and child who entered the grand hall.

All the Walkers had been here for an hour, taking pictures, and now their friends and family were arriving. He shook hands with Wade Rhinehart and introduced him to Montana. Her job was to take any gifts for Penny people had brought and put them on the table reserved for such things. She noted what the gift looked like and who'd brought it, which she'd give to Penny Walker later.

He welcomed Gavin Redd and told Montana who he

was. He introduced Brit Bellamore and several of his cowboys as they arrived.

He clapped Squire Ackerman's back with a round of laughter, and introduced Montana around to all the cowboys and their wives from Three Rivers who'd made the drive from the northern-most ranch surrounding the town.

She took Brynn Greene into a tight hug and held her for several long seconds. Then Montana went off with Brynn for a while, leaving Bishop with double duty. He didn't mind, because nearly everyone had arrived by then, including his brothers and cousins, their dates and significant others, and the cowboys who worked the ranch alongside them.

As Jeremiah took the microphone and welcomed everyone to the party, Bishop stayed near the barrels that stood sentinel in the wide doorway and drank in the crowd.

The Walkers had seven boys in their family, and they'd grown and expanded by leaps and bounds in the past decade.

Bishop felt like his family was just starting down the same path, what with Bear and Ranger married now, and already a baby on the way. He, Ace, and Cactus had girlfriends, and Bishop had met with Bear yesterday about the construction that needed to be done at Shiloh Ridge to take all twelve of them into the future.

He wanted a house for the full dozen of them, if they wanted to live there. Bishop was tired just thinking about it, and the building projects he'd thought he was almost done with had suddenly quadrupled.

The good news was that he and Montana would be finished with the Ranch House by the end of next week. The bad news was that the completion of that project meant Montana wouldn't be coming up to Shiloh Ridge every day.

She'd been dividing her time between the ranch, her family, and the new library bid for a couple of weeks now, and he knew she was looking forward to just working on the library. He was excited for her to have that opportunity too.

He located her among the crowd of people, already missing her constant companionship on the ranch. He smiled, and she somehow felt it, because she turned and waved for him to come join her.

He did, weaving his way through the crowd to her side. She slipped her fingers between his and tipped up to whisper in his ear. "Brynn said she'll take Aurora any day she can get her. Isn't that great?"

"Amazing," Bishop whispered back. He found Aurora standing next to Oliver, who watched the scene up front next to Jackie and Bob. "We're still going to the Harvest Festival with them, right?"

Montana nodded, and Bishop did too. *Good*, he thought. He hadn't had much opportunity to get to know Aurora real well. She was busy all summer up at Bowman's Breeds, and she'd spent the rest of her spare time with Oliver.

Bishop wanted to know her. He'd made great strides in

making his own peace with himself and the people around him. Montana had too.

The last piece he needed was to get to know her daughter. If he was going to marry Aurora's mother, he'd become her step-father. Instantly.

His mouth turned dry, and he suddenly wanted to flee. He held his ground, though, because he and Montana hadn't even talked about the thing troubling him.

"So let's eat," Jeremiah finally said. "Momma will be around for everyone to talk to, so don't worry. She's not going anywhere." He smiled at her with such love, and Bishop realized he needed to go see his own mother and find out what to do about Aurora.

He'd been approved to build his house, but he hadn't started on it yet. He wanted Montana to design it and build it with him, but he couldn't do that until he asked her to marry him. And he couldn't do that until she brought up the topic.

The crowd seemed to swell and move as a unit, and Bishop stepped out of the way to let the Walkers go first. He pressed his back into the wall and leaned down to talk to Montana again. His heart beat like a big bass drum, and he could barely hear himself as he said, "I got approval to build a house here on the ranch. Want to see where?"

"Yes, please," she said. "I'm going to have a panic attack in here." She looked at him with anxiety in her expression, and he smiled at her. Then he took her into the kitchen and out the door there.

The land spread before him, the stand of trees that

would be his back yard only a couple hundred yards away. "Right there."

"Right here?"

"I got an acre," he said. "Right here. Goes right up against the trees. I'll put in a road around the tower in the front there, and we'll improve the parking here. I even got Ranger and Bear to approve paving the road from the homestead to here." He smiled at her again and returned his gaze to the land he loved.

His next words could spark some danger though. In that moment, Bishop realized he was ready to get burned. "I don't want to rush you or anything," he said. "But I want the house—I mean." He cleared his throat, so much more nervous when she turned to look at him. "I'm thinking of it as *our* house."

He met her eyes as hers widened. Words poured out of him then, and Bishop couldn't hold them back if he tried. "I want you to design it. Any way you want. I want the two of us—make that three of us—to build it together. I know we're not ready for marriage yet. I know that. I still need time to get to know your daughter, and we need to talk about how that's going to work so we're all going to be happy, and I know you're not in a place where you can say you love me and you're not just happier than you've ever been."

He paused to take a breath, about to blow everything wide open. "But I love you, Montana, and I can say it and know it's true." His courage failed then, because uttering those three words took so much more than he'd ever realized. "I've never told anyone that before," he said, his voice half the volume it had once been. "But I can feel it. I know it." He pressed his fist over his heart. "I'm in love with you, and I want to build a house with you, and a family, and a future, right here at Shiloh Ridge."

Bishop sucked in a breath. What if she didn't want any of that? "I mean—"

"I heard you," Montana said. She continued to search his face, and Bishop sincerely prayed that she'd find the answers she needed right there.

"We haven't talked about any of this," he said, ducking his head so she'd stop staring at him. "I don't need to right now either. I guess I do need to know one thing though."

He took a moment to center his thoughts. "I need to know if any of that sounds appealing to you at all." He looked out over the land he loved, and the exact future he wanted. He could almost see it. They'd paint the house yellow, and it would have navy blue shutters. He'd get Aurora the black and white puppy she wanted, and they'd have Jackie and Bob over every Sunday for lunch after church.

He clued back into the present when he realized Montana hadn't answered. "If you'd rather not live up here, I can—"

"It all sounds like a dream come true," Montana said.

Bishop's gaze flew back to hers, his heart beating impossibly fast now. "Really?"

She took his face in her hands and kissed him, and Bishop wasn't entirely sure, because he'd never been loved by a woman like Montana, but her kiss sure felt like she was in love with him too.

Chapter Twenty-Four

Montana pushed into the coffee house and spotted Micah instantly. It wasn't hard, as this was more of a hipster place among twenty-somethings, and neither she nor Micah fit that description.

He rose and shook her hand, saying, "You found it," before he gestured to the seat across from him. A thick file folder sat on the table in front of him, as did a half-drunk cup of coffee.

Nerves fluttered through her stomach. "I'm not late, am I?"

"Not at all," he said easily. He didn't let his gaze roam, and his attention centered on her. "I had another meeting that ended early, and I just came here to wait." He lifted one hand to signal a barista. "What do you want?"

"Oh, uh." Montana looked up at the woman who arrived. "I'll take herbal tea, please." She'd already consumed enough coffee that morning as she tried to soothe her nerves about having Aurora and Bishop go shopping together.

But she'd spoken to her daughter about Bishop and admitted things between them were very serious. Aurora had picked up the pieces Montana had put down, and she'd instantly said, "I should get to know him better, shouldn't I, Mom?"

"Yes," Montana had said. They'd spent some time together, sure. Bishop had been at the Fourth of July picnic at Aunt Jackie's. They'd gone to the Harvest Festival together, and they'd even walked around the booths together while Montana stayed in the one Bear had set up for locally owned and operated services for the town of Three Rivers.

Aurora already had his phone number, and she'd immediately texted Bishop and asked him to take her to the mall to shop for new jeans.

Montana hated shopping with a passion, and Aurora had proclaimed that this was a perfect solution for her problem of needing new jeans and getting to know Bishop. They had a lunch date after the shopping, and Montana couldn't wait to hear both sides of how everything had gone.

It also turned out that coffee did not soothe nerves. In fact, it only enhanced them.

Micah flipped open his folder and said, "Okay, so Bishop said you're particularly skilled with custom pieces." He looked up as Montana pulled in a long breath. "Cabinetry, built-in bookcases and shelving units. Mantles. Not only that, but your attention to detail when it comes to things no one sees but that really matter."

Montana needed something to hold in her hand, but her tea hadn't come yet. "Bishop—uh, Bishop said all that?" When had Micah talked to Bishop? Why hadn't Bishop told her?

"Yeah," Micah said, his dark eyes glinting with curiosity. "When he called me and said we should partner." His words slowed near the end of the sentence, and he leaned back in his chair. "He didn't tell you he called me."

Montana felt like throwing up. The waitress arrived with her tea, and Montana lunged for it. She gulped it, ignoring the scalding temperature as it burned her mouth, tongue, and throat. She shook her head, determined not to cry in front of Micah Walker and all these hipsters in this coffee house.

She looked left and saw three cats jump up on the bench next to two women. They seemed thrilled to be sharing their coffee with cats, and Montana had no idea what world she'd entered.

One where Bishop did things for her she absolutely did not want him to do.

"How long ago did he call you?" she asked.

"I don't know," Micah said. "In the spring? Maybe early summer."

Months. He'd called Micah Walker *months* ago. Probably right after she'd started working at Shiloh Ridge.

She lifted her chin and looked him in the eye. "Had you heard of me before?"

Apology entered his expression, and Montana had her answer.

She nodded, too angry and too numb at the same time to ask another question. None of the answers would matter. She bent and reached into her purse. She took out a ten-dollar bill and set it on the table. "I'm sorry he wasted your time."

She stood and headed for the door. Once free of the insufferable coffee shop, Montana scoffed out some of her fury. "How dare he?" she asked herself as she strode toward her truck.

"Montana, wait," Micah called behind her.

She paused, inhaling to try to maintain her composure. Micah caught up to her. "I'm sure he didn't mean to upset you. I know I didn't."

"It's fine, Micah," she said crisply. "This is not your problem."

"I still want to work with you," he said. "It doesn't matter to me how I found out about you. You're incredibly talented, and I think we could dominate the marketplace together."

She did not want to say anything she'd regret later. Her ill feelings for Micah belonged to her—and she'd since passed them on to the Lord anyway. It would do no good for her to tell Micah what she'd thought of him all these months.

"I appreciate that," she said. "Perhaps we can set up another meeting."

"This one took weeks to arrange," he said. "Please. Let's

go somewhere else." He glanced back toward the coffee house. "I didn't realize there would be cats there."

For some reason, the disdainful tone of his voice struck Montana as funny. She laughed, which released some of the tension that had formed between them. "I think you were the only one wearing a cowboy hat, which is saying something in this town."

"Right?" He chuckled too. "Is it too early for lunch?" He glanced around like a suitable restaurant would manifest itself in the parking lot.

"The pancake house is always open," she said. "I think I need a lot of carbs before I talk to Bishop again anyway." She gave him a tight smile, but Micah looked nervous.

"I'm afraid I've gotten him in trouble."

"Oh, that's also not your problem," Montana said. "The man's mouth got him in trouble, and that has nothing to do with you."

Micah cocked his head to the side. "Are you serious about this partnership?"

The question took Montana by surprise. "Yes." She studied him back. "What makes you think I'm not?"

"You just walked out, because Bishop called me months ago and told me about you. You were quite cold at the library board meeting, at least in the beginning." He shrugged. "I don't know. You don't seem to like me very much."

"I don't," Montana said before she could censor herself. She clapped one hand over her mouth in the next moment.

Micah's eyebrows rose, his eyes widened, and he blinked

several times. "Oh, okay." He gave a nervous chuckle. "I don't—I don't know what to do with that." A measure of darkness entered his expression. "Maybe I should've just let you go."

"Let me explain," Montana said, her heart crashing against her ribs. She might not need Micah Walker in the future. Because she'd won the library bid, her name was all over the news in Three Rivers, and she'd already gotten a couple of calls about remodeling jobs. But hadn't she told Aurora never to burn a bridge? She might need this major connection in the future.

She sighed, grateful he hadn't walked away yet. "Let me buy you breakfast, and I'll do my best to explain."

Micah's jaw tightened, and indecision warred across his face. He finally said, "Okay. I'll meet you at the pancake house," which caused relief to cascade through Montana.

She talked out loud to herself all the way to the pancake house, telling herself she could do this. She could get this partnership on her own—with her work, her work ethic, and her explanation.

Near the end there, she chewed out Bishop for calling Micah when it wasn't his place to do so. She almost called him before she went inside the pancake house, but she decided she didn't want to punish Aurora for Bishop's mistake.

There would be plenty of time to talk to him later.

She watched Micah walk into the pancake house, and Montana got out of her truck. "Time to fix this," she said, glancing up into the autumn sky. "Any help You can send would be appreciated."

But as Montana walked into the pancake house behind

Micah Walker, she had the feeling she was on her own this time.

HOURS LATER—LONG PAST LUNCHTIME—BISHOP'S BIG black truck finally pulled into Montana's aunt's driveway. She sat in the swing, and up until she'd heard the roar of his engine, she'd been enjoying the peace of the afternoon.

Now, she felt like she'd lose all those chocolate chip pancakes she'd consumed.

She looked at the folder on the swing beside her. It held the signed contract between her and Micah Walker, who'd listened to Montana's explanation and apologized again, though he'd done nothing wrong.

I'm a bit of a bulldog, he'd said. *I just barrel through things without a lot of thought. I'm sure I took business from you unintentionally. I apologize for that.*

And because he had so much money and so much charisma and so many connections, his business had thrived while she hadn't even been able to get hers off the ground.

That situation fixed, he wisely hadn't brought up Bishop again, and they'd focused on her previous work, and he'd proposed a twelve-month contract where they worked together on select projects. They'd choose which ones they each brought to the partnership, and they'd meet regularly to keep their goals aligned.

He had one he wanted her hand in already, and she'd brought home the customer's in-take form to go over, and she and Micah were meeting in a few days to talk about their individual plans and to learn how the other worked.

Montana could admit she was excited about the partnership. It was something she'd never done before, and it could open a lot of doors for her.

Aurora got out of the truck laughing, and that too helped to center Montana. She and Bishop were supposed to spend the evening together, and Montana didn't want to break-up with him. She simply didn't know how this conversation would go.

Bishop and Aurora came up the steps, both of them carrying shopping bags.

"How much stuff did you buy?" she asked, getting to her feet.

"Mom," Aurora said, rushing toward her. "You would not *believe* the sale they were having at Williams'." She continued to gush over the prices and the cute things they had on sale.

She could talk and talk, and Montana nodded and hummed as they went into the house. As Aurora detailed the boys she ran into and what Bishop had said to them, Montana watched Bishop. He couldn't stop smiling, and he interjected some of the story too.

Montana did her best to smile and play along like she was thrilled things had gone so well that day.

"Fashion show," Bishop said. "I'm sure your mom wants to see what we got."

"Do you?" Aurora bounced on the balls of her feet, and Montana grinned.

"Of course. Fashion show."

Aurora squealed and took her bags into the bathroom, as her bedroom was on the second floor. "I'm not climbing up and down," she called.

Montana took a breath with the relief of the resulting silence.

Bishop took her into his arms. "She's fantastic."

"I think so too," Montana said. "She just talks a lot."

"I had so much fun with her."

"I'm not sure what that says about you," she said, only half-teasing.

Bishop laughed too, and Montana didn't want to say anything to ruin this day. She'd been swallowing her feelings for decades. They actually went down easily, but Montana knew what happened with them after that.

They festered and grew into resentment. The negative things she felt for Bishop right now would not simply go away. She wouldn't "get over them." Hadn't she learned that over the past several months?

The only way to heal was to speak. She could be kind and honest at the same time.

"Bishop," she said.

"How was your meeting with Micah?" he asked, his eyes bright and interested. "What did he have to say?"

Montana looked at the man in front of her. He'd made her life so much better. He'd taken a chance on her, a pathetic carpenter looking for work by knocking on doors and asking for it.

He'd taught her so much about herself, and about the Lord.

She loved this man standing in front of her, and it

wasn't because she was in pain. It wasn't because she was engaged. It wasn't because her life was just better than before, so of course her renewed happiness would feel like love.

When he'd told her he loved her a few weeks ago, Montana hadn't said the words out loud to him. She'd only kissed him, hoping that would be enough for now.

"Montana?" he asked.

"Okay," Aurora said, her voice loud and piercing. "Here's the first pair."

Montana turned away from Bishop to look at her daughter's jeans. "Oh, those are so cute." She let her gaze drip down the length of her daughter's legs, the purposeful rips in the jeans, the cute roughed-up cuffs on her ankles. "That blouse is new too."

"Yes," she said, looking down at the dark purple blouse with yellow and white butterflies on it. "Bishop found it. Isn't it so cute?" She did a little twirl, and Montana loved seeing her daughter so happy.

She was generally a happy child anyway, but this was a new level of joy Montana hadn't seen in a while. *Maybe because you never take her shopping and let her buy whatever she wants.*

Montana didn't have a lot of money for new school clothes, and Aurora had never made a big deal of it.

She knew now that her daughter loved clothes and would like new ones a lot more often than Montana had been able to deliver them.

Inadequacy filled her. This was just another gap in her

daughter's life she couldn't fill. Another space Bishop had filled instead.

"Love it," Bishop said, grinning at Aurora. She squealed and twisted to go back into the bathroom.

Montana couldn't hold back her tears, and she sniffled as the door clicked closed.

"Baby," Bishop said, pure kindness in his voice. "What's wrong?"

"Be honest with me," she said. "How much of that did you pay for?"

"I don't know the exact number." He reached for her hand. "I don't care, so I didn't keep track. You don't owe me anything."

She nodded and wiped her eyes. "When did you call Micah and suggest he partner with me?"

Bishop opened his mouth, but it fell closed a moment later.

"He told me," Montana said, some of the ice that had filled her veins in that cat coffee house returning. "And I want to know when that phone call was made. To the very hour."

"I don't remember," he said. "April or May."

"Before or after I told you about my feelings for him?"

"Before, Montana. I swear. It was before. After you told me, I was horrified I'd called him, and I thought about calling him and telling him not to say anything. But he hadn't said anything yet, and then he never did, and...." He looked down, his apology right there in his whole countenance.

"And you thought you were in the clear," Montana said.

Bishop nodded without looking at her. "You're the best carpenter in the state," he said. "I wanted him to know that. I want everyone to know that." He looked up at her. "Of course, I don't want you to work for anyone but me. And not even for me. I want you to work *with* me."

"This pair is darker," Aurora said. "I'm still trying to decide if I like the big holes over my knees."

Montana held Bishop's gaze for another moment before turning back to her daughter.

"Do they make my knees look too knobby?"

"No," Montana said, sniffling again. "No, baby, they look great."

Aurora looked at her, concern in her eyes instantly. She switched her gaze to Bishop. "What's wrong?"

"Nothing," Montana said at the same time Bishop said, "I betrayed your mother's confidence, and she just found out."

Aurora came forward, anger in her eyes. "What happened?"

"Nothing." Montana released Bishop's hand and stood up. "It's fine, sweetie. Let me see the back of the jeans."

Aurora looked directly into Montana's eyes, said nothing, and stepped around her so she was between Bishop and Montana. "How dare you? She works for you like a *dog* for months, saving every penny she can and giving *you* her very best work, and you betray her? How *dare* you?" She looked down to Bishop's feet and back to his face, as if sizing him up and finding him short.

"Aurora," Montana said quietly. "It's okay."

"No, it's *not* okay," Aurora said, her voice pitching up.

"I'm so sick of all the stupid cowboys in this town." She spun and grabbed onto Montana, her tears hot and wet against Montana's shoulder. "They think they can just do whatever they want, and because they're so cute or so nice, that we'll just put up with their crap."

She pulled away, her expression furious despite the tears. "We don't have to put up with that."

"No," Montana said. "We don't." She looked past Aurora to Bishop, who looked as perplexed as she felt. He clearly hadn't heard anything she didn't know.

"Sweetheart, did something happen with Oliver?" Montana guided her daughter to the couch where she'd been sitting.

Bishop smartly shifted over to the loveseat, which sat perpendicular to the couch. "I'll stop by and have a word with him if he hurt you," he said.

Montana shook her head, though she actually appreciated him being there.

"No," Aurora said. "Bishop, don't you dare talk to him."

"Tell us what happened," Montana said. Her mind spun with the possibilities, and she prayed mightily that it was something easily fixed, though she knew matters of the heart were unusually complicated and never easily fixed.

"Some other girl asked him to the Christmas Ball already," Aurora said, sniffling. "And because he is so kind, and so good, he didn't feel like he could tell her no." She studied her hands as a new wave of tears moved down her face. "It's not even October, Momma. How was I supposed to know I needed to ask him to the Christmas Ball so soon?" She looked at Montana with pure grief in her eyes.

"You couldn't have known," Montana said, wrapping Aurora in a tight hug. She pressed her eyes closed. "Surely he doesn't like this other girl, right? He's just going because he's nice."

"It doesn't matter," Aurora said. "How am I supposed to keep hanging out with him? Surely she knows, but he doesn't think she does. So then if he takes me to the Pumpkin Smash, or we hang out at the school dances after the football games, she'll feel stupid." Aurora shook her head. "It's a no-win situation." She looked at Bishop too, clearly wanting his input. Montana would love to know what he'd do here too.

"I really like Oliver—a whole lot. I think he likes me too. But neither of us want to make someone else feel awkward. I don't know what to do."

Bishop took a breath and hesitated. He looked at Montana, clearly seeking her permission. The vulnerability and fear in his eyes wasn't lost on her, and she nodded.

"Okay, baby," he said, sliding off the loveseat and onto the floor. He knelt in front of Aurora. "Let's establish a couple of things first, okay?"

She nodded, looking at him eagerly.

"Okay." Bishop took another deep breath. "I know I'm old and out of touch and all of that, but you're beautiful. Totally beautiful, whether you have Oliver Osburn or not. Okay?"

Aurora smiled, though her eyes kept leaking. "You just have to say that because you're old and out of touch."

"Not true," Bishop said. "I just call it how I see it. Second, I've seen you and Ollie together, and that boy is completely head-over-heels for you. He doesn't just like you a little bit, Aurora. He likes you a whole lot too." He cut a glance at Montana. "A *whole* lot."

"He still said yes to stupid Izzy." The poison in Aurora's voice almost made Montana smile. She possessed so much fire, and Montana hoped she'd learn to tame it into something that would help her in the wide world out there.

"That's because he's too nice," Bishop said. "It doesn't change how he feels about you. Now, he's fifteen, so he might be a little confused right now. I know I was at that age. It sure is nice when you—" He cleared his throat and ducked his head. "When you find out someone likes you. You feel special, you know? My guess is he's one of the very first at school to be asked to the Christmas Ball, and everyone's talking about him now. He won't know what to do with that, because he doesn't think of himself as anyone to pay attention to."

Montana hung on his every word, and Aurora did too.

"He might feel real special right now, and maybe a little arrogant. But that wears off mighty fast, and it doesn't mean how he feels about you will change."

"Maybe you just have to be patient," Montana said, looking at Bishop and quickly changing her gaze to Aurora when he looked up at her. "And just be his friend or have him over here privately until the ball is over." She reached over and tucked her daughter's hair behind her ear. "Because Bishop is right. You're beautiful, and he has no reason not to like you just because this Izzy girl asked him to one dance."

Aurora studied Montana's eyes and then dropped her

gaze back to her hands. "I got upset with him when he told me he'd said yes. I maybe told him we shouldn't hang out anymore."

"Is that what we're calling dating?" Bishop asked. "I just feel like I'm missing something. I *hung out* with friends. I *dated* girls."

Montana smiled at him and nodded just as Aurora burst out laughing. It only sounded happy for a moment, and then she dissolved into tears again. "Yes," she said through them. "That's why I told you that boy at the mall was hanging out with Rachel. They're a thing."

"They're dating," Bishop said.

"It's not called that, but yes," Aurora said. "They're together, and everyone knows they're together." She shrugged and sobered again. "I guess I just thought everyone knew me and Ollie were a thing."

"Maybe they do," Montana said. "Maybe Izzy just isn't a very nice person."

"I think she's just clueless," Aurora said. "She doesn't get how this stuff works."

"At least I know more than someone," Bishop quipped, and Montana had a hard time stifling her giggle. He wasn't going to get off the hook for what he'd done, though, just because he could have a conversation with a teenager.

"When did this happen?" Montana asked.

"Yesterday. Last night," Aurora said, glancing at Montana out of the corner of her eye. "Don't freak out okay?"

"Uh, Aurora," Bishop said. "You're going to tell her now? She's already mad at me."

"I don't keep secrets from my mom," Aurora said. "Ollie's going to be sixteen in another month, and his parents let him drive me home alone last night."

"At midnight?" Montana was indeed, freaking out.

"He's a good driver, Mom. He's been driving tractors and stuff at the ranch forever."

"I can attest to how good of drivers ranchers are by age ten," Bishop said in a monotone. "But go ahead."

"That's the part you knew?" Montana asked.

"She told me at lunch. She didn't think you'd be happy."

"I am *not* happy."

"He's a good driver," Aurora said.

"Okay, okay." Montana held up her hand as in surrendering. "So he drove you home."

"He told me about Izzy then, and that he said yes. We kind of argued in the truck. I didn't know what I was supposed to do. He doesn't know either. Then, we get here, and he walks me up to the door and kisses me."

She swallowed, but Montana knew her daughter was kissing Oliver Osburn, so she didn't get the nerves.

"I see," Bishop said. "He kissed you differently, and now it's even more confusing as to what's going on with the two of you, with him, with Izzy, and all of it."

Aurora nodded. "It was a long kiss—don't freak out, Mom."

Montana's stomach had clenched when Bishop had clarified the type of kiss. She tried to paint over everything with a smile. "I'm not freaking out."

"She's freaking out." Aurora rolled her eyes and looked at Bishop.

"I can see that," he said.

How he wasn't a little freaked out by this conversation annoyed Montana. She told herself it was because Aurora wasn't his flesh and blood, but she knew he cared about her. It was simply that he wasn't a woman. He wasn't a mother.

"What did you feel in the kiss?" Bishop asked, keeping his eyes on Montana.

"I don't know," Aurora said, shrugging again. "I guess if he'd have kissed me like that after the amazing night we'd had, without the argument and all the Izzy drama, I would think...I would...."

"Did he tell you he loved you?" Bishop asked.

Aurora shook her head. "No, but that's how it felt."

Bishop nodded. "Okay, so what we have here is a fifteen-year-old boy who really, really likes a girl. He's never been in love before, and he doesn't know how to say those words. He's also really nice, and a super great person, even at fifteen, and so he doesn't want anyone to get hurt. He's going to learn a lot from this, namely that he can't have everything all the time. If he wants you, and Aurora, he wants you. Once he realizes that, he's going to have to concede the fact that he's going to hurt someone else."

"Maybe," Aurora said.

"Not maybe," Bishop said. "I've been a fifteen-year-old boy, baby. I know what's going on in his head. I know he's mostly ruled by hormones, but that he's got adults in his life, talking in his ear and head all the time, telling him not to listen to his hormones but to act according to what he knows to be right. His mom, his step-dad, heck, probably his grandparents too. His uncles—every one of them is telling him how to act around girls. Every one of them has expectations for him. He doesn't know which way is up right now, and once he figures it out, I can guarantee where he'll be."

"Where?" Aurora asked, her voice high and filled with emotion.

"On your front porch, baby, begging you to forgive him for being a fifteen-year-old boy with hormones and values and a ton of people that care about him." He stood up, groaning as he did. "Dear Lord, I'm too old to kneel like that."

Aurora laughed, this time the sound actually sounding and staying happy. She jumped to her feet and flung her arms around Bishop. "Thank you, Bishop."

"Oh, sure," he said, wrapping her up in those arms that Montana loved. "Be kind to him, Aurora. He's doing the best he can."

That was so not what Montana would've advised her daughter to do, and she was glad she wasn't dealing with this alone.

"Okay." Aurora stepped back and wiped her face. "I'm a mess. Can we do the rest of the fashion show later?"

"Of course," Montana murmured.

"Thanks." She started to walk away, but she turned back to them. "Bishop, is that why you took me shopping? To get my mom to forgive you?"

"No, baby," he said. "She didn't even find out about my treachery until after we'd gone shopping."

"Can you fix it?" Aurora asked, and she threw a glance at Montana.

"I hope so," Bishop said. "What I told you at lunch was —and still is—one hundred percent true."

Montana stood up and looked at her daughter. "What did he tell you?"

Aurora smiled at Bishop. "She'll forgive you."

"You think so?" Bishop asked, glancing at Montana too. His eyes darted away before they'd really latched onto her though.

"Yeah," Aurora said. "She's in love with you too." She went into the bathroom and gathered her bags while Montana sputtered.

"You told her?" she asked Bishop. It was really more of a demand and not a question.

His shoulders rose and fell before he turned around. "She asked me how I felt about you, and I felt it best to tell her the truth. I saw no reason to hide it from her. I've told you. I've told everyone who'll stand still long enough to let me talk for longer than ten seconds."

Montana's pulse went back to the rapid-fire beat, and she really hated it.

"So I guess I just need to know if you think you can forgive me," he said. He sighed in the next moment. "I'm not perfect, Montana, and I'm never going to be perfect. I did not intend to hurt you, and I'm sorry. That's all I can say."

Montana nodded. "Thank you for your apology."

Chapter Twenty-Five

❧

Bishop's frustration reached the boiling point and overflowed. "That's all I'm going to get?" He knew how long it took Montana to forgive and give up the burdens she felt like she needed to carry, and the future he'd been planning vanished like the popping of a bubble.

There for a moment. Beautiful if the light caught on it just right.

Then *pop!* Gone.

Gone, with nothing left behind. Nothing to show for it.

"I'm trying to figure out what to do," Montana said, sighing as she sank back to the couch. "I feel very much like how you just described Oliver. I want everyone to have everything. I don't want anyone to get hurt."

Encouraged, Bishop sat back down too. "Tell me what else you want."

"You know what I want," she whispered.

"You interrupt me if I say something not on your list,"

he said, clearing his throat. He touched one of his finger-tips. "You want to be respected and known for your carpentry in the community, because you need a career you're proud of and that pays your bills."

She said nothing, and Bishop touched a second finger. "You want a house of your own."

He checked with her, and her eyes had started to glint with an emotion he couldn't quite name. Could've been annoyance, or it could've been desire.

Third. "You want your daughter to be happy. You want your aunt and uncle to be happy."

Still no objection.

"You want Micah Walker to know how talented you are. You want to deserve the work that comes your way, not have someone get it for you."

His big mistake, and he hadn't even known he was making it at the time.

"This is where I messed up," he said. "Because you don't need me. You don't need me to get you jobs, and you don't need me to buy your daughter school clothes." A lump formed in his throat, because what she didn't need or want from him was exactly what he wanted to do for her. To show her how much he wanted her to be happy.

"Let's see," he said, deciding to go for it. If he was going down in flames, he was going to go down fighting. "You want to be okay with God, so you've been working to release some of your negative feelings for others. You've been learning how to forgive yourself and others."

She reached up and wiped her eyes, but she didn't look away from him.

"You want to design our house. You want to build it with me. You want to get married in True Blue and have Uncle Bob walk you down the aisle. You want me to make dinner every night, and you'll make that peanut butter bacon toast in the mornings."

She sobbed then, her whole façade crumbling, but Bishop kept going.

"You want to have my children, because you're in love with me, and I want children. You want me to be Aurora's dad, so you don't have to deal with situations like the one we just experienced alone."

"Okay, stop it," she said, still crying. She got up and took the few steps to him, settling onto his lap. She wrapped her arms around him and snuggled into his chest.

"One more," Bishop whispered, his heart pounding that she'd come to him instead of demanding that he leave and never come back. "You simply want me."

Montana didn't object, and Bishop closed his eyes and held her tightly.

Finally, she said, "I also want to go wring that boy's neck," she said, her voice choked. "Just like I wanted to wring yours this morning. It doesn't mean I love you any less."

"Let's table Oliver for just a moment," Bishop said, his voice gruff. "Can you say that last part again, please?"

"I love you, Bishop." She pushed away from him and looked down at him. He gazed up at her, his angel with white-blonde hair, bright blue-green eyes, and a spirit made of pure light.

He'd been right—he felt special when Montana told him she loved him. There were no better words, in fact.

"I want to design our house. I want to build it with you. I want to live at Shiloh Ridge Ranch and build our life there together. I want your children, and I hope they're all boys so they look like you and we can teach them not to be stupid cowboys." A wobbly smile touched her lips. "I want my aunt and uncle in my life still. I want to marry you in that beautiful barn. I want to co-parent with you. I want a career in carpentry, but the scale doesn't matter to me. If it's building barns on the ranch we love, then so be it."

Tears tracked down her face. "I want to be right with the Lord, and I want to be a forgiving, kind person. I want to be the mom my kids will come to and tell me what's troubling them and what's happening so I can help them riddle through how confusing it is to be fifteen years old."

Bishop grinned at her, his own emotions so close to the surface. She loved Shiloh Ridge too.

"Basically, I want it all," Montana said. "But most of all, if I have you, then it doesn't matter about the rest. We'll figure it all out together."

"I think you just described heaven," Bishop whispered. "I love you to the moon, sun, and stars and back, Montana Martin."

"I love you, too, Bishop." She kissed him, and Bishop knew exactly what was different in her touch.

Love, forgiveness, and faith.

"YOU'VE GOT TO BE KIDDING," MONTANA SAID.

"He is not," Bishop said, glancing toward Judge, who stood a few feet away.

"We only have this week to make it right," Judge continued. "If the construction hadn't gone on so long—" He tossed a glare at Bishop, who just smiled back at him. The man had gotten his house fixed for free. Months of work, thousands of dollars of pest control treatments. A new roof. Custom cabinets from the best carpenter in the state.

If it took longer than normal, so be it.

"We would've had our regular testing stages," Judge said. "But we didn't. We have this week. I need everyone—and I mean everyone, Cactus—to come watch the show and provide notes. Preacher and I are working the lights together this year to reprogram them faster."

"He's speaking another language," Montana murmured, causing Bishop to chuckle. That earned him another glare from Judge, but he honestly didn't care.

"It makes a great date night," Judge said next. "Get dinner, go for a drive, watch the show." He nodded around at everyone. "Okay, that's it. I need your notes by Sunday night. The sooner the better, obviously."

Obviously, Bishop thought but didn't say. Judge was already on-edge, because the mistletoe he normally had hung around the ranch by now had not come into the florists on time. Or rather, it had, but it had been full of beetles, who'd eaten the plant almost to nothing.

Judge had freaked the heck out. They always decorated Shiloh Ridge for Christmas starting in October, usually with the mistletoe first and the light show at the Ranch House second.

To compensate for the late construction and the lack of a noxious weed, Bear and Ranger had agreed to this family dinner and angel tree set-up a week before the harvest was set to be finished. That alone testified how much Bear had changed, and how much more important his family was to him than the ranch.

They'd also decided to have their first family meeting before dinner. All "serious significant others" were invited. Bishop noticed that Cactus had not invited Violet, and Ace did not have Holly Ann there.

He'd texted twenty minutes ago to find out what was going on, and he'd seen both of them look at their phones and then put them away. Bishop felt like he'd been left out of the friendship, and his muscles tensed again.

The feeling only intensified when Bear said, "Bishop's going to go over our construction plan for the next few years."

"Right." Bishop stepped away from Montana and nodded to Ward. He pressed the button on the remote control and the TV brightened, with Bishop's presentation right there. "Nothing is set in stone, obviously. Bear, Ranger, and I have spoken with each of you, and this is what we've gathered. If it's wrong, just say so."

He took a deep breath and focused on the screen. "Ranger and Bear will live here, in the homestead that was designed for them to do so. Ward is going to keep Bull House." He looked around at everyone, hoping his concern for them showed in his face. "Obviously, that doesn't mean Ace has to move out tomorrow. We're thinking future plans for the ranch. Future, like, Ward has found a woman he loves and wants to have his own life, in his own house, with his own family. He'll have Bull House. Make sense?"

"Yes," several people chorused.

"Okay." Bishop looked at the screen. "Ace will need a new place. So that's one new build. We're going to partner with Montana and Micah. You can have either of them, or both, design the house. There is a budget that Ranger and Bear will go over with you, when the time has come."

He flipped slides, and his name sat there. "Montana and I are building our house out by True Blue. She's in the design stages right now, and we'll be doing the construction of that, along with the remodel on Bull House in the first six months of next year." He tapped to go to the next slide, where Cactus's name sat.

"Now, Cactus—"

"Can we pause for a moment?" Cactus asked. "Are you and Montana engaged?" He looked from Bishop to Montana and back.

Bishop grinned at her as her face flushed. "Not yet, Cactus."

"Why not?" someone else called, and Bishop was going to kill Etta where she slept tonight.

"Well, if you must know," Bishop said. "I'm waiting for her to ask me." He cleared his throat and added, "Now, Cactus wants to keep the Edge Cabin. It's far too small for a family or even a dog, so he's going to work with Montana to expand that."

"We have three designs already," Montana said. "He just needs to pick one."

"Callin' me out, I see." Cactus grinned at her.

"You did the same to me," she shot back, and Bishop burst out laughing. To his great surprise, so did Cactus, and most people in the family stared at him.

Bishop cleared his throat. "The Ranch House will go to Judge, so he can keep doing the light show until the day he dies." He grinned at his brother. "Preacher and Mister will need new houses, which makes three, because of Ace. Etta, Ida, and Zona will also need new places, should they decide to stay here or join us."

"Duke has a place," Zona said, and that caused everyone to whiplash toward her.

"Are you engaged to Duke Rhinehart?" Bear asked, plenty of surprise in his voice.

"Not yet," Zona said with a coy smile.

"Brady and I have started talking about marriage," Ida said, and Etta sucked in a breath. "Since I do the school programs, and he's a cop, I think we'll live in town." Ida smiled around at everyone, and then Brady. "I just hope we'll always be welcome up here." She reached up and wiped a tear from her eyes.

"Of course you will be," Ranger said. "Always. Everyone in this room will always be welcome at Shiloh Ridge."

The moment felt full of love and acceptance, and Bishop let it linger for a moment. He changed the slide.

"We have the old homestead from the Kinder Ranch. It's in pretty bad shape right now, and down the hill a ways, and we've talked about fixing it up for a foreman. But I think Ward's going to step into that role, and possibly Preacher, so this could be a place for someone who also doesn't mind being a bit further out. We've talked about building a little community down there for our career cowboys too, since it's right off the highway and we have the land for larger homes."

In his mind, Preacher would take the Kinder Ranch Homestead. Once Bishop and Montana could get it fixed up, which was at least a year away.

He clicked and said, "We have the house that came with the Cornish Plantation. It too is in bad shape, and it's farther out than the Edge Cabin. But it might be nice for someone who maybe likes a little more privacy." He deliberately didn't look at Mister. To his knowledge, he and Judge had not spoken in months. Mister had taken one of the newly built cowboy cabins in the south sector, and he lived up there alone. He'd met with Bear, though, and all Bear would tell Bishop was that Mister would most likely take a house farther out from the epicenter of the ranch.

"We have the Top Cottage," Bishop said. "Mother lives there now, but we'd like to move her to the homestead with Ranger and Bear once my house is finished. Then, whatever happens with Zona...that house opens up. It's also a little removed, and not nearly as large as some of the others. We could expand, or it could be perfect for someone who doesn't mind cozy."

He flipped to the next page. It only held a question mark. "So we have three potential places for the three houses we absolutely need. Etta, we haven't forgotten about you. There's always the possibility of more homes, especially down on the Kinder Ranch. Same for the other locations. If Ace or Preacher don't want to live way the heck out of the way, they don't have to. I was just told to detail the properties we have, and the possibilities."

"Thanks, Bish," Bear said. "We'll continue to collect input from everyone, especially as current construction projects start to wrap and Bishop needs to plan the next one. Circumstances change all the time, too, so be communicative and flexible, okay?"

Murmurs of assent ran through the group. Bear turned to Ranger, and said, "Ranger?"

"Our last item for this family meeting is where we want to invest our ranch money this year. Usually, Bear and I simply choose a Texas-based company that we think could use some funding, that we think has major potential for growth. That's what makes us the most money. A small start-up that basically has nowhere to go but up."

He cleared his throat, and he looked at Bear with pain in his eyes.

Oakley stood up. "This year, Bear suggested y'all take the money and invest in Two Cents." She beamed at her husband. "Ranger is uncomfortable with it, because he has no idea what kind of gold mine he's sitting on."

"That is not true," he said, giving her a dirty look. "It's because if we invest ranch money into Two Cents, you're investing it in me. I grow richer."

"So does the ranch, right?" Ward asked.

"Well, yes," Ranger admitted.

"So it's a double-win," Judge said. "How is this even a question?"

"Get your phones out," Bear said. "Bishop, put up the link."

Bishop clicked on his computer, and the link to vote to invest in Two Cents came up.

"Vote," Bear said. "It's a simple yes or no question. We typically invest twenty percent of our calf sales in this way. This year, we had a great day at market, and this would be a sixty thousand-dollar investment."

Cactus whistled, and Bishop felt the same way. He quickly called up the link and voted yes. This money would help Ranger expand his app from Three Rivers to other cities and towns. He wanted it to stay a small-town app, but Bishop knew that sometimes things took on a life of their own.

"Done?" Bear asked, and everyone nodded.

"Just a sec," Preacher said. "My internet is being dumb." He swiped and tapped, finally looking up. "Done."

Bear surveyed everyone. "Some decisions for the ranch have to be unanimous. This is one of them. When Range and I meet, we come to a consensus. When we call in Cactus and Ward, all four of us have to agree before major decisions are made. For example, where Bishop wanted to build. We lost farmland there. All four of us have to sign off on that."

He paused for a moment. "Bigger decisions like this have to have family input, and we've decided that with this much money, it has to be unanimous. So if even one of you voted no, we'll find another company to put our money into. No one will know who voted which way, so don't worry about that. There are no explanations needed. Questions?"

No one said anything, and Bishop got ready to flip to the next screen and click on the link there.

"Show us, Bishop," Bear said. He flipped, clicked, and everyone waited while the survey site loaded.

Relief rushed through him when he saw fourteen votes in the affirmative to invest in Ranger's app. No one had voted no.

A cheer went up, and Ranger grinned out at everyone. Bear took him in a hug and clapped him on the back, his smile wide. Oakley whooped and embraced her husband when Bear released him, and Bishop was happy to join his voice to that fray.

"All right," Bear said. "Etta, we're ready for food. Zona's then going to lead us in the angel tree decorating."

"Wait," Ace said. "You said we were eating at six. Holly Ann's coming."

"My family is coming too," Montana said.

"Well, what time is it?" Bear asked, practically growling the words.

The doorbell rang as someone told him it was ten minutes to six, and Ace left the family room and kitchen space to go see who it was.

"Zona," he yelled. "It's for you."

She squealed and went to meet Duke. Bishop shut down his laptop and turned off the TV. Once he'd put everything away in his suite, all he wanted was to return to Montana's side.

She was talking to Sammy about her pregnancy, with

Oakley hanging on every word. "You're so lucky you weren't sick," Montana said. "I threw up for six solid months." She looked up at Bishop, her eyes sharp. "I'm not asking you to marry me," she said. "If that's what you're waiting for, you're going to wait forever."

Both Sammy and Oakley twittered with laughter, and Bishop scoffed and pretended to be hurt. "I can't even—I don't know what to say."

She smiled and rolled her eyes. "Oh, Aunt Jackie's here." She got up from the table, pausing before she went to greet them. Bishop would go with her anyway. She put one palm on his chest, and said, "And you better make it a good proposal. I heard Ranger snuck into a forbidden garage, with dozens of chocolate desserts, all dressed up with roses and racecars." She sighed. "And Bear showed up in a suit for a simple date and was on both knees when Sammy opened the door, ring at the ready." She patted his chest and walked away.

Bishop looked at the two women who'd joined his family. "I was gone for five minutes. How fast can you guys talk?"

"Oh, Bishop," Oakley said, standing up. "I have that woman's number. I can—and have been—talking to her any time I want." She grinned at him. "If you need some ideas for great proposals, we're right here." She gave Sammy a meaningful look and took a couple of steps away. "You want a waffle with lemon curd, whipped cream, and raspberries?"

"Yes, please," Sammy said, smiling at Oakley's back as

she walked away. She looked up at Bishop. "My best advice? Include that teenager."

Bishop turned around as Aurora called his name, and he said, "Thanks," to Sammy, already distracted by the people he wanted in his life permanently. He just had to figure out the perfect proposal to merge Montana's family with his.

Chapter Twenty-Six

Montana stood near the steps in the homestead, watching as Bear and Ranger lifted a beautiful, white-flocked Christmas tree out of the box. She didn't know anyone who set up their holiday decorations in October, but she supposed she didn't know anyone like the Glovers, period.

"It's white," Bishop said quietly to both her and Aurora. "Because this is our angel tree."

"What's an angel tree?" Aurora asked.

"It's our way of putting up a physical reminder of where we came from," Bishop said. "We hang my grandmother's crocheted ornaments and remember her. She was a powerful influence on the ranch, and on all of us."

Montana gazed at him, this handsome, strong, and oh-so-loyal cowboy.

"Grandmother had two sons," Bishop said, still

speaking in barely above a whisper, and Ward said, "Bishop is going to explain the angel tree."

"Sorry," he said. "I didn't have a chance to explain it to Montana and Aurora."

"No foul," Ward said. "I'd love to hear the stories." He smiled warmly at Bishop, and Montana got the feeling that this was a very somber and silent affair, thus Bishop whispering, even off to the side, felt wrong to Ward.

"Okay," Bishop said, still watching Bear and Ranger put the sections of the tree together. "Grandmother had two sons," he said. "One was my father, Stone, and the other was Bull, my uncle. They both had a lot of kids."

Several people twittered, and Arizona, Etta, and Mister stepped forward to start straightening the branches and pulling them into a proper tree configuration once the tree was together.

"I have five brothers and a sister. Uncle Bull had three sons and two daughters. Grandmother taught us all something." Bishop paused for a moment, and Montana marveled at the emotion he allowed to show on his face.

Looking around, she saw similar expressions of love and missing on all of the Glovers' faces.

He cleared his throat. "She taught me to cook, which I still love to do to this day. She taught Mother how to deal with a lot of boys at the same time." He put his arm around his mother, and Montana missed her own mom for maybe the first time that year. Maybe in the last five years.

She mirrored him and put her arm around Aurora. Her daughter looked at her, smiled, and leaned her head against Montana's shoulder.

"She taught Daddy how to talk to his sons, and how to treat them like equals," Bishop said. "We come from a long line of Glovers who've lived here and worked this land, raising crops and cattle and families."

Arizona stepped to his side with a box in her hand. "Every year, we hang Grandmother's ornaments on the tree in remembrance of someone who's no longer with us." She smiled though her eyes filled with tears. "Some people say a few words as they hang their ornament. Some just think of the person they love and are missing. I keep trying to get us to go in order by decade of when Grandmother made the ornaments, but I keep getting outvoted."

She looked hopefully around the crowd, but Montana could tell she was about to be disappointed again. All of the men were shaking their heads, and Bear said, "We like to put up certain ones, Zona. Please don't make us go in order," in a very soft voice. The softest Montana had ever heard him use.

"Okay," she said, and she didn't seem too put out. "If you know someone likes to hang a specific ornament, don't take it from them."

"All are welcome to put up ornaments, as many as they want," Bishop said. "For your family members who are gone. Maybe for someone who's far from you that you wish you were closer to." His eyes danced over to Montana and then away again. "There's no right or wrong here, other than don't take the bear. That's obviously for Bear."

"The rocking horse is mine," Cactus said.

"I want the bird cage," Sammy said. "I put that one up for my sister last year, if that's okay." She looked only a moment from crying too, and Montana basked in the reverence and spirit that abided in this home.

Oh, how she loved this ranch, with its rich history and huge family tree. She wondered how in the world she'd gotten so lucky to land here. How had she possibly captured the attention of such an amazing man? How would she live up to the traditions they had here? How could she contribute?

Others called out the ornaments they wanted, until Bishop held up his hand. "There are plenty of ornaments. Grandmother lived until she was ninety-four, and she made new ornaments every year. She came from the Depression Era, and she was a hoarder." He smiled and chuckled. "We loved her to the end, and she loved each of us powerfully."

Bear nodded like that was the end of the story, and as he stepped back to Sammy's side, he said, "All right. Let's decorate it. Then Mother has her iced lemon cake, and I think Oakley brought gallons and gallons of leftover hot chocolate from the dealership."

People surged forward, toward the row of boxes that Arizona had put against the wall. They spoke in quiet voices, and Bishop turned back to her when she stayed put. "You don't want to put one on?"

"I do," she said. "But I'm going to wait until the others have taken their favorites." She grinned at him. "You go on."

"Aurora?" He looked at her, and Aurora stepped away from Montana to go with him.

Aunt Jackie came to her side, and Montana leaned into

her side-hug. "He is so wonderful, Montana. This is so wonderful."

"I think so too," she said.

"I want to put something on for my parents," Uncle Bob said.

"Go ahead," Montana said.

Aunt Jackie pressed a kiss to Montana's forehead. "I'm going to find something that represents a baby and hang that for the one and only baby Bob and I lost."

"Aunt Jackie," Montana said. "I didn't know you lost a baby."

Aunt Jackie's smile wavered, and her eyes looked like polished glass. "Just the one." She went with Uncle Bob, and they sifted through several ornaments until they both found one they wanted to hang on the tree.

"You have to elbow your way through them almost all the time," Cactus said as he approached. He extended his hand toward her, and Montana shook her head at him, her emotions stabilizing. "Come on, sweetheart. I'll show you how it's done."

He'd scared her for a while there, but as she'd worked with him on his home designs, she'd realized that Cactus was very much like her. Bruised and scarred, with a past hidden behind closed and locked doors.

He'd been more vigilant in keeping his doors closed, and he'd removed himself from everything in order to heal.

She'd found in him a kind soul, and someone she absolutely understood.

"Behind you," Cactus said, and Preacher moved out of the way. "See?"

"I see," Montana said. She peered down into the box and saw at least a dozen ornaments. "Wow." The skill it must have taken to make these. She reached for a couple and straightened to examine them closer. "How long did it take her to make one of these?"

Cactus's eyes shone like the sky surrounding a full moon. Deep, and dark, and navy, but bright and full of light. "She could crochet like lightning," he said. "Mother can too." He tossed her a smile, but she just shook her head.

"Not like Grandmother." She turned and hung a maple leaf on the tree.

"She used liquid starch to form them into the three-dimensional pieces she wanted," he said. "That was quite the process. If it didn't form the way she wanted, she'd wash the starch out and try again." He picked up one that looked like a toy car, complete with yellow thread woven through the circles on the front for the headlights. "Then she'd add the detail pieces in thread."

He turned away from Montana for a moment, saying, "Oakley, here's that car Ranger was talking about." He gave the car to Oakley, who looked like Cactus had just passed her a million dollars. Her cat wove through her legs, every so often giving a loud meow that no one paid any attention to.

Benny, Sammy and Lincoln's dog, wisely sat at the top of the steps, out of the fray, and Montana thought he was the smartest of them all.

She looked at the items she'd picked up. One was a barn, which seemed absolutely fitting. The only detail on this ornament was a green wreath with a red bow done with a single piece of string. "I like this one."

"Feels appropriate," Cactus said.

Montana returned the pine tree to the box and selected another ornament. This one was an apple, and it utterly charmed her. It was pure white, and reminded her of the forbidden fruit Adam and Eve ate in the Garden of Eden.

"Grandmother put that around a real apple when she starched it," Bishop said. "I watched her do it. I think I was ten years old." He smiled at her and took the apple from her hands. "She added the stem separately." He laced a hook through the dark brown stem that was done in string, not the thicker white thread the ornaments themselves were made out of, and handed the fruit back to Montana.

"I love everything about this," she said.

"It's a good tradition," he said. "Aurora put up an ornament for you," he added in a whisper.

Alarm rang through Montana. "What does that mean?"

"I don't know," Bishop said. "I didn't mean to overhear her, and I don't think she knows I did."

"What did she say?" She found her daughter down on the other end of the boxes with Aunt Jackie and Uncle Bob. They spoke with each other and then Judge as they selected ornaments. They fit here too, just like Montana had. She suspected anyone who walked through that big front door and made any effort at all would fit in here.

"She just said, 'for my mom. I love her.'"

"Maybe that's all it meant then," Montana said. "I feel close to her, but maybe she doesn't feel the same."

"Don't overthink it," Bishop said. "I have to go find Ace. Are you okay here alone?"

"I'm good, yes."

"See you in a few." He pressed a quick kiss to her cheek and ducked out the front door.

Montana turned back to the tree and marveled at how quickly it had filled. She found a spot she could hang the barn, and she thought, *Thank you for leading me to this ranch.*

She hung the barn, feeling closer to the Glovers and God in that moment.

She pinched the hook on the apple and moved around to the back of the tree. There was a little more space back here, and she closed her eyes. *For my family, wherever they are and whatever they're doing. I love you. I miss you.*

She hung the apple as a wave of sadness rolled over her. She was sad about the current status of her familial relationships. She'd been close to her sisters once, but not anymore. She wasn't sure how to be close to someone she didn't trust.

No matter what, she felt another invisible burden she hadn't known she was carrying lift from her shoulders. She rolled her neck, and there was nothing riding there anymore. No tension. No guilt. No resentment.

"Mom," Aurora said, approaching her. "They have a book." She handed Montana the book with the brightly colored A B C strung on the front cover. "You need that for the library."

"I sure do," Montana said. "Thank you, baby." She hung the crocheted book on the tree, gazing at it with such joy. She reached for Aurora's hand. "We're okay, right, Aurora?"

"Yeah, Mom."

"You like Bishop?"

"Yes."

"You can tell me stuff. Or him. I'm fine with either. I just don't want you to ever feel like you're alone. You have both of us, or Aunt Jackie or Uncle Bob. Heck, any of these cowboys here would listen to you and help you if they could."

"I know, Mom." She squeezed Montana's hand. "Look at what I got a few minutes ago." She took her phone out of her pocket and gave it to Montana.

Her heart skipped and stopped, and she looked up at Aurora's face first. She wore excitement there, so it couldn't be a bad thing she'd gotten.

She turned on the phone and Aurora said, "Ollie texted. Read it."

Montana tapped on the texting app and then Oliver's name at the top—which was Most Amazing Boyfriend (Ollie)—in Aurora's phone. She almost rolled her eyes at that nomenclature, but she managed to refrain.

Rory, I have to see you. I've made a huge mistake, and I need to apologize. Are you home? When can we get together?

Aurora had asked: *What's the mistake?*

Saying yes to Izzy.

Montana looked up. "Bishop was right." Another text came in, and she read it quickly. "Oh, dear. He's at the house right now."

"He is?" Aurora took the phone back from Montana and giggled when she saw Oliver's newest text.

"When did you start going by Rory?" Montana asked.

"I don't," Aurora said. "It's just something Ollie calls me." Her fingers flew across the screen. "Mom, how much longer are we going to be here?"

"You came with Aunt Jackie and Uncle Bob," Montana said. "But I don't want you leaving before they're ready." She looked over her shoulder and saw them laughing with Bishop's mother and aunt. "They love it here. It's the huge family they've always wanted."

"Yeah." Aurora didn't sound happy. She looked up from her phone again. "Mom...could he come here?"

Surprise lit through Montana, but she found herself nodding. If it were her most amazing boyfriend ready to apologize for his huge mistake, she'd want to talk to him as soon as possible too. "All right. Is he driving?"

"He says his dad will bring him if we can give him a ride home." She possessed so much hope in her eyes. "Please, Mom?"

"I already said yes," Montana said, not understanding where Aurora got her dramatic streak from.

Aurora squealed, and she tapped once. "I'm going to call him. Be right back." She darted across the foyer and outside, and Montana sighed.

"Everything okay?" Bear asked.

"Yes," Montana said, smiling at him. "Thank you for having us here, Bear. This is the most amazing thing I've ever participated in."

He nodded and hung a rocket ship on the tree. "You're always welcome here, Montana. Even if Bishop can't get his act together, you'll be welcome here."

"He's got a good act together," she said.

"Well, you tell me if he doesn't," Bear said. "I've looked out for Bishop for years, and I can thump him good for you."

Montana laughed, glad when Bear at least smiled. She suspected this angel tree ceremony was as hard as it was wonderful. After all, they were missing their fathers and uncles, their grandparents and aunts.

"Let's light it," Ranger said. "Then it's time for dessert." He stepped behind the tree and waited until Ida had hung her last ornament and hurried back to Brady's side. "Ready?"

"Ready," everyone chorused.

Ranger plugged in the cord, and the tree burst to life with pure, white lights. Montana pressed one hand over her heart and *ahhh*'ed along with the others.

The party did move then, but Montana didn't go with it. She cast a look toward the front door and escaped that way instead. Aurora sat on the front steps in the stiff breeze. "They're serving cake and hot chocolate," Montana said. "Sitting out here isn't going to make him arrive faster."

"You're right." Aurora got up, shivering, and followed Montana back inside. They got their desserts and joined Oakley, Etta, and Ida at one end of the table.

"All right, ladies," Montana said. "We have a dilemma and we need real advice."

"Oh, I love dilemmas," Etta said with glee. "What is it?"

"Do you want to tell them, or should I?" Montana asked Aurora.

"I guess you better. I didn't know there was a dilemma."

"Oh, there's a dilemma," Montana said. She quickly told the story of Oliver and Izzy and Aurora. "The boy is on his way here right now. He wants to quote—*apologize*. Does she take him back instantly? Or make him work for it?"

"This *is* a real dilemma," Ida said.

"I once had a boyfriend who danced with someone else," Arizona said. "While we were on a date. He didn't get why it was a problem to have a job interview on the dance floor with another woman."

Montana sucked in a breath, the weight of every woman's eye on her now.

"Sounds ridiculous, right?" Arizona said. "I made him *work* for that apology. I vote you make him work for it, Aurora. Just because he's fifteen doesn't mean he's stupid."

Montana giggled, because she couldn't stop herself. Before she knew it, Arizona was laughing too, and everyone else had joined in, even her daughter.

"What's so funny over here?" Duke Rhinehart asked, grinning at Arizona.

"Oh, nothing," she said casually. "Did you find that left-over pecan pie? Bishop likes to hide it in the back of the fridge." She got up and led Duke away before Montana could dissolve into laughter again.

"Make him work for it," Oakley said. "You want to know why, Aurora?"

Montana wanted to know why herself.

"Why?" Aurora said.

"Because it teaches him how to treat you," Oakley said. "Never let a man treat you casually. If he wants to be with you, it'll just be you. Not you and his wife, or you for lunch and someone else for dinner."

"Oakley," Sammy said, shock in her voice. "You and his wife?"

"You make him work to earn a place at your side," Oakley said, scooping only frosting off her lemon cake. "Because that place? It's worth a million bucks, and you're worth it." She nodded like that was that, and Montana couldn't disagree with her.

She met Aurora's eye, and Aurora nodded. "So no waiting on the front steps."

"Oh, no." Sammy clucked her tongue and shook her head. "No waiting out front. He has to come in here and get you from the party. In front of everyone. He has to *want* it."

"I wouldn't squeal," Montana said. "Just a suggestion." She shrugged like she didn't care if Aurora listened to her or not.

"Absolutely no squealing," Oakley said.

"You wear a mask until he's said he's sorry at least three times," Ida said. "Maybe four. Then you ask him what he's going to do to make sure this doesn't happen again, because your heart is precious, and it doesn't deserve to get broken again."

"Four apologies?" Brady asked.

"Sometimes five," Ida said coolly.

"Only when you're sure he's desperate to be with you can you smile," Etta said. "And make sure he asks before he kisses you. In fact, I usually initiate that make-up kiss. It's *soooo* good." She pointed her fork at Aurora. "Make sure that make-up kiss blows his mind. Then, next time he thinks it's okay to say yes to another girl to be nice, he'll have that to remember."

"Okie-dokie," Montana said. "I think we've gotten all the free advice we need." She glanced at Etta and shook her head.

Etta only grinned. "What? I wish I could have a make-up kiss right now."

"You could call Jericho," Ida said casually, but Etta scoffed.

"Can you imagine?"

"Yeah, I can," Ida said dryly. "That's why I suggested it. You liked him, Etta. Just because he wore a black jacket with brown boots doesn't make him lame. You broke up with him over *nothing*."

"Hmm," Etta said. "Maybe I did...."

"He's here," Aurora said, holding up her phone.

"He texted you to say he was here?" Oakley snatched the phone from Aurora's hand. "You're going to thank me for this." She tapped while Aurora looked at her phone in horror. "There." Oakley grinned and passed the phone back to Aurora.

"Read it," Sammy said.

"She said, 'Great, you can come ring the doorbell and ask for me like a Texas gentleman.'" Aurora looked up, her eyes wide. "I'm going to die."

Montana looked toward the wide, arched walkway that led into the foyer. Everyone else did too, Aurora included.

"He's not going to do that," Aurora said. "What if—?"

The doorbell rang, and Oakley pumped her fist into the

air. "Now, you stay here. Let one of the cowboys get it. In fact." She twisted, and called, "Cactus. Can you get that and give whoever it is a hard time for interrupting our party?"

"Oh, Dear Lord," Montana said at the same time as Etta and Sammy.

"Sure thing," Cactus said, leaving the kitchen.

"Mom," Aurora whimpered.

"Put your mask on," Ida said.

"No squealing," Sammy reminded her.

"Four times," Etta said.

"Make him work for it," Oakley said.

"You're worth it," Montana added last, and then Cactus was back, a very terrified Oliver holding his cowboy hat in his hands like a shield as he faced the entire Glover clan.

"This lad is looking for Aurora?" Cactus said, and everyone's gazes flew to her.

"Take a bite of your cake," Oakley hissed. "Wait. Slow. Like you couldn't care less that he's here."

Aurora did what Oakley said, a tiny smile appearing on her lips as she put the fork full of lemon cake in her mouth.

"Oh, she's good," Sammy said, glee streaming from her face.

"Good luck, baby," Montana said.

"Remember the make-up kiss," Etta hissed as Aurora stood.

She crossed the kitchen in silence, but Bear stepped in front of her. "You're okay with him?"

"Yeah," Aurora said. "I think so."

"If you're not, you come get me, okay? Bishop had to go

next door for a minute." He turned and glared at Oliver, and Montana almost burst out laughing.

"I'll keep an eye on 'em," Cactus said, glaring at Oliver like he'd just done the worst thing a person could do by showing up here.

"Thanks, Cactus," Aurora said. She shook her hair over her shoulders and straightened to her full height. "Hello, Oliver."

"Hoo, boy, we'll say a prayer for you," someone called, and Montana did burst into giggles then. Thankfully, she wasn't the only one, and she watched as Aurora left with Oliver.

"I don't know how I'm going to survive the next four years," she said, slumping back into her chair. "The drama is crazy."

"He's an adorable boy," Oakley said. "No wonder she wanted to squeal."

"That's gonna be a *good* make-up kiss."

"Etta," Ida said. "Enough with the make-up kissing." She glared at her and exchanged a glance with Montana that said, *I swear, she has no tact.*

They shared a secret smile, and Montana utilized all of her willpower to stay in her seat so she wouldn't go spy on her daughter and the most amazing boyfriend ever.

"Oliver," Montana said. "Grab that basket of rolls, would you?"

"Yes, ma'am." He did as Montana asked, and she smiled

at him. He'd been treating Aurora like a queen since they'd made up, over a month ago now. He'd been over to the house several times, and Aurora had nothing but good things to say about him.

He'd turned sixteen, and he'd passed his driving test. He'd been on the honor roll for the first term at school, and by all accounts, Oliver Osburn was a fine, upstanding young man.

"Ollie," Lois said. "We need that honey butter, baby. Can you get it?"

"Yes, ma'am," he said again, returning to the kitchen in True Blue, where Bishop still remained. Ollie came back with the honey butter and put it near Lois. "There you go."

"Thank you, baby. Now, sit down right here and tell me how your daddy's doin' with his animation."

Ollie smiled at her and took the seat she told him to. Aurora sat next to him, a smile on her face as she listened to him talk about Tripp Walker's work.

Montana adjusted all the napkins, which Aurora had folded into fanned turkey tails, sat down, and looked toward the kitchen. "What is he doing in there?" she muttered. Everything was finished and ready. The turkey was hot, as were the mashed potatoes. Bishop shouldn't have anything left to do.

No one else seemed to mind or even notice that the table in front of them could barely hold all the food, and yet they weren't eating. Montana finally got up and went into the kitchen. One step through the door, she said, "Bishop, what are—?"

The kitchen was empty.

He'd been in there, though, five minutes ago when she'd brought out the salad and asked Oliver to grab the rolls.

She walked over to the fridge and looked behind the door. "Bishop?"

"Mom," Aurora called, and Montana swept the kitchen one more time, just to make sure that Bishop was indeed, not there.

"Coming," she said as she walked toward the door. "Have you guys seen...Bishop."

Bishop stood across the hall now, wearing the same thing she saw him in on the Sabbath. Dark slacks, with a light blue shirt that pulled slightly across his shoulders. The tie around his neck was loose and not done up all the way, the top button open at the throat.

He looked up, his dark cowboy hat no longer obscuring his face. The belt buckle at his waist added the right amount of bling, and it went with the steel-toed cowboy boots on his feet.

"Oh, my," she whispered. She couldn't even look over to the table they'd set up for their intimate family dinner. Two days ago, she'd gathered here for the huge Glover Thanksgiving dinner, but she'd wanted something more intimate for Aurora to invite Ollie to, and she wanted more one-on-one time with Bishop's mother.

"Can you come over here for a minute?" Bishop asked, but Montana couldn't get her feet to move.

"Mom," Aurora said. "Go on."

"Yeah," Aunt Jackie said. "Get over there, darling."

Oliver appeared in front of her. "I'll help you." He

linked his arm through Montana's and walked her across the hall to Bishop, who tipped his hat at Ollie.

"Thanks, son."

"Sure thing." Oliver's boots clicked against the hard floor on his way back to the table, but Montana couldn't look away from Bishop.

"Montana," he said. "I remember the moment you came into my life. I'd barely eaten breakfast, and I wasn't even all the way dressed."

She grinned at him, because she remembered that moment clearly as well.

He picked up a pink rose from the barrel beside him. "I remember the moment you said you'd go out with me." He added a second rose to his hands. "I remember when you let me meet your daughter. I remember when you introduced me to your aunt and uncle." He added a flower to the growing bouquet in his hand with every statement.

"I remember the moment I knew I was in love with you. I'm a bit of a dreamer, and though I knew you didn't love me—yet—I started thinking about our life together. I know it's not always going to be rainbows and sunshine, but I only know that because Mother keeps telling me it won't be." He kicked a smile in his mother's direction.

He held a bundle of roses now, and he tied a ribbon around them with a smile. Then he dropped to both knees and held the flowers up to her. "I love you. Will you marry me?"

"Wait," Aurora said as Montana took the flowers and breathed in their heady scent. "You skipped ahead."

"I did?"

"Yes." She came running over. "You were supposed to say a line about being my dad. You don't even have the ring."

"Oh, right." Bishop looked up at her, his face turning a ruddy shade of red.

"What were you going to do? Tie a ribbon around her finger?" Aurora shook her head. "You were supposed to call me over and say—"

"I got it," Bishop said. "Do I have to stand up again?"

"I would," Aurora hissed.

Montana couldn't stop smiling, and she watched as Aurora held out her hand and Bishop used it to stand. He brushed his pants off and said, "I remember when I thought about what it would be like to be Aurora's father. I'm terrified of that, but I'm going to do my best."

"You'll do great, Bishop," Aurora said in an overly theatrical voice, moving to stand beside him.

"Oh, this is bad," Montana said, giggling. She could see the handoff of the ring box easily, as Aurora almost dropped it trying to slide it into Bishop's hand, which he held behind his leg.

"Did I miss anything else?" he whispered.

"No, you're good," Aurora murmured.

"I don't have the flowers anymore."

"Improvise."

Montana started to laugh, her joy filling her over and over again. "Yes," she said among her giggles. "My answer is yes." She closed the distance between Bishop and Aurora and together, they made a three-way hug. "I love you guys."

"I love you too," Bishop said.

"I love you three," Aurora said. "Bishop, put the ring on her finger."

"Oh, right."

Aurora stepped out of the way as Bishop opened the box and showed Montana the ring. "Bishop, it's beautiful."

"Aunt Jackie helped me," he said, sliding the ring onto her finger. She admired it as Bishop added, "I really messed that up. You're not going to tell everyone about it, are you?"

"I'm going to tell absolutely everyone," Montana said, smiling up at him. "It was perfect, Bishop. You're wonderful." She wrapped her arms around his neck. "Kiss me, cowboy."

He did, and Montana kissed him—her fiancé—right on back.

Chapter Twenty-Seven

"It has to cure for another couple of days," Bishop said, his arm slung around Montana's waist. The wind kicked up, blowing around the powdery snow that had been on the ground for a couple of days.

He turned away from the newly poured foundation of their house and closed his eyes. "We're probably going to start out behind," he said.

"That's construction in the winter," Montana said. "Don't worry about it, baby. It'll cure, and we'll frame it. It's going to be a great house."

"I know, because you designed it." Bishop had worked with her on the plans, and he was pleased with the final drawings. They'd have plenty of room for dogs and teenagers, babies and construction tools. He wanted to put a paddock on the side too, so he could have horses the way Cactus did.

"What did you get Aurora for Christmas?" she asked.

Bishop opened his mouth to answer, only cutting himself off at the last moment. "Nice try. It's a surprise, and I'm not telling anyone. She's going to love it."

"It was expensive, wasn't it?"

"It's needed," he said. They were going to live forty minutes from the high school, and Aurora would need a car to get there and back. He'd been teaching her to drive around the ranch and the road leading up to it. She was great on the highway too.

Montana's design for the library had just been approved, and she'd be splitting her time between their house up here and the library in town.

Bishop wanted to make her life as easy as possible, and if Aurora could get to school and back by herself, that would make everything easier.

"Come on," Montana said. "Your mother is waiting inside." She turned, and he went with her. They entered True Blue from the back, coming in near the bathrooms. Pretty music played through the speakers, and Bishop frowned, his curiosity increasing.

"What's happening?"

He went to the doorway that led into the big hall only to find Mother there, as he expected. He did not expect to find Ward, Judge, and Cactus there, all of them listening to Mother and then taking turns dancing with her.

"What in the world?" he asked.

"She's teaching them to dance," Montana said.

The music cut out, and Bishop quickly ducked behind the wall. "Shh," he said, pulling Montana against him. They started to laugh together, both of them keeping as quiet as possible. Bishop felt like his chest was going to burst, but he didn't dare make a sound.

Low voices reached his ears, and then they moved away. When Bishop couldn't hold it in any longer, he laughed out loud. "They were learning to dance," he said through the chuckles.

"Bishop?" Mother asked, and he went around the corner. "Come look at this layout."

"Sure." Bishop led a still-giggling Montana over to his mother, who had a book open on the counter outside the kitchen.

"The aisle goes from the back to the front," Mother said. "Did you want the stage? It was hard to see the bride and groom at both weddings earlier this year."

Bishop looked at Montana. "Do you want the stage?"

"I think so," Montana said, still looking at the book. "I want a wide aisle. I want Aurora on one side, and Uncle Bob on the other."

"That's fine," Mother said. "You said you won't have much family?"

"No," Montana said. "My aunt and uncle. Maybe a couple of friends. Former clients. That kind of thing."

"You're going to invite everyone, aren't you?" Bishop asked.

"I'm going to invite them, yes," she said. "But I don't think they'll come, and honestly, Bishop, I don't want them there. It'll just stress me out."

"We'll aim for less stress on your wedding day," Mother said. "I'd love to do the flowers for you two. Do you have a date in mind?"

Bishop looked at Montana, and Montana looked at Bishop.

"I want to wait until the house is done," she said. "We won't have anywhere to live if we don't have the house done."

"April?" Bishop guessed. "It shouldn't take that long. I won't be working on five different projects this winter. Just the house." It wasn't even Christmas yet, and they'd broken ground and poured the foundation already. Plus, if there was a date set, he'd have plenty of motivation to get the house finished.

"April third is a Saturday," Mother said. "Or the tenth. If we go to the tenth, the bluebonnets will be in bloom. Those would be lovely in this barn."

"Let's do April tenth, then," Montana said. "Does that work, Bishop?"

"Bear's baby is due the end of February, so this won't interfere with that," Bishop mused. "There will be plenty of people to look after Aurora while we're on a honeymoon, even though school won't be out yet."

"My aunt and uncle have already agreed to have her come there."

"I don't see why April tenth won't work," Bishop said. "Let's schedule that, Mother."

"Perfect," she said. "You're doing the ceremony, dinner, and dancing, right?"

"Yes," Bishop said. "You're just doing the venue, Mother. And the flowers. We'll take care of everything else, okay?"

"Okay," Mother said. "If you need any help, let me

know." She closed her book, smiled at them, and left True Blue.

"My mother has always wanted to be a wedding planner," Bishop said. "I think she's been inspired by Penny Walker, and she just wants to help."

"I don't care if she plans the whole thing," Montana said.

"Really?" Bishop asked.

"Bishop, do I seem like the type of woman that worries about her wedding?"

"I suppose not. What about your first wedding? What was that like?"

Montana cleared her throat. "We, uh, went to City Hall."

"You're kidding," he said.

"I'm not."

"We're not doing that," he said. "You must have some idea of what you want."

"Yes," she said. "I want you in a fancy black suit. Or a tuxedo. I want to wear a white dress with a long train. I want to wear flowers in my hair, and I want you and all of your brothers and cousins in cowboy hats. I want Etta and Ida and all the girls in the wedding party too. I want the music to be loud, and the food good, and I want to be a Glover more than anything."

Bishop listened to her talk, and he loved her a little bit more with every word she spoke. "Do you want me to cook?"

"At our own wedding? No," she said. "We'll hire. What about Holly Ann?"

"Oh, uh, I don't know about that," Bishop said. "Maybe, I guess. She and Ace are sort of on-again, off-again, and I guess she flipped things off a while ago, and he's trying to figure out what to do about it."

"I don't understand her," Montana said. "She really seemed to like him. How do you just turn that off?"

"I don't know," Bishop said. "He's stopped talking about her, and I don't make him talk about stuff he doesn't want to."

"Fair enough." Montana tugged on his arm. "Come on, cowboy. Show me your dance moves. Maybe you'll need to join your mother's dancing lessons."

"I'm a good dancer," Bishop said, taking her easily into his arms. "My mother already taught me to dance. I had this girl in high school I really wanted to impress, and she and Daddy demonstrated for me in the kitchen, night after night."

"Who was the girl?" Montana asked, grinning up at him.

"Her name was Cheryl, and she was gorgeous. All this blonde hair—I'm a sucker for blondes—and a beautiful pair of blue eyes. She ran track, and she had long legs, and wow."

"Okay," Montana said, chuckling. "Is that what you said to Bear when you told him about me? She's got all this blonde hair and these pretty blue eyes. But she's kind of short, and a little heavy, but *wow*."

"You are not short or heavy," he said, looking down at her in surprise.

"I'm not a runner," she said. "Or even close to a size

zero."

"I think you're gorgeous," he said. "And I did from the very first moment I laid eyes on you." He swayed with her, grinning as he spun her out, and then brought her back into the safety of his arms.

"You are a good dancer, Bishop," she said.

"Thank you, love," he said. He pressed his cheek to hers and whispered, "I got Aurora a very sensible little truck that will get her up to the ranch and back to school. Good gas mileage. Low miles."

"I knew you'd gotten her a car." Montana snuggled right into his chest.

"You're not mad?"

"I'm not mad," she said. "I've accepted that you buy things to show me that you love me, and that you want my life to be easier."

"I—well, I can't argue, I guess."

"You're a sweet, sweet man," Montana said. "I love you, Bishop." She touched her mouth to his, and Bishop leaned forward, wanting more. But she pulled away.

"Hmm," he said. "That was a terrible kiss."

"That's because it wasn't a kiss," she teased. "I was just experimenting to see if I'd want to kiss you every day for the rest of my life."

"Okay," he said with plenty of sarcasm. "You're never going to let me live that down, are you?"

"I do, by the way. Want to kiss you every day for the rest of my life." She beamed at him, and Bishop reached up and tucked her hair behind her ear.

"Thank you for completing me," he said, and when he

kissed her this time, it was a real kiss, with plenty of passion and feeling behind it. All of his love and adoration, and everything he hoped their relationship already was and all it could be.

And the best part? She kissed him back the exact same way.

<hr>

Read on for the first couple of chapters of the next book in the Shiloh Ridge Ranch in Three Rivers series, **THE SECRET OF SANTA**.

Sneak Peek! The Secret of Santa
Chapter One:

Ace Glover ignored the knock on the front door of his house, though he sat in the office only a few paces away. He knew who it was, and he didn't want to talk to Bishop. Besides his brothers, his cousin was his best friend, but Ace didn't want to explain anything.

"I'm not going away," Bishop called through the front door. "I know this thing isn't locked, and I'm coming in if you don't come open the door."

Ace sighed and pressed pause on the video he'd watched four times already. He should've known he couldn't just leave the family party without someone noticing. Truth be told, there were a ton of people at the homestead, and he'd hoped and prayed that maybe, just maybe, he would be overlooked this one time.

"Just another prayer the Lord didn't answer," he muttered to himself. Louder, he called, "Come in then," and Bishop wasted no time entering the house. Three steps later, he appeared in the doorway of the office.

"What's going on?"

"Nothing," Ace said. "I just don't want to be there."

"You missed dinner."

That was saying something too, as Ace could barely boil water. His brother, whom he lived with, was a good cook, though, and there was always something to eat next door anyway.

Ace swiveled in the office chair he'd spent entirely too much money on for how often he used it, and smashed his cowboy hat further onto his head. "I don't want to talk about it."

"Holly Ann didn't show up." Bishop entered the office and sat in the chair across from Ace. "Why not?"

"Did you not just hear what I said?" Ace growled. The more time he spent with Cactus, the more he thought the man had the right idea about everything. Live far away from the epicenter of the ranch. Give short, curt answers. Never smile. Eventually, everyone would leave him alone.

The problem was, Ace loved to laugh, and he loved living right at the heart of Shiloh Ridge Ranch. He usually liked talking, and he definitely enjoyed big family meals, movie and game nights, and horseback riding on Sunday afternoons with anyone who wanted to saddle up and go.

"It's just me," Bishop said. "You tell me everything."

"Not everything," Ace said, though Bishop was ninety-nine percent right. He sighed, his stomach growling loudly.

"Just come eat," Bishop said. "Or I'll bring you something."

He was missing the angel tree decorating too, and Ace loved that family tradition almost more than any other. "Bring me something," Ace said, and Bishop got to his feet without hesitation.

"Be right back." His cousin walked out, and Ace frowned at the laptop in front of him. Part of him wanted to pick it up and hurl it through the front windows. The other part wanted to watch the video again.

He leaned forward and pressed play, the image of his beautiful Holly Ann coming up on the screen. "She's not yours," he practically growled as a smile lit her face and she surveyed the crowd he couldn't see.

She spoke into the microphone about how "delighted" she was to be named this year's Christmas Festival chairperson, and that she pledged to do her best to make this holiday season the best one Three Rivers had ever seen.

She'd texted him an hour ago, when she should've almost been to the ranch. They'd held a family meeting before dinner, and while he was serious about Holly Ann, he didn't think they were quite to the point where he involved her in the business decisions of the ranch.

Bishop had had his girlfriend there, and of course, Bear and Ranger had their wives. Cactus had not invited his girlfriend, but Ida had her boyfriend there with her.

Ace picked up his phone, which he'd silenced after Holly Ann's first text, and found at least a dozen more.

Ida had sent the most messages, and that didn't surprise him one bit. He was close with the twins, and while they were identical, Ida was far more approachable than Etta. She was also worried about him.

I'm okay, he typed out. *Bishop is getting me something to eat, and I'm just going to hole up here for a while. I'm really fine. Hang one of the cowboy boots for Daddy for me, okay?*

If Ace was a betting man, he'd put ten bucks down that Ida had already hung the boot, and that she'd call within the hour.

Got the boot for you already, her next text said. *I'll call you on the way home, okay?*

Ace grinned at the predictability of his sister. His heart expanded too, because he knew she cared about him. Genuinely cared about him.

Just like Bishop did. He walked right into the house, no knocking or doorbell ringing, only a few minutes later, a plate laden with more food than both of them could eat.

"Here you go," he said, putting the plate in front of Ace. "What's playing?"

Ace hastened to pause the video again, but Bishop had already come around the desk to see.

"Holly Ann," he said. "She's the new chairperson. No wonder she couldn't come." He looked at Ace, their eyes meeting for a long moment. A lot was said there, and Ace should've known he wouldn't have to explain. He'd just have to look at Bishop, show him the video, and sigh.

Ace picked up the fork Bishop had brought. "She texted to say she'd been nominated and voted in as this year's chairperson, and I should go watch the press release." He looked at the plate of food, noticing the extra tall pile of shredded brisket. Bishop knew him so well.

"So I ducked out to the porch to do that, and there she was, live. *Live*. Not on her way here. Not pulling in." He stabbed his fork into a roll and split it open, then stacked meat onto that. "What's so important in Three Rivers that we need a *live* press release?" He shook his head and swiped his utensil through the barbecue sauce Ida spent hours perfecting. With that slathered on his meat, he folded his roll over and took a bite of his sandwich.

There was nothing Ace liked more than smoked meat sandwiches. Fine, maybe Holly Ann. Maybe even Christmas. She loved the holidays as much as he did, and they both volunteered at the town's six-week Christmas Festival. Ace had been looking forward to it with everything inside him.

"Can I see it?" Bishop asked.

Ace pulled the indicator back to the beginning of the video and hit play. He turned the laptop around, because he'd seen it enough to have some of it memorized already.

"This is Winn Clark with Channel Three in Three Rivers. We're live outside the City Council chambers, where we're expecting to hear who the chairperson for this year's Christmas Festival will be."

Ace rolled his eyes at the exuberance in the man's voice. Did he honestly think this was news? Was he seriously *so excited* about this announcement?

"Here we go," he said a few seconds later. "It looks like Mayor Hall is going to make the announcement."

Pause, shuffle, mic feedback.

Ace added a fork full of pea salad to his next bite of brisket sandwich, the bright pop of the peas and the addition of mayo to the meat and barbecue sauce was a match made in heaven.

"I'm pleased to announce that long-time volunteer and small-business owner, Holly Ann Broadbent, has been appointed as this year's Christmas Festival chairperson," the mayor said, his voice deep and rich and rolling with plenty of Southern accent. "She recently started Three Cakes Catering, which quickly shot to the top of the review charts online, as well as our own Three Rivers Two Cents app."

"That's not what it's called," Bishop said, which was exactly Ace's reaction. Ace had yelled some different choice words about how *he* had been the one to recommend Holly Ann and Three Cakes to literally everyone, in every online forum, on Two Cents itself, and to anyone who even got close to mentioning a party or get-together.

He'd gotten her all that business. *He'd* put her at the top of those charts, where organic visibility took over after that.

Ace wasn't an idiot. He'd earned a business degree with an emphasis in marketing, thank you very much. He knew what it took to get a business off the ground, and the power of word-of-mouth should never be overlooked.

He'd been that mouth.

She'd still be baking in her momma's kitchen without him.

Surprised at his bitterness, he shoved the rest of his sandwich in his mouth, already looking at the plate for the next thing to soothe his bruised ego. His heart had already been cracked by this woman, and he felt it starting to flake off piece by piece.

"She specializes in desserts, I've heard," the mayor

continued, chuckling. "And she comes with the greatest endorsement of all—that of long-time chairperson and founder of the Christmas Festival, Ruth Deerfield. Ruth?"

"This part is stupid," Ace said. "She drones on and on about the festival, as if we don't know what it is, and then says Holly Ann is literally the only person she trusts the festival to."

"So I can skip ahead?"

"Yeah."

Bishop did that while Ace loaded a ridged potato chip with his mother's famous frog eye salad. The salty chip only added to the cool salad, which also had a fruity tang to it.

"Oh, she's on now." Bishop sat back down. "She looks good, Ace."

"She always looks good," Ace said. That was true. Holly Ann knew how to put on the exact right shade of eye shadow to convey a message. She never wore too much lipstick, and her eyelashes always looked a mile long.

Her hair fell in soft waves over her shoulders, and Ace knew exactly what it felt like between his fingers as he kissed her. He shoved another potato chip in his mouth so he wouldn't grind his teeth together.

She wore professional clothes tonight, almost like she'd known—she'd *known*—she'd get selected as chairperson. He scoffed but ignored Bishop's curious look.

"Hello, Three Rivers," she said, her voice bright. It wasn't the same one she used when she was alone with Ace. When she wanted him to kiss her, she spoke in a low, throaty tone that made his blood burn like fire. When she was excited to see him, her voice pitched up as she laughed and squealed.

This was such a fake, fake voice, and Ace hated it. He kept his head ducked as he shook it, hating the sound of her presentation voice.

"Who's ready for an amazing holiday season?" he asked with her, waving his fork as the crowd cheered.

"Wow, you're really bitter," Bishop said.

"Yes," Ace said, deciding to own the feeling. "Read this." He used his fork to push his phone closer to Bishop.

His cousin picked it up, and it didn't take long to read Holly Ann's few texts. The one where she said she'd been appointed as the chairperson.

The one that said she wouldn't make it for dinner and the angel tree decorating.

The last one where she'd said she was so, so sorry, but she'd be so busy for the next few months, and maybe they should take a break.

"Take a break?" Bishop asked. "Why?"

"Did you read my mind?" Ace asked.

"You didn't ask her."

"I don't need to ask her," Ace said. "She gave me this exact same excuse when she started Three Cakes. It's like, she's...I don't know. She can't walk and chew gum at the same time. She can't have a boyfriend and do anything else, it seems."

"That's just ridiculous," Bishop said.

"You're telling me."

"What are you going to do?"

"Eat another brisket sandwich," he said, looking over the lid of the laptop. "What can I do?"

Bishop closed the laptop, and he hadn't even gotten to the part where she laughed like a hyena about the addition of a children's bike parade this year. A fake hyena.

"You like this woman, right?"

"Of course I like this woman." Ace glared at Bishop. "She's dominated my life for almost a year now. Even when I want to walk away, I can't. She's...." He shook his head. For him, Holly Ann was who he wanted. When they were together, she sure did act like he was who she wanted.

She'd said those words right out loud. To his face.

Then she sent texts about "taking a break."

"You don't need to explain," Bishop said quietly. "I understand." He took a long, deep breath. "Here's what I think, and it's going to go against what we always do."

"Honestly, what I always do isn't working for me," Ace said.

"You stop stuffing your face," Bishop said. "You go brush your teeth real good. Get your hair all fixed up under that cowboy hat. Make sure your clothes are clean."

"I was going to see her at dinner," Ace said. "I'm ready." Maybe he should brush his teeth, though.

"You know where she lives. You know she's still dealing with press or City Council members. You go wait in her driveway, and when she gets home, there you are. You hold up your phone, and you say, 'I don't want to take a break. Life is busy, Holly Ann. Are we going to break-up every time you get a little busy? Heck, I'm busy all the dang time. I work overnight during birthing season. I ride for twenty hours during round-up. I go out at three a.m. to start planting, which takes over a month. I—"

"I get it," Ace said, holding up his hand so Bishop would stop.

He did, and the two of them looked at one another. Hope started to collect in Ace's chest, and it pressed against his heart, which started to beat like a drum.

"I go tell her no, I don't want to take a break," Ace mused. "I don't just let her dictate to me how things are going to be."

"That's right," Bishop said. "You go fight for her. For the two of you. For your relationship." He grinned at Ace. "Women like that. And we—" He gestured between the two of them, and then around the room, likely indicating every man on this ranch. "We never do that. We never just say, 'no, that won't work for me.'"

"Ranger did," Ace said quietly. "When Oakley wanted to date him and other men...he said no. That won't work for me." He looked at Bishop, his eyes wide.

"And now she's his wife."

"This might work."

Bishop chuckled and leaned back in his chair, folding his arms across his chest. The moment sobered, and then he asked, "Why are you still here? Go. Go already!"

Ace got to his feet, his heart racing. He didn't do things like this. He wasn't even sure where to start.

"Teeth," Bishop said. "Just in case there's any kissing, you don't need that frog eye breath."

"Teeth," Ace said, striding out of the office and taking the steps up to his room.

Bishop followed him, saying, "Then you need to wipe your face. Spray some of that sexy cologne on your collar. Drive down to her house, and wait. That's it, Ace. You can do that."

Ace brushed his teeth and washed his face. He let Bishop spray the cologne, and then he was ready to go.

"Drive, wait, talk to her," Ace said, his fear diving through him. He *really* didn't do things like this.

"You look great," Bishop said, looking down to Ace's boots and back to his hat. "Everything is on-point. You've got this."

"Thanks." Ace drew in a lung full of air and held it. "Okay, well, will you tell Mister and Ward where I am?"

Bishop started to say yes, and then said, "Mister?"

"He lives here," Ace said.

"No, he doesn't," Bishop said. "He lives up in a cabin by my mother."

Ace shook his head. "He told everyone that, but there aren't even dishes in that cabin. Or toilet paper. He sleeps in one of the bedrooms in the basement." Ace started downstairs to the kitchen to get the keys to his truck. "We keep tellin' him to go get his clothes and just bring it all down here. He doesn't want anyone to know he lives here."

"Of course we're going to know. We'll see him go in and out."

"You live right next door and didn't know." Ace cocked his eyebrow at Bishop. "He's been here for months."

"Huh."

"He just needs to be left alone," Ace said. "We all feel like that from time to time."

"Yes, we do," Bishop said.

"Okay." Ace opened the drawer and took out his keys. "Here I go."

"Good luck," Bishop called after him, and Ace leaned on his luck all the way to Holly Ann's.

Her windows were dark, but she had outside lights on. He pulled right into her driveway, leaving only half for her, adjusted the radio so it wasn't quite so loud, and unbuckled his seatbelt so he could settle in to wait.

He didn't have to wait long, actually. Only about twenty minutes went by before a pair of headlights carved their way through the darkness and her SUV eased to a stop next to his truck.

"Now or never," he whispered to himself. He'd steadfastly refused to pray, because he felt like he jinxed himself every time he did. The Lord seemed to think it would be funny to do the exact opposite of what Ace prayed for anyway. He didn't see the point anymore.

He got out of the truck and rounded the back of it so he was approaching Holly Ann as she got out of her SUV. She carried an oversized purse, a forty-four-ounce soda cup, and a bag of take-out.

"Ace," she said, her voice full of shock. "What are you doing here?"

He hadn't memorized Bishop's speech, but Ace had never really had a problem speaking his mind. He held up his phone. "I don't want to take a break." He cleared his throat. "Life is busy, Holly Ann. We can't break-up every single time you have something going on in your life. That's not how real relationships work."

She stared at him, her eyes wide. She was stunning, even with only the light from her car spilling onto her, and the house lights haloing her from behind. She wasn't wearing a jacket over her nearly sheer blouse, as it was the same one she'd worn on-camera.

He'd been able to see the outline of her black camisole underneath the blouse, which was cream-colored and covered with multi-colored stars. She'd paired it with a black pencil skirt and a sexy pair of ankle boots that gave her an extra three inches.

He did not want to break up with her. He was not going to let her break up with him. He wished she'd say something.

The tension in her shoulders broke, and she eased out of the way of her door, using her foot to close it. "Do you want to come in?"

"Yes," he said instantly. "Let me help you with all of that." He stepped forward and took her drink and her food. She smiled at him, and it wasn't the horrible, fake smile he'd seen on TV. His hope rebounded and shot into the sky, because maybe—just maybe—doing something he'd never done before would get him something he'd never gotten before.

Sneak Peek! The Secret of Santa
Chapter Two:

◈

Holly Ann Broadbent put her heavy purse down on the built-in desk in her kitchen while Ace Glover set her food and drink on the counter. Her little brown and white dog, Snickers, yipped at her, jumping up on her legs in excitement.

"Yes, I see you," she said, grinning at the dog. "I left you home for so long, didn't I?" She scooped him into her arms and took him to the sliding glass door. "Go out and go potty." The little dog ran into the darkness, and she flipped the switch to turn on the lights in the back yard.

Turning around, she faced Ace. She couldn't believe he was here. He had a lot of nerve to be sitting in her driveway this late at night. She could've called the cops on him for loitering and scaring her half to death. If she hadn't recognized that half-ton truck in an unusual matte gray the color of river mud, she would have.

At the same time, every cell in her body vibrated with a new kind of energy, all of it screaming, *Ace Glover is here!*

Ace Glover didn't just give up this time!

"Did you eat?" she asked, reaching for the white paper bag her Chinese food had come in. "I have plenty." She glanced at him, but she'd never been able to just take a casual look. Ace demanded that she really soak him in, even when she tried not to.

Tonight, he wore a sexy pair of dark wash jeans that made his legs look impossibly long. He always had the cowboy boots, the cowboy hat, and the belt buckle. Always. They were three of her favorite things about Ace.

His gray shirt peeked through his jacket at his throat, only a triangle of light against the dark brown leather. He lit her up every time he walked in the room. Every single time.

"I ate," he said, and she wondered how much time had gone by while she drank him in. She hadn't even taken one container out of the bag yet, so probably not much.

"Did you hear what I said outside?" he asked.

"Yes," she said, opening the box and getting a nose full of orange mixed with fried food. Her stomach growled, and her mouth watered. "That's why I invited you in."

"So...we're not breaking up?"

"You said you didn't want to."

"I don't."

"I'm going to be incredibly busy." Not only that, but Holly Ann didn't deal well with stress or exhaustion. She would be both stressed and exhausted, constantly, from now until New Year's Day. "And Ace, you thought I was bad when I was taking care of Snickers and wasn't sleeping. This is going to be ten times worse."

"I'll come sit with you while you sleep," he said quietly.

Holly Ann saw no point in dirtying a plate she'd have to wash later, so she took the whole bag and a fork to the table and sat down. A groan came out of her mouth, because while these boots were adorable, they also pinched her toes and reminded her that she carried thirty extra pounds and doing that on a heel no wider than a penny was hard work for her feet and calves. Really hard work.

"I'll come rub your feet after a long day of baking and then Christmassing." He stepped over to the door and opened it for Snickers, who hopped inside and trotted right over to her side, clearly wanting some Chinese food too.

She grinned at Ace, and he took that to mean he could sit at the table with her, which he did. He didn't touch her, though Holly Ann wouldn't have objected to that either.

She didn't want to break-up with him, especially now that he'd shown up to fight for their relationship.

"I can support you while you're busy," he said while she opened her ham fried rice. "When I'm busy, and you're not, you can support me."

"Sounds romantic," Holly Ann said, tossing him a dry look. She *loved* the romantic things of the world, but she was practical too.

"It's called real life," Ace said, his voice somewhat sour. "You don't see marriages breaking up when someone gets too busy."

"Actually," Holly Ann said, spearing a piece of orange

chicken and rolling it around in her ham fried rice. "You do see that." She put the food in her mouth, at least a dozen things getting satisfied with just that simple action.

"Holly Ann," he said. "Not every marriage is going to end the way your parents' did."

She sucked in a breath and glared at him. "I know that."

"Okay." He backed right down, and Holly Ann wasn't sure if she liked that or not. No one usually spoke to her like that. They let her wallow in her reasons why she didn't date too seriously—or at least why she hadn't until Ace Glover.

They said things like, "You're right, Holly Ann," and "It's hard to maintain a relationship with someone who's so busy all the time."

Ace might have even said those things in the past. He hadn't tonight.

"Sorry," she murmured, pinching a tiny piece of chicken between her thumb and forefinger and feeding it to Snickers. "It's just, I...I don't know how to keep everyone happy."

"That's not your job," he said. "I know how to make myself happy, and Holly Ann, you're a big part of that. I'm very *un*happy without you, and I'd rather bring you dinner so you can keep working, or volunteer to pick up the popcorn for an event so you don't have to, or coordinate with the pastor to make your life easier, than not talk to you. Than not see you at all. Than think about you all dang day and all night, wondering why I'm not good enough for you."

He pulled in a breath, which inflated his chest, widening it the same way Holly Ann's eyes had widened with every word he'd spoken.

He thought about her all day and all night?

He'd rather bring her dinner and call that a relationship?

He thought he wasn't good enough for her?

Holly swallowed and dropped her gaze to her gooey orange chicken. "I apologize if I've ever given you the feeling that you are not good enough for me," she said. "That is simply not true, nor has it ever been true, and whatever I did to give you that impression, I'm sorry."

Ace said nothing while she rolled around another piece of chicken, popped it into her mouth, and ate it.

She fed Snickers another chicken snack and finally looked up at Ace, and he seemed to be warring with himself.

"You made me feel like that when you chose Three Cakes over me," he said. "And you did it again tonight, by suggesting we end things between us so you can run the Christmas Festival."

Holly Ann opened her mouth to deny such a thing, but her mind thankfully worked faster than her voice. She snapped her mouth closed when she realized he was right.

"You're right," she said. "I didn't realize it."

"You didn't realize it?"

"I—" She stabbed another piece of chicken, wishing it was her own eyeball. "I sometimes get caught up in things, is all," she said. "I have a hard time focusing on more than one thing at a time."

"You can use your ADD or your dyslexia all you want," he said. "I understand they're real, and they're hard for you. But I'm sitting right here, telling you that I'm not going anywhere. In fact, *I* can help you focus on us when it's the right time, and the Christmas Festival when it's time for that."

Holly Ann nodded and doctored up her next bite of chicken. "You're the one who's too good for me, Ace."

"That's nonsense," he said. "We really should stop thinking that about ourselves."

"I will if you will."

"Deal," he said, and she loved this back-and-forth between them. They'd always gotten along so well, and Ace was one of the easiest men for Holly Ann to talk to.

"I don't want to break-up," she said.

"Good," he said. "Neither do I."

She ate another bite of chicken, and then asked, "So where do we go from here?"

He grinned at her and reached over to take her forkless hand between both of his. "You open your calendar, sweetheart, and you tell me when you're available for breakfast, lunch, or dinner. I'll take you out or bring the food to you. Whatever you want. If it's twenty minutes, it's twenty minutes."

He looked at her with those beautiful, sky-blue eyes, so full of hope and desire, and Holly Ann loved being looked at by Ace. "I just want to be with you. Deal?"

"Deal," she said, a yawn immediately following. "Will you stay while I change into something that's not squeezing me like a python?"

He chuckled and slid his hands away from hers. "Sure."

"Will you stay with me until I fall asleep?" she whispered. "I'm so tired."

"Yes," he said, his voice quiet too. "Go change and come lay with me on the couch."

Holly Ann took one more bite of chicken and rice and went to do exactly what Ace had suggested. She could admit that coming home alone added to her burden, and when she'd realized it was Ace waiting for her in the driveway, she'd been almost giddy.

"Come on, Snickers," she said to the little dog, who trotted into her bedroom after her.

After closing the door, she stripped out of her confining clothes and tossed them toward the closet. The red Santa suit hanging there caught her attention, and she pulled in a tight breath. Crossing the room quickly, she closed the closet door so the suit couldn't be seen from the doorway.

Not that Ace would be there. She'd closed the door besides.

Still. "He can't know about that," she whispered to Snickers. "That's why I needed to take a break." She looked from closed door to closed door, her heart battling with her brain.

We can do it, her heart said. *He'll never know. He works up at that ranch a lot. It's fine.*

This is too risky, her brain said. *We don't care how handsome he is, or how many times he says such perfect things. He can never know you wear the suit.*

"He won't," she vowed, going with her heart for maybe

the first time in her life. She could only add a prayer to her internal debate that following her heart wasn't going to be the biggest mistake of her life.

The Mechanics of Mistletoe (Book 1): Bear Glover can be a grizzly or a teddy, and he's always thought he'd be just fine working his generational family ranch and going back to the ancient homestead alone. But his crush on Samantha Benton won't go away. She's a genius with a wrench on Bear's tractors...and his heart. Can he tame his wild side and get the girl, or will he be left broken-hearted this Christmas season?

The Horsepower of the Holiday (Book 2): Ranger Glover has worked at Shiloh Ridge Ranch his entire life. The cowboys do everything from horseback there, but when he goes to town to trade in some trucks, somehow Oakley Hatch persuades him to take some ATVs back to the ranch. (Bear is NOT happy.)

She's a former race car driver who's got Ranger all revved up... Can he remember who he is and get Oakley to slow down enough to fall in love, or will there simply be too much horsepower in the holiday this year for a real relationship?

The Construction of Cheer (Book 3): Bishop Glover is the youngest brother, and he usually keeps his head down and gets the job done. When Montana Martin shows up at Shiloh Ridge Ranch looking for work, he finds himself inventing construction projects that need doing just to keep her coming around. (Again, Bear is NOT happy.) She wants to build her own construction firm, but she ends up carving a place for herself inside Bishop's heart. Can he convince her *he's* all she needs this Christmas season, or will her cheer rest solely on the success of her business?

The Secret of Santa (Book 4): He's a fun-loving cowboy with a heart of gold. She's the woman who keeps putting him on hold. Can Ace and Holly Ann make a relationship work this Christmas?

The Harmony of Holly (Book 5): He's as prickly as his name, but the new woman in town has caught his eye. Can Cactus shelve his temper and shed his cowboy hermit skin fast enough to make a relationship with Willa work?

The Chemistry of Christmas (Book 6): He's the black sheep of the family, and she's a chemist who understands formulas, not emotions. Can Preacher and Charlie take their quirks and turn them into a strong relationship this Christmas?

The Delivery of Decor (Book 7): When he falls, he falls hard and deep. She literally drives away from every relationship she's ever had. Can Ward somehow get Dot to stay this Christmas?

Rhett's Make-Believe Marriage (Book 1): She needs a husband to be credible as a matchmaker. He wants to help a neighbor. Will their fake marriage take them out of the friend zone?

Tripp's Trivial Tie (Book 2): She needs a husband to keep her son. He's wanted to take their relationship to the next level, but she's always pushing him away. Will their trivial tie take them all the way to happily-ever-after?

Liam's Invented I-Do (Book 3): She's desperate to save her ranch. He wants to help her any way he can. Will their invented I-Do open doors that have previously been closed and lead to a happily-ever-after for both of them?

Jeremiah's Bogus Bride (Book 4): He wants to prove to his brothers that he's not broken. She just wants him. Will a fake marriage heal him or push her further away?

Wyatt's Pretend Pledge (Book 5): To get her inheritance, she needs a husband. He's wanted to fly with her for ages. Can their pretend pledge turn into something real?

Skyler's Wanna-Be Wife (Book 6): She needs a new last name to stay in school. He's willing to help a fellow student. Can this wanna-be wife show the playboy that some things should be taken seriously?

Micah's Mock Matrimony (Book 7): They were just actors auditioning for a play. The marriage was just for the audition – until a clerical error results in a legal marriage. Can these two ex-lovers negotiate this new ground between them and achieve new roles in each other's lives?

Her Cowboy Billionaire Birthday Wish (Book 1): All the maid at Whiskey Mountain Lodge wants for her birthday is a handsome cowboy billionaire. And Colton can make that wish come true—if only he hadn't escaped to Coral Canyon after being left at the altar...

Her Cowboy Billionaire Butler (Book 2): She broke up with him to date another man...who broke her heart. He's a former CEO with nothing to do who can't get her out of his head. Can Wes and Bree find a way toward happily-ever-after at Whiskey Mountain Lodge?

Her Cowboy Billionaire Best Friend's Brother (Book 3): She's best friends with the single dad cowboy's brother and has watched two friends find love with the sexy new cowboys in town. When Gray Hammond comes to Whiskey Mountain Lodge with his son, will Elise finally get her own happily-ever-after with one of the Hammond brothers?

Her Cowboy Billionaire Beast (Book 4): A cowboy billionaire beast, his new manager, and the Christmas traditions that soften his heart and bring them together.

Her Cowboy Billionaire Bad Boy (Book 5): A cowboy billionaire cop who's a stickler for rules, the woman he pulls over when he's not even on duty, and the personal mandates he has to break to keep her in his life...

Her Cowboy Billionaire Best Friend (Book 1): Graham Whittaker returns to Coral Canyon a few days after Christmas—after the death of his father. He takes over the energy company his dad built from the ground up and buys a high-end lodge to live in—only a mile from the home of his once-best friend, Laney McAllister. They were best friends once, but Laney's always entertained feelings for him, and spending so much time with him while they make Christmas memories puts her heart in danger of getting broken again...

Her Cowboy Billionaire Boss (Book 2): Since the death of his wife a few years ago, Eli Whittaker has been running from one job to another, unable to find somewhere for him and his son to settle. Meg Palmer is Stockton's nanny, and she comes with her boss, Eli, to the lodge, her long-time crush on the man no different in Wyoming than it was on the beach. When she confesses her feelings for him and gets nothing in return, she's crushed, embarrassed, and unsure if she can stay in Coral Canyon for Christmas. Then Eli starts to show some feelings for her too...

Her Cowboy Billionaire Boyfriend (Book 3): Andrew Whittaker is the public face for the Whittaker Brothers' family energy company, and with his older brother's robot about to be announced, he needs a press secretary to help him get everything ready and tour the state to make the announcements. When he's hit by a protest sign being carried by the company's biggest opponent, Rebecca Collings, he learns with a few clicks that she has the background they need. He offers her the job of press secretary when she thought she was going to be arrested, and not only because the spark between them in so hot Andrew can't see straight.

Can Becca and Andrew work together and keep their relationship a secret? Or will hearts break in this classic romance retelling reminiscent of *Two Weeks Notice*?

Her Cowboy Billionaire Bodyguard (Book 4): Beau Whittaker has watched his brothers find love one by one, but every attempt he's made has ended in disaster. Lily Everett has been in the spotlight since childhood and has half a dozen platinum records with her two sisters. She's taking a break from the brutal music industry and hiding out in Wyoming while her ex-husband continues to cause trouble for her. When she hears of Beau Whittaker and what he offers his clients, she wants to meet him. Beau is instantly attracted to Lily, but he tried a relationship with his last client that left a scar that still hasn't healed...

Can Lily use the spirit of Christmas to discover what matters most? Will Beau open his heart to the possibility of love with someone so different from him?

Her Cowboy Billionaire Bull Rider (Book 5): Todd Christopherson has just retired from the professional rodeo circuit and returned to his hometown of Coral Canyon. Problem is, he's got no family there anymore, no land, and no job. Not that he needs a job-- he's got plenty of money from his illustrious career riding bulls.

Then Todd gets thrown during a routine horseback ride up the canyon, and his only support as he recovers physically is the beautiful Violet Everett. She's no nurse, but she does the best she can for the handsome cowboy. **Will she lose her heart to the billionaire bull rider? Can Todd trust that God led him to Coral Canyon...and Vi?**

Her Cowboy Billionaire Bachelor (Book 6): Rose Everett isn't sure what to do with her life now that her country music career is on hold. After all, with both of her sisters in Coral Canyon, and one about to have a baby, they're not making albums anymore.

Liam Murphy has been working for Doctors Without Borders, but he's back in the US now, and looking to start a new clinic in Coral Canyon, where he spent his summers.

When Rose wins a date with Liam in a bachelor auction, their relationship blooms and grows quickly. **Can Liam and Rose find a solution to their problems that doesn't involve one of them leaving Coral Canyon with a broken heart?**

Her Cowboy Billionaire Blind Date (Book 7): Her sons want her to be happy, but she's too old to be set up on a blind date...isn't she?

Amanda Whittaker has been looking for a second chance at love since the death of her husband several years ago. Finley Barber is a cowboy in every sense of the word. Born and raised on a racehorse farm in Kentucky, he's since moved to Dog Valley and started his own breeding stable for champion horses. He hasn't dated in years, and everything about Amanda makes him nervous.

Will Amanda take the leap of faith required to be with Finn? Or will he become just another boyfriend who doesn't make the cut?

Her Cowboy Billionaire Best Man (Book 8): When Celia Abbott-Armstrong runs into a gorgeous cowboy at her best friend's wedding, she decides she's ready to start dating again.

But the cowboy is Zach Zuckerman, and the Zuckermans and Abbotts have been at war for generations.

Can Zach and Celia find a way to reconcile their family's differences so they can have a future together?

Second Chance Ranch: A Three Rivers Ranch Romance (Book 1): After his deployment, injured and discharged Major Squire Ackerman returns to Three Rivers Ranch, wanting to forgive Kelly for ignoring him a decade ago. He'd like to provide the stable life she needs, but with old wounds opening and a ranch on the brink of financial collapse, it will take patience and faith to make their second chance possible.

Third Time's the Charm: A Three Rivers Ranch Romance (Book 2): First Lieutenant Peter Marshall has a truckload of debt and no way to provide for a family, but Chelsea helps him see past all the obstacles, all the scars. With so many unknowns, can Pete and Chelsea develop the love, acceptance, and faith needed to find their happily ever after?

Fourth and Long: A Three Rivers Ranch Romance (Book 3): Commander Brett Murphy goes to Three Rivers Ranch to find some rest and relaxation with his Army buddies. Having his ex-wife show up with a seven-year-old she claims is his son is anything but the R&R he craves. Kate needs to make amends, and Brett needs to find forgiveness, but are they too late to find their happily ever after?

Fifth Generation Cowboy: A Three Rivers Ranch Romance (Book 4): Tom Lovell has watched his friends find their true happiness on Three Rivers Ranch, but everywhere he looks, he only sees friends. Rose Reyes has been bringing her daughter out to the ranch for equine therapy for months, but it doesn't seem to be working. Her challenges with Mari are just as frustrating as ever. Could Tom be exactly what Rose needs? Can he remove his friendship blinders and find love with someone who's been right in front of him all this time?

Sixth Street Love Affair: A Three Rivers Ranch Romance (Book 5): After losing his wife a few years back, Garth Ahlstrom thinks he's ready for a second chance at love. But Juliette Thompson has a secret that could destroy their budding relationship. Can they find the strength, patience, and faith to make things work?

The Seventh Sergeant: A Three Rivers Ranch Romance (Book 6): Life has finally started to settle down for Sergeant Reese Sanders after his devastating injury overseas. Discharged from the Army and now with a good job at Courage Reins, he's finally found happiness—until a horrific fall puts him right back where he was years ago: Injured and depressed. Carly Watters, Reese's new veteran care coordinator, dislikes small towns almost as much as she loathes cowboys. But she finds herself faced with both when she gets assigned to Reese's case. Do they have the humility and faith to make their relationship more than professional?

Eight Second Ride: A Three Rivers Ranch Romance (Book 7): Ethan Greene loves his work at Three Rivers Ranch, but he can't seem to find the right woman to settle down with. When sassy yet vulnerable Brynn Bowman shows up at the ranch to recruit him back to the rodeo circuit, he takes a different approach with the barrel racing champion. His patience and newfound faith pay off when a friendship--and more--starts with Brynn. But she wants out of the rodeo circuit right when Ethan wants to rejoin. Can they find the path God wants them to take and still stay together?

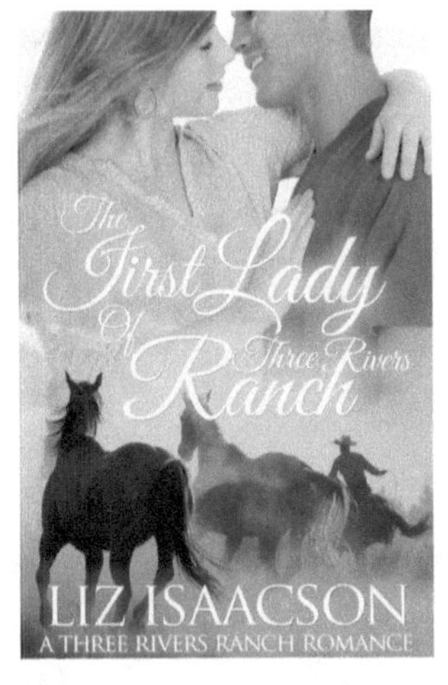

The First Lady of Three Rivers Ranch: A Three Rivers Ranch Romance (Book 8): Heidi Duffin has been dreaming about opening her own bakery since she was thirteen years old. She scrimped and saved for years to afford baking and pastry school in San Francisco. And now she only has one year left before she's a certified pastry chef. Frank Ackerman's father has recently retired, and he's taken over the largest cattle ranch in the Texas Panhandle. A horseman through and through, he's also nearing thirty-one and looking for someone to bring love and joy to a homestead that's been dominated by men for a decade. But when he convinces Heidi to come clean the cowboy cabins, she changes all that. But the siren's call of a bakery is still loud in Heidi's ears, even if she's also seeing a future with Frank. Can she rely on her faith in ways she's never had to before or will their relationship end when summer does?

Christmas in Three Rivers: A Three Rivers Ranch Romance (Book 9): Isn't Christmas the best time to fall in love? The cowboys of Three Rivers Ranch think so. Join four of them as they journey toward their path to happily ever after in four, all-new novellas in the Amazon #1 Bestselling Three Rivers Ranch Romance series.

THE NINTH INNING: The Christmas season has never felt like such a burden to boutique owner Andrea Larsen. But with Mama gone and the holidays upon her, Andy finds herself wishing she hadn't been so quick to judge her former boyfriend, cowboy Lawrence Collins. Well, Lawrence hasn't forgotten about Andy either, and he devises a plan to get her out to the ranch so they can reconnect. Do they have the faith and humility to patch things up and start a new relationship?

TEN DAYS IN TOWN: Sandy Keller is tired of the dating scene in Three Rivers. Though she owns the pancake house, she's looking for a fresh start, which means an escape from the town where she grew up. When her older brother's best friend, Tad Jorgensen, comes to town for the holidays, it is a balm to his weary soul. A helicopter tour guide who experienced a near-death experience, he's looking to start over too--but in Three Rivers. Can Sandy and Tad navigate their troubles to find the path God wants them to take--and discover true love--in only ten days?

ELEVEN YEAR REUNION: Pastry chef extraordinaire, Grace Lewis has moved to Three Rivers to help Heidi Ackerman open a bakery in Three Rivers. Grace relishes the idea of starting over in a town where no one knows about her failed cupcakery. She doesn't expect to run into her old high school boyfriend, Jonathan Carver. A carpenter working at Three Rivers Ranch, Jon's in town against his will. But with Grace now on the scene, Jon's thinking life in Three Rivers is suddenly looking up. But with her focus on baking and his disdain for small towns, can they make their eleven year reunion stick?

THE TWELFTH TOWN: Newscaster Taryn Tucker has had enough of life on-screen. She's bounced from town to town before arriving in Three Rivers, completely alone and completely anonymous--just the way she now likes it. She takes a job cleaning at Three Rivers Ranch, hoping for a chance to figure out who she is and where God wants her. When she meets happy-go-lucky cowhand Kenny Stockton, she doesn't expect sparks to fly. Kenny's always been "the best friend" for his female friends, but the pull between him and Taryn can't be denied. Will they have the courage and faith necessary to make their opposite worlds mesh?

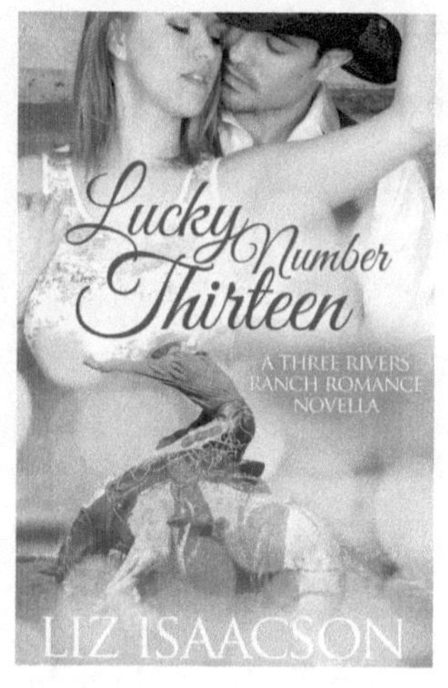

Lucky Number Thirteen: A Three Rivers Ranch Romance (Book 10): Tanner Wolf, a rodeo champion ten times over, is excited to be riding in Three Rivers for the first time since he left his philandering ways and found religion. Seeing his old friends Ethan and Brynn is therapuetic--until a terrible accident lands him in the hospital. With his rodeo career over, Tanner thinks maybe he'll stay in town--and it's not just because his nurse, Summer Hamblin, is the prettiest woman he's ever met. But Summer's the queen of first dates, and as she looks for a way to make a relationship with the transient rodeo star work Summer's not sure she has the fortitude to go on a second date. Can they find love among the tragedy?

The Curse of February Fourteenth: A Three Rivers Ranch Romance (Book 11): Cal Hodgkins, cowboy veterinarian at Bowman's Breeds, isn't planning to meet anyone at the masked dance in small-town Three Rivers. He just wants to get his bachelor friends off his back and sit on the sidelines to drink his punch. But when he sees a woman dressed in gorgeous butterfly wings and cowgirl boots with blue stitching, he's smitten. Too bad she runs away from the dance before he can get her name, leaving only her boot behind...

Fifteen Minutes of Fame: A Three Rivers Ranch Romance (Book 12): Navy Richards is thirty-five years of tired—tired of dating the same men, working a demanding job, and getting her heart broken over and over again. Her aunt has always spoken highly of the matchmaker in Three Rivers, Texas, so she takes a six-month sabbatical from her high-stress job as a pediatric nurse, hops on a bus, and meets with the matchmaker. Then she meets Gavin Redd. He's handsome, he's hardworking, and he's a cowboy. But is he an Aquarius too? Navy's not making a move until she knows for sure...

Sixteen Steps to Fall in Love: A Three Rivers Ranch Romance (Book 13): A chance encounter at a dog park sheds new light on the tall, talented Boone that Nicole can't ignore. As they get to know each other better and start to dig into each other's past, Nicole is the one who wants to run. This time from her growing admiration and attachment to Boone. From her aging parents. From herself.

But Boone feels the attraction between them too, and he decides he's tired of running and ready to make Three Rivers his permanent home. **Can Boone and Nicole use their faith to overcome their differences and find a happily-ever-after together?**

The Sleigh on Seventeenth Street: A Three Rivers Ranch Romance (Book 14): A cowboy with skills as an electrician tries a relationship with a down-on-her luck plumber. Can Dylan and Camila make water and electricity play nicely together this Christmas season? Or will they get shocked as they try to make their relationship work?

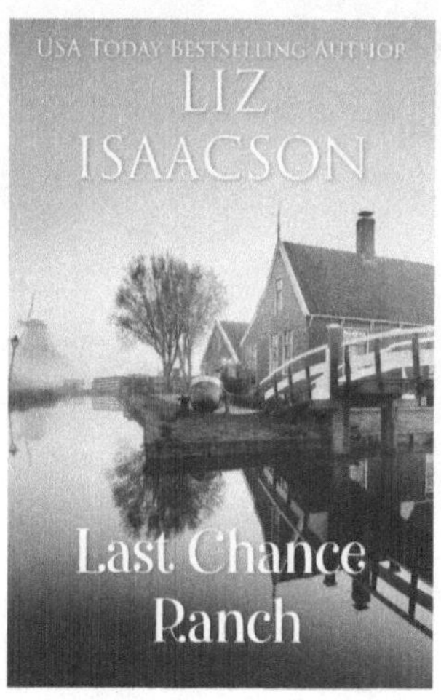

Last Chance Ranch (Book 1): A cowgirl down on her luck hires a man who's good with horses and under the hood of a car. Can Hudson fine tune Scarlett's heart as they work together? Or will things backfire and make everything worse at Last Chance Ranch?

Last Chance Cowboy (Book 2): A billionaire cowboy without a home meets a woman who secretly makes food videos to pay her debts...Can Carson and Adele do more than fight in the kitchens at Last Chance Ranch?

Last Chance Wedding (Book 3): A female carpenter needs a husband just for a few days... Can Jeri and Sawyer navigate the minefield of a pretend marriage before their feelings become real?

Last Chance Reunion (Book 4): An Army cowboy, the woman he dated years ago, and their last chance at Last Chance Ranch... Can Dave and Sissy put aside hurt feelings and make their second chance romance work?

Last Chance Lake (Book 5): A former dairy farmer and the marketing director on the ranch have to work together to make the cow cuddling program a success. But can Karla let Cache into her life? Or will she keep all her secrets from him – and keep *him* a secret too?

Last Chance Christmas (Book 6): She's tired of having her heart broken by cowboys. He waited too long to ask her out. Can Lance fix things quickly, or will Amber leave Last Chance Ranch before he can tell her how he feels?

Her Billionaire Cowboy (Book 1): Tucker Jenkins has had enough of tall buildings, traffic, and has traded in his technology firm in New York City for Steeple Ridge Horse Farm in rural Vermont. Missy Marino has worked at the farm since she was a teen, and she's always dreamed of owning it. But her ex-husband left her with a truckload of debt, making her fantasies of owning the farm unfulfilled. Tucker didn't come to the country to find a new wife, but he supposes a woman could help him start over in Steeple Ridge. Will Tucker and Missy be able to navigate the shaky ground between them to find a new beginning?

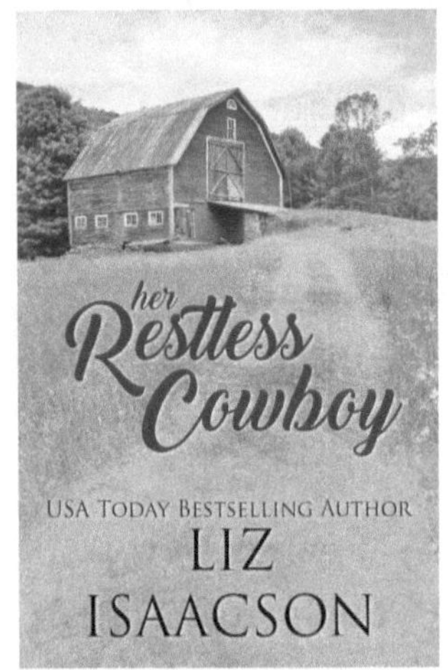

Her Restless Cowboy: A Butters Brothers Novel, Steeple Ridge Romance (Book 2): Ben Buttars is the youngest of the four Buttars brothers who come to Steeple Ridge Farm, and he finally feels like he's landed somewhere he can make a life for himself. Reagan Cantwell is a decade older than Ben and the recreational direction for the town of Island Park. Though Ben is young, he knows what he wants—and that's Rae. Can she figure out how to put what matters most in her life—family and faith—above her job before she loses Ben?

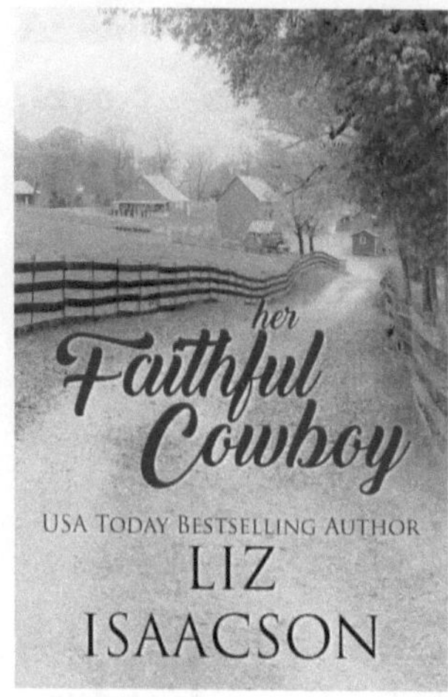

Her Faithful Cowboy: A Butters Brothers Novel, Steeple Ridge Romance (Book 3): Sam Buttars has spent the last decade making sure he and his brothers stay together. They've been at Steeple Ridge for a while now, but with the youngest married and happy, the siren's call to return to his parents' farm in Wyoming is loud in Sam's ears. He'd just go if it weren't for beautiful Bonnie Sherman, who roped his heart the first time he saw her. Do Sam and Bonnie have the faith to find comfort in each other instead of in the people who've already passed?

Her Mistletoe Cowboy: A Butters Brothers Novel, Steeple Ridge Romance (Book 4): Logan Buttars has always been good-natured and happy-go-lucky. After watching two of his brothers settle down, he recognizes a void in his life he didn't know about. Veterinarian Layla Guyman has appreciated Logan's friendship and easy way with animals when he comes into the clinic to get the service dogs. But with his future at Steeple Ridge in the balance, she's not sure a relationship with him is worth the risk. Can she rely on her faith and employ patience to tame Logan's wild heart?

Her Patient Cowboy: A Butters Brothers Novel, Steeple Ridge Romance (Book 5): Darren Buttars is cool, collected, and quiet—and utterly devastated when his girlfriend of nine months, Farrah Irvine, breaks up with him because he wanted her to ride her horse in a parade. But Farrah doesn't ride anymore, a fact she made very clear to Darren. She returned to her childhood home with so much baggage, she doesn't know where to start with the unpacking. Darren's the only Buttars brother who isn't married, and he wants to make Island Park his permanent home—with Farrah. Can they find their way through the heartache to achieve a happily-ever-after together?

Craving the Cowboy (Book 1): Dwayne Carver is set to inherit his family's ranch in the heart of Texas Hill Country, and in order to keep up with his ranch duties and fulfill his dreams of owning a horse farm, he hires top trainer Felicity Lightburne. They get along great, and she can envision herself on this new farm—at least until her mother falls ill and she has to return to help her. Can Dwayne and Felicity work through their differences to find their happily-ever-after?

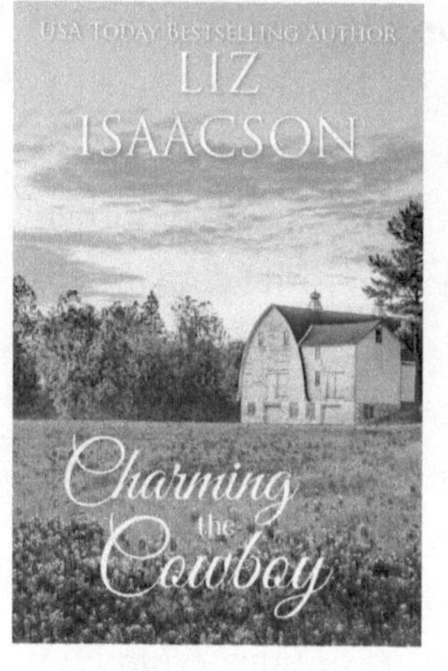

Charming the Cowboy (Book 2): Third grade teacher Heather Carver has had her eye on Levi Rhodes for a couple of years now, but he seems to be blind to her attempts to charm him. When she breaks her arm while on his horse ranch, Heather infiltrates Levi's life in ways he's never thought of, and his strict anti-female stance slips. Will Heather heal his emotional scars and he care for her physical ones so they can have a real relationship?

Courting the Cowboy (Book 3): Frustrated with the cowboy-only dating scene in Grape Seed Falls, May Sotheby joins TexasFaithful.com, hoping to find her soul mate without having to relocate--or deal with cowboy hats and boots. She has no idea that Kurt Pemberton, foreman at Grape Seed Ranch, is the man she starts communicating with... Will May be able to follow her heart and get Kurt to forgive her so they can be together?

Claiming the Cowboy, Royal Brothers Book 1 (Grape Seed Falls Romance Book 4): Unwilling to be tied down, farrier Robin Cook has managed to pack her entire life into a two-hundred-and-eighty square-foot house, and that includes her Yorkie. Cowboy and co-foreman, Shane Royal has had his heart set on Robin for three years, even though she flat-out turned him down the last time he asked her to dinner. But she's back at Grape Seed Ranch for five weeks as she works her horse-shoeing magic, and he's still interested, despite a bitter life lesson that left a bad taste for marriage in his mouth.

Robin's interested in him too. But can she find room for Shane in her tiny house--and can he take a chance on her with his tired heart?

Catching the Cowboy, Royal Brothers Book 2 (Grape Seed Falls Romance Book 5): Dylan Royal is good at two things: whistling and caring for cattle. When his cows are being attacked by an unknown wild animal, he calls Texas Parks & Wildlife for help. He wasn't expecting a beautiful mammologist to show up, all flirty and fun and everything Dylan didn't know he wanted in his life.

Hazel Brewster has gone on more first dates than anyone in Grape Seed Falls, and she thinks maybe Dylan deserves a second... Can they find their way through wild animals, huge life changes, and their emotional pasts to find their forever future?

Cheering the Cowboy, Royal Brothers Book 3 (Grape Seed Falls Romance Book 6): Austin Royal loves his life on his new ranch with his brothers. But he doesn't love that Shayleigh Hatch came with the property, nor that he has to take the blame for the fact that he now owns her childhood ranch. They rarely have a conversation that doesn't leave him furious and frustrated--and yet he's still attracted to Shay in a strange, new way.

Shay inexplicably likes him too, which utterly confuses and angers her. As they work to make this Christmas the best the Triple Towers Ranch has ever seen, can they also navigate through their rocky relationship to smoother waters?

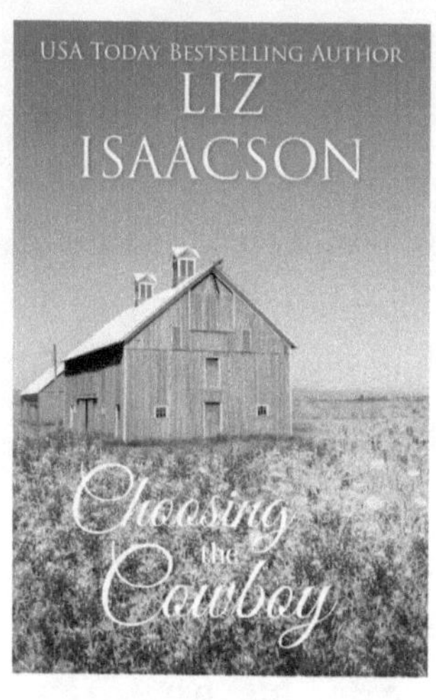

Choosing the Cowboy (Book 7): With financial trouble and personal issues around every corner, can Maggie Duffin and Chase Carver rely on their faith to find their happily-ever-after?

A spinoff from the #1 best-selling Three Rivers Ranch Romance novels, also by USA Today bestselling author Liz Isaacson.

The Redesigned Ranch (Book 1): Jace Lovell only has one thing left after his fiancé abandons him at the altar: his job at Horseshoe Home Ranch. Belle Edmunds is back in Gold Valley and she's desperate to build a portfolio that she can use to start her own firm in Montana. Jace isn't anywhere near forgiving his fiancé, and he's not sure he's ready for a new relationship with someone as fiery and beautiful as Belle. Can she employ her patience while he figures out how to forgive so they can find their own brand of happily-ever-after?

The Snowstorm in Gold Valley (Book 2): Professional snowboarder Sterling Maughan has sequestered himself in his family's cabin in the exclusive mountain community above Gold Valley, Montana after a devastating fall that ended his career. Norah Watson cleans Sterling's cabin and the more time they spend together, the more Sterling is interested in all things Norah. As his body heals, so does his faith. Will Norah be able to trust Sterling so they can have a chance at true love?

The Cabin on Bear Mountain (Book 3): Landon Edmunds has been a cowboy his whole life. An accident five years ago ended his successful rodeo career, and now he's looking to start a horse ranch-- and he's looking outside of Montana. Which would be great if God hadn't brought Megan Palmer back to Gold Valley right when Landon is looking to leave. Megan and Landon work together well, and as sparks fly, she's sure God brought her back to Gold Valley so she could find her happily ever after. Through serious discussion and prayer, can Landon and Megan find their future together?

Be sure to check out the spinoff series, the Brush Creek Brides romances after you read FALLING FOR HIS BEST FRIEND. Start with A WEDDING FOR THE WIDOWER.

The Cowboy at the Creek (Book 4): Twelve years ago, Owen Carr left Gold Valley—and his long-time girlfriend—in favor of a country music career in Nashville. Married and divorced, Natalie teaches ballet at the dance studio in Gold Valley, but she never auditioned for the professional company the way she dreamed of doing. With Owen back, she realizes all the opportunities she missed out on when he left all those years ago—including a future with him. Can they mend broken bridges in order to have a second chance at love?

The Wedding in the Winter (Book 5): Caleb Chamberlain has spent the last five years recovering from a horrible breakup, his alcoholism that stemmed from it, and the car accident that left him hospitalized. He's finally on the right track in his life—until Holly Gray, his twin brother's ex-fiance mistakes him for Nathan.

Holly's back in Gold Valley to get the required veterinarian hours to apply for her graduate program. When the herd at Horseshoe Home comes down with pneumonia, Caleb and Holly are forced to work together in close quarters. Holly's over Nathan, but she hasn't forgiven him—or the woman she believes broke up their relationship. Can Caleb and Holly navigate such a rough past to find their happily-ever-after?

The Long Way Home (Book 6): Ty Barker has been dancing through the last thirty years of his life--and he's suddenly realized he's alone. River Lee Whitely is back in Gold Valley with her two little girls after a divorce that's left deep scars. She has a job at Silver Creek that requires her to be able to ride a horse, and she nearly tramples Ty at her first lesson. That's just fine by him, because River Lee is the girl Ty has never gotten over. Ty realizes River Lee needs time to settle into her new job, her new home, her new life as a single parent, but going slow has never been his style. But for River Lee, can Ty take the necessary steps to keep her in his life?

Christmas at the Ranch (Book 7): Archer Bailey has already lost one job to Emersyn Enders, so he deliberately doesn't tell her about the cowhand job up at Horseshoe Home Ranch. Emery's temporary job is ending, but her obligations to her physically disabled sister aren't. As Archer and Emery work together, its clear that the sparks flying between them aren't all from their friendly competition over a job. Will Emery and Archer be able to navigate the ranch, their close quarters, and their individual circumstances to find love this holiday season?

The Love of a Cowboy (Book 8): Cowboy Elliott Hawthorne has just lost his best friend and cabin mate to the worst thing imaginable—marriage. When his brother calls about an accident with their father, Elliott rushes down to Gold Valley from the ranch only to be met with the most beautiful woman he's ever seen. His father's new physical therapist, London Marsh, likes the handsome face and gentle spirit she sees in Elliott too. Can Elliott and London navigate difficult family situations to find a happily-ever-after?

Brush Creek Cowboy: Brush Creek Cowboys Romance (Book 1): Former rodeo champion and cowboy Walker Thompson trains horses at Brush Creek Horse Ranch, where he lives a simple life in his cabin with his ten-year-old son. A widower of six years, he's worked with Tess Wagner, a widow who came to Brush Creek to escape the turmoil of her life to give her seven-year-old son a slower pace of life. But Tess's breast cancer is back...

Walker will have to decide if he'd rather spend even a short time with Tess than not have her in his life at all. Tess wants to feel God's love and power, but can she discover and accept God's will in order to find her happy ending?

The Cowboy's Challenge: Brush Creek Brides Romance (Book 2): Cowboy and professional roper Justin Jackman has found solitude at Brush Creek Horse Ranch, preferring his time with the animals he trains over dating. With two failed engagements in his past, he's not really interested in getting his heart stomped on again. But when

flirty and fun Renee Martin picks him up at a church ice cream bar--on a bet, no less--he finds himself more than just a little interested. His Gen-X attitudes are attractive to her; her Millennial behaviors drive him nuts. Can Justin look past their differences and take a chance on another engagement?

A Cowboy Proposal: Brush Creek Brides Romance (Book 3): Ted Caldwell has been a retired bronc rider for years, and he thought he was perfectly happy training horses to buck at Brush Creek Ranch. He was wrong. When he meets April Nox, who comes to the ranch to hide her pregnancy from all her friends back in Jackson Hole, Ted realizes he has a huge family-shaped hole in his life. April is embarrassed, heartbroken, and trying to find her extinguished faith. She's never ridden a horse and wants nothing to do with a cowboy ever again. Can Ted and April create a family of happiness and love from a tragedy?

A New Family for the Cowboy: Brush Creek Brides Romance (Book 4): Blake Gibbons oversees all the agriculture at Brush Creek Horse Ranch, sometimes moonlighting as a general contractor. When he meets Erin Shields, new in town, at her aunt's bakery, he's instantly smitten. Erin moved to Brush Creek after a divorce that left her penniless, homeless, and a single mother of three children under age eight. She's nowhere near ready to start dating again, but the longer Blake hangs around the bakery, the more she starts to like him. Can Blake and Erin find a way to blend their lifestyles and become a family?

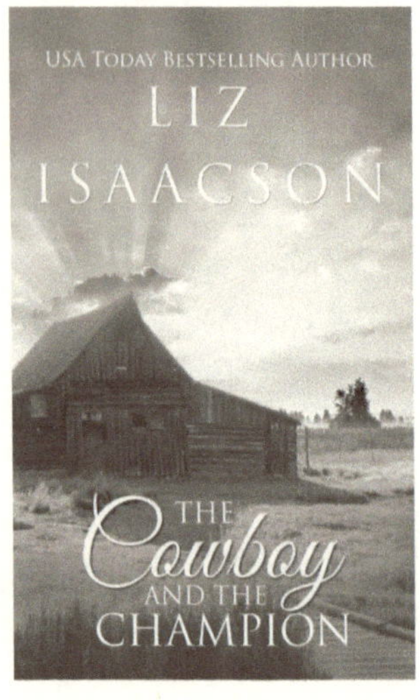

The Cowboy and the Champion: Brush Creek Brides Romance (Book 5): Emmett Graves has always had a positive outlook on life. He adores training horses to become barrel racing champions during the day and cuddling with his cat at night. Fresh off her professional rodeo retirement, Molly Brady comes to Brush Creek Horse Ranch as Emmett's protege. He's not thrilled, and she's allergic to cats. Oh, and she'd like to stay cowboy-free, thank you very much. But Emmett's about as cowboy as they come.... Can Emmett and Molly work together without falling in love?

Schooled by the Cowboy: Brush Creek Brides Romance (Book 6): Grant Ford spends his days training cattle—when he's not camped out at the elementary school hoping to catch a glimpse of his ex-girlfriend. When principal Shannon Sharpe confronts him and asks him to stay away from the school, the spark between them is instant and hot. Shan-

non's expecting a transfer very soon, but she also needs a summer outdoor coordinator—and Grant fits the bill. Just because he's handsome and everything Shannon's ever wanted in a cowboy husband means nothing. Will Grant and Shannon be able to survive the summer or will the Utah heat be too much for them to handle?

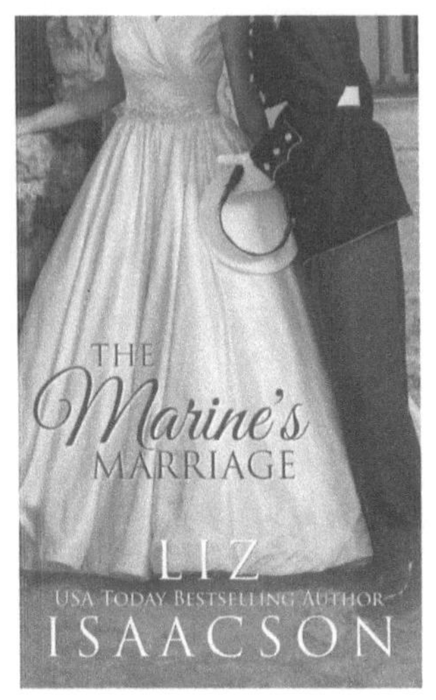

The Marine's Marriage: A Fuller Family Novel - Brush Creek Brides Romance (Book 1): Tate Benson can't believe he's come to Nowhere, Utah, to fix up a house that hasn't been inhabited in years. But he has. Because he's retired from the Marines and looking to start a life as a police officer in small-town Brush Creek. Wren Fuller has her hands full most days running her family's company. When Tate calls and demands a maid for that morning, she decides to have the calls forwarded to her cell and go help him out. She didn't know he was moving in next door, and she's completely unprepared for his handsomeness, his kind heart, and his wounded soul.Can Tate and Wren weather a relationship when they're also next-door neighbors?

The Firefighter's Fiancé: A Fuller Family Novel - Brush Creek Brides Romance (Book 2): Cora Wesley comes to Brush Creek, hoping to get some in-the-wild firefighting training as she prepares to put in her application to be a hotshot. When she meets Brennan Fuller, the spark between them is hot and instant. As they get to know  each other, her deadline is constantly looming over them, and Brennan starts to wonder if he can break ranks in the family business. He's okay mowing lawns and hanging out with his brothers, but he dreams of being able to go to college and become a landscape architect, but he's just not sure it can be done. Will Cora and Brennan be able to endure their trials to find true love?

The Trooper's Treasure: A Fuller Family Novel - Brush Creek Brides Romance (Book 3): Dawn Fuller has made some mistakes in her life, and she's not proud of the way McDermott Boyd found her off the road one day last year. She's spent a hard year wrestling with her choices and trying to fix them, glad for McDermott's acceptance and friendship. He lost his wife years ago, done his best with his daughter, and now he's ready to move on. Can McDermott help Dawn find a way past her former mistakes and down a path that leads to love, family, and happiness?

The Detective's Date: A Fuller Family Novel - Brush Creek Brides Romance (Book 4): Dahlia Reid is one of the best detectives Brush Creek and the surrounding towns has ever had. She's given up on the idea of marriage—and pleasing her mother—and has dedicated herself fully to her job. Which is great, since one of the most perplexing

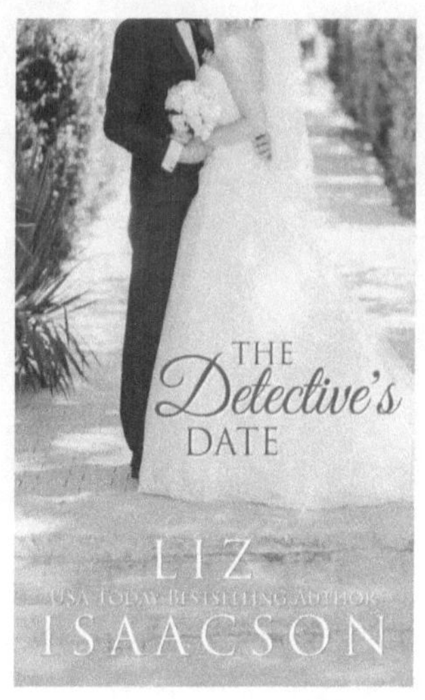

cases of her career has come to town. Kyler Fuller thinks he's finally ready to move past the woman who ghosted him years ago. He's cut his hair, and he's ready to start dating. Too bad every woman he's been out with is about as interesting as a lamppost—until Dahlia. He finds her beautiful, her quick wit a breath of fresh air, and her intelligence sexy. Can Kyler and Dahlia use their faith to find a way through the obstacles threatening to keep them apart?

The Paramedic's Partner: A Fuller Family Novel - Brush Creek Brides Romance (Book 5): Jazzy Fuller has always been overshadowed by her prettier, more popular twin, Fabiana. Fabi meets paramedic Max Robinson at the park and sets a date with him only to come down with the flu. So she convinces Jazzy to cut her hair and take her place on the date. And the spark between Jazzy and Max is hot and instant...if only he knew she wasn't her sister, Fabi.

Max drives the ambulance for the town of Brush Creek with is partner Ed Moon, and neither of them have been all that lucky in love. Until Max suggests to who he thinks is Fabi that they should double with Ed and Jazzy. They do, and Fabi is smitten with the steady, strong Ed Moon. As each twin falls further and further in love with their respective paramedic, it becomes obvious they'll need to come clean about the switcheroo sooner rather than later...or risk losing their hearts.

The Chief's Catch: A Fuller Family Novel - Brush Creek Brides Romance (Book 6): Berlin Fuller has struck out with the dating scene in Brush Creek more times than she cares to admit. When she makes a deal with her friends that they can choose the next man she goes out with, she didn't dream they'd pick surly Cole Fairbanks, the new Chief of Police.

His friends call him the Beast and challenge him to complete ten dates that summer or give up his bonus check. When Berlin approaches him, stuttering about the deal with her friends and claiming they don't actually have to go out, he's intrigued. As the summer passes, Cole finds himself burning both ends of the candle to keep up with his job and his new relationship. When he unleashes the Beast one time too many, Berlin will have to decide if she can tame him or if she should walk away.

About Liz

Liz Isaacson writes inspirational romance, usually set in Texas, or Montana, or anywhere else horses and cowboys exist. She lives in Utah, where she writes full-time, drives her daughter to her acting classes, and eats a lot of peanut butter M&Ms while writing. Find her on her website at lizisaacson.com.